Devil's Choice

M. A. Wright

termardoc press

ISBN 978-0692630211

To Terry, without whom this could not have happened.

Acknowledgements

Devil's Choice has been a long time in development and my hope is that it has now reached a maturity sufficient to make it an enjoyable experience for a wide range of readers—history buffs, mystery fans, students of human nature in its often perplexing absurdity. It grew from a tale—a brief recitation of events without elaboration on motives, without names of people or places—told by my father in the latter years of his life, long after all those important details had dissolved in the smoky fog of the past. *Devil's Choice* is a work of fiction, the product of my imagination filling in a lot of blanks, and while it was my intention to depict realistic characters, settings, and events, it depicts no actual persons, living or dead, or actual places or events.

I owe a great debt to all who helped me along the way: Assistant Professor Lynn Wallace of Gulf Coast State College in Panama City, Florida, and author Michael Lister—both opened the doors of creative writing for me and rescued me from the third person passive of technical writing; the members of the Panama City Writers Association and the Clarkesville Writers Society for their constructive criticism and encouragement; beta readers Terry Wright, Marie Kinneer and Theresa Rice for invaluable feedback. Thank you all. Your contributions were enormous. That said, any remaining faults, flaws or errors are all mine.

M. A. Wright

Chapter 1

August 1865

Home! Josiah Robertson topped a hill, rounded a bend, and looked down on his home. Tears streaked his dust-grimed, stubbled face. He swiped at them, then wiped his hand on his pants.

He'd spent almost all the daylight hours travelling these last fifteen miles. He'd gotten an early start, after the damned nightmare woke him again, but his weary horse, a large roan named Pepper, couldn't maintain much of a pace. Then sometime after midday Pepper threw his left front shoe and became too lame to ride. Josiah walked. His worn boots provided little protection for his feet, and soon he limped as badly as the horse. Together they hobbled the last four or five miles in foot-sore misery, sweating under the brutal sun until both Josiah's ragged gray uniform and the horse's speckled coat darkened in salt-circled patches.

Now late in the afternoon he had nearly reached his goal. Stepping faster despite the pain, pulling Pepper along behind him, he started down the hill toward the farmstead. With great relief and thankfulness he noted the house, the barn, the outbuildings all appeared to be in reasonably good repair. Then he noted three—no, four—children playing in the front yard in the shade of the big willow oak. The dark-haired girl had to be his Sally—bigger than he had imagined, but then she was eight years old now. Those three towheads must be Emmy and Luke's brood, Jim and Callie Belle, and—what did they name the baby? Delia? Yeah, Delia. A large black dog lay in the dust nearby, its tongue lolling and dripping as it panted in the heat. He didn't recognize the dog.

Josiah looped the reins across the saddle and left the horse to find his own way as he ran, limping, toward the children.

Sally looked up, saw him, then said something to the children that Josiah couldn't hear. Callie Belle stomped and shook her head. Sally pushed her toward the house, then gathered the toddler up from the dirt and ran onto the porch and through the open doorway, calling to the other two children, "Run! Get in the house. Right now!"

The black dog stood and faced Josiah. It didn't bark, but even from a distance he could see its hackles rise.

In seconds Sally returned to the doorway, urged the tow-headed children into the house, and closed the door. Josiah heard her shriek, "Aunt Emmy! There's a drifter after us!"

The dog retreated to just in front of the porch, turned and faced Josiah. It barked once, then growled. Josiah heard another dog barking, approaching fast. He opened the front gate and stepped through, eyeing the black dog as it crouched, tense and ready to spring. Its hackles and low mean growl dared Josiah to come closer. A scruffy brindle bitch ran around the corner of the house. Hackles up, she stopped her advance, stood her ground and growled between deep menacing barks. Josiah didn't recognize her either.

Then his sister-in-law stepped through the front door with a shotgun in her hands, her hair in disarray. Both the man and the woman stopped, stood stone still, and stared at each other. The woman aimed the shotgun at him. Josiah could see her chest heaving. His own heart hammered. A dribble of sweat ran down the side of his nose and trickled onto his lip. His right hand inched up and grasped the crown of his slouch hat, lifted it, revealed his face and his unruly thatch of curly dark hair.

"Emmy, don't you know me?"

"Should I?" she said. She squinted as she looked him up and down. Finally she ventured, "Josiah?"

Her face softened as her eyes filled with tears. She leaned the shotgun against the house and ran to embrace him. "Oh, thank God," she said. "We've prayed you'd get here soon."

"Me, too," he said as they hugged. Then he held her arms, took half a step back and looked her up and down. "It sure is good to see you, Emmy. You look well." A lie. Her face bore lines that had not been there four years ago and her dress hung loosely on her frame. The War's hard times had taken a toll on her as it had on him. And what about his beloved Mattie?

Both dogs crept forward, growling. Emmy eased from his grip, clapped her hands and yelled, "Bo, you hush now. Go on. Get back and hush. You, too, Pretty Girl." The dogs retreated a few steps but continued to watch and growl.

"Never mind the dogs, Emmy. Where's Mattie?"

Emmy paled. She covered her face with her hands and began to sob.

A shiver of alarm crawled up Josiah's spine and onto his scalp. He pulled her hands away from her face and tried to make her look at him. She shook her head and continued to cry. His dread grew but he tried to remain calm. "Hush your crying now. What's wrong?" he said. When she did not answer, he dropped her hands, grasped her shoulders and shook her. "Damn it, Emmy, tell me."

She struggled. He let her go. She backed away, out of his reach. She sniffled, then swallowed and brushed at the tears on her cheeks. "Mattie . . . ," she began, but her speech degenerated to a strangled mewl. She drew a shaky breath and kept her eyes downcast. "I don't know how to tell you," she mumbled.

Josiah's head went light. He could barely find his voice. "What's happened? Mattie's not . . . she's not dead?"

Emmy shook her head. "No." She hugged her arms to herself and backed away another step. "She's alive. But she's hurt awful bad."

"Hurt?"

Emmy nodded. "Bad."

"What happened?"

"We don't know for sure. Sally found her in the barn, all bruised and broken up."

"When?"

"Three days ago. She hasn't really waked up since. Doctor Wilson says it doesn't look good at all."

Josiah moaned and closed his eyes. Emmy stepped forward and put her hand on his arm, but he broke away and rushed toward the house.

She scrambled after him. "No. Wait. The children . . ."

Ignoring her, he charged through the front door. At the open door of the bedroom he stopped. The blood drained from his face.

Emmy caught up and laid her hand on his shoulder. She murmured, "I wanted to prepare you for this. I know it's a terrible shock."

Josiah's lips trembled as he asked, "Three days ago? I should have gotten home sooner. Why couldn't I have gotten home sooner?"

Emmy squeezed his shoulder. "We don't know God's plan."

He glared at her. "God didn't do this."

She yanked her hand from his shoulder as though it burned. "You go on to her. I'll see to the children," she said and then hurried away.

He stepped a couple of paces into the room and stared. Mattie lay in the rumpled bed under a sheet blotched with her sweat. He hardly recognized her—face covered with scabbed cuts and abrasions, closed eyes buried behind a mass of green-tinged purple bruises, jaw off-kilter and swollen, puffy misshapen lips dry and cracked. Her right arm swelled above a splint from which her fingers protruded as dark and stiff as smoked sausages. Only her shallow, labored breathing and the buzzing of flies broke the stillness. Josiah's stomach churned at the odors of urine and camphor. His throat closed around a strained groan, and he could no longer fight back his tears.

I should've been here, he thought. She'd have been safe if I'd been here.

Josiah shook with stifled sobs. Gradually he regained control and wiped his runny eyes and nose with a grimy handkerchief. He stepped to the bed, bent, and kissed Mattie's damp forehead. He drew up a chair, and took her left hand in his.

4

"Mattie?"

She didn't answer, but when he raised her hand and kissed it, she moaned softly. He swallowed and willed his voice under control before he continued.

"I've ached so to see you. It's taken such a long time to get home."

Mattie's eyelids twitched. He thought he felt a slight pressure on his hand.

"Mattie, it's Josiah."

Her fingers flexed.

A basin of water sat on the table beside the bed, a cloth draped over its rim. With his free hand he dipped the rag in the water, then squeezed it dry. He wiped Mattie's hot forehead and cheeks and fought off tears when he felt the pressure of her fingers again.

"Oh, Mattie. I love you. You're all that's kept me going."

Mattie drew a deeper breath. Her hand tensed. Josiah thought she nodded before her hand went limp.

He sat there several minutes but she gave no further indication she was aware of his presence. He kissed her again and said, "I'm going to leave you so you can rest now, but I'll be back soon. I love you, Matilda Jane."

As he arose from the chair, Emmy entered the room.

"Did she rouse?"

Josiah shrugged and sighed. "No, not really. I think she knows I'm here, though. She squeezed my hand several times." He glanced at Mattie "She looks terrible."

"I know. Every day the bruises look worse, but Doctor Wilson says they're really getting better."

"What happened?"

Emmy chewed her lip and picked at the frayed hem of her apron. She shook her head slowly. He touched her arm but she wouldn't look at him.

"Emmy? How'd she get hurt so bad?"

She drew a shaky breath and glanced up at him before she moved to Mattie's side to brush away a fly.

"We don't really know what happened. Nobody saw it." She watched the fly buzz away a couple of feet and then return to Mattie's face.

Josiah shifted his weight. "You must know something."

She brushed at the fly again and then turned to him with tears welling in her eyes. "Sally . . . she found Mattie out in the barn. Poor mite—to find her Mama like that." Her chin trembled. She wiped her eyes with the bottom of her apron, took a deep breath, and stood straighter before she continued. "She tried to rouse Mattie, but she couldn't. She came running and screaming for help. Luke was at work in the toolshed, so he got to her first."

Josiah watched as she moved to the other side of the room. "And . . . ?"

"You know Luke, how gruff he can be. He grabbed Sally and tried to get her to make sense, but she cried harder and screeched 'Mama' over and over. I don't think she understood he was trying to help. She broke away from him."

Emmy wiped her eyes again and glanced at Josiah. "Luke took off for the barn. I've never seen him run so fast, and him with his crooked leg."

She stared out the rear window toward the farmyard as though she were watching the events again. "I caught up to Sally. I held her, tried to hush her. She was shaking all over, but she managed to tell me what she'd found."

She hugged her arms around herself as she turned back to Josiah. "I ran to the barn with Sally right behind me." Her lower lip trembled and she bit it for several seconds. Josiah moved toward her, but she shook her head and held up her hands to stop him. "Mattie was sprawled on the ground, in the dust and straw, all bloody. Luke was there, trying to rouse her. But he couldn't."

Josiah moaned.

"Oh, Josiah. I'm so sorry. That's all we know."

"Somebody beat shit out of her."

Emmy gasped. "Josiah. Your language!"

Language? She admonished him about his language at a time like this? He gave her a hard stare and watched the challenge skitter from her eyes before he softened. "I beg your pardon, Emmy."

6

She nodded.

He said, "But don't you think that's what happened?"

Emmy glanced at Mattie, then back at Josiah. "Maybe. I thought maybe she fell from the loft, or maybe one of the mules or the cow? . . ." Her shoulders rose and fell as she sighed. "Luke thought it was an accident at first, but after what Jim said he's sure she was attacked. There wasn't any sign of it being anything else. He tried so hard to find the . . . the despicable cur . . . . But he couldn't."

Josiah's lips thinned into a grim white line. "What Jim said? Did he see who did it?"

Emmy shrank from him. "No. Not really. Jim saw a soldier that morning, a drifter, one of our boys. But he didn't recognize him."

"The dogs—didn't they take out after the prowler?"

Her eyes widened and she sucked in a breath. "I hadn't thought about them. They didn't. I wonder where they were?"

Josiah wondered, too. They'd sure been on watch when he arrived. "So the dogs didn't make a fuss but the boy saw a stranger. He didn't raise an alarm?"

"No. Well, yes, but . . . not right away. Not till after . . ." Emmy worried the hem of her apron, wadding it then smoothing it. "Josiah, you have to understand. After Sally found Mattie everything was in an uproar. Luke brought Mattie to the house and then he saddled a mule and raced to fetch Doctor Wilson— despite how he feels about riding. I tried to tend to Mattie. I . . . I guess I didn't do much to calm the children. I think they ran off and hid. Maybe half an hour later Jim crept in and whispered he had to tell me something."

"Why'd he wait so long?"

Emmy shook her head and bit her lower lip. "I don't know. I whipped his tail for it. 'Course that didn't do any good." She shook her head as she thought a moment. "I don't know . . . maybe if he'd told sooner? But I don't think it would've saved Mattie. The dirty cur must've already attacked her when Jim first saw him, 'cause Jim never saw him anywhere near the barn."

"Could the boy describe him?"

Emmy sighed and shrugged. "Sort of. Said he was a tall man

7

with dark hair—long and greasy-looking—and a short darkish beard, maybe with some gray in it. Faded shirt, dirt-colored pants. Barefooted. There've been dozens of men like that pass here this summer." She flicked a glance at Josiah. "Like you. Except you've got boots."

Josiah glowered. "If I ever get my hands on him, I'll kill him."

Emmy shrank from him. "That won't help Mattie."

"No. But it'll make me feel better."

They stared at each other for a long moment. Emmy turned to go. Josiah reached toward her but stopped short of touching her. "Wait, Emmy," he said. "I want to know what y'all did about finding him."

She stopped and faced him. "Luke tried. Of course he did. It's so frustrating for us all," she said. "As soon as Luke got back with Doctor Wilson, I told him what Jim had seen. He took his rifle and went looking right then. Rode a mule again—and you know how he hates to ride."

Josiah nodded. "I do know. I take it he didn't find anything?"

"Not much. Somebody had made a camp between us and the Pritchard place."

"Anybody over there see the bast—, uh, the beast?"

"Maybe. Evie Jane saw a strange man at their place the day before, prowling around their barnyard. Lem ran him off, but he didn't chase him far—figured he was stealing food, which they hated to begrudge him, except they don't have any to spare." She raised her eyebrows and sighed. "'Course now Lem wishes he had. He might've saved Mattie."

Josiah nodded.

"Lem and Andy Jack Caruthers rode with Luke—a couple of other men, too—and they followed word of that devil all the way to Henry's Ferry, but they lost his trail there. There's no telling where he went."

Josiah stepped over to Emmy, put his hands on her shoulders. "Then Luke did everything he could. I just wish he could've found the bastard."

Emmy gave him a shocked little frown. He reddened and

released her as he added, "I'm sure he does, too."

"He was fit to be tied 'cause he couldn't find the beast."

She stepped to the bed, took up the damp rag and wiped Mattie's face. The injured woman lay still and quiet, seemingly unaware of their presence, of her sister's touch.

Josiah watched as Emmy returned the rag to the bowl. "And Mattie? Hasn't she been able to tell anything about what happened?"

"No. She's been unconscious most of the time. She talks some, but she's out of her head—makes no sense." Emmy reddened and looked away from him. "I think she's hurt bad inside, too." She paused and her blush deepened. "When she makes water there's blood, too. Doctor Wilson says her kidneys are damaged, and he thinks she has other injuries. Inside, you know? There's nothing he can do. We just have to wait and see how she does."

Emmy bit her lower lip and took a few steps toward the door, putting her back to him. She wept quietly for a moment before she sniffed and wiped her eyes with her apron.

He stepped nearer her. "I swear before God, if I ever find out who did this, he's a dead man."

She turned toward him. "We all hate what he did, Josiah. But I think we've done all that can be done. He's not to be found. It's in the Lord's hands now. Leave it there."

"Sometimes the Lord don't take much heed of what's been placed in His hands."

"Don't blaspheme."

"I'm not blaspheming. Just saying the truth."

He returned to Mattie's bedside and tenderly touched her face.

Emmy frowned and opened her mouth as though to speak, but then she only sighed. After a moment she said, "Josiah, I'm so sorry about this. It pains me to see Mattie hurt this way. I know it's a terrible homecoming for you."

He nodded without looking at her.

After a few seconds she said, "You stay a while. If you need anything, I'll be in the kitchen."

Chapter 2

As Emmy's footsteps receded Josiah settled into a chair beside the bed. He held Mattie's hand and talked to her. At first he felt her fingers twitch, which he hoped was a response to his presence, but then they went limp. He wiped her face and neck and brushed away the flies that crawled over her.

For so long he'd dreamed of his homecoming, believed Mattie would be his salvation. Maybe she still would be. He had to hope. But this wasn't the way it was supposed to be. He felt helpless. He wanted to make her well, but how? After a while he scooted the chair away from the bed and rose. He bent and kissed her forehead, then slipped from the room.

He crossed the hall and stuck his head into what had been the parlor. Now it held Emmy and Luke's bed and their trundle for Delia. Several chairs remained there, but the settee was missing. Stepping back into the hall, he saw it crowded beneath the steep stairs on his right. He saw no sign of the children. He didn't even hear them. He supposed they had either gone outside or hidden in the sleeping loft.

As he continued toward the rear of the house he noted the shotgun again rested on its pegs above the back door. A rifle perched above the shotgun. An old rifle, but he didn't recognize it. It must be Luke's.

He stepped onto the back porch and paused, quickly surveying his farmstead. Little had changed since he'd left it, except the slave cabin looked deserted and run down. Luke had done well. He must have treated the place as though it were his own. Good man.

A rustle and clatter from the direction of the kitchen startled him. His head snapped toward the breezeway separating the two parts of the house. Nothing stirred there. Then he caught a glimpse of Emmy as she moved past the open door of the kitchen. He relaxed, but then heard soft, uneven hoofbeats and tensed again. With a weary sigh Pepper limped to the corner of the house and stood with his neck drooping. "Found your way home like I figured you would, didn't you?" Josiah mumbled as he stepped off the porch, took the horse's bridle, and started toward the barn. Both dogs slipped from beneath the porch and followed at a distance, watchful but no longer growling. Josiah stopped Pepper at the water trough just inside the barnyard gate and let the roan drink his fill. The dogs stopped twenty feet away.

As the horse drank, Josiah idly inspected the large log barn. The tight chinking in the feed and harness room in the near corner of the structure bespoke good maintenance. His eyebrows rose when he noticed large drifts of hay in the loft above the main level. The dry weather must have been good for haying. Then his gaze lowered to the long dark hall down the center of the barn and his shoulders sagged. Pepper raised his head from the water trough and bumped Josiah's arm. Josiah roused and led the roan into the barn.

The cooler air inside smelled of horse and cow manure tinged with a hint of pigsty wafting in from outside. A multitude of flies produced a steady drone. Josiah paced up and down the hall and looked into the stalls. Three on the east side were unoccupied, but there was fresh manure in two of them. The two on the west held a brindle cow and a sway-backed gray mare. He led the limping roan into the clean stall and removed the bridle and saddle and all his gear.

After rubbing down Pepper with the saddle blanket, Josiah took all the gear to the harness room. Briefly closing his eyes, he inhaled the familiar and comforting odors of corn and leather and neat's-foot oil. As he slung his saddle over a rack, he noticed many bits and pieces of harness hung on pegs around the room, but only one rather small set of collar and hames. There were several empty pegs.

He opened the corn barrel, found it empty, and went to the crib for several ears. He shelled them, filled Pepper's feed box and put the rest in the barrel. Then he climbed the ladder to the loft and forked a generous load of hay into the horse's manger.

Josiah frowned as he looked down into the hall from the loft. Slowly he made his way back down the ladder. As he stood in the dust of the hall he tried to visualize the attack on Mattie. He closed his eyes and imagined the sounds of struggle, of blows. Luke would have come to her aid if she'd screamed. The prowler must have kept his hand over her mouth, held her tight, stifled her cries, maybe even smothered her breath. His stomach flipped as the thought brought a recollection of another hand over another mouth. He moaned. It didn't matter whether he was asleep or awake, the nightmare haunted him. He grieved, but he didn't know whether he grieved more for Mattie's pain or his own. Shuddering and shaking his head, he tried to bring himself back to the present, out of both nightmarish worlds. He succeeded in pushing away the memory, but not Mattie's ordeal.

There must have been some noise during the attack. It wasn't far to the toolshed. How could Luke not have known what was happening? Then Josiah realized he couldn't see the toolshed from where he stood. Luke would not have had line of sight to the attack. If he had been intent on his work, he might not have heard the struggle either.

He walked back into the depths of the barn, looked at the dirt floor, scuffed his toe at bits and pieces of straw and small pebbles. What was he looking for? Bloodstains? No. He didn't want to see her blood. A clue to the prowler's identity? He snorted at the futility of such a search. The barn had seen three days of use after the assault. People and animals had walked here, milled around, stomped and shuffled. Nothing of that morning remained now.

Josiah sighed and leaned against Pepper's stall. He felt like crying, but he wouldn't. For days and weeks now he had been buoyed by his thoughts of home and Mattie. He had counted on her to help him mend his sore heart, but now she needed help more than he needed her. He closed his eyes and sagged against the wall. Would he be able to do right by her?

Pepper whickered softly and moved around the stall. Josiah heard his uneven steps and knew the lameness needed attention, but in his weariness he could do nothing about it.

He retrieved his saddlebags and returned to the house. The dogs had tired of trailing and watching his every move. They lay in the dust in the shade of the barn, panting and occasionally biting at fleas.

He stepped up onto the back porch and dropped the saddlebags in one of several chairs. A tall bench against the back wall of the house held a washbasin and bucket and a misshapen bar of brown lye soap. His old shaving mirror hung on the wall above the wash bench. A coarse sacking towel dangled from a wooden peg. He poured water into the basin from the bucket. From the corner of his eye he saw the dogs move toward the house. Taking up the bar of soap, he scrubbed his hands and face and his shaggy, greasy hair. He rinsed, then upended the bucket of dirty water over his bowed head. The black dog, Bo, had slunk close behind him, teeth bared. Now he yelped and jumped back to avoid the splash. Josiah grabbed the towel from the peg and was drying his hands and face when Emmy stepped onto the porch and motioned for him to come inside. He gathered up his saddlebags and joined her in the hall.

"Have you seen Sally yet?" she asked.

He shook his head.

She sighed. "She's hidden somewhere. The poor little thing is scared."

"Of me?"

"Not exactly, but . . . she may not have very clear memories of you. Give her some time."

"I need to see her. Do you have any idea where she's gone?"

"No. But she'll be back soon. She has to tend to her chores."

She frowned and seemed to be inspecting the floor. Then she cut her eyes up at him and continued in a softer tone. "I hope you'll be more patient with her than Luke is. He's so stern. Well, of course, so am I, sometimes. We have to be firm with children, but . . ." She sighed. "Sometimes I think Luke goes too far. She's scared, Josiah. Remember that."

"I will. I won't crowd her."

Of course he knew she was leery of him. She'd run when he first came to the house, hadn't she? Did she run from many things? He hoped his daughter wasn't the skittish filly Emmy seemed to think. The child needed grit to get through this world.

Emmy looked up at him. "I was tending to Mattie just now. She isn't really awake, but she seemed nearer this world than she has been. Maybe you should go see her again?"

He nodded.

She added, "I have to milk. She doesn't need watching every minute, but I'll feel better if you stay near her for a while. Call me if you need help."

"I will."

He was half way to Mattie's door before Emmy said, "Some supper's on the table. If you're hungry, help yourself. The family will eat after Luke gets in."

"I'll wait," he said over his shoulder. His stomach growled in protest, but once he'd said he'd wait he'd keep his word. The day was fading fast. Surely Luke would be there soon.

He tiptoed into the room and kissed Mattie's hot forehead. She didn't stir. He left her side to place the saddlebags in the corner, but returned, arranged the chair, and sat holding her hand. He talked to her about the better parts of his trip home, how his thoughts of her had kept him going, but she did not respond. After a while he could no longer make cheerful chatter to her battered, inert form.

"I guess you slipped away from us again. Come back, Mattie. Please. I need to look into your eyes and hear your voice." His eyes stung. He swiped roughly at his tears. He stood, bent and kissed her again. "You rest and get stronger, Mattie. I'll be back after a while."

In the hall he stopped and drew a deep breath. He felt he was a coward, but he couldn't bear to sit there and see her so broken. She deserved more of him. He'd have to pull himself together and try to be strong for her. He squared his shoulders and made his way to the back porch.

14

The late afternoon sunlight poured beneath the clouds in the west like warm honey. The long, broad shadow of the barn oozed toward the house. The chickens gathered near the coop, clucking and scratching, moving closer to the safety of their fenced-in yard and their roosts in the henhouse. In the barn the cow lowed as the dying day settled over the farmstead to the accompaniment of faint rumbles of thunder.

Josiah stepped to the ground and sat on the end of the low porch. He braced his elbows on his knees, massaged his temples, then rested his head in his hands and stared at the scuffed, powdery dust at his feet. He drew a deep breath and tried to quiet the hammering in his chest, the swirl of anger and confusion and despair that pounded around and around in his skull. He had thought himself free from the killing, thought it had ended with the surrender, thought he could turn away from violence and follow his conscience toward peace. But the dreams told him he couldn't put the killing behind him yet, no matter how badly he wanted to. And now he had to deal with this situation with Mattie.

How could God let someone hurt Mattie? The same way God let men cut and blast each other to bits, of course. The way He let blameless children suffer and die. The Bible said God was mindful of the fall of even a sparrow. After what he had seen and done during the war, Josiah Robertson believed God might be mindful but He seldom felt the need to intervene in the lives of sparrows or of men. God let man do what he would. Maybe He watched. Maybe He laughed or sorrowed. But He didn't interfere. He let the carnage and suffering go on. And on. And on.

Josiah moaned and raked his fingers through his damp hair. He raised his head and his eyes followed the chickens, but he didn't really see them. He wanted to catch the son of a bitch who hurt Mattie. Make him suffer. Make sure he knew why. Then kill him. An eye for an eye, and then some. He swallowed hard and dropped his head into his hands. That's what he wanted, but did he have the nerve to kill anymore? If he did, then what? The dreams tormented him now. What would they be like if he found the bastard and killed him in cold blood? Was that torment hell, or did hell come after? And last for an eternity? Either way, he didn't know if he was willing to pay the price. He pressed his throbbing temples and moaned again.

The war killing wasn't wrong. Except maybe the one time. He had tried to believe the dream didn't mean anything and only happened because of his utter exhaustion, but he felt guilty no matter how convincingly he argued he was blameless. Now, as the fierceness of his anger subsided, he knew he didn't have the stomach for more killing, not close and personal.

It was just as well they didn't know who hurt Mattie, or where he went. He had sworn he'd kill him, sworn before God and Emmy. But if he never found the son of a bitch . . . Josiah sighed and rubbed his eyes. He didn't know what was right, whether he should accept Mattie's injuries as their lot, or if he should pursue a course of vengeance. For now, Mattie needed his help, so he would bide his time and hope he would eventually find the wisdom to know what to do.

He fumbled in his shirt pocket for his stubby pipe and sack of tobacco. He filled the pipe, tamped the tobacco with his finger, and put the sack back in his pocket as he stood and walked to the kitchen. A splinter ripped from a piece of firewood and thrust into the banked coals in the stove soon flared into flame. Josiah touched it to the tobacco in his pipe. Two or three strong drags released a cloud of blue-white smoke around his head. The smoke stirred and swirled as he left the kitchen, trying to put the sight and smell of food from his mind. He returned to the end of the porch, where he sat as before and slowly puffed on the pipe. The smoke tainted the air around him.

Josiah tensed when motion at the other end of the porch caught his eye. Then he relaxed, faced back toward the farmyard but cut his eyes to the side to watch as a small dark head peeped around the corner of the house. The head disappeared. A few seconds later it reappeared and ventured farther from its shelter. Soon Sally stepped completely into view. Wide-eyed as a skittish colt, she stared through the open breezeway at Josiah. After a few moments, she stepped up onto the porch, her bare feet making no sound. Josiah did not look her way. She took two tentative steps toward him and paused, then took two more. She wrinkled her nose, perhaps smelling the tobacco smoke or the travel-grimed man. Or both. She was only about five feet from him when one of the porch boards squeaked as she stepped onto it. She froze.

Josiah slowly turned toward her. He studied her face, young and unformed and offering only hints of the woman she would become. She was pretty despite the too-large teeth at the front of her mouth. He saw Mattie in her long dark hair and greenish eyes, but the frizzy little curls near her face and the odd swirl above her forehead he recognized as his. He wanted to reach out and pull her to him, but he remembered her fright as he had run toward her earlier. And he remembered Emmy's caution. So he spoke without moving.

"Howdy, Sally. Do you remember me?"

She shook her head. She continued to study his face, and after a short pause she said in a small voice, "Well, maybe a little. I'm not sure."

"You were pretty small the last time I was here. I remember you, though. Do you still sing the song about the beautiful dreamer? I remember your mama teaching it to you. You had the tune down pat, but not all the words."

In answer, she sang the first verse, every word and every note.

Josiah smiled broadly. "You sing it very well. You're going to be as good a singer as your mama."

The child smiled shyly, ducked her head and rubbed her toe against the gray planks of the porch floor. "Nobody sings as pretty as Mama."

"Hmm. You're right. But you will, when you're a little older."

The girl continued to stand in the same spot, toeing the porch. She had almost outgrown her dress. The skimpy garment revealed the thinness of her frame but the bare feet and legs below it looked strong and healthy.

"Sally, come give me a hug."

Her eyes widened as she shook her head and sidled away.

How could he get her to accept him? He had little experience with children. His relationships with his younger siblings, long

17

ago and cut short by their early deaths, had not prepared him for this. And she had been so small when he left. The way he related to her then didn't seem right now. Yet instinctively he knew not to pressure her.

As he tried to think of something to say to put her at ease, a half-grown black pig came grunting from beneath the porch. He nodded toward the pig and said, "Reckon he got tired of the shade?"

She shook her head. "No. That's Squeaky. He heard me and came out to play."

"Came out to play?"

"Uh-huh. He's my friend. He was a runt and Mama let me feed him and take care of him 'cause the others were going to hurt him. He's a real smart pig."

"Oh, is he? Why do you think he's smart?"

"'Cause he comes when I call his name."

Josiah smiled. "Maybe he thinks you're going to feed him."

"No. I call him lots of times besides when I feed him—to come and play."

"You've made a pet of him."

She shrugged. "I guess. But he's my friend, too. One day he killed a copperhead I almost stepped on."

"That must have been scary."

"Yes." She solemnly nodded. "I didn't see the snake till Squeaky grabbed it. He bit it and shook it till it was dead. Well, I guess it was dead. It was still wiggling some. You know how snakes do? Then Squeaky ate it. Ugh." She shuddered.

"You watch for snakes now?"

"Yessir, I do. But see, Squeaky is smart. And he's my friend."

Josiah smiled. He had seen pigs do things that made him think they were smart, but he suspected Squeaky had killed the snake because Squeaky liked to eat snakes.

Before he could think of something else to say, she frowned and said, "I don't think Uncle Luke likes Squeaky, though. He says Squeaky will be bacon by Christmas." Her lower lip protruded and trembled. "I don't want him to kill Squeaky."

Josiah busied himself with his pipe, trying to coax a glow

from the gray ashes. Pigs were slaughtered, a fact of life on a farm, the reason he had never been allowed to make a pet of a food animal when he was a boy. He wished Mattie hadn't let Sally make a pet of this one. But he didn't want to lose the rapport he had started to build with the girl. And this runty pig wouldn't make much bacon anyway.

Josiah took a final deep draw on the pipe and said, "We won't slaughter your pig, Sally. I'll speak to Luke."

"Thank you." She hesitated a moment before adding, "Daddy."

Sally smiled at the grunting pig as it made its way toward the barn, then she bolted off after him. Squeaky, hearing her bare feet slap the ground, turned to wait for her and grunted happily as she scratched his ears.

The child and the pig were half way to the barn when Sally stopped and cocked her head. "I hear Uncle Luke and the team," she called back to Josiah.

Josiah listened, but heard nothing.

"Sally," Emmy called from the barn. "Draw some water and then finish putting supper on the table. Your Uncle Luke'll be hungry. Your Daddy, too."

"Yessum," Sally shouted back. She gave Josiah a strange look, one he couldn't interpret, before she padded to the well. Squeaky trotted a few steps after her, then veered away and headed behind the house toward the woodlot.

Josiah remained on the porch and took a few more drags from his pipe as he watched Sally draw a bucket of water and carry it to the kitchen. Then he heard the distant jingle of harness. He knocked the dottle from his pipe and got to his feet.

Chapter 3

Josiah ambled toward the barn, favoring his sore feet. Ahead of him Emmy called, "Jim! Jim, you get yourself busy right now. You need to draw water for the stock. Feed 'em, too."

Jim ran from the woodlot and approached the well as Josiah neared it. The bucket dangled from the windlass, still dripping after Sally's use. Jim released the brake and sent the pail falling toward the water. At the splash he grasped the crank with both hands and began to reel the full bucket back up. At the top of the crank's travel his shirttail hiked up to reveal ribs and a hollow belly.

Josiah smiled at the boy. "Hey, Jim. Want a little help?"

The boy stared at him briefly as he continued to turn the crank, heaving and pulling with his whole body. Then he lowered his gaze and muttered, "No, sir. The water's my job. Mother told me to do it. Father'll be angry if I don't."

"All right. Draw enough to fill the trough."

The boy nodded and mumbled, "Yessir."

Recalling the trough had been half empty when he had watered Pepper, Josiah added, "Water's pretty low. Maybe you should've drawn a bucket or two earlier?" He winked as he asked the question, but Jim flinched from the criticism.

As Josiah approached the barn, he heard the growing clink and rattle of the mules' harnesses and the protesting creak of the wagon before they appeared around the corner. Luke perched on the seat, reins in hand. Emmy walked along one side, the dogs

20

frolicked along the other. She had been speaking to Luke but broke off and slipped into the barn when she saw Josiah.

"Luke, it's mighty good to see you," Josiah called as he intercepted the wagon beneath the hayloft opening.

Luke pulled the team to a stop and fastened the reins. "It's been a long time, Josiah," he said with a thin smile. He removed his sweaty straw hat and ran a broad, scarred and callused hand through his damp dark blonde hair. When he replaced the hat it shaded his slightly hooked nose, thin lips, and sun-squinted eyes. Sweat rivulets streaked his dusty, chaff-grimed face and dripped from his reddish beard stubble. His shirt clung damply to his back and chest and emphasized shoulders sagging with weariness, yet his muscular broad frame projected physical strength and power. Better fed than Josiah, still he packed no fat.

Josiah stepped forward. Luke reached down and they shook hands. Then they fell into an awkward silence as though neither knew what to say next. Finally as he began to climb down from the wagon, Luke said, "We've been worried about you. Of course we always prayed. We felt better when Mattie got your letter a couple of weeks ago. We knew you were on your way, but . . ."

"I thought I might not make it, myself," Josiah answered with a short laugh. "There've been some damn hard times, and that's a fact. I'm mighty glad to be home. Mighty glad. But finding Mattie like she is . . . Of course I know it's real, but it's hard to accept."

Luke turned away from Josiah, limped to the near mule, and busied himself with adjusting the harness. He nodded and said, "I know. It's hard for us all. We've been praying for her. Seems to be about all we can do."

Josiah stared back toward the house. His throat constricted and he could say nothing. There was little they could do now, but there was a time when Luke could've done something. Why didn't he protect her? Josiah knew he was being irrational, knew he would be wrong to give in to his anger, wrong to voice it. After all, what steps should a prudent man have taken to safeguard the family? If Luke hadn't seen the prowler, hadn't known the bastard was there, how could he have intervened?

21

And from what Emmy had told him, Luke had done all he could to find Mattie's assailant. It would help nobody for him to start a fight with Luke now over what he might have done differently.

Josiah coughed and shifted his feet. He looked around the farmstead, then back at Luke. "The place looks good. You've done a good job. I can't tell you how much I appreciate that."

"Just doing what I said I would. It's been hard to keep the fruits of our labors, but we've done better than most. Nobody's starved here. And I've got crops in the field. This drought is hurting, but the Lord will provide."

Josiah nodded. "Maybe so. I'm surprised you've been able to make so much hay."

"I wouldn't have on my own, but I've been making Miz Waller's hay on the halves, too. She doesn't have as much stock as we do, and she's got a lot more grass. She couldn't very well get it in by herself, so this worked out good for both of us."

"Miz Waller's hay? Didn't Jon make it home?" Josiah asked.

Luke shrugged. "Jon came home, but he's in bad shape— lost a leg. He can't work now—probably won't ever be able to. He's fevered and . . . well, he doesn't seem right in the head. His boys try hard, but they're not big enough to take on the whole load."

Josiah closed his eyes and shuddered. "I'm sorry. Jon's my friend, and a good neighbor."

Both were quiet for a few moments before Josiah said, "I think Sally is getting supper ready. I'll give you a hand with unloading and taking care of the stock."

"I could use some help. Jim will see to the stock, though. It's one of his jobs."

"He's a mite small to have so much to do, isn't he? I saw him at the well. I thought he was going to bust a gut hauling up a full bucket."

"He's big enough. He has to do his share, just like everybody else." Luke turned to watch the boy stagger as he toted a bucket of water to the trough. "Work'll make him strong." He glanced back at Josiah. "If you want to help unload the hay . . ."

Josiah shrugged, grabbed a pitchfork and climbed into the wagon. The boy's chores were none of his business. Still, Luke's hard ways gave him an uneasy feeling. He jabbed the pitchfork into the hay and heaved a bundle into the loft.

Josiah and Luke finished with the hay, watered and stabled the mules, and walked wearily to the house. They both washed up without speaking and entered the kitchen.

Delia babbled happily in the highchair at one corner of the table. Sally sat next to her, watching as the two-year-old squeezed green beans to a pulp in her fists, only occasionally actually putting one in her mouth. Crumbled cornbread littered the highchair tray.

Emmy filled the last of seven tin mugs with milk and said, "Delia, stop messing with your food. Sally, try feeding her with a spoon."

"Yessum. She's making a worse mess than usual. Why, you reckon?"

Emmy sighed. "I don't know. Why does a two-year-old do anything? Try the spoon."

"Yessum."

Callie Belle sidled through the doorway and took the chair next to Sally. Luke limped to the head of the table and sat with a weary sigh. Josiah's face darkened as he pulled out the side chair across from Sally. This was his house, his table. He should sit at its head. He should say so, but he was too tired to start a row. Besides, Luke had been the head so long he probably didn't think about it being Josiah's place. The anger passed. Jim quietly settled in beside Josiah as Emmy took the remaining end chair.

Josiah served creamed corn onto his plate and nudged the bowl toward Emmy. He had a spoonful of the corn nearly to his mouth when he realized the family had bowed their heads and Luke was saying, "Our Father . . ." Reddening, he quickly put his spoon on his plate and bowed his head, too, but not before he caught the wide eyes of the girls. Little dickenses. Heads down but eyes wide open. Like Sally and Jim, they carried no fat and were probably more interested in the food than in giving thanks for it.

Everyone echoed Luke's "Amen," and all began to help themselves to the nearest dish before passing the bowls and platters around. No one spoke as they all tended to the business of eating, as befitted people thin enough to make it obvious there had not been an abundance of food in their lives lately. The beans and tomatoes and corn disappeared quickly, along with almost all the remaining cornbread and most of the milk Emmy had cooled and skimmed after the morning milking. The bounty of summer would not last forever. They would enjoy it while they could.

Only Delia seemed to have the energy to talk. She jabbered happily between bites as Sally spooned the mashed beans and cornbread into her mouth. Then she grabbed the spoon, which Sally relinquished with a shrug. Even as she attempted to feed herself, Delia stared at Josiah. More food went into her hair and on her face and clothes than went into her mouth. She ventured a smile at the strange man, and he winked at her. She giggled and ducked her head, then turned to Sally.

"Who dat?"

Sally answered, "My Daddy."

Callie Belle and Jim sneaked sidelong glances at their uncle. Delia shook her head. "Not Dada."

Sally sighed. "He's *my* Daddy. He's *your* uncle. Like your father is my Uncle Luke."

Jim glanced at Luke and then at Josiah. Hesitantly, he asked, "What should I call you, sir?"

Josiah smiled at the boy and extended his hand to him. "You and Callie Belle and Delia should call me Uncle Josiah."

They shook hands as Jim said, "Yessir."

"You've grown a lot since I left. Become a big help, too. I'm glad to make your acquaintance again."

The boy beamed. Callie Belle gave Josiah a shy smile and Delia squealed.

As the forks and spoons clattered on the plates, Jim took sidelong peeks at Josiah. Finally he blurted, "Why didn't you get here sooner? Soldiers have been coming home for a long time now. Father said you might've—"

Luke flushed. "Hush, boy. No one spoke to you," he said.

24

Emmy flinched and all of the children ducked their heads.

Josiah held up a cautionary hand. "Take it easy, Luke. The boy's just curious. He did no harm." Turning to Jim, he explained, "My outfit was foraging in the mountains way northwest of Roanoke and we didn't get the word of the surrender for a long time. And when we did hear we didn't want to believe it." He sighed and added, barely audibly, "But it was true, all right. Lee really had given up. It was all for nothing."

The boy watched his uncle, his mouth slightly open, his eyes wide. "What was for nothing?"

What was for nothing? All of it—the hunger, the sickness, the wounds, the deaths—all the things he couldn't talk about.

When Josiah didn't answer, Jim asked, "Weren't you in the cavalry? Where's your pistol and your saber?"

Luke frowned at the boy. "Jim, I told you to hush. Do you want a whipping?"

"No, sir." Jim stared at his plate.

Josiah coughed and ran his hand over his face as though trying to wash away the unwelcome memories that filled his head. The Yankees had taken everything—the flag, the rifles, even the side arms. He'd been lucky to have been left his horse. Finally he said, "Don't be hard on the boy, Luke. But I really don't want to talk about the War. Or the surrender." To Jim he added, "I know you've got lots of questions, but I can't answer them now. Maybe sometime later."

Jim looked up at Josiah. "Yessir. But—"

Luke's hand struck like a snake, popping the back of Jim's head, knocking the boy's face into his plate, then withdrawing just as quickly. Jim jerked upright. Some of his dinner clung to his nose and chin. His lower lip protruded and trembled as a drop of blood grew on it. He gasped a ragged breath. Luke hit him again. Jim wailed.

The other children watched, wide-eyed.

Emmy said, "Luke . . ."

"Shut up." Luke looked at Emmy and then Jim. "Stop crying. Right now. You're acting like a baby."

The boy wailed louder.

"Stop it, I said. Do you hear me?" Tears streamed from Jim's eyes, but he cut them fearfully at Luke and tried to stifle his sobs. Luke continued, "You disobeyed me. I told you to hush. Didn't you hear me?"

Jim's lips still trembled, but he managed a juddering, "Yessir."

"Then why did you keep on after I told you to hush?"

In a very small voice Jim answered, "I don't know."

The other children studied their nearly empty plates. Even Delia hushed.

Josiah couldn't hold his tongue. "Luke, you're a little—"

"This is none of your business," Luke said.

"It *is* my business! It's under *my* roof!" Josiah slapped the table, oblivious to the fact his own outburst frightened the family as much as Luke's violence had. "I know you need to discipline the boy, but I can't sit by and let you whale on him. Leave him be. You've more than made your point."

As Josiah shouted, Luke turned red. "I'll whip my boy when I see fit. He's to hush when he's told to. He knows that, but he needed a reminder." Luke glared at Josiah. Neither man blinked. The tense silence stretched for several seconds until Luke rose and stalked from the kitchen.

Emmy sat, pale and shaky, and gazed after her departing husband. Josiah had half risen, but now he lowered himself to his seat again, although he stared after Luke and gripped the edge of the table. The children sat with their heads bowed. Callie Belle and Jim sniffled. Finally Emmy said, "Go wash your face, Jim."

The boy hiccupped and swallowed. "But Father may be—"

"Your father wants you to wash your face. He doesn't want you to go around red-faced and snotty-nosed. Go on now."

"Yessum." The boy rose from his chair, pushed it back to the table. "May I be excused?" Emmy nodded. He left but paused when he got to the door and scanned the area before he stepped out.

Emmy drew a shaky breath, squared her shoulders, and not quite looking at him, said to Josiah, "You've got no call to yell at Luke. We teach our children manners. You've got no right to interfere with their discipline." Then she bit her lip and looked away.

As Josiah pushed his chair from the table its legs screeched against the floor. Emmy flinched.

"You're right about your children's discipline. I'll give you that, up to a point. But I *do* have a say about what goes on here. This is my home. My farm. My table. It was my pa's before me. It's what's kept me going through the War—it, and Mattie and Sally."

She glanced at him, then looked away, but not before he saw her jaw tighten and heard her angry sniff. "And not us. But it's worked us near to death, keeping it for you," she muttered.

"I know things have been difficult for y'all," he said. "No question. But the War's over now. We've lost. All of us have lost. Lost more than we can even understand. More than I can, anyway. It's wound-licking time." He saw her faint nod.

"I've come home hoping to find a little peace, but what's here instead? A nightmare. Mattie near to death. Who hurt her? Nobody knows. Sally afraid of me, not even remembering me. And Luke acting like he owns this place."

Emmy's shoulders began to shake. She didn't look at him as she eased out of her chair and moved to the side so the table made a barrier between them.

"You and Luke have kept this farm going. You came here when Mattie and me asked you to, and I know it hasn't been easy for you. I'm obliged. Much obliged." He sighed. "But I'm angry, too. This isn't the homecoming I deserve. I can't have survived the War for this."

Emmy wiped her eyes with the tail of her apron. After a few spasmodic breaths she wiped the tears again and stood straighter as she said, "Mattie isn't our fault. I know you're sick with worry for her. We all are. It's making us all a little crazy. But you've overstepped. You're butting in where you have no right."

"But—"

"I'm glad Luke had the sense to walk out. I don't want you two to fight. That won't help any of us. Not Mattie, not any of us."

He met her reddened eyes, rubbed his hand across his stubbled chin. "I don't want to upset Mattie," he mumbled.

"I know. So calm down."

He nodded and fidgeted under her gaze. After several seconds he said, "I guess you're right."

She reached across the table to touch his arm. He reddened and ducked his head. Shuffling his feet, he said, "I've got to get some air."

"Luke—"

"Don't worry, I'll avoid Luke," he said. "I'll be back in a little while. If you'll show me how to tend her, I can watch Mattie during the night."

Emmy nodded mutely as he turned and left the room, then she collapsed into her chair and sobbed as the tension drained.

The girls remained in their chairs, faces pale, mouths open. As Emmy's sobs subsided, Callie Belle slipped away. Sally stood and helped Delia down from the highchair.

Emmy sighed and started to clear the table, scraping the few crumbs of food left on the plates and the dabs in the bowls into a slop bucket. She said to Sally, "Here, take this to Jim and tell him I said for him to slop the sow. Tell Callie to check on the chickens and fasten the coop. Then you come back here and help wash dishes."

They were finishing with the dishes when Josiah returned. He scuffed his feet as he entered the kitchen and mumbled, "I'm sorry I was so short-tempered."

Emmy said, "I'm sorry, too, Josiah."

Sally said nothing and looked solemnly from one to the other.

Silence hung in the air for a few moments before Emmy said, "If you're serious about watching Mattie tonight, I can use the break. I feel guilty though. You look exhausted. You must be as tired as I am."

"Of course I'm serious about it," Josiah replied. "I want to be close to her. I'm tired, but I'll be able to stay awake. I don't ever sleep very well. It makes sense for me to watch over her and let you get some rest if you can."

Chapter 4

Emmy carried a bundle of rags and a lamp which feebly dispelled the deep twilight. Sally followed close behind, carrying a sleepy Delia. Emmy turned and told her to tuck the baby in and to tell the other children to come for Bible reading as soon as they had finished their chores.

Josiah frowned as he studied Emmy's drawn face and dark-circled eyes, accentuated now by the lamp light, before he asked, "Haven't you had any help since she's been down?"

"I have, thank God. Mother and Father came right away, as soon as Luke drove over and told them about Mattie. Mother helped a lot." She sighed. "But that didn't last long."

"Why not? They're not failing, are they?"

"No, not exactly. But they both got terribly tired and couldn't hold up. They went home the next day. Since then a couple of the neighbors have come by and sat with Mattie some. Every little bit has helped. And Mother sent Dorcas with some clean sheets and bandages yesterday."

Josiah stopped and his eyes widened. "Dorcas? She's still around? Mattie wrote about Samson and Dorcas leaving—said they heard about that emancipation thing and left y'all so short-handed you lost some crops."

Emmy took another step, stopped, turned back toward him, brows knit. "They did. Luke offered to let them stay on here, said they could work for food and shelter. He felt like this was kind of their home, since they'd lived here ever since your Pa bought

29

them from Father. But he couldn't reason with them. Samson said they were free and they weren't about to stay. He got mighty ugly about it, the way Luke told it. Real uppity. So they left."

She shrugged. "A couple of weeks later they showed up at Father's and wanted work and a place to stay. Father welcomed them." Emmy shook her head. "I was angry, but I guess I do understand. One of Father's slave families had stayed on, but there was more work on his place than they could do. Luke and I were here, so we couldn't help." She sighed again and shifted the load of rags. "I reckon so far it's working out all right. I'm glad my folks have some help, but I can't stop thinking Dorcas and Samson belong here."

"Mattie didn't write about them being at your father's place."

"No? Well, it happened quite a while back." She raised her brows and shrugged. "So, like I said, Mother sent Dorcas over to help, but she was nervous as a mare with a new foal. Grumpy, too. Acted like she didn't want to be here. I was right put out with her. But she did stay overnight. And she did some washing and cooking, so she helped in spite of her attitude."

As they continued down the hall, Emmy added, "I expect Mother will be back tomorrow, or maybe the next day. We've managed pretty well so far, and now you're here it'll be easier."

They entered Mattie's room, and for a moment both silently studied her unconscious form. Emmy put the rags on the foot of the bed and began to fluff Mattie's pillow and straighten her bedclothes while Josiah stayed back out of her way.

"The business about Dorcas and Samson doesn't seem right to me. I can't see Samson saying any such. You weren't there?"

Emmy shook her head. "Mattie wasn't either. I only know what Luke told me."

She bent to make a few more adjustments to the sheets, then stood upright and rubbed her lower back and sighed. "Dorcas and Samson belong here. I guess we're all lucky they're working for part of the family, but I have a hard time finding any gratitude. They act so resentful, like we've done them a great wrong. After we've fed and clothed and sheltered them." She shook her head as though bewildered. "We never did them any wrong. Father

30

and Mother treated them well, and made sure my sisters and I did, too. Luke was some rougher with them, I know, but . . ."

Josiah backed out of her way as she stepped from the bed and began to move restlessly around the room.

"What was so bad about it?" she asked. "It was just the way things were. We didn't intend any harm. And Lord knows we couldn't have worked Father's farm without their help, and you couldn't have worked this place either."

"You're right," Josiah agreed as he picked up the saddlebags he had dropped earlier in a corner. "Pa worked this farm alone for years, until I got big enough to help. Even then, we weren't able to work more'n about half of his holding till he bought Samson." He stepped over to the cupboard and placed the bags inside before he continued. "When Pa died, I had to cut back. A missing man makes a big difference."

"It does. When you left we had to let some of the fields lie barren, fields that Luke had intended to plant. Mattie probably wrote you about that?"

Josiah nodded.

"And we had to cut back even more when Samson left. Luke was fit to be tied." She picked at the edge of Mattie's sheet, the creases on her brow becoming deeper. "I don't know what's going to happen to us all now. How can we keep the farms going? It's . . . I don't know . . . everything's so different, so mixed up."

"It's the worst mess I've ever seen, and I doubt it'll get much better any time soon," Josiah said. "We've lost the War. I don't like it but I guess I have to accept it. Yankee troops have moved in everywhere. Every railroad town I came through had Yankee civilians strutting around like they owned the world. Buzzards. They're all going to be hard to live with, but I reckon we'll manage."

"Um-hum. They claim they're here to restore order, but it seems more like they're gloating. I can't bear the thought of it." Emmy raised Mattie's head and smoothed her pillow. "And yet, if they do put a stop to all this lawlessness, maybe it'd be worth having them here. I don't know."

31

"Maybe. If they can find the cur that hurt Mattie, I'll feel a lot better about them."

She shook her head. "Luke says we shouldn't take Mattie's problem to them. They wouldn't take it seriously."

"Maybe he's right. I don't know. I used to be so cocksure I knew what was right, but not anymore." He paced back and forth and stopped near Mattie. "A lot of things are going to be different now, that's for certain. We'll find ways to carry on somehow. We've got land. We can raise enough to eat. We won't starve."

"You have land. Father has land. But what about Luke? I can't help worrying."

"We're all family, Emmy. You and Luke have a place here. You know that."

With a small smile Emmy said, "Yes, and we are thankful." But as she turned away from him toward the cupboard she continued, under her breath, "But I worry."

She pulled out a quilt and a pillow and turned back toward him. "I've been sleeping in here on a pallet on the floor, but now you're here . . . ." She handed the bedding to him. "Can you make do with a pallet? Lord knows, you don't need any cover in this heat."

"It'll be fine. It's a sight better than sleeping in the dust or the mud with a saddle under my head," Josiah answered.

As Emmy instructed Josiah how to tend to Mattie, to give her laudanum for pain, to cool her brow with a damp cloth, they heard a distant rumble of thunder. "Maybe we'll finally get some rain," she said. "I hope it doesn't storm bad."

"Storm or no, we need the rain," Josiah said as he arranged the quilt pallet. "And maybe it'll break the heat."

"Yes," she said as she peered out the window. Flashes of distant lightning lit her face. She shuddered. "I'm going to freshen the water in the basin," she said. "I'll be right back."

In a few minutes she returned carrying a pitcher. She emptied the basin through the open window, then refilled it and put the pitcher on the table beside it. "If she wakes up, try to get her to drink some water—but only a little bit at a time. And there's a kettle of broth on the stove. Give her some if she'll take

32

it. Doctor Wilson says it will help give her strength. Can you manage?"

"I think so. If I can't, I'll call you. You go get some rest."

"All right." Emmy brushed her sister's hair back from her face and whispered, "Goodnight, Mattie." To Josiah she said, "We'll have Bible reading in a few minutes. Come join us. We can hear from the other room if Mattie calls out."

"I reckon I'll stay with her. I can probably hear the reading from here."

"All right. Goodnight, Josiah."

"'Night, Emmy."

Thunder rumbled as Josiah pulled the small straight chair to the bedside. He took Mattie's hand as lightning flashed, followed several seconds later by a muffled roar. Her hand remained limp. As the thunder died away, he heard Luke say in a low growl, "Will she be all right with him?" Emmy replied too softly for Josiah to understand except for a few fragments: " . . . what to do . . . so tired . . . can't watch every minute." Poor Emmy, he thought. She's worn out but Luke expects her to do everything.

Then he heard the shuffle of feet as the children gathered in the other room. Luke shushed them and announced Jeremiah 16 would be the text for the evening. Josiah heard him begin the reading in his deep voice, hesitating and stumbling over some of the words. At first he thought Jeremiah from the days of King Josiah was an appropriate selection, probably chosen in honor of his homecoming. But then he listened to the words: *They shall die of grievous deaths; they shall not be lamented; neither shall they be buried; but they shall be as dung upon the face of the earth: and they shall be consumed by the sword, and by famine; and their carcasses shall be meat for the fowls of heaven, and for the beasts of the earth.*

Josiah shuddered, chilled by the image evoked by the words. Jeremiah's prophecy had come to pass. Josiah Robertson had seen it with his own eyes and wished with all his being that he could wipe the carnage of battle from his mind. Luke could have chosen passages of love and comfort that might have made the tense, fearful inhabitants of his house feel somewhat better as they laid their heads down to sleep in the presence of sickness and pain. Even some of Jeremiah's lamentations held out hope. But Luke had chosen one of the gloomiest, most horrifying texts possible. Maybe he had started at the beginning of Genesis and this was how far he had gotten on a reading of the whole Bible. Maybe. Or maybe he thought it somehow fitting. Josiah closed his ears to the rest of the reading and hardly noticed when Luke finished and the children padded up the stairs to their beds.

He might have closed his ears, but he couldn't dismiss the Bible and religion from his thoughts. Both had been a comfort to him when typhoid fever had sickened his pa and ma and his two younger siblings, eventually killing all but his ma. Without prayer he might not have been able to take on the responsibilities of the farm in the midst of his grief. He had placed his hand in the Lord's, and felt the Lord had led him along a good path, blessed him with a good wife and a healthy child. He had taken comfort in the thought God would be with him even as he went to war. But sometimes he thought about how the Yankees prayed to the same God, with faith as ardent as his own, for the same things he sought. And the next day they would fight and maim and slaughter each other, and who could say which side God helped, or how? If God was a stern but caring Father, mindful of the circumstances of each of His children, how could He have let the conflict go on?

Yet when he looked at the stars at night, or cowered before a violent storm, or watched the new green life burst forth every spring, Josiah felt indescribably small, insignificant, but part of something vast. He didn't doubt the existence of a Supreme Being—something unimaginably larger than himself that somehow ordered the universe. But he no longer believed such a powerful entity could have any concern for something as unimportant as an individual man. He didn't spend much time reading the Bible anymore, and he seldom prayed. Although he would utter phrases like "God help me," he never intended them as prayer. He couldn't fault those who believed, though, because in the false peace of the night, with Mattie sick and the world turned upside down, he missed the comfort of his faith and wished it back.

The storm came closer. Despite his intention to stay awake,

Josiah nodded off. He awoke with a start at a particularly loud clap of thunder. A breeze stirred through the window, and he thought he could smell rain. Some time had passed, but he didn't know exactly how much. The household lay still and quiet except for the rasp of Luke's snores from across the hall.

He continued to hold Mattie's hand. He thought he felt her fingers move in his. During the next lightning flash he saw that her eyes were open a bit.

"You awake?" he asked. "How are you?"

She shifted her position in the bed and moaned. Then she whispered, "Josiah. I'm so glad you're here." Her words were drawn out on her shallow breath and hard to understand. Tears trickled from her eyes.

"Mattie. I've missed you so. I—"

Mattie interrupted him with an unmistakable, "Sh-h-h."

He rose from the chair, bent over her and kissed her forehead. She whispered haltingly, "Where's Emmy? Is Luke here?"

"Yes. They're asleep across the hall."

"You're sure they're asleep?"

"Do you need Emmy? I can call her."

"No. I want to be alone with you." She had to stop and rest during her slow, labored speech. After a long pause, she said, "Thirsty."

Josiah cradled her head and held the cup of water to her lips. A few drops dribbled out of the corners of her mouth, but she managed to swallow some.

"That's good. Doc Wilson says you need to drink whenever you can."

He continued to patiently pour the water slowly into her mouth until she breathed, "'Nough," and he lowered her head to the pillow. He saturated the rag in the basin and wrung it, then wiped her mouth and neck, her tear-streaked cheeks, her forehead.

"I'm so sorry you're hurt. I want—"

"Sh-h-h. Quiet." In the glare of the lightning he saw her eyes wide with fear.

"Don't be afraid. The storm doesn't seem very bad. Maybe it'll bring rain. We certainly need it."

She moved her head from side to side. "Not the storm."

"Well, what then? What's scaring you? Tell me, please."

"Sh-h-h. Be quiet." Mattie closed her eyes and took several breaths before she added, "Don't know. Just afraid. Not the storm. Evil."

Josiah listened closely, trying to hear all she said and piece it together to make sense. He assumed her fright stemmed from the attack. "Don't be scared, Mattie. I won't let anyone hurt you. You concentrate on getting well. I'll be here to protect you."

She nodded, then rested again before asking, "Will you be here all the time?"

"I'm home for good now. Of course I'll be here all the time."

"Right here? With me?"

"Here, holding your hand all the time? No. I have work to do. It's not right to expect Luke to do all the work now that I'm home. And I'm trying to get to know Sally again." He smiled. "Mattie, she's a beautiful child. She's so much like you."

Mattie's fleeting smile gave way as her frightened frown returned. "Here. I need you here."

"I will be here every night. And Emmy will see to you during the day."

"She's only a woman. No good against a man."

"You'd be surprised. When I got here today, the children didn't recognize me. Sally herded them into the house and yelled for Emmy, and she came a-running with her shotgun. She was ready to blow a hole in me as big as a barn door. I could see that in her face clear as day. Damn near scared me to death. You'd better believe I was real careful how I spoke to her, and I didn't make a move—except to take off my hat—until I was sure she recognized me." He chuckled. "Woman or no, she's a good guard."

"Maybe so," she whispered.

The storm drew nearer. The frequent lightning flashes illuminated the room, and the rumble of the thunder never completely died away. The wind gusted, whipping the branches of the trees, as a few big raindrops plashed through the leaves and plopped onto the dirt of the yard. Then with a hiss the downpour began.

Josiah rose from his chair and lowered the window where the rain blew in. He breathed deeply the fresh damp scent. Despite his doubts, he raised his eyes and thought a prayer of thanks.

"Rain," Mattie whispered.

"Yes. It's pouring." He returned to the bedside and stood there for a few moments, quiet, enjoying the roar of the storm. As the first fury passed and the wind died down, he remembered Emmy's instructions.

"Do you think you could take some broth? There's some in the kitchen. It won't take but a minute for me to get it."

"Maybe. Still thirsty." She rested for a moment or two. "Give me some water before you go."

Josiah again raised her head and poured the water slowly into her mouth. She seemed to be able to swallow more easily than before. When she had drunk enough, he made her comfortable and then left for the kitchen.

As he passed down the hall, he heard Luke's bass growl but could not make out his words nor Emmy's soft reply.

The storm had come out of the southwest and the rain blew onto the back porch, drenching him as he crossed to the door of the kitchen. The lightning continued to flash so frequently he did not need to light a lamp. He went directly to the kettle of broth and poured half a cup of soup.

As he returned to Mattie's room he heard a soft murmuring. Emmy stood beside the bed, stroking Mattie's forehead with a damp cloth and speaking very quietly. She turned at Josiah's approach and smiled. "She's awake. Has she been awake long?"

"No. Not long. The storm woke her. She's taken some water. I've just gotten some of the broth from the kitchen."

"I'll feed her, Josiah. You take a break."

"I don't need a break. I thought you were going to try to sleep tonight?"

"I was, but the storm woke me. I don't like loud thunder. Not at all. But since it brought the rain, I guess it wasn't so bad

37

this time. Anyhow, I'm up now. I don't mind sitting with her a bit. I'm so glad to see her awake. You stretch your legs. When you come back in a few minutes, I'll go back to bed."

Mattie gazed at Josiah. She still looked frightened. "Don't go far. You said you'd be here at night."

"I remember. I won't be far away. I'll go out on the porch and have a smoke. You drink your broth, now." She nodded, and he handed the cup to Emmy.

As he left the room, he heard Emmy ask, "Did you and Josiah have a good talk?" His eyebrows rose in surprise as he heard Mattie whisper, "No."

Chapter 5

Josiah returned to the kitchen and lit his pipe at the stove, then found a dry place in the breezeway between the house and the kitchen and squatted with his back against the wall. The storm had passed on. The lightning flashed farther away and the thunder grumbled like a grouchy grandpa. He sat enjoying the pungent tobacco and the sound of the gentle rain. He felt less angry and depressed than he had at supper. Mattie had awakened. She had talked to him, and she had managed to take a little nourishment. He felt a rising current of hope. Maybe tomorrow would be a better day.

He knocked out his pipe and went back to Mattie's room. Emmy stood by the bed, the broth cup in her hands. When she saw Josiah, she put a finger to her lips and nodded toward Mattie, whose eyes were once again closed. They both stepped back into the hall.

"She took most of the broth, but she's so tired. She fell asleep with the cup at her lips," Emmy whispered. "She's definitely getting better. This is the most she's eaten since it happened. You're a good tonic for her." She smiled, but her forehead creased with worry lines. "She'll probably sleep till morning. I'll change her and bathe her after breakfast."

Josiah resumed his watch in the chair by Mattie's side. He noted her breathing seemed steadier, which he deemed a good sign.

Although he thought he stayed awake, he must not have, for the next thing he knew the roosters crowed in the gray light of a drizzly dawn.

He squirmed in discomfort as he awoke. Mattie slept peacefully. He stood and stretched to loosen the kinks in his neck and shoulders, and then he quietly walked around the room to wake up his butt and legs. He vowed to find a more comfortable chair before his next night vigil.

The storm was long past, but a slow rain continued. The wind had died, so he raised all of the windows he had shut when the storm hit. Gradually the air in the room began to feel cooler and smell fresher as the stench of sweat and stale urine diluted. A multitude of flies, becoming more active with daylight, buzzed throughout the room. Two lit on Mattie's face. He quickly brushed them away. He heard mutterings and stirrings from the room across the hall.

Emmy appeared in the doorway. "How is she this morning?"

"Maybe a little better. She seems to be sleeping peacefully. I'm trying to keep the flies off her face without waking her," Josiah replied. "They're probably drawn by the smell. It stinks in here."

"I know. I'll clean her up after breakfast. I've got to stir up the fire and get the children up and off to do their chores."

"I can build the fire for you. You could clean her up while I do that."

"Thank you, Josiah, but it'll be better if I wait till after breakfast to tend to her. It takes quite a while. Luke'll growl if breakfast isn't ready soon." She turned and left the bedroom. Josiah heard her calling up the stairs, "Wake up, Sally. Jim, you and Callie, too." A chorus of muffled, sleepy "yessums" answered as the soft thuds of small feet hitting the floor thumped over his head.

"Jim, you get on out to the barn and feed the stock. Then draw some water for the trough and for the kitchen. Sally, after you milk you come help me with breakfast. Callie Belle, you let the chickens out of the coop and don't forget to gather the eggs." Emmy gave orders in a cross voice that assured anyone failing to do his duty would have cause to regret it.

The noise had not wakened Mattie. Josiah tried to remember what mornings had been like before he left for the War. He didn't think they had been so raucous, but of course they had had only Sally to awaken. He was certain Mattie had usually been more cheerful than her sister, but given the pressures on Emmy he reckoned her crossness might be understandable.

After he assured himself Mattie slept, he left to go to the outhouse and to bring in wood for the kitchen woodbox. When he returned he found Luke standing in Mattie's doorway.

"Morning," Josiah said. He wondered if Luke was still pissed.

"Morning." Luke's brows were drawn together, but he sounded friendly.

"This rain should do some good. At least it's cooled things off a little." Including the two of them.

"Yep. It'll do some good, though the hay I had cut over at Miz Waller's will be ruined." Luke turned and headed for the back door.

Josiah went to Mattie's bedside. She appeared to be sleeping, but he realized she breathed irregularly and her face showed traces of tension. He bent to kiss her and whispered, "Hey, Mattie, why are you pretending to sleep? Don't you want to see me this morning?"

She opened one eye. "Bad dream, I guess. Thought I heard something scary."

"Not here. There's no one here but those that love you. We'll all take care of you. Please don't be afraid anymore."

Mattie weakly nodded. "All right. I'll try. It's easier when you're here. But you go get your breakfast."

He stood quietly by her side for a few minutes until she truly slept.

The stifling blast of heat from the fire in the cookstove greeted Josiah as he entered the kitchen. The aroma of ham sizzling in a skillet overpowered the smell of biscuits in the oven. Sally set the table while Emmy tended to the ham and added a dollop of lard to another skillet.

"Good morning, Daddy. How's Mama?"

"Morning, Sally. I think she's a little better. She took some water and some broth during the night. She's sleeping again now." Sally smiled. He added, "Did you hear the storm last night? Were you afraid?"

Sally scurried to the pie safe to bring preserves and the spoon caddy to the table. "I never saw such bright lightning," she said. "And the thunder was so loud! I hid my head under the sheet, but that didn't shut out the lightning. And it sure didn't shut out the thunder. But it didn't scare me—much."

"I'm glad to hear you weren't scared—much. I see you've already been enjoying the mud. I'll bet Squeaky is having a great time."

"Oh, he is. He's out there grunting and rooting around in it. He's covered in clay," Sally said. After a short pause, she asked, "How'd ya know I've been enjoying the mud?"

Josiah laughed. "I can see it squished up between your toes. I remember when I was a boy I liked to squish the mud with my bare feet, mush it all up between my toes." His eyes briefly took on a faraway look as he added, "It felt good then, but I don't enjoy mud much anymore."

Sally giggled but she looked a little skeptical. She probably thinks I could never have been a child, Josiah thought.

Emmy said. "Sally, go back outside and clean your feet before you come in this house. Right now. You hear me?"

"Yessum." Sally scampered out the door.

As Emmy broke eggs into the second skillet, Luke came in, his hat wet and his shirt plastered across his shoulders. "It looks like it might rain all day," he said.

"Then we can't hay or cultivate," Josiah said. "What else needs doing?"

"How do you want your eggs, Josiah?" Emmy asked.

Luke tossed a nettled glance at Emmy.

"Any way you want to fix them. It doesn't matter to me. Having eggs at all is a treat," Josiah answered.

Luke said, "Smokehouse roof's been leaking. Should be able to spot the bad section now. We can work on that. Rain's light enough." He pulled out the side chair for himself and motioned for Josiah to take the chair at the head of the table.

So Emmy told him, Josiah thought, as he took the offered

chair, thankful Luke seemed to want to smooth over their relations. "If it keeps on like it is now, I'm for tackling something else. I'm mighty tired of the heat and drought, but I'm not ready to work all day in the rain if I don't have to. I noticed there's practically no corn shelled. One of us could work on that."

"I hope somebody shells some corn and goes to the mill soon," Emmy said. "I'm low on meal."

"We'll tend to the shelling, Emmy. And I'll go to the mill soon," Luke answered with a quick frown. Then he turned back to Josiah and said, "I've been trying to get around to oiling the buggy harness and making a new halter for the cow. The wagon needs greasing, too. I reckon there's plenty for us to do."

"If it's all the same to you, I think I'll work on the harness. After we take a look at the smokehouse roof, that is. Do you have some shakes split?"

"Yes. Plenty for the job."

The older children entered and noisily scraped their chairs as they took their seats but quieted quickly at Luke's frown. Emmy served the ham and eggs onto platters as Josiah asked, "Where's Delia?"

"She didn't sleep well last night, with the storm and all," Emmy said. "I'm letting her sleep a little longer today. I'll get her up and feed her after I've seen to Mattie.

Josiah remembered to wait until Luke had said grace before digging into the breakfast. Soon they were all buttering biscuits, slathering on preserves and shoveling ham and eggs into their mouths.

"This sure is fine," Josiah said after his first few bites. "It's been a long time since I've eaten such a wonderful breakfast."

Emmy smiled shyly. "Thank you, Josiah. We did try to make it special, in honor of your safe return, didn't we, Sally?" The girl nodded as Emmy continued, "But don't go getting spoiled. We have enough to eat, but we don't make a feast of breakfast— or any other meal—every day."

Luke nodded and continued to eat. Few other words were spoken as everyone savored the unusual bounty. As the food disappeared, Emmy got up and poured more coffee—the real thing, to Josiah's delight. Too soon they had consumed the meal and all but Sally left the kitchen to begin their chores.

* * *

Sally thought about her father as she cleared the table, placed the remaining usable food in the pie safe and scraped the other leavings into the slop bucket. She had told him she didn't remember him, or maybe remembered him only a little, but she hadn't been completely truthful. She remembered Daddy, but the Daddy she remembered looked like the portrait Mama treasured, the one they looked at often while they talked about Daddy, the one she was never allowed to touch. This man didn't look like the picture. He had a stubbly beard, a gray one. Some of his hair was gray, too. He looked old. Older than Uncle Luke. Almost as old as Grandfather, she thought, as she scraped the last bit of tough, salty ham rind into the slop bucket.

She stepped on a low stool and hefted the water bucket to fill the deep basin she had placed in the sink, and as the water splashed she continued to think about Josiah. His face looked skinnier now. And his eyes looked . . . well, different, somehow, kind of like he was angry, or sad. Except when he talked to her. Then he got crinkly around his eyes, like he was smiling, even when he wasn't smiling. And he sounded like Daddy. He sounded like Daddy even when he got mad.

She didn't know how she knew about his angry voice, she couldn't remember any specific time he had been angry, but when he got mad at Uncle Luke last night she recognized his voice. She had kept her head down and her mouth shut as he had lashed out at Uncle Luke and then at Aunt Emmy, but she had sneaked a peek at first one and then another of the family around the table. Uncle Luke was plenty mad, too, no mistaking that. Jim was really scared. Callie Belle, too. Even Delia. Aunt Emmy looked . . . how? Hard to say. Kind of like scared. Well, a lot like scared. But kind of mad, too. At Daddy, she guessed. But she looked at Uncle Luke like she was kind of mad at him, too, before he left the kitchen. And scared of him. Nothing unusual about that.

As she rubbed a wet rag over the dishes, a smile crept across her face. She was glad Daddy and Uncle Luke argued last night. She wasn't glad Jim got whacked into his supper. He didn't deserve that. But she was glad Daddy stood up to Uncle Luke and made him angry.

She didn't like Uncle Luke, but of course she couldn't ever say so. She had told Mama once, and Mama had looked so odd— kind of like Aunt Emmy looking mad and scared at the same time—and Mama had told her she must never tell anyone else she didn't like Uncle Luke. Mama had said it like she meant it, like when she said "Don't play with snakes" or "Don't walk close behind the horses," so Sally had taken the admonition to heart. But she didn't really understand why Mama had looked kind of scared, too.

Uncle Luke always got his way. Mama said a man was head of his wife and family, and that made it right for Uncle Luke to boss everybody. Who made such a rule? Sally didn't like it and she told Mama so. Mama said for her to hush.

Now she mused that Daddy was the head of his wife and family, too. And Daddy could be mad at Uncle Luke and tell him so, 'cause he was a man. And this was Daddy's farm, and his house. Daddy didn't have to do everything Uncle Luke said. A small, quiet smile lit her face. Maybe Uncle Luke was supposed to do what Daddy said. Maybe Daddy had come home now to make Uncle Luke do right.

When she finished the last dish, Sally poured the greasy dishwater into the slop bucket. She stepped to the door and called, "Jim! Your Mama said you should come take this to the pigs." From a distance she heard Jim's grumpy response. She grabbed a towel and began to dry the dishes. Maybe she could sneak off when she finished the dishes. She'd get Squeaky and they'd go to their secret place. She would tell him all about what had been happening. She bet he'd be glad, too.

Squeaky knew all her secrets. He was a good friend. He wouldn't tell.

Chapter 6

Mattie stirred as Emmy pulled back the sheet. "How are you this morning?" Emmy asked.

"Some better."

"Would you like to get cleaned up?

"I guess."

As Emmy turned her sister to remove the soiled linens, Mattie moaned and bit her lip.

"Am I hurting you?" Emmy asked.

"Yes. You can't help it. I'll try to be quiet."

Emmy worked with care and tenderness, but she saw the pain reflected in Mattie's face. Before she finished the job, Mattie had passed out again. Emmy said aloud, although she knew her sister couldn't hear her, "Oh, Mattie. I'm sorry I can't tend to you without hurting you. How I wish I could make you well. I wish you could forget everything bad that has happened."

As she stood beside the bed and made needless small adjustments to Mattie's gown, Emmy feared neither wishing nor praying nor performing sacrifices would have effect. What exactly had happened to Mattie? She wondered, and yet maybe she didn't really want to know—it might be too terrible to bear.

She had envied Mattie's prettiness, her liveliness, her self-confidence, even though she knew envy was a sin. Mattie had been a flirtatious girl, had even flirted with Luke a little bit before she had married Josiah. Emmy had told Mattie to leave her Luke alone. Mattie had laughed and said, "Oh, he's yours,

46

Emmy. Don't you worry." Did that mean Luke was devoted to Emmy, or that Mattie didn't want him? Emmy suspected the latter. Mattie had thought she could have him if she'd wanted him, but she didn't want him. It must be nice to have so much self-confidence.

Or maybe not. Out in the barn, was Mattie too bold, too defiant? Could she have provoked the attacker?

Emmy wanted to hold Mattie blameless. That's what she wanted, but . . .

One thing was certain—she didn't envy Mattie now.

She shook herself, stroked Mattie's forehead and whispered, "Please get well. Please, let's get this all behind us."

When she entered her own room to wake Delia, she found Callie Belle playing with her rag doll and talking to her baby sister.

"Callie, I want you to take your dolly and go play in Aunt Mattie's room. When you see flies bothering her, you wave the fly whisk and scare them away. Don't let the whisk hit her, though. Just scare the flies away. Can you do that?"

"Yessum. My dolly will help me."

Callie Belle trotted across the hall, dragging the tattered doll by one arm. Emmy heard the chair creak as Callie Belle climbed up to sit beside Mattie, heard her daughter chattering to the doll about Aunt Mattie being hurt and having to stay in bed all the time, heard the swish and crash as the child dropped the whisk on the floor. She hoped Callie Belle was doing more good than harm.

Emmy picked up Delia. Wet again. As she changed the child's clothing she prayed in a whisper, knowing Delia couldn't understand her words and Callie Belle was too far away to hear them clearly. "Dear God, help me. It seems like everything in my whole world is going wrong. I'm so tired of cleaning up messes—the children's and now Mattie's. I know this isn't a proper way to pray, but I need to talk to You. Trouble is, I don't know what to say, or promise, or ask.

"Mattie is so sick. I love her—I don't want her to die. But what if she hangs on but doesn't really recover? I'm afraid I haven't the strength to care for her on and on like she is now.

"And here's Josiah back to take over his farm. I do thank You for his safe return, but where does that leave me and Luke? We've worked so hard here. It feels like it should be our place, at least in part. It would've gone to ruin without our work. Josiah says we have a place here, and he means it—today. But what about later? I'm afraid to trust him and afraid not to. Please help me."

She finished changing the child and frowned. Delia had been using the chamber pot dependably. Why was she wetting herself now? With a sigh, Emmy bundled the toddler's soggy clothing and swept the babbling Delia onto her hip. She walked out into the breezeway and hung the wet clothes to dry before she went to the kitchen to feed the child.

While Emmy tied Delia into the highchair she thought about all she had to do. She feared she was not coping very well. Unable to sort out any of her questions and concerns, she had to push them aside, at least for a while. The daily chores demanded attention. And energy. She would gather vegetables first, so she could finish the day's cooking, bank the fire and let the kitchen cool a bit. Josiah spoiled Mattie, having an iron cookstove shipped here so she could be the first in Red Lick to have one. It was nice in the winter, but in August it was nothing but a curse. Before the War, Mattie had had Dorcas to do the cooking and bear the heat. Now Emmy had no such luxury.

She heaved a big sigh. Early morning and she was worn out already. "Please God, help me. Give me strength."

Chapter 7

Josiah and Luke walked across the farm yard through the drizzle. The dogs tagged along. They had become friendlier in Luke's presence and wagged their tails and ran circles around the two men. Bo even pushed his nose against Josiah's hand, asking to be petted. Josiah obliged with a few pats and a ruffling of the shaggy black ears. Satisfied, the dog bounded on ahead.

"I see Jim's already let Pepper out," Josiah said.

"Yep. Looks like he's lame, like you rode him hard and rough."

Josiah reddened. "We've had a long way to travel. I didn't push him any harder than I pushed myself."

"Um-hum. And you're both lame," Luke said, noting Josiah's tender-footed gait.

The muscles at the back of Josiah's jaws bunched as he clenched his teeth. Why that bent-legged son of a . . . But there was no profit in such a train of thought. Luke had a weird sense of humor. Maybe he thought the remark funny. Josiah made himself relax and smile.

"I reckon we are. But my feet may heal quicker than his. I need to trim his hoof and re-shoe him, but I don't much look forward to working on him while he's so sore—he'll be jumpy. I'm not looking forward to firing up the forge, either. Maybe I can borrow Samson for a day. I'd rather him sweat than me. Not to mention he's a good hand at shoeing—does a better job than I can."

49

Luke hacked and spit off to the side. "You can't 'borrow' Samson anymore. McLain accepts the Yankee yoke, says the niggers are free and have to be 'hired' now. He even promised to pay Samson and another buck something at the end of the year. I wouldn't give the black son-of-a-bitch nothing but a whipping. He's one uppity nigger. He belongs over here, you ask me. Your Pa bought and paid for him."

Josiah sighed wearily and waited for a few seconds before he replied, "Lord knows I don't like to lose what my Pa worked hard for. What I worked for, too. But McLain's right. The blacks are free. That's the law now."

"But that ain't right."

"Doesn't matter whether it's right or not. We've lost that argument already."

"Lee should've never given up."

"I've come to think he didn't have much choice."

Both men turned red and set their jaws. Josiah stopped and took a deep breath, then said, "Look, Creed McLain is old and can't work his farm without help, so I'm glad a few of the darkies stayed with him."

"Right charitable of you, Josiah."

"Resigned might be a better word for it. Still, I reckon a man can tell his hired hand to go over and help out at a neighbor's place. Always could before. I can't see why he couldn't now. And if the hand wants to stay hired he doesn't have much to say about it."

"All right. Go ahead and ask for Samson. I don't want anything to do with the black bastard, though. And I advise you to watch him like a hawk. He ain't above stealing your tools or botching the shoeing out of spite."

What Emmy told must not've been the half of it, Josiah thought. And yet the Samson Luke and Emmy described didn't fit with the Samson he'd known. He'd never had any problems with the man. Of course, he'd never dealt with a free Samson.

By the time they arrived at the smokehouse, the drizzle had soaked their hats and shoulders. Luke said, "Inside we can tell where the leak is. It's mostly in the back left corner, I think. I've had my eye on it for a while but never could get time to fix it."

50

Josiah entered first and smiled as he inhaled the smoky smell of cured meat. He thought he could taste salt on his lips and tongue without having touched anything. And he could smell a musty dampness. In the darkness he could see little, but gradually he made out the long salting trough along the right wall. And then he could see two hams—one having been cut—and two sides of bacon hanging from the rafters along with several cylindrical sausages. Not much meat to carry eight people till hog killing in the fall, even if four of them were children. He might have more trouble saving Sally's pet than he had thought.

As Josiah's eyes adjusted to the darkness he saw the damp rafters in the back corner, and he heard an occasional drip. Luke followed him as he went to examine the leak more closely.

"How much do you think we need to do here?" Josiah asked.

"It looks to me like a couple of these purlins are rotten. I think we should remove all the shakes on the rear three or four feet of the roof. Then we can scab in some new rafters if we need to. Replace the rotten purlins. With new shakes it'll be in good shape again."

"It'll take a heap of shakes and purlins. You're sure we've got enough?"

"'Course I'm sure," Luke answered.

"Want to start on it now, or wait a while to see if the rain will let up?" Josiah asked.

"It ain't going to let up anytime soon. Why don't you work on the harness, and I'll get Jim and shell some corn. Maybe this afternoon we can get to it without drowning," Luke said.

"Sounds good to me."

Luke yelled for Jim, and the boy met them as they came to the barn. Josiah could not see well enough in the dark tack room to clean and oil the harness. He took his supplies and tools out into the better light of the hall.

Luke sent Jim for the wheelbarrow and started to the corncrib. Soon the man and the boy returned with the barrow full of corn, which they dumped on the tack room floor. Luke watched and instructed Jim as the boy began to feed the ears into the iron chute of the sheller while turning the crank. Then he started back to the crib for another load of corn.

"Takes a lot of arm, doesn't it?" Josiah asked the boy.

"Yessir. But I can do it," Jim said as he kept turning.

"I see you can."

Though he was doing a good job, Josiah expected Jim to wear out soon. And from what he had observed of Luke, he figured the boy would be made to labor long after he tired. Well, it won't hurt him, he thought. I'll stay out of it.

The three worked quietly for most of the morning, neither man having much to say, and the boy apparently knowing better than to make any comment. Soon Jim switched from one arm to the other to turn the crank, then used both arms together to turn more and more slowly. Josiah admired his toughness, but he felt his tension ease when Luke said, "I think I've got enough corn from the crib. I'll shell for a while now. You can go, boy. Ask your mother if she needs you to do any chores."

"Yessir."

Jim left for the house. Well away from the barn, he looked back, then rubbed his upper arms and flexed them and slowed his pace.

Josiah had oiled the harness and had cut the straps for the new cow halter when they heard Emmy calling the family to the midday meal.

"Let's see what Emmy has fixed," Luke said as he placed the lid on the corn barrel.

"I don't much care what she's fixed, as long as there's enough of it. I'm so hungry I could eat this harness leather," Josiah said. Both men laughed.

After Josiah had washed up, he checked on Mattie and found her quiet, her eyes closed. He kissed her forehead and she stirred but did not wake. He assumed she truly slept, so he left without disturbing her further.

In the kitchen, everyone took a seat at the table and Luke said grace. He thanked God for the bountiful spread before them, and indeed it was bountiful—a heaping bowl of green beans seasoned with salt pork, another of black-eyed peas, and another of fried squash, and a platter of roasted corn, a plate of sliced ripe tomatoes, and a basket of cornbread accompanied by a crock of butter and another of preserves. Buttermilk filled the tin mugs.

Josiah noted the absence of meat except the small amount of fatback in the beans. Both men heaped the vegetables on their plates and took large pieces of cornbread. Emmy and the children did the same. For several minutes they all remained quiet as everyone ate.

After his hunger pangs dulled, Josiah commented, "I notice there's not a whole lot of meat left in the smokehouse. Those pigs with the sow out by the barn—they going to be enough meat come winter?"

"We'll have about a dozen hogs, I reckon," Luke replied as he sopped bean broth with a piece of cornbread. "Enough for us and some to sell, too. Some of them are running loose out in the woods. 'Course, you know how hard it is to get 'em gathered up. I haven't penned any up to fatten yet."

Jim said, "Father couldn't pen 'em up 'cause—"

Luke raised his brows and pointed at the boy. Jim shut up. Luke swallowed a bite of cornbread, then picked up Jim's explanation.

"Every time I penned some up during the last couple of years, along came another bunch of soldiers. They'd take every pig they could find. Didn't matter whether they were our boys or Yankees. 'Course our boys were supposed to pay for what they took, but most of 'em didn't. That's why we're short of meat—had a hard time getting any of the hogs butchered for ourselves—and keeping the meat when we did."

"Daddy, Uncle Luke hid the meat from the soldiers," Sally said.

"Hush, Sally. Were you spoken to?" Emmy said.

"Nobody spoke to you, either, wife. Be quiet and let me talk to Josiah," Luke said.

Emmy frowned, but she kept quiet.

Luke waited a moment, then continued. "Yep, we had a hard time keeping meat for ourselves. When we butchered, we had to pray none of them soldiers would come around while we were curing it. Luckily they never did."

"Tell about the hidey-holes, Uncle Luke."

Luke scowled at Sally but went on, "I had to find a way to hide most of what we cured. I hung it in the barn, the toolshed,

53

up in the sleeping loft. I even built a coffin, figuring if we had advance warning we could stash some of the meat in it and fake a funeral. Never got to use it, though. Never enough warning. If any of the patrols had searched hard, they'd have found what was in the barn and the shed, maybe even what was here in the house. I guess most of them were too lazy, or in too much hurry, to look beyond the smokehouse. They cleaned that out more than once."

"So why risk keeping meat in the smokehouse now? I mean, more than a few day's supply?"

Luke shrugged. "There haven't been many patrols close by for a while now. And there was no way to keep the rats from chewing on what was in the toolshed and the barn. I've left some in the loft"—he motioned toward the main part of the house— "but I brought the rest to the smokehouse. I hope I haven't made a mistake."

"We've had some losses from the smokehouse," Emmy added, "but it's mostly been small amounts. We figured drifters stole 'cause they were hungry. We didn't like it, but we didn't begrudge 'em too much." She fell quiet for a moment, then sighed. "Of course, now we know we should've been more vigilant about drifters."

Luke frowned, avoided Josiah's eyes, but said nothing. The silence grew awkward. He cleared his throat and continued, "There wasn't much I could have left in the other places—a ham and a couple of sides of bacon and a few sausages."

Josiah nodded. "You probably did right. I'd hate to lose the rest of the meat, though."

Luke shrugged. "A risk worth taking, you ask me." He gnawed another mouthful of corn from the cob and chewed before he added, "Anyhow, I stored the coffin in the shed. It'll be usable for something. I worked hard building it—sawing and fitting and planning those boards."

Talk of coffins brought Mattie's plight too close. Josiah stared at his plate. Emmy sniffed. Luke reddened. The silence grew uncomfortable.

At last Josiah took a gulp of buttermilk, glanced outside, then said, "We got a lot done this morning. It looks like the rain is letting up. Maybe we can get the smokehouse roof done this afternoon if we both work on it."

Luke nodded, and Josiah continued, "Then tomorrow I'd like to ride over to McLain's place—pay my respects to them and see about getting Samson to shoe Pepper."

"They'll be glad to see you," Luke said. "But I don't know what you're going to ride. Your roan's not up to travel. And you sure don't want to ride our old sway-backed gray. I guess you could take one of the mules, but they're not much good for riding. I rode one when we searched for the b—" He glanced at the children and Emmy and backed up a bit. "—searched for the stranger Jim saw when Mattie . . ." He fell silent for several moments, then finished. "Well, the mules can be ridden. I don't think much of them but I'm not the best judge of a saddle animal."

Josiah gazed out the window for a long moment. Emmy held her breath.

Josiah turned back to Luke and said, "It's hard for me to talk about what happened to Mattie. I can see you trying not to remind me, tripping all over your tongue when you realize you have. But the facts are there all the time, even though I can't quite get it all in my head, can't quite understand exactly what happened." He paused, noticed Luke had turned even redder. He drew a breath and went on. "I want you to know I appreciate what you did, Luke, how you tried to find the dirty low-down snake. Emmy told me about your search, you and the neighbors. You tried. I appreciate it."

Luke flushed and ducked his head, avoided Josiah's eyes, and muttered something unintelligible.

Same ol' stiff-necked Luke, Josiah thought. Prickly over any little criticism, but you can't praise him or thank him, either. He sighed and caught a glimpse of Emmy's pinched expression. He gave her a sad smile as he said, "I thank you both for how you've tried to help Mattie."

Emmy's face relaxed. "We've done what we could," she said. "I hope we've helped her."

"Of course you have," Josiah murmured, and they all fell silent.

After a few moments, Josiah cleared his throat. "What happened to all the decent horseflesh? When I left and took Pepper, you still had another good saddle horse, and a pretty bay carriage horse, and two fine teams of mules. Now we only have those two scruffy mules and a miserable old gray mare."

Luke shifted uncomfortably and avoided Josiah's eyes. "I reckon we've done the best we could. All the decent horse stock was confiscated by our boys early on. It's been dang nigh impossible to get horses or mules fit to work. We didn't have much left after our boys had withdrawn. And then the Yankees came and took the rest—all of our horses and most of the cattle."

"It's a wonder you were able to keep the farm going."

"I did whatever I could think of. I tried yoking a couple cows, but that didn't work out very well. They had never been trained to the yoke, and I didn't have any experience with oxen. We had to let most of the fields go, just worked a big garden to feed ourselves and a plot of corn for the animals. When I got an opportunity to trade your one-horse wagon and two cows for this team of mules we have now, I jumped at it."

Josiah scowled.

Luke hurried on. "I hated to let the wagon and those cows go, but they'd have been confiscated anyway. The cows, I mean. Trading for the team seemed the only thing to do."

"I'm surprised you've been able to keep the mules, after all you've told me."

Luke shrugged. "The team is old, but they're good enough to be taken by the danged Yankees, or by anybody wandering through here, for that matter, and that's been a worry. But we've been lucky. Once when the foragers came looking for stock I had taken a load of corn to the mill, so I missed them. And a couple of times we got word they were headed this way and I had time to take the team out in the woods and hide 'em."

Luke paused and took a deep breath. "I hate we don't have stock as good as you left, but I've done the best I could."

"I believe you." Josiah said. "I try not to think too badly of our boys taking our stock, even food. The army had to eat and it had to travel. My outfit did some confiscating, too, truth be known. We got so we didn't let ourselves think about the

56

hardship we might cause the folks we took from. And my unit didn't take everything a family had. I guess some did. I can't feel much charity toward them. And I don't feel any charity at all toward those damned Yankee sons-of-bitches."

"Josiah! Watch your language! The children," Emmy said.

"I'm sorry, Emmy. You, too, young-uns. I'm not much used to being around ladies and children here lately. I used some bad words just now, children. I don't want to hear you repeating them. Understand?"

"Yessir," chorused the three older children.

"Sumbitches!" squealed Delia.

"Delia, that's one of the bad words Uncle Josiah shouldn't have said. You're not to say it." Emmy turned to Josiah. "See what you've done?"

"Emmy, I said I was sorry."

"Well, you should know better."

Luke snorted. "Yep, you should. I think I'd better get you out of here before you get into any more trouble."

"You're right. Let's see about the roof. I'll look in on Mattie, and then I'll join you at the smokehouse.

Chapter 8

Josiah found Mattie awake, writhing and breathing raggedly. "Mattie! What's the matter?"

"Ohhhh. Don't worry. It'll pass." She groaned as she seemed to make a strong effort to be still and to compose her features. "Sometimes I hurt. But the pain eases after a bit."

"How can I help you?"

"There's nothing you can do." She tried to shake her head but only managed a feeble twist. "Except the medicine." She weakly motioned toward the laudanum bottle on the table. He loosened the cork and poured some of the liquid into a spoon, then helped Mattie raise her head enough to take the dose. Her skin felt hotter than it had last night— he hoped that was because of the heat and humidity in the room. Mattie's face glistened and her sheets darkened with sweat.

"I'll be all right. Go. Work."

But Josiah stayed and watched her struggle with her pain. Gradually her face relaxed, but she looked exhausted. Her eyes closed and she slept. He quietly turned and walked out through a misty drizzle to meet Luke at the smokehouse.

As much as Josiah felt indebted to Luke for maintaining the farm in his absence, as much as he was obliged to treat him as a brother, he found himself trying to find fault with the man's work. When they inspected the shakes in the shed, he hoped to find Luke had been sloppy with the froe, but the uniformity of the shakes told him otherwise. The large stack of shingles spoke of industriousness. As they began the repairs, Luke didn't let his twisted leg get in his way as he worked, and he accomplished as much as Josiah did. Josiah grudgingly recognized Luke as a good and skillful worker. He supposed he should be thankful, not jealous. Mattie and Sally had been better cared for in his absence because of it. He should thank Luke, but Luke had already shown he didn't accept thanks gracefully.

The two men worked throughout the afternoon, limiting their conversation to what was necessary to coordinate on the job. They both frowned in concentration, and measured and cut and nailed. The rain stopped completely. The sky brightened. The work progressed quickly, and they were nearly finished when Emmy sent Sally to ask if they were about ready for supper.

"Well, I'm ready to call it a day," said Luke as he pounded the last nail into a shake. "I'm plenty ready to finish off those beans and peas. How about you?"

"Sure am," agreed Josiah. "We only have a few more shakes to nail to finish this job, so let's do it."

They sent Sally back to say they would be in for supper soon. They finished the job, then gathered the tools and put them away, and headed to the house.

The family gathered in the kitchen as they had the night before, tired and hungry. After Luke said grace they served themselves cold leftovers. There was no meat, but there was butter for the cold cornbread and buttermilk to drink. Everyone concentrated on eating and said little other than to ask for a dish to be passed.

As the clink and scrape of cutlery on plates diminished, Josiah sopped the juice from the black-eyed peas with a piece of cornbread and said, "We made quick work of the smokehouse roof this afternoon. I thought it'd take till tomorrow. Now we're set for the butchering this fall."

"Yep," Luke said. "We can bait the hogs as soon as we gather some of the corn. It'll be ready in a couple of weeks."

"It looks to me like the crib's full for this time of year. Why don't we bait 'em now? Gather 'em up and see what we have. We could sell off some of what we won't need and pen a few to start fattening," Josiah said.

"I don't want to have to feed 'em till the corn is in."

Josiah looked around the table at the lean faces of his household. "But it looks like we all could use some meat."

Luke made no comment.

Josiah sat looking at his plate for a few seconds before he continued. "I haven't gone over the field yet, but from a distance the corn doesn't look too bad, considering the drought."

Luke frowned. "By the grace of God, we'll have a harvest, but I don't know how good. We had fine weather at planting, and for a few weeks after. Got a good stand of corn that looked strong when it tasseled. Then the rain stopped. We're going to have a lot of half-filled nubbins. There ought to be enough to get us through till next year, but I don't think there'll be any extra."

"Enough is all right."

"No, it's a disappointment. I planned to have some to sell, but now I doubt we will. It's a shame—there's going to be a market for it. Maybe not a cash market, but there'll be a big need for corn. We could have used it for trade. But the Lord will provide sufficient unto our needs," Luke answered.

"Amen," murmured Emmy, but her knitted brows suggested her doubt.

"He'll provide, but it behooves us to help ourselves as much as we can," Josiah said. "I still think we ought to round up those hogs and sell some now. The pen out in the woods is big enough they should be able to shift for themselves without too much extra feed. I'd like to be ready to butcher as soon as we have suitable weather."

Luke flushed. "You're wrong. Take a look at the crops before you decide to waste corn. And this drought has hit the oaks, too. There won't be many acorns in the pen for any hogs you put there." He paused, then smiled. "If you're so hungry for meat, kill that runt that runs around the yard and roots under the house. There's no sense wasting feed on him. He's so dang small we could eat him up in a couple of days—no need to wait for cold weather."

"No-o-o-o! Not Squeaky!" Sally shrieked. "Daddy, you promised."

Luke scowled and half rose from his chair, drawing his open

hand back as if to slap the girl, but caught Josiah's glare and sat back down.

Josiah frowned as he looked from Sally to Luke and back again. He wished he hadn't promised Sally he'd save her pet. Luke was right—anything they fed the runt was wasted. And if they killed him now, he wouldn't last long enough to spoil. Josiah could almost taste fresh pork, just thinking about it. He looked at Luke and knew saving the pig would be costly, one way or another. But he had promised Sally. What a minor thing to start a family feud over. He looked at Sally's pleading eyes and knew it would be a long time before the child would trust him again if he did not keep his promise now. He really didn't have a choice. He took a deep breath.

"I reckon I'm not meat-hungry enough to eat the runt, Luke. And I reckon you're not either."

Luke turned red. "Josiah, you're a danged fool!" His eyes flashed and the cords in his neck stood out.

Josiah kept eye contact with Luke, but he grinned sheepishly when he said, "I 'spect I am. But I promised Sally we wouldn't kill her pig, and we won't. We can trade him off for another pig."

"Who's going to trade for such a runt?" Luke rose from the table and stomped from the kitchen.

Sally stared after him, then looked back at Josiah. Tears ran down her cheeks and her lips quivered. Jim and Callie Belle remained rigid, hardly breathing, their eyes downcast. Delia stared open-mouthed at the doorway, her spoon clutched in her hand halfway to her mouth. Emmy, with a look of dread, watched her husband depart, then turned to Josiah and opened her mouth, but he cut her off.

"Don't you start, too, Emmy. Nobody's going to touch Sally's pig. You understand?"

Emmy grimaced but nodded and kept quiet as Josiah stood and fished in his pocket for his pipe and tobacco. After he filled and lit the pipe, he slowly walked out and stood on the porch. A few strong draws on his pipe got it well started. Looking around the farmyard, he saw no sign of Luke. The scruffy gray dog, Pretty Girl, nuzzled his hand and licked grease from his fingers. Josiah could hear Emmy in the kitchen assigning chores to the children and cleaning up after the meal. From her tone of voice he knew she was exasperated by the events at supper. He heard her say to Sally, "Your Daddy is the most pig-headed, childish man I've ever known." He let out an angry snort. She had no business saying such. But in his heart he knew she had some justification, though he'd be damned if he would ever admit it to her.

As Josiah ambled across the back porch he eyed each of the chairs set back against the wall of the house, remembering how uncomfortable he had been last night. He sat in one but found it offered little improvement over the little slipper chair. He moved to a rocking chair with a curved splat back and a woven hickory splint seat comfortably dished by years of use. Rocking, he drew on the pipe, tobacco smoke drifting off into the night on the barely perceptible breeze. The chair fit well, and when he had finished the pipe and knocked the dottle out into the yard, he picked up the rocker and carried it with him on his way to Mattie's bedside.

He found her asleep. Her discolored, swollen face, now dry, wore a tight, pained look even in sleep. Josiah set the rocker down and moved the small chair aside. As he placed the rocker by the bed, it bumped the table. Mattie woke.

"Josiah. I'm so glad to see you." She turned to the window, then back to him. "It's getting dark."

Josiah leaned down to kiss her forehead. Her skin burned his lips.

"I told you I'd be here. How're you feeling?" he asked as he soaked the cloth in the bowl of water and wrung it. He wiped her face and laid the rag on her forehead.

"Not too bad. Hot. It's been getting hotter in here all afternoon."

True enough. The air had heated quickly when the rain had stopped and the sun had finally broken through. But he knew her fever was worse. He stirred the air with the fly whisk and asked, "Do you want some water?"

"Maybe a little."

He helped her raise her head and held the cup to her lips. She only swallowed a few drops.

"Mattie, please try to drink a little bit more. Doc Wilson says you need water."

"My belly hurts when I drink."

"Do you need some medicine?"

"I think so," she said as she squirmed.

Josiah opened the vial, raised her head, and administered the dose of laudanum. "Maybe when the pain goes away you can drink some more."

"Maybe." She closed her eyes and moved restlessly again.

Josiah watched in the deepening darkness and was relieved to see her face begin to relax after a few minutes. She squeezed his hand once. Then her breathing became more regular and she lay still.

He released her hand, leaned back in the rocking chair and wiped at the sweat on his own face. His skin felt oily and gritty and his eyes burned. He dropped both his hands to the arms of the chair, tried to relax. After a while he saw his knuckles whiten as he gripped the chair arms. He forced his muscles to loosen. Mattie had seemed better last night and this morning, but high fever was a bad sign, a very bad sign.

With a rustle of her skirts Emmy entered carrying a lamp. "Josiah, you look terrible. You need to get some rest. I can sit with Mattie tonight."

"No. I promised her I'd stay."

Mattie stirred restlessly. Josiah put his finger to his lips as he quietly rose from the chair and motioned for Emmy to come with him out into the hall.

When they were well away from the bedroom door he said, "She feels hot as fire to me. You feel her forehead, see what you think."

Emmy nodded and murmured, "All right. I'll check."

"She only took a few drops of water. She said it hurt to drink. I'm worried something awful."

Emmy returned to the bedroom and removed the damp rag from Mattie's forehead. She placed the back of her hand on Mattie's brow, then withdrew it, frowning. She freshened the damp cloth and returned to the hall.

63

"She's burning with fever. I'll go get some cool water from the well. Maybe keeping the cloth cooler will help."

Josiah nodded as she left, then he returned to Mattie's bedside.

In a few minutes Emmy returned with freshly drawn water. As she dipped and wrung the rag they heard Luke call from the other room, "Emmy, what are you doing? Get on in here!"

"Go on. I can do this," Josiah said.

Emmy left.

Josiah could hear rumblings and murmuring but nothing distinct. Then he thought he heard Emmy crying, and a little wail, followed by more bass rumblings. Then he distinctly heard Luke say, "You've got other duties. Josiah can sit with her tonight."

Again he heard the children gathering in the other room, and Luke beginning his reading. Jeremiah 17:1. *The sin of Judah is written with the pen of iron, and with the point of a diamond . . . .* So he probably was reading the whole Bible, each book and chapter in its turn. Josiah's mind wandered. He only caught part of the reading, a word, a phrase, a sentence. *. . . enemies . . . cursed be the man . . . he that getteth riches, and not by right, shall leave them in the midst of his days, and at his end shall be a fool . . . .* His attention drifted. He couldn't tie it all together—didn't even want to. He did not hear the ending and prayer and was unaware of the children's departure afterward.

In a few minutes Emmy returned, her eyes red and swollen. "I want to sit with her a while, Josiah."

"Fine. But I'll stay here. I don't know why, but it seemed to be important to Mattie for me to stay. I don't want her to wake up and find me gone. It might really upset her, and I don't think that would be at all good for her. She's acts so scared."

"We all are," Emmy murmured as she brought the small chair close to the bed. "Maybe not scared exactly, but leery. Wishing we could see the future, but then, maybe not."

They tended to Mattie, keeping the damp rag cool, but said little. After a while Emmy observed, "She's sleeping through this, not waking at all when we change the cloth. Is she sleeping, or? . . ."

"I'm not sure. I gave her laudanum before you came in a while ago. I think it's what's keeping her asleep. You want to try to wake her?"

"Maybe we should. I hate to, though. She needs her rest."

Josiah shook his head. "Somehow, I need to know." He took Mattie's hand and, leaning over her, whispered, "Mattie. Matilda Jane. Can you hear me?"

Mattie stirred and her eyelids fluttered. "Jos . . . i . . . ahh." She soon lay still again.

Emmy sighed.

They resumed their wordless watch. After an hour or so, Josiah noticed Emmy nodding in her chair, sagging to the point he feared she would fall. He whispered to her. "Emmy. Emmy Louise." She jerked upright and opened her eyes.

"Wh-what is it? Is Mattie? . . ."

"Sh-hh. She's the same. There's no need for both of us to stay up. You're exhausted. Go on to bed. I'll watch. If Mattie needs you, I'll call."

"I feel like I should stay with her. And how can you keep working through the days and not sleep at night?"

"I never sleep much, Emmy. I reckon I nap a little without knowing it. You go on. It'll be all right." In truth, he was exhausted, but he didn't want to sleep and allow the nightmare to come again.

Emmy looked back and forth between Mattie and Josiah. They could hear Luke's loud snores in the other room. Finally she nodded and whispered, "You'll wake me if there's any change, won't you?"

"Of course."

She left and Josiah heard only the faintest rustlings as she slipped into her bed. Luke's rasping snores continued without interruption.

Josiah changed the damp cloth again and settled into the rocking chair. The house was so quiet he could hear every little disturbance. One of the children—he couldn't tell which— mewled as it stirred in its bed, rustling the shucks in the mattress. Between Luke's snores he could hear the faint hiss and sputter of the flame in the lamp.

An owl hooted in the woods. Death's messenger. Josiah shuddered. Just an old superstition. He didn't lend much credence to such superstitions, but . . . Damn bird sounded so eerie, could be a haint calling. He listened anxiously for Mattie's shallow but regular breathing.

Chapter 9

Josiah tried in vain to clear his mind of the worries and doubts plaguing him. How could he *not* worry about Mattie?

In the stillness of the night, disturbing questions and doubts began to gnaw at him like rats chewing an unattended ham. What had happened to her, really? He supposed it remotely possible she was injured by a fall or by the cow, but he didn't believe either, and neither did anyone else. Somebody beat her. Who? The barefoot stranger? Why? Maybe she caught him stealing? But then wouldn't he have simply shoved her out of his way and run? Unless he intended rape.

Josiah's mind recoiled from the thought, but he had to consider the possibility. It might explain the ferocity of the beating. It might explain Mattie's fear. Did Luke think of rape? When he raised an alarm, did he tell the neighbors they were after a batterer, or a rapist? Maybe, even if he suspected rape, he kept quiet about it to keep Mattie's honor intact. Emmy hadn't mentioned any suspicion of rape, but she was so constricted by her sense of propriety, she might not have been able to voice the word.

Mattie's honor. If she'd been outraged, it wasn't her fault, wasn't any of her doing. He understood, and yet . . .

He poured fresh water into the bowl, soaked and wrung the cloth. Cooled her brow again. Sat back in his chair. His mind whirled round and round over what had happened, over the lack of certainty. He couldn't break from the rut. Round and round . . .

Tense, unquiet dark. Leaves rustle. Twigs snap. Dank air, still and threatening. He strains to see, but there is only the fog, gray, growing denser, swirling into patterns that dissolve as soon as they form. The gray morphs into a face—a face he knows too well now. Its twisted mouth whispers, "I hope you burn in hell, you miserable coward." The 'burn in hell' repeats like a fading echo. The fog thickens, reddens, transforms itself into blood that spews like a fountain. Slimes his skin. Fouls his eyes, his mouth. Takes his breath.

He awoke panting, bathed in sweat, his throat raw and tight around a scream, his hand firmly grasping the knife from his boot. Mattie shrank from him, eyes as wide as her bruises allowed, looking first at his hand and then at his tortured face and back again. His eyes followed her frightened stare. His hand shook as he returned the blade to his boot.

"Josiah?"

He kept his eyes down and muttered, "I had a bad dream." Slowly he raised his head and looked at her. "I didn't hurt you, did I?"

"Hurt me? No. But you sounded so . . . terrified, so lost. You scared me."

"I'm sorry. I had a dream." He moaned and ran his hands over his face, rubbing deeply across his eyes. "I have bad dreams. That's why I don't like to sleep very much, but a body's got to sleep sometime." He drew a deep breath and expelled it forcefully. "I'm all right now."

"Tell me the dream. When Sally has a bad dream, it helps her if she tells about it. Maybe it'll help you, too."

"I'm not a child, Mattie."

"No. Of course not."

He looked around the room, out the window into the darkness, anywhere to avoid looking into her eyes. He shifted in his chair, then twisted to yet another position. He clasped and unclasped his hands. Minutes passed.

"It was about . . . It wasn't about anything real."

"But it was frightening."

He nodded. "Yes." He leaned forward, rested his elbows on his thighs, buried his face in his hands. "Lot's more frightening than . . . than what I think might've caused it."

"Something from the war?"

He remained silent for minutes. Then he nodded and mumbled, "Yes."

"Oh, my poor Josiah."

He mumbled through his hands, "Mattie, it was more terrible than I could ever tell you. I don't want to think about it."

"But you do think about it, or you wouldn't have these dreams." She stretched her hand to touch his bent head.

He slowly raised his head and clasped her hand between both of his. "I'm so ashamed, Mattie." He swallowed hard, blinked, and continued with a quaver. "I did a bad thing. I think it was a really bad thing." He coughed out an ironic little laugh. "I don't know why this is so hard to tell you. For months I've dreamed of telling you about it, having your forgiveness. But now I'm so afraid . . ."

"Josiah, I doubt you could do anything so terrible I couldn't forgive you."

"But what I did was bad. Dishonorable."

He swallowed again and bowed his head so his forehead touched their clasped hands. The bedding muffled his words as he made his confession.

"I killed a man."

She stirred and began, "But—"

"I know. War requires killing. I think I killed several men— enemies. Mostly it didn't bother me too much. But one time . . . I've thought about it and thought about it, and I don't think I could've done any different. I think I had to do it. But it was still terrible."

Once started, he raised his head and began his story, at times pausing so long it seemed as though he would not go on. Mattie listened, silent, as he relived his story.

*   *   *

Riding single file. The trail is narrow, and steep, but wide enough the one-horse wagon can get through, although

69

sometimes the hubs of the wheels scrape the bluff on the left. Josiah can't believe anyone who lived in these mountains could have any supplies worth taking, but orders are orders. Ride in, grab corn and hogs and anything else they can use, ride out again. Shouldn't be any resistance to speak of.

The crack of a rifle. The man in front of him slumps and slides off his horse. Then more shots. From where? The bluff above? The steep, brush-clogged ravine on the right?. More men fall.

Keep moving. Pepper whirls and leaps at his command.

Return fire. Where? Anywhere. The dense woods allows only brief glimpses of smoke and motion. Somebody yells, "Retreat!" A couple of riders rush by him.

Pepper falters, falls. The ground rushes up at Josiah, the ground and a big boulder at the edge of the ravine. He kicks free of the stirrups and tries to roll away from the hunk of rock, but his head smacks it hard. A flash like lightning. The world goes black.

Later—how much later? still daylight, but maybe late afternoon—he gradually becomes aware of his throbbing head, then of stones and deadfall jabbing his body, finally of the silvery undersides of laurel leaves above him.

Quiet. Keep quiet.

Wind sighs in the trees. A squirrel chatters somewhere nearby. The little creek burbles in the ravine. No voices, footsteps, horses' snorts.

Where did everybody go?

He rolls over as quietly as he can—God, his head hurts!—and eases his way up to the edge of the trail, thankful that the laurel hides him. A horse lies dead in the road. Not Pepper, thank God. The acrid stench of gun smoke no longer taints the air.

He is about to crawl from under the laurel when he hears them. Voices. Men not trying to be quiet. Not close, but not far away, either. The clink of a horseshoe against stone. A nervous laugh. And then he sees them, coming around the bend up the trail. Yankees. Rear guard? Burial party? Scavengers? What difference does it make? If they see him, he's either dead or captured. No witnesses. He'd bet on dead.

He slithers on his belly backward, away from the road, thankful that recent rains have softened the earth and the dead leaves beneath the laurels. Inch by inch. So careful. No noise. Down the steep side of the ravine. Peek to see what lies farther down. Move. Peek again. Up on the road a wagon creaks, horses plod, men talk. Good. All that will help cover any little sound he makes. His feet suddenly find no purchase. He turns his body enough to see that he is at the edge of a stone outcrop. How high? Can't tell. Creek sounds close below.

Above, someone says, "Get that horse out of the way." The order is followed by the mutters and grunts of men straining at hard work and a scraping, sliding noise. And then the body of the dead horse comes crashing down through the brush, straight at him. Out of options, he rolls a few feet to the side and drops over the edge of the outcrop with the horse right beside him.

His landing is soft! He finds himself on top of a Yankee, looking into the man's wide eyes. Josiah clamps his hand over the Yank's opening mouth. The man—no, more like boy—tries to shake Josiah loose, but his efforts are feeble. Then Josiah notices the blood soaking the blue uniform.

"Be quiet," he mouths.

The boy struggles harder. His feet kick, dislodging stones at the edge of the creek. The body of the horse settles, moving a rock and masking the noise the boy makes.

"Shh," he hisses and bears down harder on the hand covering the boy's mouth. With his free hand he searches for a weapon on the Yankee, finds none.

"Quiet. I don't want to hurt you, but you've got to be quiet. You're going to get me killed," he whispers. The boy continues to kick and squirm without much vigor but hard enough to shift small rocks. Josiah can't let him make any more noise. He reaches into his boot and draws his knife. "Be still, boy!" The Yank's eyes open wider and his struggles become more frantic.

Where'd he get this sudden strength? Got to quiet him.

With a quick slice he cuts the boy's throat. Blood spurts in pulsing arcs, diminishing with each beat of the Yankee's heart until it slows to a trickle, then stops.

* * *

"He was going to kill me, as sure as if he had a gun," Josiah said.

He swallowed hard several times as he fought down his nausea. Then he continued, his voice dull. "I cut his throat."

He stared, unseeing, and after a long pause continued. "Blood all over both of us. Where'd he get the strength to buck and twist?" He shook his head.

"I held him to keep him quiet till he finally went limp. He'd already bled out so much, it couldn't have taken long, but it seemed like an eternity to me."

Josiah shuddered. "I kept him quiet and the Yankee troop didn't find me. It got dark. I slipped away. It took me a few days, but I made it back to my company. They had Pepper. We both healed."

He paused for a few moments. "I had to do it. But God have mercy on me, he was unarmed and nearly helpless."

Tears ran from Mattie's swollen eyes. "Oh, my dear Josiah. What a terrible thing."

He stared out into the darkness. "I shouldn't have told you. Now you'll despise me."

"No, I don't despise you." She reached for his hand again. "I love you."

"But I killed an unarmed man, Mattie. Unarmed. Looking right into his face."

"To save yourself. I can't feel you were wrong."

"Then why does he curse me every night?"

She drew a shaky breath. "Maybe because you feel so bad about it."

He nodded and buried his face in his hands again.

"Josiah, listen to me."

He looked up, afraid of what she might say.

"I worried, afraid you wouldn't come back to us. I prayed and prayed you would be kept safe. Selfish, but . . ." She paused to catch her breath, and panted for a few seconds before she could continue. "My prayers were answered. Don't you see? God saved you. We can't know the mystery of His ways."

Josiah blinked and turned away. "You can forgive me?"

72

"There's nothing for me to forgive, only your return to rejoice in." Mattie rested a few moments before adding, "But I wish I could ease your pain. You must forgive yourself."

"When I'm awake I do. I know I only did what I had to. But when I sleep the dream comes and . . . ."

"Then pray for God's forgiveness. And your own. Pray."

He shook his head. "I'm not . . . ." He couldn't tell her how he felt about God's indifference. She had strong faith and she needed it now in her distress. He dared not risk damaging her beliefs. He clasped her hand again. "Yes . . . Yes, I will." He closed his eyes and continued. "And I feel better having told you about it."

They remained quiet for several minutes, their breathing becoming more steady. At last Josiah said, "You sound stronger than you did earlier this evening. Do you think you could take some water or some broth?"

"Maybe a little water," she answered. He poured fresh water into her cup and held it to her lips. She sipped a few drops, then drew away, as she had in the evening. "Hurts."

"I know you hurt all over, Mattie, but you must drink."

"No. My belly hurts. My stomach. It's so sore. It hurts when I move. It hurts when I'm still. I'm thirsty, but it hurts to drink." She paused and closed her eyes for a bit, depleted by her speech. "Sorry. I shouldn't complain. But I can't bear to drink."

"All right." Josiah looked away from her, then back again. "I feel so helpless. I want so much to help you get well, but I don't know what to do."

"I know. You do help." She closed her eyes.

Josiah stayed silent for several minutes. The clock ticked, then struck midnight. Except for Luke's snores, the house was quiet. She was so weak, so tired. He felt terrible about doing it, but he touched Mattie's hand, gently stroked it until her eyes opened.

"Mattie, I want to know what happened to you."

Her eyes widened, as much as the bruised flesh would allow, then closed again. She slowly shook her head back and forth. "I don't remember. I went to the barn to milk. But then . . . I don't remember."

"Try, Mattie. Did you fall? Did the cow turn on you? Or did somebody do this to you?"

Eyes closed, she shook her head again. "I . . . don't remember."

"Someone attacked you, didn't he? Jim told Emmy he saw a stranger prowling around that morning."

Her eyes opened a slit and she studied him for several seconds. Then she closed them again before she repeated, "I don't remember. Please, Josiah . . ."

"Luke chased him, you know. Gathered some of the neighbors and searched for him, but they never found him." He paused for a few seconds. "They didn't know enough about him. The way Emmy told it to me, Jim's description of him wasn't very good. What did he look like?"

She sighed. "I told you. I don't remember what happened. It doesn't matter now, anyway. It's done. Can't be undone." She turned her head away from him.

He felt she remembered more than she was telling.

"It matters to me, Mattie. I want him to pay." Josiah kept his voice down with difficulty. He didn't want to wake the rest of the household.

"Let it go, Josiah. The Lord will take care of it all. Who hurt me doesn't matter now." She shook her head slightly, kept her face turned from him, kept her eyes closed.

"It does matter. There has to be some way to make him pay." He was certain. She knew. She knew something about the bastard.

Mattie turned back toward Josiah, her eyes pleading with him. "Pray, Josiah. Pray. You've told me about killing a Yankee, one who was probably dying anyway. You're heartsore over that. You don't want to stir up another mess of trouble for yourself." She had to catch her breath before she could continue. "Pray for forgiveness in your heart. Just as you want to be forgiven. I will pray for you, too. as I always do."

"You've forgiven him?"

Mattie didn't respond for several seconds, maybe a minute or more. Tears ran from her closed eyes. At last she said, "Yes."

He kissed her hand. "You're so good. If you can forgive, then maybe I can, too."

"You must."

"There's something else I have to tell you. When I first got home and found out about this, I was so furious I know I would've killed the bast—" He hesitated, searching for a less offensive word, then continued, "—your attacker right then and there if I could've gotten my hands on him. But now . . . He has to be punished, but I don't know if I have the stomach to do it myself. That bothers me. I should be willing to do anything to avenge your injuries. Anything. I feel weak, not wanting to kill that scum. It's going to be hard to forgive what he did but hard to forgive my own weakness if I do nothing."

"But you must forgive. For your own sake, and for mine. For all of us. It would take great strength, not weakness. I want you to let it go."

Josiah couldn't agree, so he remained silent for a while. God, help me, he thought. I know I've done wrong. I do need forgiveness. And I guess I need to forgive the low-down snake. Maybe he's as sorry for what he did as I am. But, Lord, it's so hard.

"Mattie, can't you tell me something to help us find him?"

"No. I can't." She steeled her voice, but the effort seemed to exhaust her and she had to pause to gather her strength before she continued. "You must try to forgive. If you don't, the hurt and anger will get worse." She closed her eyes and lay panting for a few moments, but when he started to speak, she slowly shook her head and added, "Too many could be hurt. Pray for help."

Josiah patted her hand while he mulled over his response. He didn't want to make the situation worse for her. And he didn't really know what was right. He wished he could close his eyes and she'd be well and this would be over. It'd be a lot easier to forgive then.

The silent seconds passed into minutes. At last Josiah shrugged and sighed. "Mattie, I'll try. I'll pray for forgiveness to come to my heart."

She nodded weakly and tried to smile.

He hoped she believed him.

He held her hand, felt it slacken as she fell asleep. He reviewed their talk, trying to sort out what he had learned, if anything. For sure she was attacked. Otherwise, why all the talk of forgiveness? She wasn't a saint. Never had been. It didn't seem quite like her to be so forgiving for such a terrible assault. He knew she believed she should *try* to forgive, but he didn't think she could succeed. Not really. She'd never been meek.

Mattie moved restlessly, grimacing in pain.

"Do you need more medicine?"

"Yes."

He provided the dose of laudanum and watched as she began to relax, then drifted into sleep, or unconsciousness. Sometimes he couldn't tell the difference.

Josiah sat for a while and thought about what Mattie had asked of him. Then he sank to his knees and tried to pray, even though he had little confidence he would be heard. He thanked God for his safe return to his home and asked for Mattie's recovery. He asked for help in forgiving Mattie's attacker but his plea was weak and unconvincing, even to himself. He suspected—and reckoned God did, too, if He paid any attention at all to the doings of mortals—Josiah Robertson was not really ready to give up his anger, the canker. It felt right and just, no matter how much it burned and smarted.

The bastard deserved death, plain and simple. But could Josiah kill again? He knew he didn't want to face the guilt his conscience would heap on him if he took another life, knew he didn't want the torture of new nightmares. Knew he was afraid. He could turn to the law for vengeance, to lift his burden, but what would the authorities do? The occupation troops seemed more interested in punishing Johnny Rebs and stirring up the blacks than maintaining law and order.

He sighed and rubbed his tired eyes with his fingertips, pressing hard and welcoming the stinging ache that resulted. Maybe an answer would come eventually.

He rose from his knees and paced about the room as he planned the coming day. First he would find Doc Wilson, have him come out and see if there was anything more they could do for Mattie. He'd ask Doc about all he had seen and heard. Josiah sank back into his chair, rehearsing questions, but his thoughts came slower and slower and he covered the same points over and over again.

Chapter 10

Luke awoke with a start as the scream pierced the night. Emmy grasped his arm so tightly her fingers dug into his flesh, and even in the dark he could see her wide white eyes. The scream died, but Luke's heart hammered on. "What was that?" he whispered.

"Josiah. It was Josiah. Oh, my God. Mattie's . . ." Before Emmy could finish expressing her fear, Luke heard voices, both Josiah's and, much more faintly, Mattie's. Emmy began to relax her grip on him, but he could still feel her quick, shallow breathing.

"What's going on?" he asked.

"I don't know. Maybe there's a problem with Mattie. Shh. Be quiet, let's listen."

Emmy held her breath, and put her finger on his lips. They could hear Josiah and Mattie talking, but they couldn't make out the words. The tones seemed calm enough. It didn't sound like an emergency.

"Maybe you should go check on them?"

"No. I don't think so. Josiah would call me if they needed help." Her hand continued to rest on his arm. He could feel her trembling.

"If she's awake, even though it's the middle of the night . . ."

"All right." Emmy quietly slipped from the bed and padded into the hall. In a couple of minutes she returned and slipped back into bed.

"It's all right. I think he had a dream—a war dream. I heard a little of what he told her about it. Now he's trying to get her to drink some water. It's good she can talk to us some, now, don't you think?"

"Um."

"She sounds tired, though."

"Uh-huh. I am, too. I don't like being waked up in the middle of the night by a grown man's screams. Maybe he's a little crazy. They say Jon Waller's kind of crazy now, from the War. Maybe Josiah shouldn't be staying in there with Mattie?"

"He wants to be there. And I can't tend her day and night and keep going myself." Her whisper held a cranky edge.

"Well, I don't like it," Luke muttered. "Why'd he have to come home now and butt into everything?"

Emmy paused for a few moments before she said, "We all prayed for his safe return."

Luke sighed. "Yes, and the Lord heard us. Praise Jesus. But why's Josiah have to push his nose into all our business?"

"He's concerned."

"Uh-huh, and while he's concerned he's interfering with the raising of our children, telling us what to do, rubbing it in about this being his farm? So many men got killed. Why didn't he?" Luke's whisper, barely audible, crackled with anger.

"Shh! You don't mean that!" Emmy put her finger over his lips again. "Besides, we knew he was coming home. Mattie got his letter saying he was on his way."

"I know. But he could've gotten bushwhacked."

"Shh. Hush." They both lay still, barely breathing, listening to the murmurs from the other room.

"All the work we've put into this place. Now he's going to take it back. Where will that put us?" Luke hissed.

Emmy groaned. "I know. It worries me, too. I told him so."

"What did he say?"

"He said we'd always have a place here. And I think he meant it, too. But he could change his mind. What if Mattie doesn't get well? What if she dies and he marries someone else? Where will that leave us?"

"Sucking hind tit."

"Hush."

Nearly complete silence enveloped them. No more sounds came from the other room. If Josiah was awake, he might hear their conversation, which Luke certainly didn't want. He rolled over, putting his back to Emmy, and whispered, "Go to sleep." He could feel her nod assent.

He wanted to stay awake for a while, listen for more talk in the other room. Soon he could feel Emmy's breathing become regular, not too deep, and he knew she was asleep. He lay there straining to hear anything said across the hall, but in the quiet his weariness overcame him and soon he snored.

Chapter 11

Josiah awoke with a start as something banged and clattered in the hall outside the room. Roosters crowed although the sun had only begun to tint the pearlescent sky. The clock struck once at four-thirty.

The noisy activities of the family arising and going about their early morning chores irritated Josiah every bit as much as they had the day before. He left the house and went to the barn where he found a measure of peace and quiet. Luke and Jim, feeding and watering the stock, grunted greetings and went on about their work. Josiah interpreted Luke's general silence as anger left over from the argument they had had at supper. He remained riled himself, in the way he sometimes did when he knew he was partly wrong but would not admit it. He felt more justified if he held on to his anger.

Josiah entered Pepper's stall. The roan snorted and turned his head to him. "Hey there, boy. Let's see how your hoof is today," Josiah murmured as he stroked the horse's neck and right shoulder, encountering a patch of caked dirt. "Been rolling in the mud, have you?"

The horse tossed his head up and down, as though he were saying yes, before he stuck his nose back in the feed trough to continue crunching corn. Josiah passed around behind the animal, stroking and murmuring softly, and lifted the left front hoof to take a look. In the dim light he could see very little. He gingerly prodded the softer tissue in the center of the hoof. Pepper didn't flinch.

"Let's go outside in the light so I can take a better look at this." Josiah tied a line on the horse's halter and began to pull him out of the stall. Pepper resisted momentarily, stubbornly keeping his muzzle in the feed trough.

As Josiah led the horse into the hall he noticed Jim at the well drawing water and Luke disappearing in the direction of the outhouse. Josiah sighed, glad to have the barn to himself, although he knew his solitude wouldn't last long—he had caught a glimpse of Sally leaving the back porch with the milk bucket.

He led the horse to the fence and tied him to a post. Speaking quietly, almost as he would to a child, he once again lifted the left front leg. Although sound enough to take a new shoe, the hoof needed careful trimming and reshaping. The roan shouldn't be ridden in his present condition.

Josiah left Pepper tied to the post and started to the tack room for a currycomb. As he walked soundlessly along the soft dust of the hall, he heard the rhythmic "psh-h-h-ht, psh-h-h-ht" of milk squirting into a bucket. "Good morning, Sally," he called into the cow's stall.

Sally gave a little startled cry and a crisp "psh-h-h-ht" changed to a soggy "sh-h-h-h" as one squirt missed the bucket. "Daddy! You scared me. I didn't know anybody was out here."

"Sorry. I came to check Pepper's hoof. I thought you saw me," he replied as he stepped into the stall with her.

Sally continued to milk for a few moments, her face hidden against the cow's flank, before she said, "Unh-uh. But I didn't mean you really scared me. I was just startled because I didn't think anybody was out here." After several more squirts she said, "But sometimes I think you are scary. Not as bad as Uncle Luke, though."

"Uncle Luke is a little gruff sometimes, but he loves you and wouldn't really hurt you. He wants all of you children to mind. So do I."

"I s'pose."

"You 's'pose' I want you to mind?"

She raised her head to look at him. "I know you want me to mind."

"And Uncle Luke?"

Sally put her head back against the cow's flank and resumed pulling and squeezing the distended teats. After a few moments she whispered, almost inaudibly, "Sometimes he scares me."

Luke's too rough with the children, Josiah thought. He patted Sally's thin shoulders and said, "I want you to be a good girl and mind all of your elders. But if Uncle Luke or anybody else yells at you, or scares you, or hits you when you don't think you've been bad, you come tell me. Understand?"

Sally again looked up. "Yes, Daddy. But what if you're not here?"

"I'll be here."

"You haven't been."

Josiah's face reddened. He could feel the heat of it, and he clenched his teeth. Sass. But her worried frown told him Sally meant no sass. He bit back his rebuke. "I'm here now," he said.

Sally nodded and resumed milking.

The quiet moment stretched into a minute or more. Josiah shifted his feet and slapped his hands against his thighs. "I'm going to comb Pepper before breakfast." He patted Sally's head and ambled out to the tack room where he retrieved the comb. Then he returned to the horse and began to work the comb along the roan's neck, shoulders, flanks, and rear. When he finished, Pepper's coat was dirt-free and smooth. He led the horse back into its stall.

He heard no sounds of milking, only the buzzing of the flies, so much a part of the barn he scarcely noticed it. Sally had finished her chore and gone on to the house. He returned the comb to the tack room and followed after her.

The family ate breakfast in silence. The children kept their heads down; the adults did the same. Even Delia seemed subdued. As soon as Luke had finished his biscuits and eggs, he rose and left without a word. Emmy cut her eyes after him but said nothing. Jim briefly looked up to watch him go, then returned his attention to his nearly empty plate. Sally did the same. Callie Belle hunched over her breakfast and didn't acknowledge her father's departure in any way.

Finally Josiah spoke. "I'm going to take the buggy and go over to Doc Wilson's. He's got to take another look at Mattie. Maybe there's something he can do."

Emmy glanced up, then cast her eyes down again. "Yes, maybe so."

"Then I'll go on by your folks' place. I want to get Samson to shoe Pepper. I can bring your mother back if she wants to come. It shouldn't take me much longer than the drive over and back, so I should return by late morning, early afternoon. Unless Doc is able to come right on when I ask him, I should be here before he arrives, but in case I'm not, pay close attention—I want to know everything he says."

She nodded, but made no other move.

He looked in on Mattie before he left. She slept lightly and stirred when he entered the room.

"Mattie, I hate to wake you," he said as he leaned down and brushed her cheek with a kiss.

She moved again. Through her swollen lips she whispered, "I'm awake. I'm glad you're here."

"I have to go over to your parents' place this morning. I want to pay my respects to them, and I need to get Samson to shoe my horse. Is there any message you want to send? Or is there anything I can get for you while I'm there?"

"But you promised to stay. You said you would be here."

He took her hand, "I promised to be with you at night, remember? But there're other things I have to do."

She closed her eyes and frowned.

"Anyway, I won't be gone long. Emmy will be around if you need anything." He hoped that was true. Emmy had so many things to tend to, and she seemed more and more distracted.

"I'm scared here alone."

"How about if I send Sally in to sit with you? She's big enough to do some things for you, and she could call Emmy if you need her."

She inhaled sharply and shook her head. "I don't want Sally to see me like this."

84

"Mattie, she's seen you. She found you after you were hurt. She's a strong girl, real grown-up for her age. She'll be all right."

"She'll be scared."

"She'll be all right, Mattie. You'll see."

"Do you really think so?"

"Yes."

Mattie nodded and closed her eyes.

Josiah brushed her cheek with another kiss and said, "I'll go get her."

Returning to the kitchen he found Emmy and Sally cleaning up after breakfast. Jim and Callie Belle had gone to tend to chores. Still tied in the high chair, Delia banged a spoon on the tray and jabbered.

"Sally, your mama needs someone to sit with her for a while. How about you do it? Aunt Emmy has lots of other things to do."

"Josiah, Sally has chores to tend to," Emmy protested.

"Go on to your mama, Sally. I need to talk to Aunt Emmy a minute. I'll be right there."

Sally looked back and forth between Emmy and Josiah with an apprehensive frown, but she nodded and put away the dish she was drying and left.

Josiah waited until he heard her padding footsteps recede before he said, "Emmy, Mattie's scared. I guess it's natural after what happened. She needs somebody nearby. I know Sally has chores, and she's kind of young to do this, but it seems to me you have your hands full with the house and your children. You can't spend all of your time sitting with Mattie. And I've got things I have to do, too. Sally can stay with her, brush the flies away, call you if Mattie needs you. I'm going to try to bring back your mother or Dorcas to help. Taking care of Mattie is more important than gathering eggs or picking beans, don't you think?"

Emmy sighed. "You're making a mistake, Josiah. Sally has acted like she didn't want to see her mama. She seems to be afraid to go to her. And Mattie hasn't asked for Sally, not any time I've been with her."

"It'll be all right, Emmy."

She murmured, "I hope so."

Josiah knew he hadn't convinced her.

He found Sally waiting for him in the hall instead of in Mattie's room. Her lower lip trembled.

"Is Mama going to die?"

Josiah placed his hands on the girl's shoulders and leaned his head down to her level. "Mama's very sick, but we're trying to help her all we can. She's very strong. She'll be all right."

"When . . . when I found her in the barn, she looked so awful. She was all bloody. She wouldn't talk to me. Daddy, I thought she was dead. I was so scared."

"Are you scared now?"

Sally looked at the floor and nodded. Then she raised her head, and he could see tears glistening in the corners of her eyes. "Daddy, I'm afraid to see Mama. I'm afraid she'll be dead. Really dead."

Josiah knelt and drew her to him. "Shhhh. Sally, don't cry. Mama's not dead. I talked to her only a few minutes ago. She needs someone to sit with her while I go to Grandfather's house. She needs someone to keep the flies from bothering her so much, and to keep a fresh damp cloth on her forehead. But most of all, she needs someone to get help if she needs it. You can do that, can't you? You can stay with Mama and call Aunt Emmy if Mama needs help?"

Sally stiffened in his embrace, her face against his shoulder, her arms at her sides. She shook her head back and forth as she tried to stifle her crying. "I don't want to," she whispered.

"Sally, you—"

"Daddy, you said you'd be here. You told me, in the barn. You said you'd be here," she blurted before bursting into sobs.

"I am here."

"But you're fixing to leave."

Josiah hugged her tighter. "I didn't mean I'd be right here every minute. I meant I'd be here . . . generally. You know— every day, or at least every night." He paused, saw no signs of acceptance or agreement, and blundered on. "I'll be nearby—I'm only going to Grandfather's. Aunt Emmy and Uncle Luke are here. They'll take care of you and Mama."

"I'm still scared," Sally whimpered. "And you said—

"Sh-h- h. You'll upset Mama."

Maybe Emmy was right—maybe this was a bad idea. Maybe he should wait a few days before going to McLain's. But he didn't see how things would get much better in a few days, and they might get a lot worse.

"Sh-h-h," he shushed again. Sally quieted, except for hiccups. He patted her back and whispered to her, "Sally, I'm going to tell you a secret. Can you keep a secret?"

She nodded.

"From everybody?" he asked. She nodded her head up and down more vigorously this time.

"Well, Mama's scared, too. She needs someone to stay with her like she used to stay with you when you were little and you had a bad dream. Do you remember?"

"Yes. She still does." Sally hesitated, then added, almost inaudibly, "Except now, when she can't." After a moment she asked, "But why's it a secret?"

"It upsets Mama to talk about whatever is scaring her. So we need to pretend she isn't scared. Do you understand?"

"No. But I can stay with Mama if it will help her not be so scared," Sally answered. "And I won't say anything about being scared."

"That's my brave girl," Josiah said as he kissed her and got to his feet. He took her hand and led her into Mattie's room.

Mattie lay still with her eyes closed.

Sally stared wide-eyed at her battered mother and squeezed Josiah's hand tighter. He heard her draw her breath and hold it as she took a step backward.

"Mattie, I've brought Sally to see you."

Mattie's eyes opened.

Sally resumed breathing, and her grip relaxed. Then she turned loose and ran to her mother. Josiah caught her before she grabbed Mattie's splinted arm.

"Mama!"

Mattie feebly raised her good hand and smiled.

"Mama's very sore. Don't bump her," Josiah cautioned.

"Mama."

Sally tried to hug Mattie despite Josiah's warning. He gently held her off enough to keep her from doing any damage. Mattie touched the child's head and stroked her hair.

"I told your daddy I didn't want you to see me like this. I didn't want you to be scared."

"I'm not scared now."

Josiah showed Sally how to soak a rag, wring it out and place it on Mattie's forehead. Sally tried it, and Mattie told her she did well, even though the rag wasn't quite dry enough and rivulets ran from it into her hair. Satisfied Sally would tend her mother well, Josiah took his leave.

He had intended to go immediately to the barn, but as he walked down the hall he stroked his itchy, bristly chin and decided he could stand his scraggly beard no longer. Besides, he didn't really want to call on his in-laws for the first time in four years looking like a homeless drifter. He went to the kitchen and asked, "Emmy, could you heat some water so I can shave?"

"Yes," she answered. Then she continued with more warmth, "The kettle is nearly hot enough now. It won't take long."

"Thanks," he called as he started back to Mattie's room, where he found Sally standing by the bed, aimlessly fiddling with the items on the bedside table.

"Don't bother Mama's medicine and things."

Sally jumped at the sound of his voice. She turned away from the table and, eyes downcast, murmured, "I'm sorry, Daddy."

"I know you meant no harm, but I don't want you to risk spilling the medicine. If you can't get to the water basin very well, I'll help you move it to a better place."

"No. I can reach it all right. I-I was curious, is all." After a pause, she asked, "Did you decide not to go to Grandfather's?"

"No, I'm going on to see Doc Wilson and then Grandmother and Grandfather, but I decided I really need to shave before I go. What do you think?"

"Yessir, you do. You look all gray and hairy like Pretty Girl."

"I hope not." Pretty Girl was the ugliest dog he had ever seen, but he had to admit that his unshaven chin did kind of look like the grizzled whiskers raggedly frosting her muzzle.

"You do. I'll bet you feel all rough and prickly like she does, too." Sally giggled.

"Well, if you want to know how these whiskers feel, you'd better come here and feel them now 'cause I'm about to shave 'em all off. I came back here to get my razor from my saddlebags."

Mattie smiled weakly as Sally held her hand up toward his face. He bent down, and she ran her fingers over his chin. "Yessir, you feel like Pretty Girl."

"He looks more like a 'possum," Mattie said.

Sally and Josiah laughed.

Josiah opened his saddlebags and found his razor. He stepped to the bedside and kissed them both. "I'm going to shave now, then get on down the road. I'll be back around midday."

* * *

As her father walked away, Sally levered her rear into the small slipper chair. Despite the chair's low seat, her feet dangled, and she squirmed to get more comfortable.

"Mama, do you want me to wash your face?"

"No, baby. Not right now."

A cicada began its chirring in the willow oak outside. It droned on and on. The multitude of houseflies hummed and buzzed as they flew about the room, lighting on Mattie's face often. Sally picked up the fly whisk and fanned them away. The heat built in the room as the sun rose higher, and Mattie's fever still raged. The sour, fetid smell of stale fever-sweat filled the room.

Sally took the cloth from Mattie's forehead and soaked it in the bowl again. This time she did a better job of wringing out the water—it only dripped a little bit. She twisted and squeezed the cloth again, managing to wring another small stream from the rag. She gently dabbed at Mattie's face, wiping the sweat away. She soaked the cloth again, this time not wringing it quite so dry, and placed it back on Mattie's forehead.

Mattie tried to smile. "Thank you. That feels good," she whispered.

"Y' welcome."

Sally resumed waving the whisk over Mattie's head, shooing flies and stirring the stale air.

Time dragged on. Sally wriggled in the chair, but continued to move the whisk. Mattie's eyes were closed, but she breathed irregularly. Sally didn't think she was asleep. A deer fly droned into the room. Sally got up and found it, swatted it with the whisk. Swack!

Mattie's eyes popped open as she gasped.

"Mama, I'm sorry! I was swatting this ol' deerfly so it wouldn't bite us."

"It's all right. The noise startled me, though," Mattie whispered.

Sally continued to move around the room, idly swishing at flies here and there, not looking at her mother. She fingered the torn curtain at the back window and spoke again.

"I'm sorry. Not for the . . . well, for that, too . . . but . . ." She continued to study the curtain, her throat working as she fought back tears. Finally she choked out, "Mama, I'm sorry I didn't keep you from being hurt."

"Oh, baby. You couldn't have. There's no way. You had nothing to do with what happened to me." Mattie paused to gather strength before she continued. "I know you don't want me to be sick. It may scare you, me being like this. But it has nothing to do with you. You couldn't have done anything to help me. I promise you."

Sally turned toward Mattie as tears welled and ran down her cheeks to drip from her chin. "But, Mama—"

"Hush. Don't cry. Come here."

Sally ran to her mother, knelt at the side of the bed and pressed her damp face against Mattie's hand. Mattie stroked Sally's hair. "But, Mama . . ."

Mattie rested her hand on Sally's head and whispered, "Hush. Hush. There's nothing for you to be sorry for."

They remained quiet for some time. Mattie dropped off to sleep. Then Sally stirred, and once again took up the fly whisk. The morning passed as she fanned and thought about all the things she wanted to tell Squeaky.

Chapter 12

After Josiah picked up his razor he returned to the kitchen to ask Emmy for the hot water. She brought the kettle immediately and filled the basin on the washbench, then wordlessly retreated, barely acknowledging Josiah's "Thanks" with a nod.

Pretty Girl slipped from under the porch, eyed Josiah suspiciously and growled softly. Josiah watched the animal with amusement. He wondered who's sense of humor was responsible for her name. Probably Mattie. The animal certainly wasn't pretty, but he had to give her credit for being protective.

"Here, Pretty Girl. Come here. Hush your growling."

She quieted and inched toward him, muzzle extended, nose twitching. He held out his hand toward her, palm down, alert should he need to withdraw it quickly. She took another step closer and gave his hand a thorough sniffing. At last she seemed satisfied with his scent, his manner. She licked his offered hand.

"Good girl. I'm not here to cause any harm. You're a good dog," Josiah murmured as he rubbed her head and scratched her ears. He hit an itchy spot and her right hind leg raised and kicked toward her head as she scratched a phantom flea. Her tail wagged tentatively, then with conviction. "Good girl. I can't scratch you all day, though. I have to get rid of these whiskers so Sally won't think I look like you." He laughed as he gave her a final pat. She whined, then lay down and watched him.

Josiah stropped the razor, then rubbed the soap furiously in an attempt to produce enough lather. At last he deemed the foam

91

sufficient and applied it to his face. Carefully he scraped the rough whiskers away. The harsh soap caused his skin to sting. The burning eased after he rinsed, but an irritated rash remained. He inspected his reflection, his bloodshot, sleep-deprived eyes staring back tiredly above sun- and razor-reddened cheeks. He looked like cold hell warmed over but more civilized now he was clean-shaven. After rinsing the razor and drying it on the sacking towel, he folded it and stuck it in his pocket. He finger-combed his hair back from his brow, placed his hat firmly on his head and started for the barn. Pretty Girl followed.

As he entered the barn, Pepper whinnied from his stall, which reminded Josiah to let him out. Josiah turned him into the pasture and watched while the horse took a few steps and lowered his head to crop the newly greening grass.

Back in the barn, Josiah brought the gray mare out of her stall and tethered her to a post near the tack room. He looked in the horse's mouth and sighed. She was twenty-five years old if she was a day. Her ribs showed, her back sagged, and she held her head low with no arch to her neck.

"Old horse, you are one sorry sight," he murmured as he began a cursory currying. "I hope you can get me as far as Doc Wilson's and McLain's. Don't you go dropping dead between the shafts."

The gray made no move except to shift her weight off her right hind foot, resting the hoof on its tip, ankle bent, bony hip sagging. She didn't even swish her tail at the flies plaguing her.

After Josiah combed her he strapped on the buggy harness. He led her to the wagon shed and backed her between the shafts and fastened the traces to the singletree. After leading her forward until the buggy cleared the shed, he climbed up to the seat, took the reins and urged the old gray mare forward. He was mildly surprised when she actually moved.

Pretty Girl let out a couple of barks as she danced around the buggy. Then she quieted and trotted alongside.

"You'd better stay here, Pretty Girl," Josiah remarked, but the dog trotted along for several hundred yards. Then, distracted by a rabbit running into the weeds at the side of the road, she left the buggy and eventually wandered back toward the house.

The morning freshness had not yet burned away. The clear sky promised a hot day, but now the dew sparkled on the brush at the side of the road. Birds busily fluttered in the bushes and sang their various songs. A mockingbird, perched in a wild cherry tree, ran through a broad repertoire of calls indistinguishable from those of the birds it copied except that each thrice-voiced song was immediately followed by a different triplet. A goldfinch flew with its rhythmic, dipping pattern along the roadside fencerow, its bright yellow body in sharp contrast to the gray rails of the fence. A red-tailed hawk sat motionless in a dead chestnut tree to watch for a mouse, a vole, a small rabbit. The dew glinted on a huge spider web woven completely across the road, its maker lying well off-center, waiting for the telltale jiggle of entrapped prey. The old gray hit the web and tore it asunder. The spider scrambled for safety.

Josiah inhaled the morning air and smiled to himself, glad to be back in his home country. The roadside vegetation stood greener now after the rain. The crops in the fields looked stronger, healthier than they had two days ago. He heard the bird songs and the scurrying rustles of the small creatures in the brush near the road and the steady clop-clop of the mare as she plodded along. For a short while he almost felt content.

But contentment was beyond his reach. He had far too many worries, far too few solutions.

There was Sally, bright, beautiful and older than her years. He knew she was trying hard to please him, which seemed strange, since she had claimed she didn't remember him when he first got home. She had enough grit to object when he wanted her to sit with Mattie, though. He had always thought girls should be docile and sweet, and all children ought to obey their elders and keep quiet; and yet he found he admired her spirit. He understood why she didn't want to sit with Mattie. He hoped he hadn't put more on her than she was able to handle.

He didn't even understand why he had felt it so necessary that the child sit with her mother. In part it was Mattie's fear of being alone. And he couldn't help it—he did feel she was safer in Sally's company. It didn't make rational sense to him, but he couldn't deny the feeling. So he was glad Sally overcame her fears when she actually saw Mattie. Glad for Sally and glad for Mattie, too.

The old mare had been walking slower and slower. Josiah suddenly realized she had almost stopped and was lowering her head to a clump of grass. He flicked the lines and called, "Get up there." She raised her head and moved on. He flicked the lines again as a reminder, and she trotted a couple of steps before she settled back into a slow walk.

As the mare plodded on, Josiah's thoughts turned to the reasons for his trip this morning. Mattie was so terribly ill. He wanted her to get well, but she might not. How could he go on if Mattie died? He didn't want to think about her death, but he couldn't get it out of his mind. And he couldn't stop thinking about what had happened to her.

He chided himself for wallowing in such misery. If Mattie died, he'd have to keep on doing whatever had to be done. When his siblings died, when his pa died, when his ma died, he had gone on, not always knowing exactly how he would, but muddling along, doing the familiar, doing what was necessary until somehow he survived the trial.

He came to a fork in the road and turned the mare to the right. Doc Wilson's place was only about a mile farther. Even at the mare's slow pace, he would be there in twenty or thirty minutes. Josiah returned to his ruminations.

He needed to do something. He didn't want to simply mark time till it was over, however it might end. He'd promised Mattie he would forgive the low-down bastard, and he knew it was his Christian duty, but . . . He couldn't help it—he wanted to see him pay and know what he was paying for. There had to be a way.

Josiah formulated the start of a plan but in his weariness it was difficult to keep his thoughts straight. He needed to find out all he could about what happened—talk to Doc Wilson, talk to Luke, talk to Jim, and even the neighbors. Then he could go to the sheriff. Or, as much as it galled him to think about it, maybe he could go to the Yankees.

Engrossed in his thoughts, Josiah almost drove past Doc Wilson's place, hardly recognizing the decrepit old house. Peeling Paris green paint on the trim underscored its neglect. One rotting corner of the front porch sagged almost to the ground, pulling its roof away from the front of the house. Bricks missing from the left chimney gave it a snaggled top line. A cow grazed on the grass and weeds that grew nearly knee-high in the front yard. She'd been undeterred by the bedraggled broken fence. A gaunt, gray-bearded man sat in a rocking chair on the front porch, a book open on his lap.

"Morning, Doc," Josiah called as he drove through one of the breaks in the fence and up to the house. He barely had to pull the reins to stop the mare. She immediately slumped and began to crop the grass near the porch.

Doc peered at Josiah without recognition but returned the greeting with a nod and quiet, "Morning."

"I'm Josiah Robertson, Mattie's husband. You may not remember me."

"Ohhh. Now I recognize you, Josiah. 'Course I do. My eyes aren't as good as they used to be. It's getting so I can hardly see to read, and then when I get my eyes all set for reading, I can't see a damn thing when I look up. When did you get home?"

"Two days ago."

"Well, I'm glad to see you back. How're you doing?"

"All right, I guess. It damn near killed me to find Mattie like she is," Josiah answered as he climbed down from the buggy.

"I'm sorry for Mattie's misfortune. How is she this morning?"

"Not very well, Doc. That's why I've come."

"Um-hmm. Tell me about her."

"Her fever's awfully high. And she's in pain."

"'Course she's in pain. You can't get hurt as bad as she is and not be in pain. That's why I left the laudanum for her."

"The pain's worse, though. The laudanum helps, but she still hurts."

"You're sure?"

"Yes. She tries not to show it, but she can't keep me from seeing how bad she hurts. And she finally admitted it."

"It's a good sign she's talking to you. She was unconscious the last time I saw her, three days after it happened. The day you

95

got home, I guess. Emmy said she had hardly been conscious at all."

"She seemed to perk up some right after I got home. She's talked to us—well, mostly to me. Night before last she took some broth, and she drank some water. We felt like she had gotten better. But last night she said her belly hurt. She would only take a tiny sip of water, no broth. And she's burning up with fever. Doc, can you come look at her, see if there's anything you can do?"

"Of course I'll come. Let me get my bag," Doc said. He rose from his chair and turned toward the doorway.

"Doc, d'you have a horse you can ride, or a buggy? I had hoped I could get on to McLain's to see if Mother Lorna or one of the black women could come over to help. Emmy's going in a hundred directions at once, what with taking care of Mattie and the children and the cooking and all. Mattie seems scared. I . . . we don't like to leave her alone. I left Sally sitting with her, but Sally's really too young to have to take on such responsibility."

Doc stopped in the doorway, then turned back to Josiah. "I have a horse. You can go on. I'll get to your house all right."

"Thanks, Doc. I'll be back home before long. I hope you'll still be there. I'll want to hear what you think."

Doc remained where he stood, looking thoughtfully at Josiah. "I'm concerned about Mattie's fright. She needs to be as quiet and calm as possible. What's she afraid of?" he asked. And then he answered his own question. "I 'spect she's scared of dying."

"Maybe, but I think there's more to it than that. I think it's about what happened to her, but I can't get her to tell me." Josiah's brows knitted, and he glanced away from Doc and then back again. "I guess I have some questions for you, Doc."

"I can see how you might," Doc said as he returned to his seat. "Sit a spell, Josiah," he said as he motioned to another chair.

Josiah pulled the chair up to face Doc's and sat, leaned his elbows on his knees and absently rubbed his hands together. "Doc, nobody seems to know exactly what happened to Mattie. Everyone agrees it didn't seem like an accident. She must've been beaten. The stranger must've done it, the one Luke's boy saw. The one Evie Pritchard saw in the neighborhood."

Doc laced his fingers together in his lap and nodded.

"Mattie won't talk about it, though. I asked her what happened. She said she didn't remember. I'm sure she was beaten, and I told her I would avenge her if she could just give me some clues about who did it. She told me to forget vengeance, to forgive instead. Very Christian of her, and I guess I should admire her for it, but it seems to me she as good as said it was no accident and she knows something about her assailant." He fisted his hand, then looked up at the doctor. "There's not a finer woman around than Mattie, but I can't believe she really wants to forgive the brutal bastard." He sighed and opened the fists. "Maybe she really does, but I can't accept it." He rubbed his right thumb against a callous on his left hand. "It almost sounds to me like she's protecting someone. I can't get that out of my head."

Doc stared into the distance and stroked his beard. "I've always thought Mattie is a really good person. This is a small community. People talk. And yet I never hear anybody speak ill of Mattie. I think she tries to live a Christian life. You may be doing her a disservice by not believing in her mercy, Josiah. You know her better and closer than I, of course, but don't you think she could really mean it?"

Josiah shifted uncomfortably in his chair. "Maybe. Maybe she does forgive him." He tapped his fingers together, then balled his fists. "But she ought to be angry. I'm angry. I'd kill the bastard if I could get my hands on him. At least I think I would. How can I forgive him? I want to make him pay for what he did. And . . . and I don't even know exactly what he really did, if you know what I mean?"

Doc slowly shook his head and looked puzzled. "He beat the stuffing out of her. We know that's what he did."

Josiah grunted, glanced quickly at Doc and then stared off into the distance. "I mean, the details of what he did. Maybe I don't even know, myself, what I want to know. I just have some questions about what happened when they found her. I know what Emmy told me, but . . . maybe you saw things she didn't?"

Doc cleared his throat, frowned in concentration. "Luke came to get me all in a lather. Told me about Mattie. Said he wanted to ride on to McLain's to let them know, her being their daughter and all. He said for me to rush on over to tend to Mattie. I grabbed my bag and saddled my horse and rode.

"When I got to your house—well, your household was in a heck of an uproar. Emmy was trying to tend to Mattie in spite of the children's hysterics. Emmy wasn't far from hysteria herself. I saw right away Mattie's right arm was broken. Her face was a mess—bad cuts and bruises, lots of blood. I wanted to do a thorough examination, but Emmy wouldn't hear of us removing any of Mattie's clothes—said her sister was a modest woman."

Josiah nodded and said, "She is. You know, she wouldn't let me get you when Sally was born, made me go get the granny woman. Said she couldn't bear for a man to see her, even if he was a doctor." The tension around his eyes eased and a hint of a smile curled his lips as he remembered.

Doc raised his eyebrows and grunted, "Um-hum." Then he shrugged and continued. "We cleaned the wounds we could see, and I set her arm. I felt of her chest and belly, but I couldn't tell how bad her injuries were, what with the clothes and all, and her not being able to tell me what hurt. She had some swellings. I thought there were abdominal injuries, but I couldn't be certain. She had a couple of broken ribs—I could feel them move and grind when I pressed—but there's not much I could have done about them. Bind 'em, maybe, but I'm not at all sure that does any real good. I did the best I could, Josiah, but she was bad hurt. I'm so sorry."

"Did you think maybe she'd . . . Did you see any reason to think she'd been outraged?"

Doc shook his head. "No way to know, what with Emmy insisting all her clothes remain intact."

"But you suspect?" Josiah pressed as he inched forward in his seat.

"Well, she'd taken a hell of a beating and her clothes showed it—ripped shirtwaist, torn skirt, everything dirty—front, back and sides."

Josiah's face reddened and his jaw clenched. He started to

rise from his chair. Doc reached out, placed his hand on Josiah's arm. "Now Josiah, I know this is hard for you. But you did ask."

Josiah slowly lowered himself back into the chair. "Go on," he said.

"I saw smears on her skirt. There's a lot of things it could've been, but . . . Well, I smelled something, faint but—like a man's seed, you know? I didn't see her undergarments. But I had to wonder."

"You didn't say anything?"

"I didn't have to. The boy had told about seeing a stranger. When Luke got home and heard, he acted like he understood the implications immediately. I assumed Emmy did, too, but it didn't seem like a topic I should discuss with a lady."

Josiah swallowed hard. "So it was as bad as my worst fears."

Doc nodded. "I believe so."

Josiah kept quiet for a while before he asked, "And nobody had any idea who the bastard was?"

"No. Luke grabbed his shotgun and searched around your place, found a campsite in the woods. Evie Jane Pritchard had seen the stranger, too, so he got a more reliable description than a scared boy could give, but she hadn't seen him up close, nor had Lem. Luke saddled a mule and got some neighbors together and tore up and down and all around, but they couldn't find him. They followed him all the way over to Henry's Ferry, but he disappeared. Nobody knew his name, or where he came from, or where he might be going. Mattie was unconscious. She couldn't tell us anything about him. Luke finally had to give up the search."

Josiah groaned. He drew a deep breath and said, "How can she ask me to forgive that snake? I want the son of a bitch worse than ever."

Doc nodded. "I understand. But there's no way to know who he is unless Mattie tells us, and she may not know."

"I'll have to get her to tell whatever she does know," Josiah said through gritted teeth. He grimly stared out over the ragged dooryard, yet blind to his surroundings. Doc let him work through his thoughts without interruption. Gradually some of Josiah's tension eased. In a less strained tone he said, "I appreciate you telling me what you have, Doc. I don't know how I'm going to deal with it, but . . ." His voice trailed off. Then he shook himself as though trying to clear muzziness of sleep from his head and said, "I don't want to delay you any longer. I'll let you get on your way to see Mattie, and I'll go on over to McLain's." He stepped from the porch and climbed into the buggy.

"Don't forget Mattie's own wishes, Josiah. She's a good woman," Doc called after him.

Josiah grunted and waved. He slapped the reins and clucked, and the swaybacked old mare reluctantly moved forward. He steered her in a circle and exited the yard at the same broken place in the fence by which they had entered. Then he turned her back the way they had come, towards the fork in the road.

*   *   *

Jethro Wilson stood on his porch and watched until Josiah was out of sight. He shook his head sadly and muttered, "That man's a powder keg waiting for a spark. I don't think I want to be around when it finds him."

"What?" His wife had quietly come from the house and stood behind him.

Doc continued to stare up the road where Josiah's buggy had disappeared. After a bit he turned to her and explained, "It's Josiah Robertson, finally come home. He's in a state—wants vengeance—bad. But Mattie's asked him to try to forgive what's happened. If he ever figures out who attacked her . . ." He shrugged and shook his head before finishing, "I don't know what he'll do."

"You didn't tell him what you told me?"

"No. I answered his questions, but I didn't mention my suspicions. I have no proof. The consequences would be bad enough if I'm right, but if I told and I'm wrong . . ." He shook his head. "I don't think I could live with that."

She put her hand on his arm. "It's so hard to carry other people's pain on top of our own, isn't it? And hard to know what's right. So many people could be hurt."

He nodded. "Yes, many would be hurt." He shook his head.

100

"Such a brutal attack. And it could happen again, to some other woman. If I was certain, I would tell. I'm coward enough to hope I never know."

"I don't want to know, either. And I don't want you mixed up in it." She patted his arm and turned to go back into the house, stopped abruptly and turned back to him. "But what of Mattie? She hasn't? . . ."

"Oh, no. She's alive. But he said her fever is worse, and she has gut pain. He wants me to go take a look at her."

"Well, you better go on. You saddle your horse, I'll bring your bag out to you."

"Thank you. Dear, make sure there is laudanum in it, would you?"

"I will."

He stepped off the porch and started for the barn.

Chapter 13

Josiah returned to the fork and took the other branch. He thought back over everything Doc Wilson had said. Doc had all but told him Mattie had been raped. All the evidence he recounted pointed to that. He'd seemed forthright, and yet Josiah was sure he held something back. What? And why?

The air became hotter minute by minute as the sun climbed higher in the clear sky. Fewer birds flew about now; they perched in the bushes, sheltered from the intense heat, rustling as they shifted on their perches or moved from one branch to another. The dew had burned off. Three buzzards soared in circles. Hawks still perched on high snags and watched for prey. The swaybacked old mare plodded on, sweat now dampening her withers and flanks. Josiah sagged with exhaustion. He nodded off and only woke when the buggy stopped.

The old gray had come to a small creek, waded in a few feet, and stopped. She pulled at the lines, trying to lower her head to drink. Josiah gave her slack and let her drink her fill, even though he recognized this as the edge of Creed McLain's farm and knew she could soon drink her fill from McLain's trough. The creek, running across its gravel bed, would seem cooler than the water in any trough; and the shade here refreshed both man and horse.

Knowing the mare would not move until urged, he looped the lines around the brake handle and got down. He stepped off into the underbrush a few feet and pissed against a gum tree, his stream almost striking a dark cottonmouth lying loosely coiled at

102

the tree's base. He didn't see it until the insulted snake tightened its coil and opened its white-lined mouth. Josiah retreated hastily. He looked for a long, sturdy stick, but couldn't find one. The cottonmouth lowered its head after a while and slowly slithered away, as though it recognized safety and dismissed Josiah from its attention. Josiah's heart slowly returned to its normal rhythm. He remounted the buggy and took up the reins.

As the mare pulled the buggy up out of the little creek hollow, Josiah saw Creed's farm unfold before him. The corn in the field on the right had already turned brown in its maturity, the browning no doubt hastened by the recent drought. The ears looked small, as Luke had reported their own to be. The cotton on the left bore small green bolls. Josiah couldn't tell how good the crop would be, especially from the distance of the road, but he suspected it wouldn't be abundant—the plants looked scraggly, sparse, shorter than they should be.

Beyond the cotton four large oaks rose. Their leafy crowns shaded the two-storied McLain house—no mansion, but larger and finer than Josiah's. Creed McLain had come from North Carolina as a young man, supposedly the son of a wealthy planter. He had bought this farm and sent for a half dozen slaves from his old home. They built him a comfortable house with four rooms and a hall on each of the two floors. They planted corn and cotton and cleared more fields. Upon the completion of the house he brought his bride, Lorna, to live there with him, to bear their children—seven girls. Before the War it had been rumored he still held property in North Carolina, but McLain kept his business matters private so Josiah did not know if it was true. He knew McLain as a man of some substance but not what he'd call a wealthy one. And now, after the War? . . .

As he drew nearer, Josiah saw the rose garden had grown undisciplined but the large kitchen garden beyond was well kept. Someone wearing a bright scarf moved along the rows of beans and corn, stooping and rising, stooping and rising—probably Dorcas or Mamie, the other Negro woman Emmy had mentioned. Josiah laughed when he saw the large yellow-green leaves filling the tobacco patch between the kitchen garden and the road. Creed wasn't likely to be without his tobacco patch. He might not grow enough to market, but he'd have enough for personal use.

Five small cabins, each with a door, a window, and a squat chimney, sat behind the kitchen garden. Only two of the cabins had open doors and seemed to be occupied. The barn and a number of sheds and outbuildings straggled off beyond the cabins. A calf bawled, a jack brayed, a Negro man walked from one of the sheds to the barn.

Josiah turned the mare into the drive and neared the house. As he pulled the weary old animal up to the hitching post, Lorna McLain stepped through the front doorway, shading her eyes with her hand as she peered at her visitor. Her brows knit as she stared at him, and then both hands flew to her face.

"Josiah! Is it really you? Oh, thank God you're home."

Josiah stepped down from the buggy and rushed to her. They embraced and Lorna cried. At first she seemed joyous, but then alarmed. "Mattie! She's not . . ."

"No. No. Mattie's still with us. Don't faint. Here, let me take your arm."

The old lady sagged against him and Josiah led her into the house and eased her down on the sofa in the parlor. The color had drained from her face, and she sat there gasping.

"Let me get you a drink of water."

She nodded but managed to whisper, "Dorcas. Salts."

Josiah arranged a pillow so she could lie on the sofa, but she shook her head.

"No. It's easier if I sit up," she said.

He stood and stepped into the hall, calling, "Dorcas! Dorcas!"

A tall, neatly groomed black woman stepped into the hall from the back porch.

"Mistuh Josiah!" she cried and smiled broadly, but the smile quickly faded.

"Miss Lorna needs a drink of water and her smelling salts. Right away."

"Oh, Mistuh Josiah! It's not Miss Mattie?"

"No. Get the water and salts quickly."

"Yessuh."

104

Dorcas sped to the dining room. Josiah heard her pouring water, then her quick steps as she returned to the parlor with the full glass.

"Here, let's get you a little whiff of the salts first, Missus," she said as she set the glass of water down.

"I don't know where they are," Lorna panted.

"They's right here in your apron pocket, Missus, right where you 'most always keep 'em," Dorcas said as she retrieved and opened the small vial. "'Cept when you leave 'em on the center table, but I already checked for 'em there." She passed the vial beneath Lorna's nose two or three times.

"I believe I'm somewhat better, now, Dorcas." Her breath came more evenly, and she seemed less panicked.

"Yessum. Now you have a little sip of this water." Dorcas brought the glass to the old lady's lips.

Lorna took the glass in both of her own shaking hands, and she took several good swallows before she said, "Thank you, Dorcas. Oh my! What a shock you gave me, Josiah."

"I should have realized you might think the worst when you saw me. I should have found Creed first, or Dorcas or Samson. Are you recovered now?"

Lorna nodded, her sausage side curls swinging to-and-fro like pewter pendulums. "Yes, I believe I am." She took another sip of water and smoothed her plain calico skirt with a wrinkled hand browned and roughened by outdoor work. "Oh, Josiah, I do apologize. What an absolutely inexcusable welcome after your long absence. Please forgive me." Her face, composed now, displayed pale, thin skin netted with tiny wrinkles, a forehead lined with traces of the frowns of sixty years, and cheeks deeply furrowed with smile lines.

"Mother Lorna, there's no need for your apology. I should have given you some warning. I apologize for the fright I gave you."

"Oh, no lasting harm done," Lorna said with a wave of her hand as the color began returning to her cheeks. "Tell me, when did you get home?"

"Two days ago. I would've come by sooner, but there's been so much . . ."

"I know. How is Mattie?"

"She's not doing very well."

"I feared that." The old lady moaned.

"The first night and day after I got home she seemed better—she came to, and she talked to me, and she drank water and broth."

"Then she's much improved," Lorna said.

"Not really. Her fever's gotten higher—a lot higher. And her belly pain is worse. Now she won't drink."

"That don't sound good. No suh."

"No, it doesn't. I've been by Doc Wilson's to ask him to take another look at her. He's probably there by now. I told him I wanted to come by here before I went home."

"How's Miss Emmy holding up?"

"She's worn to a nubbin. She's trying to see to Mattie and take care of her children and tend the garden and do the cooking. Sally's big enough she doesn't seem to need quite so much tending, in fact she helps a good bit. Luke keeps Jim busy most of the time, but Callie Belle and Delia need a heap of seeing to."

Both women nodded.

"The last two nights I've sat with Mattie so Emmy could get a little rest, but I don't think it's helped much. She looks exhausted, and she's ill as a hornet. Cranky with everybody."

"My poor baby," murmured Lorna.

"I left Sally sitting with Mattie this morning. What with cooking and all, Emmy can't stay with her. Mattie's afraid to be alone. I hope I didn't do wrong by leaving Sally with her. She didn't want to stay with her mama, but I insisted. She was doing fine when I left, though."

"Oh, my poor girls!" Lorna moaned and began to cry, holding her apron up to her face. "My babies."

"Now, now, Missus. Don't you be getting yourself into a state. We have to be putting you to bed and waiting on you, too," Dorcas murmured as she patted the old lady's shoulder. Turning to Josiah, she asked, "Can we help out some way, Mistuh Josiah?"

"I hope so. On my way over here I was thinking you or Mother Lorna could come give Emmy some help. But now, I

106

don't know. I'm worried about Mother Lorna. It looks to me like she needs you here."

Lorna sniffed and wiped her eyes. "No, don't y'all worry about me. I'm not as strong as I used to be, but I'll be all right. I'll have Mamie to help me. My girls need you, Dorcas. You go help with Mattie." She sat up straighter.

"Yessum. Mistuh Josiah, you're going to be home for good now, ain't you? 'Cause I ain't going if you're not going to be there." Dorcas avoided Josiah's eyes, but she sounded resolute and she stood quietly, with no turning away, no shuffling feet.

Josiah's eyes narrowed. What had gotten into Dorcas? How dare she even consider refusing Lorna's order? He stared at her for several seconds, the muscles at the corners of his jaws knotting as he gritted his teeth. Finally he spat out, "Whether I'm home for good is none of your concern. And it has no bearing on whether or not you go to my house."

Dorcas flinched but she didn't back away. "Yes it does, Mistuh Josiah. No matter how much I love Miss Mattie and Miss Emmy, I ain't going to work for Mistuh Luke again, not if you ain't there."

"That's not for you to say. You'll go where you're told."

Dorcas held her ground. "No suh. I's worried 'bout Miss Mattie and Miss Emmy, and I want to help, but not if you ain't there to keep the peace. I chanced going over there once. I ain't going again."

Josiah's face had reddened. Lorna looked questioningly from Dorcas to Josiah and back again. With a frown she said, "You hush now. That's no way for you to talk. What's come over you?"

The black woman flicked a resentful glance at her but said nothing.

Josiah glared at Dorcas, who glanced up at him but could not continue to meet his gaze. She lowered her eyes but she maintained her composure and did not back down. He was puzzled—and yes, offended—by her impudence, but he knew Dorcas had served the McLains and the Robertsons long and well, and she and Samson were here helping Creed and Lorna when they could have kept going after they left his and Mattie's place. He didn't like her sass, but if she had an explanation he would listen to it. He took a deep breath. "What's brought this on, Dorcas?"

Lorna added, "Yes, what *is* this all about? What is this about 'keeping the peace?'"

Dorcas looked from Lorna to Josiah, then back to Lorna, and said, "I guess I'd better tell you." She sighed. "I know you're not going to want to believe me."

"Just tell us," Lorna said.

"Yessum. I don't know where to begin, though. It goes back a long way. To bad things, worse than just wrong."

Josiah rolled his eyes and shifted his weight on his feet. "Get on with it."

"When you went away to the war and Miss Emmy and Mistuh Luke came to live at your house, it seemed like everything got bad for me and Samson. It wasn't too good to start with, anyhow."

"Dorcas, we've always treated y'all kindly." Lorna's mouth pressed in a grim line and her neck flushed.

"I don't mean you was bad to us. Mostly you wasn't. If that wasn't so, there's no way me and Samson would be here now. What I'm trying to say is you all tried to treat us kindly, except Mistuh Luke—he's nasty mean. He's always yelling at me, and Samson, too. He hit us both with a buggy whip more'n once."

Lorna gasped, but Josiah motioned for her to be quiet.

"Miss Mattie was terrible mad when she found out the first time he hit me. She stood right up to him, told him she had a good mind to take the whip to him, and she would, if he ever did it again. Mistuh Luke, he's so mad—red in the face, fists all balled up. I's sure he's going to hit her."

Josiah scowled. "He hit Mattie?"

Dorcas shook her head. "No suh, but Miss Emmy, she's scared he's going to hit Miss Mattie. She's trying to calm him down, but she wasn't doing a lot of good. Finally she got him to go on in the house with her, and Miss Mattie took me to the cabin and put salve on the welts."

Dorcas' lips trembled as though she could still feel the lash of the whip.

Lorna said, "Oh, Dorcas. We didn't know."

Josiah balled his fists. "And was that the end of it?"

Dorcas shook her head again. "No suh. We heard Miss Emmy scream. Miss Mattie started to run back toward the house, but I held her back." Dorcas wrung her hands. "We both wanted to help Miss Emmy, but we's scared, so we just held each other and cried, for I don't know how long. After a while Mistuh Luke come storming out of the house and hurried out to the barn. Then he come tearing toward the road in the buggy, whipping the horse. I don't know how he got the horse hitched up so fast. Me and Miss Mattie ran up to the house and found Miss Emmy crying and her eye all swelling shut."

"You're saying Luke hit Emmy?" Lorna asked.

"Yessum. I didn't see it, but how else she get that eye?"

Josiah scowled. "Sure sounds like that's what happened."

Dorcas shifted nervously.

"Is there more?"

Dorcas nodded. "Yessuh. Mistuh Luke, he stayed gone a couple days. When he come back he's good as pie to Miss Emmy—for a while—but he wasn't good to me and Samson. And I don't think he was good to Miss Mattie, either. I heard them arguing lots of times, 'specially after he'd hit one of us again, but I don't think she actually tried to whip him like she said she was going to. As time went by, I'd see a bruise on Miss Emmy's face, or she'd favor one leg when she walked, and I knew Mistuh Luke had done something to her again. She never said nothing about it, though."

"She's never let on about this to me," said Lorna. "Surely she would have."

"Maybe not," said Josiah. "After all, what could you have done?"

"Let on or not, it's true. That's why, soon's we heard Mr. Lincoln said we's free, we took off, me and Samson. Mistuh Luke near foamed at the mouth like a mad dog. He tried to get us to stay, said we belonged on your place. But we didn't want nothing more to do with Mistuh Luke Elrod. There was enough Yankee soldiers around right then to protect us—or so we thought. But they didn't protect us, and we's scared and hungry, so we come back here. Mr. Creed said he needed some help, and if we'd stay, we could have a cabin, and he'd pay us shares when the crops come in. And that's what we're doing."

"I see," Josiah said, but he didn't. This tale resembled Emmy's report, but the background—the whippings, the beatings—that was hard to take in.

"Mistuh Josiah, I ain't going back where I'm under Luke's thumb again."

"But you went the other day."

"Yessuh. Missus begged me to go help tend to Miss Mattie, and I went. Luke Elrod was meaner'n ever. I's trying to help Miss Emmy, and he's just skulking around, being mean. Mostly he did his meanness where Miss Emmy couldn't see. Said I's sassing him once, and punched me in the stomach. Pinched my titty when I had my arms full of laundry and couldn't do nothing, too."

"Dorcas, what an unseemly thing to say!" Lorna said, blushing.

"It was an unseemly thing for him to do," Dorcas shot back. She closed her eyes and shuddered with disgust. "I wanted to come right on back here, but I couldn't tell Miss Emmy why. She begged me to stay the night and help her. So I stayed. I sat up with Miss Mattie so's Miss Emmy could get some sleep. And I did a few more chores the next day, and then I walked on home."

Ashen, Lorna closed her eyes. "Oh, dear God. I had no idea."

Dorcas looked up at Josiah. "I ain't going back to no such, no matter how much I care about Miss Mattie and Miss Emmy. You've got to be there to keep the peace. You might not be happy about it—you either, Miss Lorna—but it's the way it is."

Josiah drew a deep breath, then puffed it out slowly. Did he believe this tale? It was hard to give it credence. But the way Emmy looked so cowed around Luke . . . It might be true. She'd even been jumpy around him. Surely she knew he wouldn't hit her? Wife beating wasn't uncommon, but Josiah thought it was wrong, low. And it didn't fit the pious image Luke tried to project.

"Dorcas, are you positive Luke hit Emmy?"

"I didn't ever see him hit Miss Emmy, but sure as I'm standing here, he did. 'Course, Miss Emmy, she never talked about it."

"You think he might've hit Mattie, too?" Josiah asked as he watched Dorcas' eyes.

Lorna gasped, clasped her hand to her mouth and whispered, "No."

Dorcas leveled her gaze on Josiah. "No, Mistuh Josiah, I'm not saying that. No suh. But I am telling you Luke Elrod is a mean man, no matter how much he reads his Bible or how often he prays. And I ain't going over there unless you're going to be around to see he don't take his meanness out on anybody, 'specially me."

Josiah grunted and studied on the situation before he said, "We need you, Dorcas. Mattie needs you. Emmy needs you. You have my word I'll be there. Luke won't harm you. I swear it."

"Yessuh. I believe you will take care of things, now you know."

Josiah frowned, deep in thought. Either Dorcas was spiteful, or reckless, or just plain crazy—or she was telling the truth. How could he know which? If he went straight to Luke, he was bound to deny the accusation. If he went to Emmy, what would she say? Even if it was true, she might not want to admit it, for fear of what Luke might do to her. The only thing he could think of was to ask Mattie. Surely she'd tell him the truth.

His frown deepened. And what would he do if he found out the tale was true? Wasn't this something between Luke and Emmy? Emmy was a bit of a harpy, but she didn't deserve to be beaten. He couldn't let that go. And what about Mattie? Had Luke ever hit her? And this business about mistreating Dorcas and Samson—he couldn't let that go on, either. He needed their goodwill too much.

They all were quiet for a few moments before Lorna turned to Dorcas. "You swear this is true?"

"Yessum. You oughta know I wouldn't make up no such story." It seemed to Josiah she looked and sounded resentful.

Lorna nodded. "Yes. I do know. I've never known you to be untruthful."

Dorcas' expression eased a bit.

Lorna turned to Josiah. "It's true, Josiah. Dorcas isn't a liar."

He nodded grimly. "Yes, I know. I'll see what I can find out about all this."

"Do. I don't doubt Dorcas, certainly not about Luke's treatment of her and Samson." Lorna shook her head and mused, "All the time Emmy and Luke lived here there was a tension in him, as though he kept himself reined in. Creed said I imagined it, but I don't think so. I always figured it was because Luke hadn't really gotten comfortable with us yet, hadn't really felt himself become part of the family. Some people are distant like that, you know."

"Luke has always seemed stiff and standoffish to me, but then I never have lived close to him, day to day. Till now, of course." Josiah raised one eyebrow. "Maybe when he lived here he forced himself to be on good behavior out of fear of Creed."

Dorcas nodded as Lorna picked up the thought. "And when he didn't have us so near all the time, he didn't feel the need anymore. My poor Emmy. I never suspected there might be that kind of trouble—that Luke would strike her. She's never let on to us there was anything wrong between them. Can you find out if it's true, Josiah? And if it is, can you help my Emmy?"

"If Luke really has beaten Emmy, I'll make him see the error of his ways—teach him a lesson he won't soon forget."

"You take care, Josiah. Even though he's got a bent leg, Luke's a strong man, and stubborn. He won't take kindly to correcting, especially by you. I think he's always been jealous of you."

"Don't worry about me. I can take care of myself."

Lorna said, "I wish I hadn't told Dorcas to speak. I wish I didn't know what might be going on. I wish . . . oh, so many things, none possible." She sighed, and shook herself. She looked at Josiah and asked, "Do y'all need anything like sheets or bandages? Or some of the liniment Mamie makes?"

"Emmy said we might need some sheets. Mostly I think she needs help with the cooking and the laundry. It's hard to keep Mattie clean. She's as helpless as a baby."

"Dorcas, go out to the garden and tell Mamie I'll be needing her to do the cooking for a few days and to do like you do, help me get up and down the stairs and so on. Then gather up some sheets," Lorna said. "They don't have to be the best ones."

"Yessum."

As Dorcas left the room, Josiah asked, "Lorna, where will I find Creed this morning? And Samson. I need to talk to both of them."

Lorna frowned. "Oh, what did he tell me he planned to do today?" she mumbled. "He told me, but all of this has made me forget." After a few seconds her face brightened. "I believe he said he would work on the cornfield fence. And Samson or George will be helping him."

"Thank you, Mother Lorna. I'll find him and then head home. I'll take my leave of you now," Josiah said as he pressed the old lady's hands between his and bent to kiss her cheek.

"Yes, Josiah. You hurry on home. I'm so glad you're back with us now, safe from the War, safe from your journey."

Chapter 14

Josiah found Creed McLain at the back of the cornfield where he supervised Samson's repair of the rail fence. Josiah called out to them as he strode across the field to the work site. Creed turned to stare at the approaching figure, squinting in the bright sunlight and clearly not yet recognizing his visitor.

Samson placed a rail and stood. He put his hands to the small of his back and bent backwards, left and right, to stretch out kinks. His extremely dark complexion glistened with sweat that streamed from his face and ran down his broad chest and muscular arms to soak his dingy frayed shirt and dark baggy pants. He removed his shapeless, sweat-stained hat and ran one hand over his close-cropped graying hair as he watched the man approach from far across the field. Then he said, "It's Mistuh Josiah, Boss."

"By Jove, you're right," Creed said as he shaded his eyes with his hand. "Josiah, my boy! Welcome home!"

They met and embraced, then held each other at arm's length. Josiah saw his father-in-law now showed his sixty years. Long yellow-white hair hung lankly from beneath his grimy straw work hat. A tobacco-stained, frizzy beard covered his lower face. Watery green eyes peered from beneath bushy white brows. A scaly white lesion marred the right cheek of his wrinkled, sun-reddened face.

"Father Creed, you're looking well," Josiah said.

"It's mighty good to see you, son-in-law," Creed said. "Even

114

if you are as thin as these rails." And then, "You've not come about Mattie?"

"Oh, no. No. She's not doing well, but she's hanging on." Josiah went on to repeat what he had told Lorna.

"It hasn't made a very joyous homecoming for you, has it?"

"No. But I'm glad to be home, none the less. Get to know Sally again. See you and Mother Lorna. And Luke and Emmy. They're well. The children have really grown. My farm looks good, too, considering. Luke's done a good job, but it's really more than one man can handle. Maybe I can rebuild it now. One more man and a good horse should help a lot. Which brings me to part of the reason I came over here today—I need some help."

"You know I'll do anything I can."

"I need to borrow Samson to shoe my horse."

Samson had returned to his task, but at the words 'borrow Samson,' he hesitated and cast a resentful look at Josiah.

"Pepper threw a shoe and went lame on me a few miles from home. His hoof needs trimming and he needs a new shoe. I can't ride him till it's done. And I can't ride that miserable old swaybacked mare Luke scrounged up somewhere. Nor the mules—we need them in the fields."

"Ha. You don't think that mare is a fine animal?"

Josiah grunted. "She pulled the buggy here today—just barely."

Creed chuckled. "Of course Samson can go tend to your horse." Then McLain tossed back over his shoulder, "You go with Josiah right now, Samson."

"Yessuh," Samson said, as he pulled another rotten rail from the fence. "Only we needs to get this here fence done. You know them cows been getting into the corn."

"Well, I'll have George work on it this afternoon," McLain said.

"Why not send George to shoe the horse, let me finish this here fence?"

"Samson, I need you to work on Pepper," Josiah said. "You're a blacksmith. I don't know about this George. He know anything about shoeing?" Samson shrugged and Creed shook his head. Josiah continued, "I know you'll do a good job. Besides, you can ride along with Dorcas so you only take one mule."

"Ride along with Dorcas? Dorcas ain't going over there where Luke Elrod is."

McLain stared at Samson as his face grew redder and redder. "What are you talking about, boy? You're overstepping."

Josiah scowled and his own face reddened, but he intervened. "Hold on a minute, Creed. There's something you should know about. It doesn't excuse Samson, but . . . well, I need to talk to you both about it."

Samson stood with his head bowed, but his jaw muscles clenched and unclenched repeatedly as he watched both white men.

McLain stared stony-faced at the black man for several seconds before he turned to Josiah and asked sharply, "Well, what is it?"

"Dorcas refused to help Emmy with Mattie unless I promised to be there to 'keep the peace.' Lorna made her explain herself, and she told a worrisome tale, Creed. She said Luke had mistreated her and Samson, and when Mattie had stood up to him Luke got boiling mad. Emmy tried to calm him down, and before it was all over, he hit Emmy—hard enough to black her eye. Dorcas said Emmy has had other bruises since then, too."

"What?"

Josiah shook his head as he went on. "I don't know whether to believe it or not. Dorcas admits she never actually saw Luke hit Emmy, but she insists that's what happened. It might be true. If it is, it makes my blood boil. We need to look into this, Creed."

McLain looked over at Samson, then back at Josiah. "I knew there'd been some trouble between Samson and Luke. I heard that from both of them, figured the truth of it lay somewhere between the two tales. I thought the trouble mostly sprang from Samson and Dorcas leaving your place. I never heard anything about Luke hitting my girl."

Samson shifted his weight from one foot to the other.

McLain continued to stare at the black man. Finally he asked, "Is your woman making up this tale out of spite?"

"No suh. She's not making it up. Luke whipped Dorcas with a buggy whip. And he whipped me. And lots of times I saw Miss Emmy with a black eye or a swollen lip or favoring an arm or leg. She never said how she got them bruises, but we knew, me and Dorcas. I don't want to work for Luke Elrod, and I don't want Dorcas to work over there, either. She went the other day against my will. I knew it was a mistake. Now I don't want him to have another chance to hit her—or worse. 'Specially if he knows she told—we've told—about what he's done. He'll be worse'n ever."

"Damn it, Samson, why didn't you tell me this before?" McLain asked.

"How much good would it've done, Mistuh Creed?"

Creed's face reddened. "You should've told me."

"Yessuh." Samson kept his head down, but his back had stiffened and his fingers had curled almost into fists.

McLain turned to Josiah. "You seem willing to believe Dorcas and Samson."

Josiah answered, "I am. This story kind of explains some of Emmy's behavior, and her tale of how Dorcas acted at my house a few days ago. But I hate to face Luke with this kind of accusation without more than the word of two blacks."

Samson's fists drew tighter.

"Nobody else would know except Emmy and Mattie—and maybe the children," McLain said.

"I know," Josiah said. "I can't ask the children. They're so obedient, they're almost what I'd call cowed. I think they'd be scared to answer any such questions. And I don't want to put them in a position to raise Luke's ire. He's kind of rough with them. I've seen that with my own eyes."

Josiah thought for a few seconds. "I can ask Emmy, but since she hasn't said anything about his abuse I suspect she'll be inclined to cover up for him even if it's true. I'll have to be very careful about how I go about asking her. Even so, I don't think I can trust her word if she says he never laid a hand on her. Or on Dorcas and Samson."

"Maybe I should ask her? She wouldn't lie to me," offered McLain.

117

Josiah shook his head. "I don't know, Creed. The more I think about it, the more I think maybe it's best for us not to question her yet. Her situation might be kind of similar to the children's."

McLain moved restlessly, removed his hat and raked his fingers through his hair. "It's hard to accept this. Luke's a good man—church-going and religious. He's been a good son-in-law, best I could tell. And he lived right here with me. If he's mean, I ought to have seen some sign of it. I'm going to need some proof before I can believe this tale."

Josiah sighed. "I know. We've never been really close friends, but I've never thought of Luke as anything but a good man. He's raising good children, even if his methods seem too strict to me. And I'm indebted to him. He's taken care of my place—maybe saved me from ruin. I don't want to think he's been so rotten. Still I have to give some credence to what Dorcas and Samson have said."

"We need some proof, son. It's not fair to Luke to believe this charge without question."

Josiah nodded. "You're right. Let me try asking Mattie if Luke has beaten Emmy. And if he's mistreated Samson and Dorcas. If she's able, she'll tell me the truth." But would she? He was certain she was holding out about what happened to her. "If she says he's done any of that, I'm going to beat Luke Elrod within an inch of his life. What he does to his wife is their business, in a way—"

"No it's not. Not if he's beating my daughter," Creed said.

"Exactly. And I won't stand for any such in my house. I'll teach him a lesson he won't forget."

"You better figure some way to protect Miss Emmy, then. Mistuh Luke's a proud man and he ain't going to 'preciate you correcting him. He's likely to take it out on her," Samson said.

"She can come to me and her mother," McLain said.

"She could've all along, but she hasn't," Josiah said.

"She might ought to come to you before Mistuh Josiah teaches his lesson," Samson said.

"I'll watch out for her. I'll bring her over here to safety if he tries to get violent with her."

118

"Yessuh, you do that. But I do think you ought to get them ladies and chilrun out'n the way before you light into Luke."

"If it comes to that, I will."

McLain pulled a tightly twisted loop of tobacco and a small knife from his pocket and cut a chew for himself, offered one to Josiah, then one to Samson. The tension which had risen during their conversation waned as each of them chewed and worked the tobacco over into his cheek.

"I still need your help, Samson. And Dorcas's. Y'all come on back with me. I think we need Dorcas to stay for a while, so if you want to, if it'll make you feel better about it, you can stay, too."

Josiah frowned as Samson shook his head. He looked over at Creed. "You can spare Samson, can't you, Creed?"

McLain nodded.

"I'll study on it, Mistuh Josiah. But I want to talk to Dorcas before I decide," Samson said. "I reckon I'll go do that right now, Mistuh Creed." He turned and walked toward the farmstead.

"Whsssshhhht!" Josiah let out his pent breath. "That boy needs to have his chain jerked up short," he muttered as the black man strode away, but he realized he hadn't done anything about the assertive black, nor had McLain.

"Samson's a little full of himself," McLain agreed, "but he's basically a good hard worker. I've never had him defy my order before, though. I don't like it—not one little bit. Sets a bad precedent. I reckon I can understand he's worried about his wife's safety, but it seems like I should've done something about his insolence."

"Maybe it's better to let it ride this time," Josiah said as they started toward the house. "He'll come around and do what's right. Give him time to work it out for himself. But he's bound for grief if he acts out around other folks. He'll get himself whipped—or worse."

*   *   *

As Samson neared the house he saw Dorcas leave the back porch and go to their cabin. He turned that way. By the time he reached the doorway, she was already coming back out carrying a small bundle.

"Go back inside. I need to talk to you," Samson said as he grasped her upper arm and pushed her back into the dark little cabin.

"About what?"

"Josiah says you're going over to his house, over where Luke Elrod is. Why you want to do that? Ain't we had enough trouble with them folks already?"

"Samson, Miss Mattie's awful bad off, and Miss Emmy can't do all that needs doing. I want to go help 'em. They's good women. Miss Mattie was always good to us, and Miss Emmy, she tried. I . . . I think Miss Mattie's going to die. I want to give her a little comfort." Dorcas began to cry.

"I know they's good, as good as any white women can be. But we don't belong to them no more. Let them take care of theirselves. We don't need to be 'round Luke Elrod, risking him going off on one of his rages. Josiah wants me to shoe his horse, but I don't want to, 'cause I don't want to be anywhere near Luke. Josiah knows how to shoe a horse hisself."

"But not as good as you," Dorcas murmured between sniffles.

"No, not as good as me, but he knows how. I reckon if it's his own horse, he'll be careful and do it right."

"But Mattie and Emmy need me," Dorcas said. "I can't just pay 'em no mind. Josiah swore he'd be there to see Luke don't do no bad—gave me his word."

"You think that white man's word is worth anything? That white man still has a deed says we belong to him, same's his farm does. You think he wouldn't be still claiming us as property if it wasn't for the Yankee soldiers whipping his sorry ass from here to Virginy and back?"

"I do think Josiah's word is good. He ain't never been bad to us."

"Woman, you ain't got no sense. You softhearted and you ain't got no sense." Samson sighed, shaking his head.

Dorcas pulled a handkerchief from her apron and dabbed at her eyes, then blew her nose. She stood straighter and looked him in the eye. "You're right, I am soft-hearted. I want to help 'em, and I mean to. Josiah'll protect me, but I wish you'd go along and take care of the horse. Then I'd have you to protect me, too."

"Dorcas, you ol' mule."

She looked into his eyes. "I'm going over there. You coming?" She headed for the door with her small bundle.

Samson remained in the dimly lit cabin for a while, his fists clenched, muttering, "A mule. A damn mule." But he wasn't going to change her. He heaved a heavy sigh, shrugged in resignation and followed her. "I'll put a bridle on a mule and come to the back porch. You come on out when you're ready to start," he called."

*   *   *

As Samson led the bony mule toward the back porch he met Josiah and Creed. "I reckon we'll be coming with you, Mistuh Josiah."

"Good." Josiah glanced at Creed, saw that he, too, felt easier now that the black man had come to the right decision. "I need to get started. Where's Dorcas?"

"She went back in the house, to see to Miss Lorna, I reckon."

"Creed, would you send Dorcas out when you go in? I'm going to hit the road. Samson, y'all catch up. It won't be any trouble, as slow as my old mare is." Josiah shook hands with McLain, and started on his way.

Before he had gotten back to the creek, Samson and Dorcas caught up with him, riding double on the mule. Dorcas sat astride behind Samson, her lower legs and feet exposed. Her hands lightly touched Samson's waist, not really holding tight. Her small bundle had been tied to a larger one and they had been thrown across the mule's withers in front of Samson, one bundle on either side, but the larger bundle slipped lower, which pulled the smaller one across the mule's shoulders. Samson grabbed them and pulled them back into position.

"Samson, you'd better put those in the buggy," Josiah called.

"Yessuh, boss," the black man replied, and swung the bundles into the buggy behind the seat.

They proceeded slowly, at the old gray's pace, with no

conversation. The heat built, they all sweated. A raccoon ambled across the road in front of them. The mule pricked its long ears, but the old mare gave no sign of noticing.

"Kind of odd to see a 'coon out this time of day," commented Samson.

Josiah grunted. "Yep." Extreme weariness dragged at him. As long as he kept moving he could hold off the sleepiness. But now, as he sat still and hardly had to give attention to the mare, staying alert had become impossible. His eyes, dry and burning, felt like they'd been filled with ashes. The heat of the day, the steady clop of the animals' hooves, the rhythmic creak of the harness, all conspired to lull him. Soon his chin dropped to his chest.

"Mist—," Samson began, but Dorcas swatted him on his back and whispered, "Shhh. Let him be. He's 'bout exhausted. Let him sleep whilst he can."

"What if he falls out'n the buggy?" Samson whispered back.

"He won't. I reckon he's learned to sleep on a horse, or in a wagon, or anywhere else he happens to be. He'll be all right."

Josiah did sleep, but not deeply. The jostling of the buggy kept the nightmares away, and all other dreams besides. As they neared his house, Pretty Girl came running up, barking. The old gray paid no mind but the mule danced and side-stepped. "Whoa," Samson said while he brought it under control. Josiah woke up.

"Hush! Stop barking, Pretty Girl, you stupid old bitch. Hush," he called to the scruffy dog. She looked at him and whined, then took another turn around the mule, barked again. "Shut up! Come here, leave the mule alone." The dog bounded toward him but turned to bark again. Josiah urged the mare on to the barn. Recognizing home, she moved more quickly than she had during the entire trip.

Josiah jumped down from the buggy. He noted a saddled horse tethered near the water trough. Doc's horse, he hoped.

Samson and Dorcas dismounted but kept wary eyes on the dog. Josiah caught her by her scruff and held her.

"Come on and let her get a good sniff of you."

They approached and tentatively held their hands toward the animal.

"Hush, now, Pretty Girl. You ought to remember us, you think about it a minute," Samson murmured. Pretty Girl quieted and began to wag her tail. Samson patted her head and the wagging increased.

Dorcas said, "Good dog," but she stepped back and made no attempt to touch the animal.

Josiah entered the barn and took a quick look around. No sign of Luke, or anybody else. The stalls were empty, and he had not seen the mules in the pasture with the cow, so he assumed Luke had them out working somewhere. He went back to the buggy.

"Samson, you unhitch this mare and turn her into the pasture—your mule, too—then come on up to the house. I'll go on to the house with Dorcas, and I'll have somebody bring you out a plate of dinner," he said as he lifted the bundles from the buggy. Dorcas had already started toward the house, but she turned and waited as he caught up and handed the bundles to her.

Josiah went into the kitchen for a dipper of water. The heat almost pushed him back out. Several pots occupied the eyes of the stove, steam drifting lazily from their lids. The table was set with six places. He was in time for dinner. But Josiah saw no sign of Emmy.

Chapter 15

As Josiah entered the back door he heard the murmur of voices from the front of the house. He paused at Mattie's door and watched as Doc Wilson gently pressed her distended belly, his hand separated from her flesh by her nightgown and the sheet. Mattie clamped her jaw tight and emitted a strained, high-pitched moan, her body writhing away from Doc's hands. The movement brought on another stifled scream. Josiah could see sweat beading on all of her exposed flesh. A thin trickle of blood oozed from the corner of her mouth. She must have bitten her lips or her tongue. And then, mercifully, she fainted. Emmy, who had watched with tears streaming down her face, turned away, her shoulders shaking with the sobs she no longer could hold back. Dorcas drew her close, held her, murmured something that sounded soft and comforting.

Josiah stood there, stunned. Why was Doc hurting Mattie? And my God! How could her belly be so big? She'd hardly eaten for days, had only taken a few sips of water in the last twenty-four hours.

He shakily entered the room. "Doc?"

Doc turned and looked sadly at Josiah. "I've been observing Mattie for some time now. We need to talk." Turning to Dorcas, he instructed, "Wipe her with damp cloths and fan her. That'll help keep her cool. Keep the sheet pulled up off her feet. Wipe them, too. When she comes to, give her another dose of the laudanum. I'll leave some more of it with you. She'll need it."

Dorcas nodded over Emmy's shoulder. "Yessuh. I'll take care of Miss Mattie."

Doc continued, "Emmy, Josiah, will y'all step on out of here so we can talk without disturbing Mattie?"

Josiah nodded but hesitated for a moment before he turned away from the scene in the bedroom. Emmy wordlessly moved toward the doorway.

Doc led the little group down the hall and out the back door and well onto the back porch.

"I don't want Mattie to hear. She might not be as unaware as she looks. I've known folks to hear things when I've thought they were unconscious."

Josiah recognized the prelude to bad news. He reached for Emmy's forearm. Emmy moaned and put her hand over his.

Doc continued, "I know y'all can tell. You could tell last night. She's much worse. There are some terrible complications."

Josiah worked his dry mouth, finally got his tongue to move. "What's happening to her, Doc?"

"You remember I said I thought there might be abdominal injuries?"

Josiah nodded.

"Well, I'm sure of it now. And they're really bad."

Emmy moaned and squeezed Josiah's hand, hard.

Josiah felt his head go light, his scalp prickle with dread. "What do you mean, Doc?" he asked, but he already knew the answer.

Doc looked at Josiah, then at Emmy, then down at the scuffed, weathered floorboards. "It's kind of like when a man's gut-shot."

Josiah's mind reeled away from this, ran from it, didn't want to face it. How could he? He had seen men take a bullet in the gut—messy wounds, and extremely painful. He had heard the moans and screams of the wounded, smelled the horrible stenches as he passed the hospital tents, the ambulance wagons. And he didn't know of many who had survived gut wounds. He swayed, felt so light-headed he thought for a moment he would black out.

125

"But what does that mean?" Emmy asked, very softly, almost holding her breath.

"There's bad infection in her belly. Real bad. Probably her bowels are broken open. They're leaking and the filth causes suppuration."

At this Emmy gagged and moaned, her eyes rolled back, and her legs gave away. Josiah's grasp on her arm allowed him to pull up and keep her head from banging hard on the floor. His action had to have hurt her, but she made no sound. He eased her on down to the floor, in a dead faint.

"Emmy?"

"Emmy'll be all right, Josiah. It's the shock. She'll come to in a bit," Doc said as he turned her head to the side and checked to be sure her breathing was unobstructed.

"But Mattie?"

"The way her belly is swollen, and the great tenderness of it, and the high fever—I don't think she'll make it. I'm so sorry." Doc put his hand on Josiah's shoulder, but Josiah shrugged it off and turned away.

His eyes burned, but he would not let himself cry, not in front of Doc. He stared ahead, out over the farmyard, over his property, but he saw nothing—he saw only a succession of memories of Mattie and their life together, culminating with the scene of Mattie standing bravely, trying not to let him see her tears as he rode off to the War. How he wished he hadn't left her alone, left her without his protection. How could such a beautiful, dear creature have to suffer so cruelly and die such a horrible death? How could God allow that?

The agony Mattie must endure until she would slip from life had no redeeming aspect, unlike labor and childbirth, where the pain brought a new life, a child to love, a hope, a reward. Mattie would experience unbearable pain, an unreasonable punishment laid on the finest person he had ever known. His grief and rage and bitterness overcame him, and he punched a porch post, hard, repeatedly, until his knuckles bled and he left ragged scraps of his skin on the weathered wood.

Emmy stirred and started to come around. Doc bent to tend her. Then he helped her up, and he led her, almost carried her,

126

back into the house and deposited her on the settee in the hall. He retrieved his bag and passed smelling salts beneath her nose. She drew several shaky breaths, then shook her shoulders, sighed, and set them in an attitude of determination.

"Well, we'll have to carry on as best we can. Maybe you're wrong," she said, and stood.

"Do you feel up to standing?" Doc asked.

"Yes. Thank you, Doctor Wilson. I'll be fine. There're things to tend to. I have to get everybody in to dinner. You will stay for dinner with us?"

Doc blinked. He nodded. "Why, yes. I'd be most glad to take dinner with you."

Emmy smiled. "Good. I already told Sally to set a place for you." She massaged her wrenched arm and started for the kitchen while Doc repacked his bag.

On the porch she found Josiah sitting on the floor. His legs dangled over the side, his torso rocked back and forth. He held his hands together and drawn to his belly. "Josiah, dinner is about ready. Get washed up."

He blinked hard, then braced his hands on the edge of the porch as he rose unsteadily. She looked at his battered knuckles in bewilderment for a moment, and then seemed to remember his beating the post as Doc had helped her into the hall.

"Josiah, your hands!"

He nodded dumbly, looked at his bleeding knuckles, and went to the washbasin.

"You come on in the kitchen when you're done. I'll salve those before I feed Delia." He nodded again. Emmy rang the dinner bell and called the children before disappearing into the kitchen.

Doc returned after tying his bag on his saddle just as Josiah finished drying his hands on the dirty, bloodstained towel. "Josiah, I'm so sorry."

"I know." Josiah blinked. "Emmy called dinner."

"Yes, she did. And I think we'd better give some attention to those hands of yours."

"Emmy has some salve in the kitchen." Josiah sounded distant, barely there, even to himself.

127

"All right. It's probably as good as anything in my bag."

As they started for the kitchen, all four children rounded the corner of the house. Sally and Callie Belle each held one of Delia's hands. Jim trotted behind, carrying a sturdy stick. Their high-pitched laughter dwindled as they saw Josiah and Doc.

"Daddy, I didn't know you were home," Sally said as she pulled Delia and Callie Belle to a stop. Jim went around them and on into the kitchen where he propped his stick beside the door.

Josiah forced a smile. "You didn't see the buggy?"

"No," she answered, then bent down to Delia and said, "You go with Callie Belle," and motioned for Callie Belle to go on. She turned back to Josiah and said, "We were playing over in the edge of the woods. When the doctor came, Aunt Emmy said we had to go out and play somewhere away from the house so we wouldn't bother Mama." She glanced over toward Doc. "She said I didn't need to stay with Mama. It was all right for me to leave Mama then, wasn't it, Daddy?"

"Yes," Josiah answered.

Doc said, "You did a fine job of taking care of your Mama this morning. She told me so."

Sally beamed.

Josiah smiled and asked, "What were you children doing in the woods?"

"Oh, nothing. You know, just playing." Then her face lit with excitement. "Jim found the strangest little red snake under a rock. It looked almost like a wiggly worm. Callie Belle and Delia ran away, but I wanted to see it up close. Jim poked at it with a stick and it tried to crawl back under the rock. He said to move the rock, so I did. The snake crawled so fast Jim couldn't keep it turned back with the stick and it got away under the leaves."

Josiah and Doc both frowned.

"What kind of markings did the snake have?" Josiah asked. "It didn't bite any of y'all, did it?"

"No, it didn't have any kind of spots or stripes. It looked like a big red worm." Sally paused briefly, then added, "And it didn't even try to bite anybody. It just tried to get away."

"That's what most snakes do, if you don't corner them,

except cottonmouths, or sometimes copperheads," Josiah said as he thought about the cottonmouth he had encountered that morning.

"Maybe, but I think most folks are like me when they come across a snake" commented Doc. "They grab something to whack it with and don't give it much chance to get away. All serpents are evil."

"Ah, come on, Doc. You surely don't believe that. What about the corn snakes that keep down the rats and mice in the crib?" Josiah said.

"I do believe it," replied Doc. "They have been evil since the Garden of Eden. It's right there in the Bible."

"But—"

Emmy poked her head out of the kitchen doorway and called, "Y'all come on in here and get your dinner."

"Yes, ma'am," Josiah answered, then turned to Sally as they neared the kitchen. "Dorcas and Samson came back with me from Grandfather's house. Dorcas is with your mama now, and Samson is tending to the mare and putting the buggy away. He'll be up here in a little bit. I want you to take a couple of tin plates and load 'em up with some of this dinner Aunt Emmy has made and give 'em each a plate. And you wait till Samson is here to give him his. Don't put his dinner down on the porch. Those dogs will get it."

"Yessir," Sally said as she went directly to the cupboard to get the plates.

"Emmy, you don't have enough places set," Josiah said.

"Luke won't be here. After you left this morning he came in and said he would carry some corn to the mill. I fried a couple of eggs and put 'em in biscuits for him to take with him, because he said it would probably be late afternoon before he gets back," Emmy said. "I don't know why it takes so long, but I'm glad he went. I need the meal," she added. Then she turned to a shelf over her sink and found a tin of salve. "Here, let me see those knuckles," she said.

"Aw, Emmy, I really don't need any salve. It stinks!" Josiah protested.

"Well, it'll keep the flies off. You ought to use it," commented Doc.

"Hmmmff!" Josiah snorted, but he extended his hands.

Sally stared at his bloody knuckles. "What happened, Daddy?"

"Um, nothing. I bumped into a post."

Sally nodded and kept her mouth shut as she filled the plates, but her raised eyebrow suggested she doubted his explanation.

"Emmy, this is a fine dinner," Doc said as Josiah sat at the head of the table and motioned for him to take the chair on his right. The children clambered into their usual places. Sally was the last to take her seat after she took the plates to Dorcas and Samson.

Josiah started to take up his fork put paused when he noticed Emmy's small frown and slight shake of her head. He said, "Let us bow and give thanks," and proceeded with a perfunctory prayer. Emmy gave him a critical frown when she raised her head.

The meal consisted of vegetables and cornbread and was eaten mostly in silence. The children ate hungrily, as did Doc, but Emmy and Josiah spent much of the dinnertime staring at their plates.

Sally asked, "What's the matter, Daddy?"

Josiah looked up, tried to smile and failed. "Nothing. I'm kind of sad about Mama." Emmy's eyes flashed a warning as she gave him a small shake of her head. He cleared his throat and finished, "About her feeling so bad."

Alarmed, Sally asked, "Didn't I take care of her good?"

Now what should he say? He didn't want her to feel like any of their troubles was her fault. But Mattie was worse. All of the children would be aware of that soon enough. This wasn't the right time to tell her, though—not with everyone else looking on.

He cleared his throat again. "You took care of Mama very well this morning. You did such a good job she told Doctor Wilson about it. Don't you remember? Doc told you? She's proud of you."

"But why are you so sad?"

"Because Mama isn't getting better yet."

"But she will get better, won't she?"

"We hope so." True, but it was a mighty thin hope.

Emmy added, "We pray so. You can pray for your Mama, too."

"Yessum, I do pray for Mama," Sally said.

Josiah saw her frown, her glance from one adult to another. He suspected she knew they were lying to her.

After a few moments of silence, Doc spoke up. "Emmy, thanks for the delicious dinner. I hate to eat and run, but I've promised Miz Waller I would look in on Jon this afternoon."

"Thank you for coming today," Emmy said. "Please give my regards to the Wallers."

Josiah walked out with Doc. "Thanks for seeing Mattie. I wish your news were better. I can't help hoping maybe you're wrong."

"I don't usually enjoy being wrong in my profession, Josiah, but in this case, I'd be glad."

Josiah nodded several times, quickly. "I know. I know." After a long pause, he asked, "Doc, how much do I owe you?"

"Oh, how about two dollars? I know you just got home and you probably don't have your affairs straightened out yet, so don't worry if you don't have it now."

"I've got nothing right now, Doc, I'm ashamed to tell you. We're planning on selling some hogs soon. As soon as we do, I'll bring you your money. Or I could give you a pig."

"I know you'll be good for it. We'll work something out. I can wait. You concentrate on getting your family through these next few days." They shook hands. Doc turned and strode toward his horse.

Josiah waved as Doc rode past on the way to the road. He leaned against a porch post and gazed across the farmyard. At first he really saw nothing as his mind grappled with thoughts of Mattie, contemplating the evil and injustice of her agony and near-certain death, then flinching as his mind protested the unbearable pain her suffering inflicted in his heart. He couldn't think about it. He couldn't bear it. But it was the only thing on his mind.

He made himself take in the details of the farmstead, the barn and outbuildings, the fields beyond. His farm, his Pa's farm. He had been home two days, and he had not really inspected his farm. He had seen to relatively unimportant tasks and had taken Luke's word about the work that needed to be done, the state of the crops, their personal economy. How could he have been so neglectful? This was his life, Sally's life until she married, and maybe even after. This would have to be his anchor after Mattie passed. And there it was, the thought he couldn't escape no matter what.

Yet the contemplation of his farm was a distraction, a way to keep his sanity. He resolved to go over his fields in the afternoon, inspect his crops, form his own opinions about their status.

He only now noticed Samson sitting on the edge of the porch, finishing his dinner. Josiah and Doc had paid the black man no more mind than they had the lean red rooster that strutted around his feet on the alert for any dropped morsel. Now Josiah focused on him.

"Samson, we need to tend to the shoeing, I reckon."

"Yessuh, we should get started, for sure. I'll give this plate back to Miss Sally and—"

"You go fire up the forge. I'll catch Pepper and bring him around," Josiah said as he started for the barn.

Chapter 16

Samson erased his resentful frown as he got up from the porch and took the plate to the kitchen doorway.

"Miss Sally?" he called into the room. Sally quickly appeared, and he handed the plate to her. "You tell Miss Emmy I sho did enjoy her dinner."

She took the plate and smiled up at him. "I will."

Samson ambled toward the smithy. He was in no hurry to fire up the forge on such a hot day. Why was he even here? He should've been stronger, not knuckled under to Josiah. Shouldn't have given in to Dorcas, neither. These white folks' troubles weren't none of his concern. Wasn't nothing but trouble going to come of this. Nothing but trouble.

He stepped into the smithy and looked around. Little had changed since he last worked there. The bellows waited beside the stone forge, ready to the smith's hand in case he didn't have a helper. For sure he wasn't going to have no helper. A poker and shovel hung from hooks set into the stonework. The anvil hunkered nearby, an ugly beast of iron and wood, its darkly snouted head shrugged into its heavy wooden body, its splayed timber legs braced against the burden to come. Hammers, tongs, chisels, and files dangled conveniently from the low rafters above the anvil. All in good order. He'd better get on with it.

He took a scorched and stained leather apron from its peg and tied it around his body. Then he took down a broad-brimmed leather hat, floppy and shapeless and sweat-stained, and jammed it on his head. Sweat already beaded on his face and upper body. He pulled a few sticks of pitchy kindling from a bin and laid them carefully in the forge, and then he covered them with charcoal he found in another box. With an expert flick of the flint against the striker he lit the tinder. As he pumped the bellows bright little flames leaped and the charcoal began to smolder.

A few iron bars and rods and horse and mule shoes hung on pegs scattered about the shed. He ought to be able to fit one of those shoes to Josiah's horse. Maybe the work would go quickly and he could get out of there.

He worked the bellows again and smiled as the charcoal began to glow. He didn't enjoy the scorching heat of it, he thought, but dang if he didn't actually like smithing. Didn't really know why, except maybe it was satisfying to take an old piece of iron and make something useful out of it. Sometimes something pretty, even. He wished he could've been a blacksmith all the time, like his daddy. His daddy had taught him the trade, but Creed McLain had said he couldn't afford to put two men to smithing full time when the cotton needed chopping and the corn needed working.

Samson pulled the bellows once more and watched the glow brighten, then dim as the ash layer cooled on the surface of the coals. He continued to muse. McLain had his daddy smithing for the whole county, seemed like. He made money off the man's sweat, for sure. Had him working from sun up to sun down and couldn't get everything done, even with Samson helping some. Why couldn't McClain have put Samson in the smithy all the time? He'd have earned enough money to buy more help for the fields.

He pumped again and frowned as he remembered being sold to Robertson and the even broader variety of endless work that brought. His lips turned up in a little smile as he thought about how glad he'd been to find this smithy, almost as good as McLain's. He'd worked the iron a lot, especially in the winter when there hadn't been so much to do in the fields—and when the heat of the forge was more welcome.

Samson's smile faded to an ironic grimace. This sure wasn't winter, and horseshoeing wasn't real smithing. But by God's mercy, he was free. Seemed like he was still doing what the white man said, though.

He pumped the bellows slowly until the coals glowed cherry red, then he released the handle and turned to a wooden bucket upended over a stake, suspended above the damp of the earth. Lifting the bucket, he gave it a sharp rap without turning it over. Nothing fell out, so he cautiously turned it upright. He shuddered when he saw sheets of spider web, cottony egg sacks, and lively brown spiders scurrying, trampling the husks of prey long since sucked empty and dry.

He dropped the bucket, which landed on one edge of its bottom and wobbled to rest right side up. Grabbing a long stick of kindling, he swiped it around inside the vessel to dislodge webs and egg sacks. Spiders ran in every direction. He smashed them with the end of his weapon as he danced about to make sure none of them got on his bare feet. Then he raked the stick back through the wrecked webs and egg cases, gathering them up into a tacky mass, and threw the whole agglomeration into the fire. As he pumped the bellows, the pine quickly flamed and the webs threw bright crackling sparks. Grimacing, he drew a deep breath and slowly let it out again before he picked up the bucket and took it to the well.

As he returned with the filled bucket, Josiah brought the roan from the barn.

"Pepper looks a bit older and a lot thinner than he did when you took him away," Samson commented as he rubbed the roan's neck.

"Yep, like me," agreed Josiah.

"Uh-huh," Samson grunted as he began to examine the animal. "He's got some bad scars. He get shot in the war?"

"He did—three times. Twice he was only grazed—see the scar across his rump and that little hairless patch on his front leg here?—but that shoulder wound was bad. He went down under me and . . ." With a faraway look in his eyes Josiah remembered pitching from the falling horse, then the blackness, then . . . He shuddered and said, "Well, the details don't matter. I didn't find him for a long time in all of the confusion. The wound was still bleeding, so I cauterized it, which may be why the scar is so wide

135

and puckered, and dang if he didn't heal up just fine. He's one tough horse. We've been through a lot together, and that's the truth."

"Did you get hurt in the war, too, Mistuh Josiah?"

Josiah didn't answer right away. Finally he muttered, "No. Not like Pepper. Not like . . ." His voice trailed off as he stared at the horse's scar for several seconds. Then he shook his head and bent to show Samson the ragged, shoeless hoof. Pepper swung his head and nuzzled Josiah's back, nibbling his lips over the man's neck and making snuffling sounds.

"Cut it out." Josiah pushed the animal away. "If you don't behave yourself, I'm going to tie you up tight."

Pepper snorted and tossed his head.

"You're going to have to tie him kinda close, anyway, for me to do this here shoeing," Samson observed. "You want me to do just the one shoe?"

"No, I want you to go ahead and do them all. I reckon at least two of the others are not far from coming loose."

"Yessuh. And them hoofs, they look like they be needing some trimming, too."

"Yep. See if you can get them evened up. You got enough shoes here?"

"Think so. And I reckon the fire's 'bout ready. I guess I'll get started on this."

"You need my help?"

"No suh. Me and Pepper'll be fine, specially if we tie him up close so's he can't go jumping around. He ain't picked up no bad habits like kicking or biting, has he?"

"No, I've never seen him give a horseshoer any trouble."

"We be fine then."

"Good. I've got some other things I need to tend to before Luke gets home."

"Where *is* Mistuh Luke?"

"Went to the mill."

"Uh-huh. I's glad he wasn't around here at dinner time, but I wondered why not. Mistuh Josiah, you're not going off nowhere now are you? You do plan to be around when Mistuh Luke gets back here, don't you?"

"I'm going to walk the fields. I'll be in earshot. I'll be finished before late afternoon when Emmy's expecting him home. Soon's you finish with Pepper, put him back in the pasture, and then you go on over to the cabin. Do what you can to make it livable. If Luke comes home before I get back, stay away from him."

"Yessuh. Only I don't feel right about hiding out in the cabin, doing woman's work."

"Just keep out of his way, Samson. That's all I'm asking."

"Yessuh."

Chapter 17

Luke cut his gaze upward and watched the dingy droplet of sweat swell, suspended from his right eyebrow. He bent forward slightly, and the droplet quivered, then fell to his cheek. He felt it trickle toward his jaw. He sighed and flicked the lines against the sweaty rumps of the scrawny mules. One backed its ears as it stepped up its pace and dragged its teammate along. Bo, open-mouthed and tongue lolling, trotted beside the wagon, slipping in and out of the skimpy pools of shade cast by the scraggly roadside trees. Dog, mules, and wheels all raised swirls of dust as they moved along the rutted road. The dust hung in the still air long after they passed but eventually settled onto the weeds, brush, and trees to deepen the reddish film obscuring equally the green of leaf and the gray of bark.

Luke set the brake as they started down a rough grade. No fields bordered the road here, and the trees arching across the dirt track provided, if not coolness, at least a break from the insistent pounding of the sun. As they moved around a bend Luke heard the murmur of the creek in the hollow, its soft whisper almost obscured by the rasp of the iron-rimmed wheels as they rolled over the outcropping stone of the road. The mules pricked their ears and quickened their pace toward the welcome sound. Around one more bend the road leveled and they broke from the shade into the white-hot glare of the midmorning sun. Luke blinked several times as his eyes adjusted to the bright light. He pulled on the right lines, and the mules turned into the chewed-up dust wallow that served as the mill driveway.

The creak of the mill wheel and the low rumble of the turning stones joined the burble of the stream. Luke straightened his spine and set his mouth in a grim line as he saw the two men on the loading dock at the side of the weathered mill. One leaned against the far roof post. The other sat on a bench, hunched forward, whittling a stick in a steady rhythm—whick, whick, whick—forming a point on the stick, then cutting it off and starting over. He figured somebody'd be here. He wished it wasn't these two. Lige saw too much and knew too much—or thought he did—and he gossiped worse than an old woman. And nosy Jay took too much joy from other folks' sorrow.

Luke stopped to let the mules water at the trough fed by a branch of the sluice. Bo propped his front feet on the edge of the trough and lapped alongside the mules. Luke let them drink their fill. Then he drove the wagon around a cart and a yoke of oxen and stopped alongside the dock between the oxen and a small bony mule. Bo flopped into the dust in the shade of the wagon and panted, saliva dripping from his tongue. Luke nodded to the men as he wrapped the lines around the brake handle.

"Morning, Lige."

"Morning, Luke," the whittler said with a nod.

"Morning, Jay."

The post leaner nodded.

As Luke stepped over the seat into the back of the wagon, a black teenager padded from the mill on bare feet. Luke lifted four bags of corn onto the dock, one at a time. The boy, eyes on the ground, muttered, "Morning, Mr. Luke," and carried the first bag into the mill, then quickly returned for another. Sweat rivulets drew black lines through the pale corn dust powdering the boy's face. Luke stepped over the side of the wagon onto the dock and hefted the remaining bags. He limped after the boy into the mill.

Jay watched as Luke disappeared, then turned to Lige, his brows raised. "Reckon we might find out some news?"

Lige's knife hand maintained its rhythm as he nodded. "Could be." He made three more strokes with the knife, then

139

paused and looked up at the younger man. "If you don't piss him off."

The younger man straightened from the post and turned toward the whittler. His empty right sleeve, folded and pinned to the shoulder of his shirt, fluttered as he moved. "I don't have much use for him, Lige. He didn't serve in the War."

"I know, Jay. But by all accounts, he took care of Josiah's farm and family." Lige cast a quick glance toward the mill door. "Mind your mouth is all I'm saying."

Jay grunted and leaned back against the post as Luke thumped unevenly from the mill.

"Take a load off, Luke," Lige said as he motioned toward the bench beside him.

Luke shook his head. "Been sitting too long this morning. Reckon I'll stand a while." But instead of standing, he limped a few steps to the end of the porch and spat tobacco juice into the dust. He pulled his knife from his pocket, opened it, and trimmed a twig from the beech that shaded the end of the mill, then ambled back to the other men and leaned against the wall beside Lige's bench.

Lige had resumed his whittling. Without looking up at Luke, he spoke. "Lem Pritchard said he seen some coming and going at your place. Said he thought he recognized Josiah's roan out by the barn. Josiah get home?"

"Yep. Couple days ago."

"He all right?" Jay asked.

"Seems fine. Thin."

"Ain't we all?" Lige said as he rubbed his belly. Jay chuckled.

"He say anything 'bout where he's been? I mean, taking so long to get back, and all?" Lige asked as he whittled.

Luke touched the tip of his knife to the beech twig and peeled a thin sliver of bark into a tight curl before he answered. "Said they got word of the surrender late. Said he had a long, hard trip. Said he didn't want to talk about it much."

The curl flicked from the end of the stick and rolled across the floor. Jay watched it for a moment, then turned and stared off into the distance. His Adam's apple bobbed slowly, and after a

140

few seconds, again, quickly. He gave a slight shrug, almost a shiver that fluttered his sleeve, and turned back to Luke.

"Sure was sorry to hear about what happened to Mattie."

"Real sorry," Lige agreed, nodding. He continued to whittle without breaking his rhythm.

Luke glanced at Jay. "Thanks."

"Lem said y'all chased the s.o.b. all the way to Henry's Ferry," Lige said.

"Uh-huh. We lost his trail there. He disappeared."

Jay shifted his weight and rubbed his back against the post. He wet his lips, looked at Luke, then dropped his gaze to the floor. "When he beat on Mattie, did he, uh … do anything, uh … you know?" He glanced at Luke only to shrink back as Luke stopped his whittling and glared at him. Jay shuffled his feet, and a flush crept up his rough cheeks. After a long pause, Luke viciously cut the end off the beech twig.

"So, how's she doing?" Lige asked.

Luke shrugged, still frowning. "Hard to say."

"She gonna live'?" Jay asked.

Luke peeled another curl of bark from the twig. "Who knows? It's in the hands of the Lord."

"Amen. We'll be praying for her at our house," Lige offered, pausing in his steady whittling.

Jay glanced at Lige before adding, "We will, too."

"I appreciate it," Luke said without taking his gaze from his beech twig.

Jay shifted, hawked, and twisted to spit into the dirt, then resumed his slouch against the post. Without looking up, he asked, "So. How did Josiah take the way Mattie is?"

Luke stopped whittling and stared at Jay, who reddened more. As Jay began to fidget, Luke raised one eyebrow and said, "How you think?"

Jay shrugged. Luke continued to stare at him for several seconds before returning to his whittling, now forcefully slicing the end off the twig a half inch at a stroke.

"Josiah don't talk much. Thanked me for chasing the dirty . . ." Luke paused, shook his head. "You want to know how he feels, you go ask him yourself."

141

Jay flushed even darker and balled his fist. He clamped his jaw shut, the muscles oddly bunching in front of his ears like the ridges of a washboard. Just as he stood away from the post, the black boy emerged from the mill carrying two bags of meal.

"All done, Mr. Jay. You want me to tie 'em on your saddle for you?"

Jay stared at Luke for a moment, then shrugged as he turned toward the steps at the end of the dock. "Yep. Tie 'em on."

The boy produced a cord from his back pocket and tied the two bags together, slung them across the mule's withers, and tied them to the saddle. By the time he finished, Jay had descended the steps and stood beside the mule with the reins in his hand, ready to mount. He grasped the pommel, put his foot in the stirrup, and swung easily into the saddle.

Lige sat with his stick in one hand and his knife in the other, solemnly watching the scene play out. Jay nodded to him as he turned the mule toward the road.

"See you around, Lige."

"Yep."

Luke returned to the destruction of his beech twig. Lige watched Jay leave, then measured Luke with a long stare. Luke turned to him briefly, then sliced the twig again.

Lige rose from the bench, folded his knife, and spat into the dust. "Jay don't have a lot of consideration."

"Nope." Luke made a final slice of the twig and tossed the butt away.

"Need to make some allowances for him. He's had a rough time."

"I suppose."

Luke turned and ambled off the dock and wandered down by the mill sluice. He cut another twig and idly sliced bits from it into the water and watched them rush along on the surface of the fast-moving stream.

After a few minutes the black boy brought Lige's meal from the mill and loaded the sacks into the oxcart. Lige climbed into the cart and called to him, "See you around, Luke."

Luke turned and waved. He watched until Lige disappeared

142

from sight, then he returned to the dock and claimed the bench where Lige had sat.

Chapter 18

Josiah left the smithy and headed for the cornfield, which, from a distance, looked about the same as McLain's. As he walked between the rows, he examined the ears on first one stalk and then another, here and there along the row. He parted the almost dry shucks at the dark brown dried silk, then pulled them open further down the ears and looked at the kernels. Few of the cobs had grown to normal length, and many had gaps where the kernels had failed to form or had shriveled before they had fully developed. And of course the worms had done their usual damage. Yet almost every stalk held at least one ear, some several. The worms and the drought had taken their toll, but the crop was a long way from a total loss.

He continued to the end of the field, then crossed the ends of several rows and turned back into the corn, again checking the ears. His evaluation remained the same: there should be corn for the two families and their stock, although there probably wouldn't be much surplus to sell. Luke had planned well by planting more than he thought would be needed. It was frustrating there wouldn't be a cash crop, but at least their needs would be met.

He walked on to the cotton field and similarly inspected it. It looked like McLain's—a thin stand of undersized plants. The rain had revitalized them to some degree and the leaves had a healthy resilience. The greenish cotton fiber swelled the bolls, but few of the bolls had actually opened. Maybe the rain came soon enough to save it. Maybe. He admired the clean rows, cleaner than the corn. The weeds wouldn't be robbing the crops of water. Luke must have worked endless hours cultivating. Emmy and Mattie and the children, too. But it would be a miracle if the crop was bountiful.

He started back toward the farmyard thinking they'd probably be able to sell some of the cotton, but it would be poor quality. The price would be low. He sighed and flicked sweat from his eyes. They needed the money. Somehow they had to get better horse stock. And a cow or two if they were going to rebuild a herd.

He removed his hat and used his soiled handkerchief to wipe the sweat from his forehead and his neck. Cramming the rag back into his pocket, he settled the hat on his head and tugged the brim down over his eyes. And he owed Doc Wilson. He pulled out his wallet, opened it and confirmed what he already knew. One half dollar, two half dimes, three pennies, U.S., and forty-five paper dollars, Confederate.

He thought about the hogs he and Luke had argued over last night. If he could sell a few hogs now there might be enough cash to tide them over until the cotton could be sold for whatever it would bring. He didn't need to fatten the hogs. He'd only need enough corn to bait them into the pen out in the woods. Luke was too pessimistic about the corn crop. There'd be enough. It wouldn't hurt to use a peck or two to bait the hogs.

As he ambled toward the smithy, he heard Samson's hammer beating against the horseshoe on the anvil. Ting ting ting *clang*. Ting ting ting *clang*. Then silence. Then the hammering would begin again. By the time he got to the smithy, the clanging had been replaced by the much lighter tap-tap-tap of the shoeing hammer.

"How's it coming?" he asked, his words giving both Samson and the horse warning of his approach.

Samson stooped beside the roan's hindquarters. He had the horse's left hind leg raised and the hoof rested in the pouch formed by the leather apron as it sagged between his knees. He carefully drove nails through the iron shoe and into the horny rim of the hoof.

145

"We doing fine," Samson answered as he hammered. "I got them front hooves trimmed even and the shoes on. Now I'm working on these hind uns. Pepper, he been behaving hisself. I ain't had no problems with him."

"Good." Josiah rubbed the horse's velvet nose and took a close look at the front hooves. "These look kind of short, Samson. I hope you haven't trimmed too much."

"No suh, I's real careful. I had to kinda even 'em up, you know, and that 'un he threw the shoe, it had to be trimmed a good bit. I led him around after I did 'em, and he moved real good. They's not too short."

"Well, keep at it. You reckon the wild hog pen is still out in the woods?"

"Was a couple years ago, but it wa'n't in good shape."

Josiah nodded. "When you're through with the shoeing, you come on out there. We'll see what needs to be done to put it right."

Samson drove another nail before he answered. "Yessuh."

Josiah gave the horse another pat, then turned and walked toward the toolshed.

*　　*　　*

Samson finished with the left rear shoe and released the leg. As the horse shifted weight onto it, the black man stood upright and stretched the kinks out of his back. Dang if Josiah didn't gall him, demanding he shoe his horse and then picking at the work he did. And expecting him to ready the cabin. Woman's work. And now he'd got some wild hair about the hog pen. Can't the man make up his mind? Well, the hog pen suited fine. He'd a lot rather mend a hog pen than sweep out a house. 'Sides, it didn't matter if'n he did sweep out the cabin, Dorcas'd do it over 'cause whatever he did wouldn't suit her. And, if'n he was out there in the woods working on the hog pen he sho wouldn't be running into Luke when he got home.

He stretched again and noted Josiah leaving the toolshed, carrying both an axe and a hatchet. He resumed his work, fitted the last shoe, heated, hammered, quenched, rechecked the fit. As he worked, he saw Dorcas fill the wash pot and build a fire under it. White folks sure knew how to put the hot work off on both of them.

He finished the shoeing and took the horse to the pasture. Returning to the smithy, he raked out and quenched the charcoal that had not been consumed, and he placed all of the equipment where he had found it. Then he sauntered toward the wash pot.

"It's late in the day to start a wash, ain't it?"

"Sho is. But it needs doing bad."

"I thought you's supposed to help out with Mattie."

"'Course I'm helpin' out with Miss Mattie. I sat with her whilst they all ate, and now Miss Emmy's sittin' with her. They's 'bout out of clean linen, and I 'spect the situation will get worse. I'm going to boil some sheets and rags. I'll get 'em up on the line this afternoon, but I doubt they get dry before night. They'll be dry soon's the dew burns off in the morning though. I hope no bird roosts over the line."

"How's Miss Mattie?"

Dorcas looked up at Samson, fighting tears. "She's not doing no good at all, not at all." She bit her lip and sniffed. "Samson, she's going to die." She gave in to her sobs, gathered the tail of her apron to her face and moaned. Samson awkwardly hugged her and patted her back. She regained her composure.

"She's going to die, and it may be God's blessing when she does. She's in such pain. I don't know how anybody could set out to hurt another human being so bad."

"What you mean, anybody set out to hurt somebody? I thought she's s'posed to been kicked by the cow."

Dorcas huffed. "That's what Luke said at first, when he first come to tell Mistuh Creed and Miss Lorna about Miss Mattie, but now ain't nobody pretending any such. Somebody beat on Miss Mattie, for sho. They don't know who. They say it was a stranger, nobody knows his name or nothing. Miss Mattie, she can't say. Or won't. I asked her."

Samson raised his eyebrows. "You didn't."

"I did. Whilst the white folks was at their dinner. But she just shook her head and moaned. I think she might know, but she won't say. Why wouldn't she tell who did such an evil thing?"

"'Cause if it's a stranger, she don't know who he is either."

"I s'pose that's right."

"This whole family's got troubles. We ought to go back home," Samson said.

"I can't. Miss Mattie and Miss Emmy, they need me. Miss Emmy, she's going to need me more in the next few days. Don't worry. We'll be all right."

Samson looked away, scratched his ear. "I feel sorry for Miss Mattie's misfortune. I feel sorry for Miss Emmy. I even feel kinda sorry for Mistuh Josiah. It's just that damned Luke . . . But you're right. We should stay."

"Course we should."

"I'm supposed to go help Josiah fix the old hog pen in the woods. You reckon you could sweep out our cabin and fix us a bed soon's them sheets is boiled?"

"I's planning on doing that very thing."

"Well, me and Josiah's going to be out in them woods, so you keep an eye out for Luke. If he comes home, you go in the house with the others, even if you're not done with the wash or the cabin."

Dorcas stared at her husband, frowning. "All right."

Samson gave her a quick hug and turned away toward the woodlot. He looked back just before he entered the trees and saw she still watched him.

Chapter 19

Sally finished cleaning up the kitchen after dinner. She had no help, and it had taken a long time. The dishwater stood in the pan, no longer hot. She had poured a separate pan of rinse water. Rainbow films of grease floated on its cold surface. Sally wiped the last plate dry and put it in the cupboard, then hung the towel over a peg to dry. She emptied the rinse water into a bucket and lugged it, sloshing, to the garden, where she poured it on the tomatoes. She refilled the bucket at the well. When she returned to the kitchen she left her water bucket, poured the dishwater into the slop bucket filled with parings and scrapings, and carried that to the sow in the pen by the barn.

The sow grunted and pushed her snout into the trough when Sally poured out the slop. The piglets ran up, squealing in their excitement, but they were not yet tall enough to stand beside the trough and reach into it. One climbed entirely into the trough. His mother rooted him back out as she gobbled the parings. Sally laughed. Then she returned to the kitchen but she avoided the wash pot and tubs where Dorcas labored.

The house seemed to hold its breath, so deep was the silence. Jim had taken advantage of his mother's distraction and had disappeared before she could assign more chores. Callie Belle and Delia played mutely in the hall outside the bedroom where Emmy tended Mattie—Sally had spied them as she came past the back door with the slop bucket.

Sally stood in the kitchen and absorbed the unusual silence.

149

The other children normally played noisily, chattering and laughing, and Aunt Emmy usually scolded and gave orders. She closed her eyes and drew a deep breath, then exhaled slowly. So much had happened around her in the last several days. She had been assigned chores and kept busy till she hadn't had much time to think, and the diversions had been welcome. Now the pushed-aside worries rushed in on her. She was so sad. And scared. And sorry. She'd like to tell Mama how scared she was, but she knew she shouldn't worry her. All the other grown-ups were always busy, and they argued and carped. She couldn't talk to any of them. They'd just scold. Or tell her she was being a baby. Or worse, tell her everything would be all right. She knew better.

Sally heaved a deep sigh. She wanted to crawl into her bed and pull the pillow over her head, away from all the rest of the world. But the attic would be so hot now, in the middle of the day. And somebody would sure find her, and Aunt Emmy would fuss something awful.

Her face crumpled as she began to cry. She sniffled for a minute or so before she began to regain control. As she wiped her nose with her sleeve, her face brightened. She'd go to her secret place in the woods. No one had ever found her there, not even Jim. Squeaky might follow her, but that was all right. She could talk to him. He'd listen.

She padded onto the porch and saw Dorcas had not noticed her. She quickly scampered into the breezeway and out to the far side of the house, away from easy detection. She slipped into the edge of the woods and followed a very faint path. She had been this way before. Many times. She didn't think she had ever been followed, except by Squeaky, of course. Before she had gone far, the pig trotted up behind her and squealed softly. "All right, you can come, too, but you have to be quiet," she whispered.

They made their way through the woods on a clear path, then veered off onto a barely discernible trail. Sally ducked below branches and skirted thickets, in no hurry, as she moved among dead leaves whispering beneath her bare feet. She came to another thicket. Thorny bushes grew in a great impenetrable tangle, covered by the billowing drapes of virgin's bower that were not yet in bloom. They all but surrounded a copse of two

150

small pin oaks and several spindly dogwoods. The pin oaks' lower limbs swept almost to the ground on the side away from the thicket so their deep-lobed, rich green leaves concealed their limbs and trunks.

Squeaky trotted ahead under the oaks. Sally heard him grunting and the undergrowth rustling as he pushed his way into the thicket. She gathered her skirt and hiked it above her knees, then dropped to all fours and crawled beneath the drooping oak branches.

The shelter beneath the young trees—dark and still, cooler than the surroundings—smelled musty. Leaves and acorns from last year littered the ground. Sally crawled past the trees and into the bushes, taking care not to be snagged by the thorns, and entered a small clear space completely hidden from the rest of the world—her really secret place. Secret from all but Squeaky, who happily snuffled and rooted at the ground.

"Stop rooting, Squeaky," Sally said. "You're messing up my floor and making it all dirty."

On previous trips to her retreat Sally had brought armloads of hay to soften the prickling of the curled dead leaves dropped by the thorn bushes. Now she sat on the hay cross-legged, her skirt pulled above her knees. Squeaky tired of his rooting and came to lie beside her and rest his head across her thigh. She idly scratched his ears and he grunted and twitched his kinked tail.

"Squeaky, I'm so scared Mama's going to die," she whispered to the pig. "I thought she was dead when I found her, you know. It scared me so bad. I didn't know what to do."

The pig gave a soft grunt and shifted so her fingers found a particularly itchy place as she continued to scratch.

"And it's been scary seeing her all bruised and hurt. A couple of times I peeked into her room, and she was so still. She didn't move at all. And I whispered to her, 'Mama,' and she never would answer me."

Squeaky grunted again and pushed his head against her belly.

"I really didn't want to stay with her this morning, but it wasn't so bad. Mama talked to me some. I'm glad Mama talked to me. But she sounded so weak and sick. It's really scary, Mama being hurt and sick. And . . . and . . . I think . . . I think it's my fault." She began to cry. Tears ran down her cheeks and her nose dripped, but she did not sob aloud. She quit scratching the pig and used the hem of her skirt to wipe her eyes and nose.

Sniffling, she whispered to Squeaky in a brighter tone of voice, "But Daddy's home now. For the longest time he's been gone. But I prayed he would come. And after I found Mama all hurt, I prayed harder because Mama really needed help. Me, too. I think God up in heaven heard my prayers and told Daddy to come home and save Mama and take care of us." The pig stirred and nudged her hand. She scratched his ears again as she continued. "Yes, I do, Squeaky. I think God told Daddy to come home and take care of us. You, too."

After a long pause, she added wistfully, "I wish God would tell me what to do. I asked Aunt Emmy how I could tell what God wanted me to do. She said. 'About what?' 'Course I couldn't tell her. I just said, 'Oh, things.' She looked cross and said, 'God tells us in the Bible how we should live. If you'd pay attention when your Uncle Luke reads the Bible to us, you'd know.' Hmmff. There's a lot of Bible stuff I don't understand—it sounds all weird. The words are strange. I asked Mama to explain some of it one time—when Uncle Luke had read the Ten Commandments. I asked her what was 'adultery,' and she said, 'You'll understand when you're older.' That's no answer. What if I do adultery and don't even know it?"

She heaved a big sigh. "If the Bible tells me, I don't understand it, and if I ask a grown-up, they either say I don't need to know or I'll understand when I'm older. What'm I supposed to do about now?"

Squeaky shifted against her side and rooted his head under her hand, which had grown idle. She resumed her petting and scratching him, and continued to whisper to him. She really could tell Squeaky anything.

After a long time Sally heard voices and the brush rustling. She held Squeaky and froze as she listened, but relaxed when she recognized Josiah's voice, and then Samson's. It sounded like they were cutting brush, over near the old hog trap. Then their voices ceased and she heard someone moving along the path back toward the farmstead.

Believing herself once again alone, she began to sing softly. She jumped when Josiah called out to her from quite nearby. She scrambled out of the bower and hurried to him, hoping he hadn't spotted her hiding place.

"What're you doing out here in the woods?" he asked.

"Nothing. Talking to Squeaky."

"What about?"

Samson arrived with a sack of corn and saved her from answering the question. The three of them spread the corn to bait the hog trap. Squeaky fell hungrily upon the grain as though manna had fallen from heaven. Sally had a hard time persuading him to leave the baited trap—until they heard the grunts and rustlings of a couple of the wild hogs nearby. Then he pushed close against her, and all of them made their way back toward the farmstead.

Chapter 20

The sun sank below the treetops. Its slanting rays knifed through the lace of the roadside foliage and spattered bright splotches on the tree trunks. Luke, sweat dripping from his brows, sat on the hard unsprung wagon seat and occasionally flicked the lines to remind the weary mules to keep moving. What was it about going to the mill that was so tiring? It wasn't hard work, not for him. He simply had to drive the wagon to the mill, sit around while Culpeper ground the meal and raked off his share, then drive home. Maybe the inactivity wore him out. And today, the tension, having to fend off those two busybodies, them wondering was Mattie raped. And how Josiah was taking it all. None of it their business.

He had a lot of good reasons to hoard the secrets of Mattie's misfortune, but he'd seen no sense in causing hard feelings that could end up being costly. He'd tried to be civil, but he knew he hadn't succeeded. What else could he have told them? He didn't know how Josiah was taking it. True, Josiah had thanked him for trying to catch the prowler. Said he thought he'd done all he could. Seemed calm enough. But Luke hadn't talked to him about any of it since then. He didn't know what to say, how to act. And he had a lot at stake.

He clucked at the team, almost strangled on his tobacco quid, coughed and spit over the near wheel. The spittle almost hit Bo. The dog bunched his hindquarters and bounded out of the

154

way, then turned his head and threw a reproachful look back at his master.

Of course, calm wasn't necessarily accepting. What Josiah told Emmy about the stranger being a dead man if he ever caught up to him—that sounded like he was madder than a riled cottonmouth. So what? He couldn't do anything—not without knowing who to go after.

He sniggered and grinned. If he thought he could sic Josiah off on a hunt for the drifter, he would. Let him have a go at it, maybe get his head shot off.

He shifted to set the brake as the mules started down a hill. The harness creaked and the chains clinked as the wagon pushed into them. They stiffened their backs, squatted in resistance, and shuffled stiff-legged down the grade while Bo trotted easily ahead. At the bottom Luke released the brake. The mules waded into a small stream where the dog lapped noisily. He let them stop long enough to put their heads down for a good drink, then flicked the lines and started them up the other side. His grin had disappeared.

Oh yeah, he wouldn't mind seeing Josiah get his head shot off.

He sighed and stared glumly at Bo as the dog caught up, dripping from the stream. It was a strain always watching what he said. One little slip and he'd be in shit up to his ears with nobody to reach him a pole. He didn't want to rile McLain. Didn't want to rile Josiah. Didn't want to make Emmy any crankier.

He rolled his chaw from one side of his mouth to the other and spat. He shifted both reins to his left hand and raised his right arm, stretching out the stiffness. It was a relief to have a few minutes without having to watch his every move and every word. He sighed. Too bad he'd be getting home soon.

"Home, sweet home," he growled aloud. "Bitter and sour's more like it."

He made a wry face, as though he tasted a faulty crabapple, and fought an impulse to rein in the mules. The Bible told him to value a worthy woman far above rubies. There could be no more worthy woman than pious, dutiful, responsible Emmy, but she

155

was often surly and disagreeable now. He still controlled her, but . . .

He rocked from side to side a couple of times to relieve the growing numbness in his buttocks. Nothing had ever worked out for him the way he wanted it to. Something, or usually somebody, always got in the way, screwed things up.

Born a second son. Why'd God even let there be second sons, anyway? As spares, maybe. First-born sons got everything—new clothes, the best horses, the father's property.

He snorted, remembering. It had looked like fun, the hell-for-leather way his brother rode his half-wild stallion. He wanted a taste of the fun. His illicit ride had been exhilarating until he realized he couldn't control the animal. And then it shied at a rabbit. How could a horse move sideways so fast? Suddenly he had been hurtling toward the ground and an outcropping boulder.

He shuddered and gritted his teeth. He'd be able to hear his leg bones snap till his dying day. His stomach lurched almost as it had when he was twelve years old and his world changed forever. He'd been sick, puking and shaking and sweating. It had taken hours for his father to find him. And more hours to fetch the doctor, who had set the bones crooked. What a quack. Any half-blind fool should've been able to see how his leg curved.

As if to underscore his thought, he stretched his crooked leg, then bent it and rubbed the ache always lurking there. His father said he was lucky to be alive after what he'd done. Put all the blame on him. Never a word against his brother who'd made the damned horse so wild. And he never spoke a word of regret for the crooked leg. Old fool.

Scowling, he spit with such force the spittle bounced in the dust before it settled and soaked into the side of the road.

So he'd grown up with a limp and no prospects. It had been hard to find a wife, until he met Emmy McLain—plain, fearing spinsterhood, and set to inherit something from her prosperous parents because she had no brothers.

Luke smirked as he remembered. It hadn't taken a lot of courting to win Emmy. No, it had been easy. She'd been sweet and her parents agreeable. She had looked small for childbearing, but . . . well, maybe she wouldn't die before she popped one out to insure the inheritance from McLain.

He shifted on the wagon seat and flicked the lines on the mules' backs. He needn't have worried. Three already, and about time for another. But she got crabbier with each one.

They had lived with the McLains. He'd never had a minute to himself. And the big, prosperous farm had to be worked. McLain acted like he owned him. No easy overseer's job for Luke. He'd worked nearly as hard as the slaves. That had pissed him off, but he'd gritted his teeth and kept McLain happy. Figured it would pay off eventually.

Luke was brought back to the present when two Yankee cavalrymen appeared around a bend. They looked over the mules, then stared at Luke with their eyes narrowed. He tensed but met their gaze and nodded at them as they passed. Bo growled, but trotted along with the wagon between him and the Yankees.

He hadn't seen what a problem the War would be for him, not at first. Emmy already had Jim and was well along with Callie Belle, so he had the heir he needed. But Josiah wanted to volunteer, and he didn't want to leave Mattie and her brat alone. So they—Mattie and Josiah, Creed and Lorna—cooked it up that he and Emmy would go live at Josiah's farm. Figured he wouldn't be conscripted because he was crippled. Not too crippled to work, though.

He looked over his shoulder. The Yankees receded out of sight around a curve. Luke sighed.

It hadn't mattered what he thought, so he didn't even try to get out of it. Besides, it got him and Emmy out of McLain's house. And they were right, he could work. He worked till he thought his arms would fall off and his back would break, till his leg throbbed, all to keep Josiah's farm going. And then it got worse when the niggers took off and he had to help McLain, too.

His grip tightened on the reins and his shoulders tensed. He sucked his teeth and spat. Oh, yeah, Mattie and her brat weren't alone. Neither was he. Screaming, whining, puking brats surrounded him all the time. Many's the time he had wanted to pinch their heads off. But he hadn't. He'd tried to raise them up in the way they should go. Read them the Bible. Maintained discipline. Besides, the brats weren't all bad—they could be put to work. But they were as bad as niggers—he had to watch them all the time so they'd keep at whatever he'd set them to do.

The wagon jolted across a ledge of rock protruding from the road surface. Pain shot up Luke's spine and down his leg and brought his attention back to the road, the team, the wagon. They neared another steep descent. He set the brake and drove carefully to the bottom of the hill where he released it and let the mules find their own way.

He continued to fume. Yeah, he'd slaved like a nigger. Made the women work, too. More responsible than the children, still they often claimed they had to go tend to the cooking or the washing or the gardening, or they ailed, or a sick child needed them. He couldn't keep them out in the field. They'd both gotten thin, looked exhausted all the time. Emmy didn't have much looks to lose, but he hated to see Mattie so drawn, see the lines begin to form in her pretty proud face.

He scowled and squirmed on the seat. Shrews. Both of them. 'Course they had different ways, like they did about everything else. Emmy knew better than to stand up to him, but she'd be bitter and cranky and make snide remarks when she was out of his reach. Mattie would stand right up to him and argue, always more concerned about the children or the niggers than she was about him or the farm. He'd thought time and again she needed to be put in her place, had come near to seeing to it more than once.

"Bitch got what she deserved," he muttered. A mule turned an ear back toward him. He realized he had spoken aloud and clenched his jaw.

He had driven within a half mile of the farm now. Bo lagged behind the wagon, panting, his tongue hanging out and dripping into the dust, but the mules picked up their pace without urging. Luke reined them in.

Why'd Josiah come home when so many others hadn't? Luke had kept the farm productive. Without him, Mattie would've probably wanted him to stay and run it. Maybe someday, if anything happened to Emmy . . . He knew he

158

shouldn't think about Mattie that way. She was a bitch. Too proud, too stubborn. He shouldn't even consider wanting her damned farm. Emmy was a good woman. Dutiful. More precious than rubies. He grimaced and spat his whole chaw into the dust. Bo ambled over to sniff it, found it uninteresting, and trotted to catch up.

He looked back over his shoulder once more. Those damned Yankees were all over the place now, coddling the niggers and trying to squash the whites under their heels. No matter how hard farmers worked, without the niggers they couldn't make crops big enough to pay their taxes. How long could McLain keep his farm? If Creed failed, there went his inheritance. He groaned and wiped sweat from his face. All his work. All those years with Emmy. Was it worth hanging around in hope of something that might never be? He'd asked that question many times. The answer seemed to be inching closer to no.

Luke composed his features as he turned the wagon off the road and drove beside the house. Both mules raised their heads and trotted toward the barn. He sighed and straightened on the seat, readying himself to be welcomed into the bosom of his family.

Chapter 21

As Josiah, Sally and Samson entered the farmyard, they saw Dorcas stirring the sheets in the wash pot. Sweat dripped from her chin and tears ran from her eyes as the smoke hung over the fire in the still, oppressive air. The corrugated wash board and bar of harsh soap waited nearby, along with another pile of jumbled fabric.

Josiah wanted to go inside and see about Mattie, but he had told Samson and Dorcas he would be around when Luke came home, which could be any time now. His stomach growled, reminding him that suppertime neared. Turning to Sally, he said, "Go inside and ask Aunt Emmy if she needs some help. She may want you to sit with Mama, or she might want you to put supper on the table. And ask if she or Mama needs to see me. Fetch me if they do."

"Yes, Daddy." Sally ran toward the house with Squeaky right behind her.

Josiah assigned some chores to Samson, then whistled and called for Jim. After several minutes the boy had not answered. He whistled and called again. Pretty Girl crawled from beneath the house and ambled toward him, lazily wagging her tail. When she rubbed against his leg, he patted her head. "I didn't call you. No, I didn't." The whole dog wagged joyfully. At last Jim appeared, shuffling his feet, kicking up dust, as he sauntered from the direction of the cornfield.

160

"Time to start evening chores. What does your father usually have you do?"

"Um, uh, put water in the trough and get the stock into the barn. And pitch down hay to 'em. And feed 'em."

"That's a lot. Samson and I will divide up some of those chores so you don't have to do so many, what do you say?"

"I don't mind doing 'em, Uncle Josiah. 'Sides, Father might be mad if he gets home and finds I didn't do 'em all."

"No, he won't, because I'll tell him you did as you were told. It only makes sense for Samson and me to do a fair share of the work. Why don't you get the cow and the horses and the mule into the barn and pitch the hay. I'll draw some water for the trough. Samson'll feed the sow. Get busy now."

"Yessir." Jim grinned and trotted through the barn and on toward the pasture.

After Josiah had filled the trough, he went into the barn to check on Jim's progress. The boy worked in the loft, forking hay into each of the mangers. Then he disappeared from Josiah's view, but Josiah heard the hay rustling and knew the boy was playing before returning to his chores.

"Eeewwww!"

"What's wrong, son?"

Jim appeared at the edge of the loft, near the ladder. He wiped his sleeve with his hand, then wiped the hand on his pants. Josiah saw slick grayish-yellow stains and smelled the sulfurous stink of rotten eggs.

"Uh, I rolled into some eggs. They don't smell too good."

"No, they don't. Your mother's not going to be very happy about your clothes."

"It's all Sally's fault."

"Oh? How so?"

"She's supposed to come up here and check for the hens' hidden nests, but she hasn't been doing it."

"Maybe she just overlooked an egg."

"Unh-uh. There were several eggs in the nest. She hasn't gathered 'em for a long time." Jim started climbing down the ladder.

"If they were so obvious, why'd you roll in them?"

The boy reached the ground and turned to face Josiah. "I didn't see 'em till I rolled in 'em 'cause y'all piled the new hay up there. I rolled off the top of the pile and it was too late to miss 'em. It's not my fault. It's Sally's fault. She should've gathered up them eggs a long time ago."

"I'll speak to her about it."

Josiah knit his brows and glanced toward the house. From what he'd seen of her, he didn't think Sally would neglect a chore. Maybe she was afraid to come into the barn, after Mattie . . . No, that wasn't it. She came out to milk. Of course, they would know if she didn't come back with a bucket of milk and she'd be punished, but they wouldn't know if she didn't get every egg. Maybe she didn't want to be in the barn any longer than she absolutely had to be. Josiah couldn't blame her.

Jim stood as though waiting to be dismissed. They had the barn to themselves.

"Jim, I need to ask you about something, son."

Jim glanced up at Josiah and immediately dropped his gaze to the dusty, hoof-marked dirt. He became so still it almost seemed he had stopped breathing.

"I'm not angry with you, son. You haven't done anything wrong."

"Yessir," the boy mumbled so softly Josiah could hardly hear.

Josiah squatted before him, put a forefinger to Jim's chin and lifted his head so he could see his eyes. "Son, your mother told me you saw someone prowling around the day Aunt Mattie was hurt. I want you to tell me exactly what he looked like, what he did."

Jim's eyes flicked to Josiah's, then dropped again. "Mother said I should've told sooner," he whispered.

"I know she thought so at first, but she's had more time to think about it and she doesn't think that anymore."

"She was mad."

"I know. But she isn't now. I'm not either." Josiah paused. The boy wouldn't meet his gaze. Josiah continued. "But Jim, I need to find out all I can about the man, and you're the only one who saw him."

The boy looked directly at Josiah and kept his gaze steady for several seconds. Finally he nodded, then moved his head so Josiah's finger left his chin. Josiah withdrew his hand. The boy dropped his eyes again. Flies buzzed. They both breathed slowly, shallowly. Jim said nothing.

"Your mother sent you to the garden . . ."

Jim nodded and drew a deeper breath. "Uh-huh. To get some onions."

"And what happened?"

"The dry tops kept breaking off. I had to scratch the onions out with my fingers. My back got tired, and I stood up. And then I saw the man. . . ."

"Where was he?"

"Over close to the smokehouse."

"Not near the barn?"

"No, sir."

"Did you recognize him? Could he have been a neighbor?"

"No sir. I didn't know him."

"Were you scared?"

"Yessir. He looked . . . To me he looked mean."

"Can you describe him?"

A nod. "Kind of. He was a soldier, I guess—his clothes were like yours. 'Cept he was barefoot."

"Could you see what color hair he had?"

"Yessir. Sort of. He had a hat but I saw brown hair hanging out below it. Maybe there was some gray in it, or yellow. Gray, I think. It looked greasy and dirty."

"Did he have a beard?"

Jim scrunched up his face as he thought. "Yessir. Kind of. Kind of like you had when you first came home, only maybe a little longer."

"A week or two's growth, then?"

"Um, I guess so. I don't really know."

"But it wasn't a long beard, one he'd been growing a long time? Like Grandfather McLain's?"

Jim shook his head. "No, it was short, but kind of messy."

"And what color was his beard?"

"Kind of like his hair, only—well, he turned so the sun

163

caught it, and it looked redder than his hair, but with more gray in it."

"You're doing well, Jim. You really noticed a lot about the man."

A shy smile tipped the corners of the boy's lips.

Josiah picked up a stiff hay stem and idly doodled in the dry dust. He didn't know why he was asking about the bastard's beard. If he shaved it, or let it grow more, it'd look different. Color'd probably stay the same, though.

"If you saw that man again, do you think you would recognize him?"

"Maybe." Jim paused. "Yessir, I'm pretty sure I would."

Josiah nodded and smiled. "You keep on remembering him, Jim. Someday we may catch him. We'll need you to remember."

Jim stared solemnly at Josiah. "Yessir. I will."

Josiah looked at the boy, then looked away, then back again. He sighed. "Why didn't you run tell your father about the prowler, Jim? Or your mother, or Aunt Mattie?"

The boy ducked his head, but not before Josiah saw a tear roll down his cheek. "I was scared." Josiah had to strain to hear the words.

"I guess I understand, son, but you know it would've been a lot better if you had—"

"I was scared, Uncle Josiah! Mother and Father had said we should tell them right away if we saw anybody poking around the place, and I wanted to, but . . . I thought Father was in the toolshed, and the drifter was between us. And . . . and I didn't think I could run to Mother in the kitchen without him seeing me. He could've caught me. I ducked down behind the pole beans and tried to watch him without him seeing me."

"What did he do?"

"He looked all around and then he went into the smokehouse."

"Couldn't you have run for help then?"

"I started to, but he came back out and I had to duck back down again."

"So he didn't stay in there very long?"

"No sir, not long at all."

"Did you see what he did next?"

Jim nodded. "Yessir. He looked like he had something in his hand—a hunk of bacon, probably—and he looked all around again and then he kind of slipped over behind the outhouse. I started to go to the house then, but he came out again and I had to stop."

"But he didn't see you?"

"No, sir. I watched him. I don't think he saw me."

"So where did he go from the outhouse?"

"He walked kind of quick but bent over till he got to the muscadines. He went under the vines, like he was trying to stay hid from the house and the barn both. He stopped for a little bit at the far end of the grapes and looked around again, kind of sneaky. Then he slipped over to the edge of the woodlot and disappeared."

"So then you went to tell your father?"

Jim's face crumpled and he stepped back, away from Josiah. Tears spilled from his squinted eyes as he shook his head.

"Why not?"

The boy drew a shuddering breath as he watched Josiah warily. He wiped his nose on his sleeve. "Because . . . because he didn't seem so scary anymore. And I didn't have as many onions as Mother had told me to get."

"So you dug some more onions?"

The boy nodded and sniffed.

Josiah doodled in the dust again while he thought. The boy was telling pretty much what Emmy had. More detail but pretty much the same. He wondered if Jim really could recognize the bastard. Seemed like when he was a boy, most men looked pretty much alike to him. But there was still something . . .

"Jim, you're certain you didn't see the stranger near the barn? Maybe when you first saw him? Could he have been coming from the barn toward the smokehouse?"

The boy shook his head. "No sir. He was almost at the smokehouse when I first saw him. He looked like he came from over toward the grapes."

"And your father didn't see the stranger from the toolshed?"

Jim tipped his head to one side. His brows drew together in a frown. "I know he didn't see the man—he would've chased him away."

Josiah nodded. "Yes. He would've."

The boy sniffed again, and wrinkled his nose. He rubbed at the smears of rotten egg.

Josiah reached out and ruffled his hair. "You've been a big help to me, Jim. Now you go wash the rotten egg off of your clothes. Don't forget to wash your sleeve where you've been wiping your nose, too. Draw a bucket of water from the well and clean up at the washbench—don't go fouling the water trough."

"Yessir."

Josiah stood, but the boy didn't move right away. Then Josiah heard the creak and clatter of a wagon moving up the road, approaching the house. "Hurry up, now. Your father's coming. Don't let him catch you with those smashed eggs on you."

Jim scampered toward the well.

Samson entered the barn just as the boy was leaving. He held his nose. "Eeww! What that boy been into?" He laughed.

"You know very well what he's been into," Josiah answered. "Luke's coming. You go fill the woodbox and see if Dorcas needs any more wood for her washing. Stay out of his way."

"Yessuh, I'll sho do that," Samson said and took the long way around to the woodpile, out of Luke's path as the wagon turned into the yard and pulled up near the kitchen. Bo trotted beside the wagon and flopped to the ground, panting, tongue lolling and dripping, as soon as it stopped.

Josiah stood in the end of the barn hall and watched as Luke got down and toted a large sack of meal into the kitchen. A few moments later he came back out of the kitchen empty-handed, climbed back into the wagon and drove on toward the barn.

Do I believe Dorcas and Samson? Josiah wondered as Luke neared. He saw no answer in Luke's face, only the same Luke he had known for years—tawny brown eyes no more nor less hard than they had ever been, no new expression to speak of great cruelty and brutality. Nor one that proclaimed innocence. All he knew at this point was that a pair of disgruntled former slaves

166

had accused him of mistreating them—and Emmy. There was no proof.

And yet he watched Luke with less respect than before. He couldn't help it, the accusations rang true to him. Maybe because he'd always slightly disliked Luke but didn't know why. Maybe because, under his surface, Luke always seemed to think he was owed something. Josiah grunted, looked quickly around the farmyard, then back to Luke. Well, now he was obliged to the man. He owed him the courtesy of looking into the matter before he made any accusation.

Forcing a smile, he nodded at Luke and asked, "How was the trip to the mill? Culpeper must've been busy for it to take you all day."

"Yep. He's always busy, it seems. I knew it would take about all day—always does. And it does pay to stick around and watch the milling. His idea of ten percent kind of grows if nobody's watching."

"Yep, that's how I remember him." Josiah chuckled. "Jim has already put feed out for the mules. I'll help you unhitch. It shouldn't be long till supper."

"All right. Let me pull on up a little bit so it'll be easier unloading the rest of the meal."

As Luke drove the mules past him, Josiah could see two more large meal sacks in the wagon. He had lifted one out before Luke climbed down from the wagon seat. He lugged it to the tack room, where he placed it in a bin with a close-fitting lid. Luke followed with the remaining sack.

Luke wrinkled his nose. "Shew-ee! I smell rotten eggs."

"Yep. One of the hens managed to hide one when she started to get broody, and nobody found it. Jim knocked it out of the loft accidentally when he was forking hay. Stinks like hell, don't it?"

"Yep, pure brimstone. For once your blasphemous language is appropriate, Josiah," Luke said. With a disgusted look, he added, "Sally's supposed to gather those eggs. She needs a switching for missing a nest."

Josiah stopped in mid-stride and gave Luke a narrow-eyed stare. "She maybe shouldn't have missed it, but after all, the hens do hide them. And why hadn't the hens' wings been clipped?

167

They couldn't get to the loft if they couldn't fly." Luke's face reddened. Josiah added, "I'll speak to Sally about it. If she needs a switching, I'll take care of it. It's not your call."

Luke squinted at Josiah. He grunted and spat a stream of tobacco-stained spittle onto the dirt. "You do that. Straighten her out. The girl's just plain lazy." Then he turned to the task of unhitching the mules.

Josiah made no move to help. "She's not lazy," he said. Emmy worked her hard, and he'd never heard her complain or seen any evidence of her shirking. He turned toward the house and tossed back over his shoulder, "I reckon you can see to the mules yourself."

Josiah stomped to the house, fuming. How could Luke rile him so easily?

He stopped at the back porch and sluiced the dust and grime from his hands and face without much soap. He grabbed the towel and slowly dried off, waiting until he had calmed down and felt he could trust himself to be near Mattie without upsetting her.

Chapter 22

Emmy heard the wagon turn in from the road and creak and clatter toward the barn. She drew another shuddery breath and swabbed at her eyes with her damp and wadded handkerchief, then blew her nose. She wanted to get herself under control. Luke would soon come clomping in, demanding supper. She looked at Mattie and her face crumpled and she sobbed anew. She found a dry handkerchief and wiped again. Why couldn't she control her tears? She couldn't afford to collapse into weeping uselessness—there was too much to be done, too many people depending on her. She breathed deeply and pressed the fresh handkerchief to her face as though to dam her eyes and runny nose.

All afternoon she had grieved and worried. Grieved for more than Mattie. Grieved for Luke. Their marriage. She pressed the handkerchief to her face and let her thoughts swirl through their endless whirl yet again. Luke didn't love her—not the way Josiah loved Mattie. He used to care for her. She knew he had. She sighed. Well, she *thought* he had.

Mattie moaned. Emmy rinsed the fever cloth and wiped her sister's face. Mattie mouthed something. Thanks? Emmy rinsed the cloth again and wiped her own face before placing the rag on Mattie's forehead.

She wasn't wildly in love with Luke, either, but he was her man. She did care for him. She'd been a dutiful wife. She sniffed and wiped her nose and smiled wryly. Three children proved that. And she hadn't bled in weeks. That and the way she'd been feeling the last several mornings—she thought there was another one on the way. That's all she needed.

She shifted in her chair. Flies buzzed. Several crawled on Mattie's face. She picked up the whisk and shooed them away. She laid the whisk across her lap and sighed. She shouldn't dread another child. She had three beautiful children. Sometimes she feared for them. Luke wasn't so harsh in the beginning. She sighed again. When did everything start to go wrong?

She idly swished the whisk once again, shook her head slowly and bit her lip. Now Luke was so stern, so harsh. They didn't get along very well anymore. He blamed her. But that wasn't right. Plenty of the discord was his fault. Plenty of it.

She pressed her lips together grimly. It might not be right, but she had to put up with it. She got so mad at him sometimes, but she couldn't leave. Where would she go? What would she do? Maybe to her parents, but they'd be mortified she would leave a godly man like Luke. The world was full of widows and orphans. She saw their misery all around her. It would be so much worse for a grass widow.

She shuddered. She could only imagine what she might have to do to live, and even so she might not be able to feed her babies. She could damn her own soul and yet that not be enough of a sacrifice.

Tears began to blur her vision again. She sniffed and wiped her eyes. The simple truth was she needed Luke. Needed him to provide for their family by the strength of his labors. She'd have to give him that—he was a good provider. But she couldn't help resenting being under his thumb.

Emmy noticed the flies gathering on Mattie again and whisked them away. She frowned. She even resented her sister, resented living in *her* house, working for *her* dreams, keeping up *her* farm. Didn't she ever get to have anything of her own?

Mattie moaned and moved restlessly. Emmy bowed her head into her hands and sobbed for several seconds before she recovered and wiped her nose and eyes. Forgive me, Mattie, she thought. You know I love you. I truly do.

Emmy raised her head as she heard Jim run to the porch and

slosh water. What she hated most was the way she behaved toward her children—always carping at them, riding them, driving them. She took out all of her frustration and resentment on them, and that was wrong. She loved her babies. Sally, too. She wanted to hug and cuddle and kiss them, but always ended up yelling at them, smacking them. It was wrong but she couldn't make herself stop.

She sniffed and snuffled and wiped her eyes again. Maybe that's how it was with Luke. Maybe he wanted to treat his family better. He revered the Bible, took seriously his duties to his family, but his methods were harsh. Maybe he would like to change, but he didn't know how. Maybe . . . maybe he really did care about her, about all the family. Maybe he couldn't help the hard things he did.

Emmy nodded and sniffed. She rinsed the cloth and wiped Mattie's face and hands, feet and legs. She sat and stared at Mattie for a few seconds, and then her gaze wandered to the front window, to the willow oak and the road beyond. She sighed. Dear God, the truth was she did love Luke. He was handsome, even if all of his hard work has roughened him. He had been good to her in the beginning. And despite all that had happened, she needed him. Not just for his providing. She needed him, his body, his company. What did that say about her?

She heard Josiah out at the washbench. She rinsed the cloth and wiped Mattie's face again. What was to become of them all? She and Luke, and Josiah? She retrieved her handkerchief, blew her nose as quietly as she could, and sat wearily beside Mattie's bed.

Chapter 23

Josiah found Emmy sitting beside Mattie's bed, nervously twisting a damp white handkerchief. Her swollen eyelids, their rims like raw meat, and her bloodshot eyes left no doubt she had been crying. She looked up as Josiah entered the room.

"How's Mattie?" he asked, but he could see she had not improved. She lay sweating, her gown rumpled and hiked up to expose her feet and lower legs. In good health she would have been mortified to be seen by anyone, even her sister and her husband, so exposed, in such disarray, but she seemed to be unaware of her circumstances. She looked eight months gone, her belly a mountain beneath her wrinkled gown. A wet white cloth lay across her forehead. It blended with her pale skin but accentuated the fever flush in her cheeks. Her eyes, open and glittery, seemed unfocused, and didn't turn toward Josiah when he spoke.

Emmy shook her head and nodded toward the door as she rose from her seat. Josiah stepped back out into the hall and Emmy joined him there.

"She's no better. I think she may be some worse." Tears welled in Emmy's eyes and she roughly swiped at them with the soggy handkerchief. "Her eyes have been open much of the afternoon, kind of bright and darting, but I don't think she's really very aware—the fever's so high. I've been doing as Doctor Wilson said, keeping her hands and feet and face washed, but she's burning hot." She paused to wipe more tears. "If only there were something more we could do."

Josiah nodded. If Doc was right—and all signs indicated he was—they could do nothing. Death would win this waiting game. He looked away from Emmy. If he saw any more of her anguish, he would be unable to conceal his own.

"I know. All we can do is try to hold her fever down. Maybe Doc's wrong. Maybe she has a chance."

"Maybe. If we pray hard enough."

Josiah nodded. He stared toward the bedroom door for a while before he swallowed and drew a deep breath. "I told Sally to start supper. You go see to her and the children. I'll sit with Mattie. Maybe Dorcas can spell me while we eat. I'll sit with her again tonight. We'll take care of her the best we can. And hope."

"Hope . . . and pray."

Josiah nodded. "And pray."

"I heard the wagon pull in. Luke'll be tired and hungry. He'll be wanting his supper. Thank you for sending Sally to get it started." She paused, then added, "I'll bring some fresh water first, though."

Josiah entered Mattie's room and drew his rocking chair up close to her side. He took her hand and whispered, "How are you?"

She shifted her head slightly and her eyes moved in his direction. They looked very sad. She answered, "Not too bad," but it seemed to take all her strength. Her gaze dissolved into a blank stare.

Josiah continued to hold her hand and only glanced up when Emmy brought the water. He drenched and wrung the cloth and wiped Mattie. She seemed hardly aware of his ministrations, which he repeated frequently. After a while, Dorcas came in, smelling of wood smoke and lye soap. She sent him to supper while she took over the nursing tasks.

The family sat at the table in their usual positions. Luke bowed his head, then raised it again and asked Josiah, "Do you want to say grace?"

Josiah shook his head. "No, you go ahead."

Luke did. Then he helped himself from the dish nearest him

and passed it in Josiah's direction. Josiah stared at his plate and made no move to take the bowl.

"Josiah?" Luke prodded.

Josiah shook his head. Then he roused enough to take the bowl and pass it on without taking a helping. "I'll get some in a little bit."

As had become the norm, little conversation punctuated the meal. Luke dug in heartily. The children ate hungrily. Emmy and Josiah served themselves after everyone else had taken what they wanted. They picked at their food, pushed it around their plates. They seldom actually raised a fork or spoon to mouth. When Luke had finished they still wore worried, far-away expressions, and uneaten food lay on their plates. On the table crowder peas remained in one bowl, and corn in another, and okra in a third. Even some cornbread remained.

Luke bristled as he turned on Emmy. "What's the matter with you? You haven't eaten anything, hardly. The sow will be glad of your wastefulness."

She looked at him with anger timidly sputtering from her eyes. "The food will keep till tomorrow," she said, then added, "Mattie's worse."

Luke stared at her, his harsh, angry frown softening only slightly. "I'm sorry to hear that," he said, but no tenderness shaded his voice. In a few moments he added sternly, "Then you'll need your strength. Eat your supper."

Emmy glared at Luke for a moment. But then she lowered her head and spooned a few peas into her mouth.

Josiah felt sure he had seen a flash of hatred in Emmy's eyes. No wonder. Luke gave her good reason to be riled. But it all looked like a familiar pattern—his anger, her submission.

He forked the last of the okra and peas from his plate. He shouldn't make too much of their spat. All couples have fights, but . . . Something in their eyes—something he couldn't quite name—almost looked like warnings given and taken, in both directions. He paused in his chewing. He had to find a way to ask Emmy if Luke ever hit her. And then he'd have to figure out what to do.

The children had warily watched the tense exchange

between Emmy and Luke. When the adults stopped talking, the silence drew out tense and taut, a hot wire drawn thin. Finally Jim asked, "May I be excused?" followed by a "me, too" chorus from the others, even Delia.

Luke frowned and raised his hand. Jim flinched. Luke lowered the hand as he breathed slowly a couple of times and then mumbled, "See to the rest of your chores."

Jim, Callie Belle, and Sally quickly scooted their chairs back. Jim and his sister left immediately, while Sally stayed long enough to release Delia from her high chair.

Emmy said, "Sally, don't get far. I'll need you here to clean up."

"Yessum. I'll take Delia out to the swing."

Sally grasped her little cousin's hand and led her toward the door. As she left the room she glanced back at Josiah and Luke.

Josiah watched the children leave. He pushed a piece of cornbread around his plate to soak up the pot liquor, frowned, and bit off the soggy portion. He suspected Luke thought about carping at him too for not eating. Wonder why he didn't say anything? Because he'd get as good as he gave? Probably. They were going to have to sort some things out before long. Maybe now. He swallowed the cornbread and took a drink of buttermilk, then turned to Luke.

"Me and Samson fixed up the hog trap in the woodlot today and put out some bait. I reckon we can catch a few of those hogs and take them to market, bring in a little cash. I'm flat broke." He watched Luke redden, his mouth tighten.

"You brought that nigger here? Did he cripple your horse yet?" Luke snapped.

"He shod Pepper. Did a fine job of it. And he helped mend the hog trap. He'll be around for a few days to do whatever we need while Dorcas is here to help with Mattie."

Luke glowered. "I don't want him here."

"It's not your call. He's here. I reckon he can help catch the hogs and drive 'em to market."

"How much corn do you figure on throwing away on this scheme?" Luke demanded, his face growing even darker.

"Oh, we didn't use much for bait—maybe a peck." Josiah

175

gauged Luke's anger, and his own. And then he thought about Mattie and her needs. And Sally's. It wasn't the right time to provoke a fight.

"I reckon you were right about not using too much to try to fatten a few hogs for ourselves now. We'll take the ones we want to sell and let the others fend for themselves a while longer. But I checked the fields—they look mighty clean, by the way—and I don't think we're going to run short of corn. We can afford the bait, and we need the cash."

Red-faced and scowling, Luke roughly pushed back his chair, stood, and stomped out.

Emmy released a pent breath. "Josiah, you oughtn't needle Luke. He's got an awful hot temper."

"I know, Emmy. I can take care of myself." He took a deep breath and released it slowly. "But can you?"

Emmy nodded and murmured, "I reckon I can, but sometimes . . . the children . . . You ought to think before you go crossing him, think if you've got a good reason."

"I do, Emmy. He doesn't treat you right. Are you sure you can take care of yourself?"

She nodded but wouldn't meet his eyes.

She was lying, for certain, he thought. "If ever you have anything you want to tell me . . ."

She shook her head. "Go away, Josiah. Go smoke your pipe. Leave me be."

Chapter 24

The late afternoon sunlight washed gold and copper over the weathered buildings of the farmyard. Their long shadows formed blue and purple smudges, like bruises, yet somehow comforting, lending depth and definition. Josiah sat on the porch and smoked, savoring the peaceful appearance of his small domain. The pipe finished and knocked out, he sighed and braced himself to confront its unpeaceful reality.

He found Mattie much as he had left her before supper. Dorcas was gently laving her sweaty face, murmuring something comforting-sounding that Josiah could not make out. No matter—it wasn't intended for him. Dorcas spoke more distinctly, "Here's Mistuh Josiah, Miss Mattie. I knows you be happy to see him." Mattie turned her gaze in his direction. Her lips twitched into the semblance of a smile.

Josiah took Mattie's hand and bent to place a kiss in her palm. "How are you?" he asked, although he could see her condition had deteriorated.

"Better now you're here."

He patted her hand, surprised she had been able to respond. Turning to Dorcas, he said, "I'll sit with Mattie tonight. You can go, Dorcas. Did you get any supper?"

"Yessuh. Miss Sally brought me a plate a while ago. Said she took Samson one, too. I'll just take mine on back to the kitchen as I go." Dorcas retrieved her empty plate. Before she left, she turned back toward Josiah for a moment and said, "I been giving her medicine. It seems like it helps her some. I 'spect you better keep on giving it to her when she awake enough to take it."

Josiah nodded. As she left, he turned his attention back to Mattie, whose eyes had grown vague again. He wanted to ask her about Luke's treatment of Emmy and of the blacks, but clearly she could not talk. Maybe she'd be a little more alert when the laudanum began to wear off. It was a conversation better held in private, anyway, after the household was sound asleep.

He continued to cool Mattie's brow and hands and feet. He vaguely heard Luke's reading—more Jeremiah—and the gradual quieting of the household. Occasionally he dozed off, only to wake with a start as his head dropped forward, sometimes after the red fog became the Yankee's bloody face but always before the chilling curse. At such times he found himself as sweaty as Mattie. Exhaustion overwhelmed him, and yet he dreaded sleep. He rose shakily from his chair, paced, finally picked up the pitcher and ambled through the darkened house and out to the well for fresh, cool water. He poured a bucketful over his head and then drew more to fill the pitcher before returning to the sickroom.

Once again he sat and watched Mattie twist and moan. Maybe the laudanum was wearing off. Maybe. But she didn't wake up. What if she never woke up? Josiah wiped her exposed skin with the fresh water. She moaned, and her eyelids fluttered. Poor Mattie. Her agony was so unjust.

Josiah grieved. And he seethed in fury at the nameless dark-haired phantom who had brought such suffering on her. Did she really forgive the bastard? How could she? How could she forgive such a brutal attack? He rinsed the cloth and wiped her face again. But if she knew she was dying? Believed she must forgive for the good of her soul?

His eyes smarted and he rubbed them, pressing so hard they ached. Maybe she really did forgive. Maybe he shouldn't doubt her. Maybe she truly wanted him to forgive, too.

"Oh, Mattie, how can you ask that of me?" he whispered. "How can I watch your suffering and not hate the man who caused it?"

"What did you say?" Mattie turned her face toward him. Her eyes, bright and startled, seemed to be focused.

"You're awake."

"You said something." She inhaled, shakily. "You sounded . . . angry, but sad."

He leaned over her, kissed her forehead. "I was thinking about the man who did this to you. How you've asked me to forgive him. That seems impossible."

"It's not." She closed her eyes tight, clenched her teeth, and twisted her body as another lance of pain skewered her. "I have."

"Even in your agony?"

She managed a feeble nod. "Yes." She panted shallowly, and gradually her face relaxed somewhat. "I've prayed for him. And you must, too." She tentatively drew a deeper breath. "Promise me."

Tears welled in Josiah's eyes. He blinked them away. How could he deny her? This might be the last thing she ever asked of him. His hands shook. His lips trembled. He moaned and buried his face in the bed beside her. His tears dampened the sheet as his body shook. He inhaled, almost a hiccup. "Yes-s. I - I will forgive him. I will."

He felt Mattie's hand gently touch his head, stroke his hair. This time he meant his promise. His breathing calmed. A kind of peace and acceptance enfolded him. Someday he might find out who the assailant was. Someday he might find him. He did want the bastard to be punished, but he could let the law do it. He'd take no pleasure in his suffering. And for whatever good it'd do, he'd pray for his soul. He raised his head and looked into her fever-bright but focused eyes.

"I'll forgive him. And I'll pray for him, too. I truly mean it, Mattie."

Her hand slipped to his shoulder. Through his shirt he could feel it, weak, limp, hot. "Thank you." She blinked slowly, and tears beaded in her eyelashes. "That means so very much to me."

She closed her eyes and let her hand drop to the bed. He eased back into his chair, then placed his hand over hers. After a while he no longer felt an answering tension when he squeezed her fingers. He studied the slow rise and fall of her chest and felt reassured. He continued to watch her for minutes, maybe hours.

He had intended to ask her about Luke, about whether he had struck Emmy, but there had been no opportunity. He didn't know how he should handle the matter, but he would keep his promise to look into it.

He did feel better, now he had decided to forgive Mattie's attacker. He wouldn't have to find out whether he could kill again. Maybe, just maybe, the nightmares would go away.

His butt became numb. He rose from his chair and paced around the room for a few minutes, then sat again and wiped Mattie's face. She moaned and her eyelids fluttered, and she squirmed, but she remained unconscious. Later she seemed to be resting easier, more as though she simply slept.

As the hours passed, she stirred and seemed to wake a few times, but the raging fever had stolen her mind. Once she struck out at Josiah in fevered panic, weakly screeching, "No! Stop!" His heart broke as he restrained her. Occasionally she muttered a few words to her older sisters who had married and moved away years ago. She became a child again, calling for her mother. Although Josiah talked to her and told her he loved her, she didn't seem to hear. He wiped her brow and put the laudanum to her lips, but he could not make her well, or even truly ease her suffering. He wept quietly. The household slept. No one saw his shoulders shake or heard his muffled sobs.

Chapter 25

Luke stood in the kitchen doorway and watched as Emmy set a platter of eggs in front of Josiah and then took her seat. The children were already in their usual places. Josiah slid a couple of eggs onto his plate and reached for a piece of cornbread. The man looked beaten. Working days and sitting nights with Mattie must be taking their toll.

Luke ambled to the table, sat, and said grace. Josiah and Emmy hardly looked up. The children ate quietly, glancing from Josiah to Luke to Emmy, who barely picked at her food. Jim dropped his fork. He looked fearfully at Luke before he bent to pick it up, but Luke didn't say anything. Sally stared at her father. Luke heard Josiah's stomach growl and knew he must be hungry. And yet Josiah stared into space, hardly touched the eggs. When he did bring a forkful to his mouth he dribbled yolk down his chin and did nothing about wiping it away.

Luke bolted his breakfast. He helped himself to the eggs Josiah left on the platter. He finished his coffee and Emmy poured his cup full again. As he drank it, he glanced at Josiah—haggard and exhausted, staring at his plate—and he flicked a quick look at Emmy's tense, forbidding back as she stood near the sink and began to scrape garbage into the slop bucket. It was quiet, but it sure wasn't peaceful. There wouldn't be peace for a long time, if ever.

He could read the weariness in Josiah's eyes, the sorrow, the dread. But if he knew Josiah, there was violence festering in him,

181

too. Josiah was near to coming apart, that was clear. Probably he should pity the man, but he didn't. He'd like to drive him to action. Like lancing a boil. Let whatever was coming spew out. Get it over with. He fiddled with his fork, rattling it against his plate. Jim glanced at him, looked surprised, but kept quiet. Provoking a fight with Josiah would be rash. There'd be a better time. Still, he couldn't resist a little jab.

"I reckon you'd better check on your hog trap, Josiah. If you caught any, they'll wreck that spindly fence in no time."

Josiah roused from his reverie. His eyes focused on Luke, not with the anger Luke half hoped for, but with what looked like gratitude. "You're right. Give me something to do. I'm so worried about Mattie, I almost forgot the hogs."

Luke turned to Emmy. "Is there any more coffee?"

She nodded.

"Well, pour another cup for me and Josiah."

She did as bidden.

Luke raised the steaming cup to his lips and blew on it. He took a sip of the bitter brew, watched Josiah do the same. Yeah, he wanted to lance the boil, but he knew the danger. It was getting harder to control himself. He took another sip, found the coffee to be cooler, and took a big gulp. The hogs might be a way to get away, put some distance between them, even if it did mean putting in more hours on the wagon seat. Given the troubles that were sure to be coming, it'd be tempting to sell the hogs and just keep going.

"I guess you could use some help," he ventured. "I'll help you catch the hogs, and if you'd like, I'll take 'em to town to sell. You can stay here with Mattie."

Josiah studied Luke. "I can send Samson with the hogs." He raised his cup to his lips again.

Luke made a wry face. "It'd be better for a white man to do the trading."

"Can't argue." Josiah lowered his cup to the saucer, stared at it, nudged the handle with one finger. "I don't know, Luke. You must've had other work planned. I can take care of the hogs."

Luke shrugged. "Sure I did. But things change. Since you've

started this hog thing, it needs to be finished. We'll catch up the other work later."

"All right. Let's get to it." Josiah pushed back his chair. Its legs scraped shrilly on the floor. Luke rose, too. Josiah turned to Emmy. "We'll be out in the woodlot at the hog pen. You can send one of the children to fetch me if . . . if you need to."

"All right," she said. "Luke, I'll need Jim around close."

Luke nodded and turned to the boy. "You run on and tend to your chores now, Jim. Then you come back here to the house so's your mother can find you if she needs you."

"But, Father, I wanted—"

"Do as you're told."

"Yessir. May I be excused?"

Luke nodded, and the boy left. The men finished their coffee and followed. As they stepped down from the porch, Josiah said, "I'll go tell Samson to come on out and give us a hand."

Luke glared at him. "We don't need that lazy black son of a bitch underfoot."

"He's an extra pair of hands to catch hogs."

"We don't need him. Bo's a damn fine hog-running dog. We'll take him. The lazy nigger'd be in the way."

Josiah shrugged. "Suit yourself."

Luke whistled for the dogs. Bo came out from under the porch, yawning and stretching. He stopped to scratch, then trotted to Luke. Pretty Girl also emerged from beneath the porch, but she stopped and watched, not joining the activity.

As they started for the hog trap Luke said, "We catch any, we can put 'em in the holding pen over by the sow. Then we'll run 'em up the loading chute into the wagon. I don't much look forward to smelling their stink all day. I'd walk and drove 'em, but I don't think my leg would hold up."

"Yep, Sand Springs is a long hike," Josiah said as they entered the woods.

*   *   *

A half hour later they had seven hogs in the holding pen near the barn. Both men sweated. Bo ran back and forth outside the gate, barking, keeping the hogs in turmoil. They squealed and milled and raised a choking cloud of dust.

183

"Bo! Hush!" Luke yelled.

The dog yipped once more, then settled on his haunches and watched, his tongue hanging out and dripping.

Josiah and Luke brought the mules out of their stalls and harnessed them, led them to the wagon, and hitched the double trees. Luke drove the wagon to the loading chute, turned and backed up to the gate, pulling and sawing on the reins to make the mules step backward. One brayed in protest.

The tall sideboards remained in place from the haying. Josiah removed the tailgate, then opened the chute. He and Bo entered the pen and drove the hogs up the chute and into the wagon, cutting out one that had Waller's ear notch. When he had loaded four he replaced the tailgate. Leaving the gate open, he left the pen and came to the side of the wagon.

The remaining two hogs sprinted for the open gate. Bo chased after them until they scattered into the woods.

Josiah looked up at Luke, squinting in the early light. "Don't trade. Get cash."

Luke nodded, said nothing. His frown suggested irritation.

Josiah continued, "I appreciate your doing this. I would've let it wait, but we need the money. I owe Doc Wilson. Did you pay him for the other times he came?"

Luke shook his head and muttered, "No money. I thought about borrowing it from McLain, but I don't think he's too well fixed, either. He put a lot of money into Confederate bonds. There's probably not much left."

"That's what I figured. Well, good luck. We'll look for you back late in the afternoon." Josiah reached up and shook Luke's hand. "Take care." He winced at the pain of the grip and knew the scabs on his knuckles had split and bled again. Luke seemed not to notice.

Emmy stepped out of the kitchen and called, "Be quick, Luke."

Luke scowled and muttered, "Shrew."

"Luke." Josiah hesitated a moment, his mouth a grim line and his eyes hard. "When you get back, we have to talk. About how you treat Emmy. And the children." He hadn't meant to get into those issues. Not yet. He wished he hadn't said anything.

"They're mine, Josiah. I'll do with them as I please, and it pleases me to keep them in line." Luke glared down from his perch on the wagon seat. "And how I do it is none of your concern."

"This is my household. It is my concern. I've heard some disturbing reports."

"If you've been listening to those niggers, you're a fool."

Josiah's face darkened. He slapped the rump of the nearest mule. She jumped ahead, jerking the wagon into noisy motion and startling her teammate. They lurched without coordination. The hogs squealed and braced against the heaving of the wagon. The trace chains clinked and rattled and the wagon creaked.

Luke braced his feet against the dashboard as he swayed on the seat. He hauled on the lines and brought the team to a stop. He turned to look back at Josiah.

"What've they been telling you?"

"We'll talk when you get back."

Luke clamped his mouth shut, his jaw muscles bunching as dark and rough as walnuts. He raised the reins, then slapped them down hard on the backs of the mules. They leaped forward, coordinated this time, and the wagon moved ahead smartly. The iron tires clattered and complained and the hogs stumbled drunkenly and squealed in fright. Bo dashed alongside, twirling and barking. The noisy parade crossed the yard, passed the house, and turned into the rutted red road.

185

Chapter 26

Josiah watched until Luke and the wagon disappeared from sight, then ambled across the farmyard toward the house. He saw the wash Dorcas had done last evening, hanging limp in the morning stillness and damp with dew. The sheets reminded him of something, but his weary mind couldn't think what image they almost evoked. He stood and stared at them. Samson strode up beside him and interrupted his musings.

"'Mornin', Mistuh Josiah. What you want me to do this morning?"

Josiah jumped. "Oh, morning, Samson. Did you get breakfast?"

"Yessuh. What you want me to do now?"

Josiah stared blankly at Samson. He tried, but he couldn't think of a task to assign. God, he was tired. He continued to stare. At last, he blinked and said, "I started that halter for the cow. You can finish it. It's out in the tack room."

He retraced his steps toward the barn. Samson followed. It only took a couple of minutes for him to show Samson what needed to be done.

He wandered back toward the house, unsettled in his alien aimlessness. He had always been an energetic, motivated worker, taking pride in his farm and his ability to provide for his family. Suddenly he was . . . what? Kind of disconnected. He'd done what he could, and it had no effect. He rubbed his face and shook his head. He was going to lose Mattie. His eyes stung, but he

186

blinked quickly and warded off tears. Home didn't feel like home anymore.

He stopped at the well and drew a bucket of water. He immersed the gourd dipper and lifted the cool water to his mouth. It tasted good.

"Daddy, keep the bucket up for me. I want a drink, too."

Sally emerged from the chicken coop, carrying the egg basket with exaggerated care.

Josiah smiled. Sometimes he felt he had gotten to know Sally now, and she had accepted him back in her life. Other times he wasn't so sure. He had been gone a long time. It seemed a long time even to him. How long had it been for such a little girl?

He nodded at the basket. "I thought Callie Belle gathered eggs from the coop," he said.

Sally raised her face from the dipper. Water dripped from her chin. She took a quick swipe at the rivulet.

"Yessir. It's supposed to be her job, but she's so cranky this morning—whining and crying and pulling on Aunt Emmy's skirt. Aunt Emmy got tired of it and smacked her. 'Course then she really cried and her face got all red. Aunt Emmy hugged her, and then she felt Callie Belle's fever. I guess Callie Belle's sick. Aunt Emmy put her to bed."

"And I suppose you have to do all of your own chores now, too?"

Sally shook her head. "Uh-unh. I'm all done with 'em."

"Really? It seems kind of early to be done with chores."

Sally nodded. "It is, but, well . . . I tried to help Aunt Emmy fix dinner, but she kept on crying. And every time she looked at me she cried harder. Finally she told me to get these eggs and then I could go play." She looked down, rubbed her toe in the dirt, and frowned. "Only Jim has to stay close by, for some reason or other, and Callie Belle's sick, and Delia's too little to be much fun to play with, so I guess I'll play with Squeaky." Her lower lip protruded. She sighed and added, "I don't much feel like playing though."

"I know. I don't much feel like working or anything, either."

Without looking up she asked, "Daddy, is Mama going to die?"

Josiah's eyes swam. He looked away, then took a deep breath, let it out in a rush. He sat on the well wall and drew Sally to him.

"Yes, I think Mama's going to die."

Sally's face screwed up and she cried, "No-o-o! No-o-o! I don't want Mama to die!" She dropped the basket and beat her fists against his chest.

He wrapped his arms around her. "I know. I know. I don't want Mama to die either. But she's hurt bad. The doctor has done all he can. We've all done everything we can think of. But she's getting worse and worse. The kind of hurt the doctor says she has . . . Baby, nobody gets well from such a hurt." He paused and swallowed hard. "I wish it wasn't true." He held the sobbing child close and stroked her hair. He wanted to comfort her, but how? He held her tight and drew solace himself. Gradually her sobs subsided.

"When? When will Mama die?" she asked.

"I don't know. She seemed much worse last night and this morning. I don't think she can hold on much longer, maybe a day or two."

"I don't want Mama to die. Daddy, you've got to save her." The sobs began again.

"Child, I wish I could." His tears dripped onto his daughter's head.

They clung together. Josiah had lost his parents and his siblings but that sadness could not compare to this, and Mattie still lived. How terrible would his grief be when she died? How could he bear it?

Sally sniffed and wiped at her nose with her hand. "If we pray, won't God help Mama?"

Josiah nodded. "Maybe. Praying won't hurt. But we have to remember when we pray, we ask that God's will be done. You remember?"

A nod.

"God's will may be he doesn't want to help Mama. We have to be prepared for that."

"But why wouldn't God want to help Mama?"

"I don't know. Maybe God needs someone good and strong like Mama to help him up in heaven."

Hogwash! He couldn't believe he'd uttered such drivel. He thought such expressions pathetic, but now that it had popped out of his own mouth he understood it as an attempt to give comfort. Everyone had to die sometime. The timing never seemed good. He had simply tried to give his child some comfort.

"Maybe so," she answered.

She sniffled and leaned against him for a while longer. Then she stirred. Her eyes focused on the dropped basket and she moaned, "Oh, no. Some of the eggs broke. Aunt Emmy's going to be mad."

"No, I'll tell her it wasn't your fault. Here, I'll go with you to give them to her."

"Oh, would you, Daddy? I'll bet she won't yell at you."

"She might, but it won't bother me."

About half way to the kitchen Sally tugged on Josiah's pants leg and stopped. "Would you like to see my secret place in the woods?"

A secret place in the woods? He'd feel like a fool. He almost blurted out a refusal before it hit him—she trusted him. She felt safe to share her secret with him.

"Yes, I'd like to, if I'm not too big."

"You can scrunch up real small. You don't have to go all the way in."

"All right, let's go, as soon as I hand these eggs in to Emmy."

Josiah took the eggs into the kitchen and explained quietly how some of them had gotten broken. Emmy frowned at the eggs, but she sighed, "Poor child." Josiah told her he and Sally would be walking in the woods, in case she needed to send Jim for him.

Sally took Josiah's hand and led him along the clear trail going toward the hog trap, but several yards into the woods she veered off onto her secret path. They hadn't gone far when Squeaky joined them, softly grunting, occasionally stopping to root, then trotting to catch up.

Josiah now saw the woods in a way he hadn't in a long time, a nostalgia brought on by the warm grasp of his daughter's hand.

"Did you know I used to play in these woods, too?"

"These same woods?"

He nodded. "Yep. My Ma fretted because of the snakes and the wolves. Pa, he just told me to keep my eyes open and be home in time for chores. The wolves and the snakes didn't get me, so I reckon Pa was right."

"Did you have a secret place to go in the woods?"

"Um, kind of. Mostly because nobody cared to look for it. I didn't have a brother close to my age, and my sisters were afraid of the woods. I guess they listened to Ma too much."

"I don't think the woods are scary." Sally said.

Josiah laughed. "I know you're not afraid, but you should be cautious—because of the hogs."

"Squeaky warns me when they're around. We don't go near them."

"Then I feel some better about you wandering around out here by yourself."

He gazed up at the leafy canopy far above their heads. It did seem peaceful. "When I was a boy the woods were much bigger—or so they seemed to me. And more dangerous. I guess now I understand some of my Ma's concern. I probably should have been . . . not afraid, but . . . more cautious."

"Are you cautious in the woods now?" Sally asked as she skirted a spicebush and approached the pin oaks and thorn thicket. Squeaky darted ahead and disappeared beneath the skirt of the oaks.

"Sure. I watch for snakes, watch where I put my feet. I stay out of the poison ivy. But I've always liked the woods. You must feel the same way if you've found a favorite place to play out here."

Sally nodded. "Uh-huh. Um, Daddy?"

"What?"

"You've got to promise not to tell anybody about my secret place. 'Cause it's my secret, and it's all right for you to know, but I don't want anybody else to. D'you promise?"

"I promise."

190

"Cross your heart?"

Josiah solemnly said, "Yes, cross my heart," and made the familiar gesture.

Sally nodded. "Well then, we're here. We have to get down and crawl."

She pulled her skirt up out of the way and dropped to all fours and scrambled beneath the pin oaks. Josiah dropped to his knees and followed, pushing a branch aside. He had barely enough room under the drooping limbs of the trees to make his way. A twig scratched his head. Another raked along his back. He stopped in a small space slightly more open than the rest and carefully twisted himself around to sit cross-legged. Sally scurried toward the entrance to her bower in the thorns but stopped and turned to face him.

"What do you think?" she asked, as she sat with her legs curled to one side.

Josiah smiled. "It's a good secret place. It'd be hard to find you here."

She beamed. "This isn't really my most secret place. It's over here," she said as she waved toward the thorns.

"But that's a thorn thicket."

"That's what makes it such a good secret place. It's really hidden, and it's hard to get into. But there's an open space back in there big enough for me to sit. I think Squeaky went there already. Squeaky, come here," she called. With a grunt and a rustle the little pig emerged from the thorns.

Josiah laughed and scratched behind the pig's ears. "You can hide from Jim and Callie Belle in here as long as you want to, can't you?"

"Uh-huh. And from Uncle Luke and Aunt Emmy. And Mama."

Sally's smile faded. She bit her lower lip. "If Mama dies, will she go to live with God?"

"The Bible says the righteous have a reward in heaven. Your mama . . . she's among the righteous."

Sally screwed her face up in thought. "God sees everything and knows everything, doesn't he?"

Josiah nodded, thinking He sees but He don't care much.

"Will Mama see everything and know everything, too? After . . . after she's dead?"

Josiah hesitated before he said, "Maybe. I don't know. And there's not any way to know."

"Do you think Mama might be able to see me when I come out here? Will she be able to find my secret place then?"

Will her ghost be here, follow us around? He didn't think he believed in ghosts, but to be honest, he'd seen and heard things he couldn't explain. He frowned, picked up a twig from the ground, stirred the dead leaves and sighed. "I don't know. Maybe so."

"Will she know everything, like God?"

How could he answer such questions? He drew a deep breath and tried. "I don't know, Sally. I don't know if she will know everything. I think maybe people, even dead people, aren't supposed to know everything. That's God's job."

"But will she know what I'm doing?"

"She might. If she's able to watch anything, she'll keep track of you because she loves you so much."

Sally's eyes widened. Almost in a whisper she asked, "Will she know things I've done before . . . before she dies?"

He shrugged. "Maybe."

"But I don't want her to know." Sally broke into sobs. Josiah pulled her to him and tried to comfort her. She continued to blubber, "I don't w-want her to kno-o-ow!"

"What don't you want Mama to know? All little girls do things their mamas wouldn't like, but mamas forgive. Daddies forgive, too. Don't worry about Mama being angry. She loves you. She has always loved you, and she will love you when she has gone to live with God."

Sally wailed louder. He hugged her and stroked her hair, tried to shush her. She controlled her crying enough to gasp, "She might not, Daddy. Cause it's my fault."

"Hush now. What's your fault?"

"It's all my fault Mama's hurt and she's going to die."

"No, baby. How could it be your fault?"

"It is. I should've stopped him."

"You weren't there. Even if you had been, you couldn't have stopped such a mean man. He would've hurt you too."

"But I was, Daddy. I was there."

Chapter 27

Josiah froze. He grasped Sally, then forced his grip to relax. Could she have been in the barn, seen what happened to Mattie?

He hoped Sally had not seen the terrible attack. No child should see such a thing. And yet, if she had, could she give him a better description of the bastard? But what about his resolution to forgive? Wouldn't knowing more about the beast tempt him to try to find him, make it harder to forgive? And did he really want Sally to relive the horror of anything she might actually have seen? No.

"You've been so worried about Mama, you dreamed you were there."

Sally lay quietly in his arms, sniffling as her sobs subsided. He felt her head press tighter against his chest.

"I was there, Daddy. I should have stopped him."

Josiah rocked her. "You couldn't have stopped him, Sally. Please believe me. You mustn't feel guilty."

"But I do. Because I am."

"No, no. You can't be." He hugged her and stroked her hair, all the while trying to think of a way to make her see she could not have been responsible for Mattie's injuries. He thought about Mattie telling him it helped Sally to talk about her nightmares. He shuddered. He didn't want to do it, but maybe he should encourage her to talk about whatever she thought had happened. He kissed the top of her head and asked, "But why don't you tell me about it. I'll bet we'll see you couldn't have changed anything."

Sally sniffed and wiped her nose with her hand. She turned her face up to Josiah, studied his face. "If I tell, will you punish him?"

"Sally, your Mama has asked me to forgive whoever injured her. I promised her I would. And I'm trying to. Yet I want him to be punished. I don't know how that fits in with forgiveness. I'll have to work on that, but I'll try to find a way."

Sally's brow wrinkled in a worried frown. "You won't tell him I told? You won't let him hurt me?"

"I'll protect you. I swear it." He would kill the bastard if he threatened Sally. Of that he was certain. And he was certain he'd have no recriminating nightmares. But how would the stranger know if Sally told? The snake had gone on to Henry's Ferry and beyond.

Sally nodded, then drew a shaky breath. "All right." But she fell silent.

After several seconds Josiah said, "I know it'll be hard. You're the only one who knows what happened, except Mama, and she's so sick she can't tell."

"No, Daddy. He knows."

"Well, yes, but he isn't likely to tell." Josiah paused. "Does he know you know about it?" He held his breath.

"I don't think so. I think he would have . . . done something, if he did."

He released his breath in a quick burst. He waited a few moments, then led her into the story. "Were you nearby when? . . ."

Sally nodded, sniffed again. "Uh-huh. In the loft. Looking for eggs. It was warm and quiet up there and I got sleepy. Maybe I went to sleep, just a little bit. And then . . ." She stopped, closed her eyes, shook her head. She began to cry again.

"Shhh. Don't cry." He held her and rocked her until she wiped her eyes on her sleeve, sniffed hard, and continued.

"I heard a man and a woman arguing. It sounded like Uncle Luke and Aunt Emmy. They argue a lot. But when I peeked over the edge of the loft, I saw Mama. She didn't sound like herself."

"But you didn't know the man?"

She looked up at him as though she thought him dense. "'Course I did. It was Uncle Luke."

"Mama argued with Uncle Luke? Are you sure?" Josiah could hardly breathe. He knew what Sally would tell him, something too horrible to be true, and yet . . .

Sally nodded. "Uh-huh. Uncle Luke sounded real mean, but Mama wasn't scared. She was just mad. I'd never heard Mama so mad."

"What were they arguing about?"

She shook her head. "I don't know. It was like they wanted to yell loud but were trying to keep quiet. And you know how Uncle Luke doesn't cuss? He said to Mama, 'Damn bitch. I'll teach you your place.' Not like himself at all." She paled. "I'm sorry about the bad words. But it's what he said."

Josiah hugged her. "It's all right." He waited, but she remained silent. Giving her another squeeze, he asked, "Can you tell me more?"

"Uh-huh. Mama yelled back at him. 'This *is* my place. Don't you forget it.' She sure sounded mad. She wasn't keeping so quiet anymore. He grabbed her and put his hand over her mouth. She slapped him. He took his hand off her mouth and slapped her, hard enough her head snapped to the side." Sally pressed her head into Josiah's chest. He felt her tremble, heard her strained moan. "I was so scared, Daddy. He was hurting Mama, I knew he was, but I was too scared to do anything. And Mama—she was so mad. She didn't cry. She tried to jerk away from him but he had her arm. She called him a bastard and slapped him again. He hit her with his fist. And . . . and . . ." Sally sobbed again.

Josiah rocked and hugged the child. He couldn't stand this, asking Sally to recall the horror, but he had to know. "Shhhh. Don't cry. Try to go on." As he comforted her, his hands twitched with a mind of their own, wanting to strangle the life from Luke, the treacherous son of a bitch.

"I . . . I was so scared. Uncle Luke would whip me good if he caught me snooping. I ducked back down in the hay and stayed still." She stopped and seemed to hold her breath.

Josiah squeezed her and murmured, "It's all right. It's all right."

She shuddered. "No, it's not all right. 'Cause I heard a noise, like when Mama pounds the meat to make it tender. You know, like 'whump.' And Mama made a squeaky, moany sound. And then I heard a scrabbling scuffling sound. And more 'whumps.' And like a rag tearing. And grunts and moans and mumbly, squeaky sounds. And then lots more 'whumps.' And I stayed still because I was too scared to do anything."

Josiah had shut his eyes tight. He moaned, and nodded slightly. Sally drew a shaky breath and continued.

"Then it got really quiet. I could hear the flies buzzing, and the cow swishing her tail. I couldn't hear Uncle Luke anymore but I was afraid to move. Then I got worried because I couldn't hear Mama, so after a while I peeked over the edge again. She was sprawled on the ground, bloody and all bent funny, with her dress pulled up."

Sally stared wide-eyed, unblinking, quiet. Josiah held his breath, fascinated by the horrible tale, not wanting to hear it, unable to force himself to tell Sally to stop. She trembled, but she continued her narrative in a calm voice, uninflected, as though she were in a trance, and once started would go to the end.

"I got closer to the edge and looked all around, to be sure Uncle Luke wasn't there anymore. Mama was lying there so still. I climbed down the ladder and went to her. Her breath blew bubbles in the blood in her nose. I touched her and nothing happened. I shook her shoulder and her head wobbled. She quit blowing bubbles. I whispered, 'Mama. Mama, wake up.' She didn't open her eyes. She didn't move. I shook her again, and I yelled, 'Mama.' She still didn't open her eyes. I thought she might be dead. I screamed and ran and yelled for help.

"That's when Uncle Luke grabbed me. I thought he was going to hurt me, too. I screamed and screamed. But Aunt Emmy pulled me away from him and he went running to the barn. I tried to tell Aunt Emmy he might hurt Mama again. I don't think she understood anything except Mama was hurt, but she went running with me to the barn.

"Uncle Luke was on his knees beside Mama, like he was

praying. Only he wasn't praying. He had his hands on Mama's neck. I saw. But he heard us coming and he turned loose.

"Aunt Emmy ran up to Mama and knelt down and touched her neck and her arm. She told Uncle Luke we had to get Mama to the house, so he picked her up and carried her. But you know what? He had pulled Mama's skirt down to her ankles before we got there."

Sally lay quietly in Josiah's arms, her breath becoming more even. No more sobs.

Furious, Josiah could hardly breathe. Luke? Surely Sally couldn't make this up? But could Sally have misunderstood what she heard? Could she have mistaken someone else for Luke? He needed to be absolutely certain.

"I'm so sorry you saw such a terrible thing. But I'm glad you told me. This is a serious matter."

"I know, Daddy." She shuddered. "I was so scared."

Josiah hugged her and whispered, "Of course. And when you're scared, it's easy to make mistakes. Are you absolutely sure you saw Luke arguing with Mama?"

Sally nodded. "Yes. I'm positive. I saw Uncle Luke."

"But then you ducked down and hid in the loft. Maybe Uncle Luke left and someone else came in and hurt Mama. Could that have happened?"

Sally shook her head. "No. I ducked down and right away I heard the meat-pounding sound." With a mewing cry she asked, "That was Uncle Luke hitting Mama, wasn't it? He hit her and hit her. He's so mean." In a terrified whisper she added, "I'm so scared of him." She quivered and cried again.

Josiah hugged her and rocked back and forth. "Hush, hush, baby. I won't let him hurt you," he murmured, even as he trembled in fury.

He had seen a few faint clues. He understood them now. Should he have seen them before? Mattie's feigning sleep when Luke had stood in her doorway. Her panic after she heard Luke's voice, and her fear of being left alone, especially in the night. Those supported Sally's story, but by themselves they didn't point to Luke.

Luke's frantic search for the dark-haired stranger—that

might have been Luke's opportunistic use of Jim's frightened tale. The stranger had been real but guilty only of stealing meat.

What would Luke have done if he had caught the man? Shot him, probably. Or hanged him on the spot. Shut him up forever.

And if there hadn't been a stranger? Luke would have invented one.

Why hadn't he killed Mattie outright? He probably thought he had. Then, when Sally raised the alarm, he discovered Mattie had survived but he didn't have time to finish her off.

What would he have done if Mattie had accused him when she regained consciousness? Had he planned to finish his dirty work before that could happen but never found the opportunity? Josiah remembered Luke standing in Mattie's doorway, studying her while Mattie feigned sleep or unconsciousness. No wonder she hadn't wanted Josiah to leave her.

But why didn't she name Luke? She was afraid, pure and simple. Josiah had seen her fear. Now he understood it stemmed from present threat, not past.

And through everything the sly bastard had seemed so normal, had not made a false step, had shown no guilt. He had been as he always had—touchy and stiff-necked and righteous. Righteous? What an act! Cold. A rapist and a murderer. There could be no sympathetic explanation for his behavior.

Did Emmy know? Or had he fooled her, too? Surely she had to suspect. But maybe not. Luke had been so normal.

And now the bastard was heading off with almost all of the farm's profit. With Josiah's own blessing. At his own insistence. Oh, God! How could he have been so blind?

Josiah hugged Sally and fumed. Would Luke come back? Did he feel that triumphant, that safe? He was controlled enough, cold enough. He might. Or would he take the hog money and keep on going? He surely feared Josiah would eventually find out what happened.

Josiah had no intention of waiting for Luke's next move. He would catch the murdering bastard. He would cut out his heart, and make sure he knew why. Forgive such vile treachery? Never.

Sally squirmed and cried out, "You're hurting me. I'm sorry. I didn't mean to let Mama get hurt."

Josiah came to his senses and realized his hands throttled Sally as if she were Luke. He relaxed his grip, caressed the child, murmured, "I'm so sorry. I didn't mean to hurt you. I'm sorry. I'm so sorry."

Sally nodded, breathing shakily. "I know I was bad."

"Baby, you weren't bad. You were scared, just like you should've been. You couldn't have stopped Luke, and him so worked up. You'd have had to knock him out. How could you have done that?"

And yet, at exactly the right moment, before the argument escalated, if she had made her presence known . . .

Trembling, he felt Sally shaking, too. He held her close and continued stroking her. "I'm really sorry I hurt you, Sally. I truly didn't mean to. I was thinking about how much I hate Luke, hate what he did to Mama. I was thinking about what I want to do to him. I guess my hands didn't know they were holding you. I'm so sorry."

"I'm all right, Daddy." She seemed more calm, less frightened. "You don't blame me? You really don't?"

"No, baby. It wasn't your fault."

"Really?"

"Really."

They sat quietly for a while. Sally wiped her hand under her runny nose. Josiah found his handkerchief and wiped the tears from her face, then held it to her nose and commanded, "Blow." She did. He put the handkerchief away.

Sally squirmed and pulled away a little bit. "But you see why I don't want Mama to know about . . . about me not helping her? I tried to tell her yesterday, but she didn't understand. And then I got to thinking—she might not love me anymore. You won't tell her, will you?"

Josiah sighed, looked up into the leafy canopy of the oaks, then back at Sally. He sighed again. "I won't tell, baby. I'll avenge her, but she doesn't need to know. We talked about it once—revenge—and she said I should forgive. I didn't think I had the guts to kill whoever hurt her, so I promised I'd do as she asked. It would upset her if I was to tell her I'm going back on

200

my word. So we won't tell her. But I can't forgive Luke, no matter what I promised your mama."

"Me, too. I hate Uncle Luke."

They continued to sit under the oaks, faces tinged green by light reflected from the leaves around them, each lost in private thoughts. Josiah itched to pursue Luke. Regardless of the cost to himself, he had to confront him. He had to. But with Mattie's condition deteriorating, he should stay with her. What if she called for him, needed him? Luke wouldn't travel fast with a wagon and a load of hogs. He could overtake him easily, riding Pepper.

From far away Jim called, "Uncle Josiah. Uncle Josiah."

Josiah's heart gave a frightened bound and his scalp prickled. Mattie!

Chapter 28

Wide-eyed, Sally turned to Josiah. "We have to get out of here quick. I don't want Jim to know about my secret place." She scrambled from beneath the tree. Josiah followed.

They moved as quickly as they could through the clinging, ripping briars and underbrush to the larger path. Then they ran toward the house. When they had left the secret hiding place well behind, Josiah called out to Jim, "Here, boy! Where are you? What's wrong?"

The boy called again, and Josiah heard him running through the woods toward them. Sally fell behind. Josiah waited till she caught up to him, then picked her up and ran on. They nearly crashed into Jim, who was running as fast as he could, his eyes bugged out and his nostrils flared.

"What's wrong?" Josiah asked as he lowered Sally to the ground and grabbed the boy by the shoulders.

"Mother says you should come quick. Aunt Mattie's . . . " But he didn't have the wind to finish.

"What? Speak up, boy."

"Aunt Mattie's calling for you," the boy managed between gasps.

Josiah ran toward the house so fast the children could not keep up. Mattie was alive. She was calling for him. Maybe she was better.

He leaped up on the back porch, ran down the hall, turned into the bedroom, and stopped abruptly. A fetid odor, like rotting meat, assailed his nose. His stomach heaved, but he swallowed hard and managed not to vomit. Mattie lay much as he had last seen her, but pain lined and pinched her face even more than before. Her eyes widened slightly and shifted to look at his face. Emmy stood on the other side of the bed along with Dorcas. They both looked drawn, exhausted, tense.

Josiah walked to the bed and took Mattie's hot, limp hand. He could barely feel her answering squeeze.

She drew several irregular, shaky breaths, finding strength from reserves that must be nearly depleted, and said, "I had to see you before I go."

"Mattie, you're not going anywhere."

She shook her head, the motion barely perceptible. "I'm dying. You know. I know."

Mute, he squeezed her hand.

She struggled for strength again and whispered, "You must take care of Sally."

Dorcas and Emmy both had tears running down their faces. Dorcas was silent, but Emmy made a strained soft squeal, trying to control her crying. She lost her struggle and turned away to hide her weeping.

Josiah's eyes brimmed as he answered, "Of course. Don't worry."

Mattie managed a tiny nod.

Josiah drew a shaky breath and bit his quivering lip. Tears blurred his vision, but he refused to cry. "Mattie, you are my life, my dearest one. How I can live without you?"

Mattie shook her head. "You must." She paused, her breath labored. "For Sally."

Josiah nodded. "I know. Don't fret. I'll take care of her." He patted her hand, kissed it.

She nodded but then moaned and twisted in pain.

He shook his head and clenched his teeth. "Mattie, it's wrong that you should suffer so for what that bastard Luke has done."

At the mention of Luke, Mattie's eyes briefly opened wider, then squeezed shut. She tried to shake her head. Emmy whirled to stare at Josiah, her eyes wide, her mouth slightly open.

Josiah went on, his voice shaking. "I'll make him pay for what he's done to you. I'll make sure he knows who's doing it and why. He won't get away with this."

Emmy shrieked and ran at Josiah, clawing, screaming, "What are you saying? Luke didn't do this."

"He did. I'm going to kill him for it."

"You can't kill him! You can't! I won't let you! I'll kill you first!"

Josiah threw his arm up to ward off Emmy's blows. Dorcas tried to pull Emmy off him, but without success. Josiah took in Emmy's frantic denial with growing suspicion. He flung her back, hard. She crashed against a chair, lost her balance, fell to the floor. Dorcas, thrown off balance, righted herself and stepped to the side, her attention skittering between Emmy and Josiah.

"You bitch. You've known all along. You pious witch."

"No." Emmy scuttled away from him.

"Pretending to pray to God to save Mattie. You didn't want her well—she might tell on Luke. You ran to warn him when I got home. Warn him so he wouldn't be surprised, wouldn't betray himself. You're disgusting."

Emmy gathered her feet under her and tried to stand. Dorcas reached to help her, but Emmy shook off her touch. Weeping bitterly, shaking her head, she said, "You're crazy. You don't know what you're talking about. Luke wouldn't do such a terrible thing. Never. How could you say such a thing?" But even as she protested, her eyes narrowed and clouded. "What gave you such a crazy idea?"

"Sally. She was in the barn, hidden. She saw. She heard. She's been terrified, afraid he would hurt her, too."

Emmy moaned "No-o-o-o." She had gotten to her feet, but now she wobbled as though she would fall again.

Behind him Mattie gasped.

"She felt guilty because she thought she should have stopped what happened. Could she have stopped him, Emmy? How many times has he beaten you? Can you hold him off when he's riled up? What kind of chance would a little girl have?" As he asked his questions his voice softened. Maybe she really hadn't known. He couldn't be certain. But surely she had suspected?

204

Mattie writhed and feebly shook her head, mouthing "No" with every twist of her head. Dorcas moved to her side and tried to hold her still.

"Now, now, Miss Mattie. Don't you fret. You rest easy. Don't you fret," she murmured as she stroked her hair.

Mattie's gasps, her thrashing about, her trying to say something finally got Josiah's attention. He took an unsteady breath and forced himself to be calm. He returned to her side and whispered, "Shhh. Shhh. Be still Mattie. Please be still. I didn't mean to upset you so. You're going to cause yourself damage. Please be still."

Mattie grasped his sleeve. "Josiah, you must forgive. Let it go. It's done. Can't be undone. What'll happen to Emmy and her children if you kill Luke? They'll starve."

Josiah closed his eyes and tried to shut his ears to her pleas. "They won't starve. Your father would never let that happen. *I* won't let it happen." He clasped her hand and hoped she would calm down.

While Josiah tried to calm Mattie, Emmy muttered to herself. "I didn't know . . . Oh, God. What am I to do now? He's my husband. My children's father. And . . . and I don't really know. Why should I believe this? Sally's a child. She doesn't like Luke. She never has. She could be making this up. She could be."

Mattie breathed in shallow, raged gasps. "You can't be sure Emmy and hers will be taken care of. Father's nearly ruined. We're nearly ruined. Emmy and the children need Luke. You must forgive Luke."

Forgive Luke? He couldn't. Not knowing the viper did this and then stayed on in his house, sat at his table, smug and safe, thinking he would never know. "Mattie . . . ," he began, but couldn't go on.

"Promise me." She panted, struggled for breath. "Promise you won't kill him. Promise me. For Emmy."

His hands shook as he held her. He knew he had made her last hours a greater trial. Why had he said anything about Luke? He knew better. But he couldn't unsay it. Couldn't let her suffering go on, either. "Mattie . . .," he began again. He could hear his doubt. He knew she could, too.

"Promise," she demanded with unexpected strength and determination.

Josiah knew this turmoil was costing her too much. If he loved her, how could he refuse her dying request? Then again, how could he let her killer go unpunished? He whispered, "I'll try to forgive him, my dearest. I'll try."

He didn't lie. He would try—sometime. Sometime might be long after the worms had feasted on Luke's flesh and his bones had turned to dust, but sometime he would try to forgive Luke.

Mattie nodded. "Thank you."

She closed her eyes and rested for nearly a minute before she spoke again. "Sally? I want to see Sally."

*   *   *

Dorcas looked back and forth from Josiah to Emmy. Neither was making a move to find Sally, bring her to Mattie. She slipped into the hall to look for the child. The girl sat on the settee, bent double as though her belly hurt, her fists jammed against her mouth. Tears rolled down her cheeks.

"Miss Sally, baby, your Mama's asking for you." Dorcas curled her arm around the child's shoulders.

Sally nodded and mumbled, "I know. I heard." She made no move to get up, but raised her face to Dorcas and whispered, "I don't want to see Mama. I don't want to see her dying."

"She's not dying right now and she wants to see you. You come on and kiss your Mama. I know you're afraid, but it's important for you to go see her now. You trust me. You trust what I'm telling you."

Sally rose from the settee and took a few hesitant steps toward the bedroom. She stopped and looked back up at Dorcas. "Do I have to?"

"Yes, baby. You'll be fine, and it'll make your Mama feel better."

"Will it help her get well?"

"No, baby. But it'll make her feel better, in her heart."

206

Sally swiped her sleeve across her face, wiping away some of her tears, took a deep breath and stood straight. "All right."

She tiptoed to the bed and put her hand on Mattie's shoulder. "I'm here, Mama."

"I'm so glad." Mattie eyes swam and wandered. She fought for breath and continued, "I love you. Never forget that."

Sally climbed on the bed and kissed her mother. "Mama, I'm so sorry I didn't save you. Please don't die."

Josiah reached for Sally, intending to lift her from the bed. Mattie put her hand on the child and feebly shook her head.

"Sally, you couldn't have done anything. I'm glad you were hidden. I'm thankful you're safe."

"But Mama . . ."

"Shh. It's all right. Don't worry. Daddy will take care of you now."

Exhausted, Mattie lay still, struggling for each ragged breath. Her hand rested on Sally. Josiah started to lift Sally away from her, but her eyes focused again and she whispered, "Always . . . love . . . you." Then her eyes closed and her hand went limp, but her chest continued to heave unevenly.

Josiah lifted Sally away and carried her out into the hall. She wept, her face against his shoulder. He hugged and comforted her as best he could. At last her crying diminished. "Is Mama dead now?" she asked.

"No, baby. Not yet."

"When?"

"We can't know. I think not much longer."

Josiah had come to think of Mattie's passing as inevitable. He hoped she would not suffer much more, hoped her ordeal would be over soon. But he didn't want Sally to have to know every detail of the final hours.

"I guess you don't much feel like playing, but maybe you could take Squeaky out in the woods, out where you showed me? Stay away from the house for a while. But be careful. Pay attention if Squeaky warns you about any danger. Can you do that?"

Sally nodded and sniffed.

"If you're needed, we'll ring the dinner bell. Aunt Emmy may need you to get dinner for the children. You can do that, can't you?"

Sally sighed. "Yes, Daddy." She pulled away from Josiah and slowly walked down the hall, dragging her feet, and out the back door. He heard her calling Squeaky.

Josiah went back into Mattie's room. She lay still, unconscious, but breathing.

Through tears Emmy looked at him with what appeared to be a mixture of fear and guilt and hatred as she rubbed her arm and her hip where they had crashed into the chair. Josiah studied her. At the moment he hated her because he felt she had been complicit in Luke's evil. Yet he recognized she must be torn between loyalty to her husband, loyalty to her sister, responsibility toward her children, fear of hellfire, fear of starvation. He pitied her, but not enough to forgive her just yet.

She whispered, "I didn't know. I still don't."

He glowered at her and said nothing.

Dorcas moved away from Mattie's bed and stood in front of Josiah. "Mistuh Josiah, why don't you step outside for a little bit? Get you some air? We'll be all right here," she cajoled.

Josiah scowled, took a deep breath, then slowly released it. "I reckon you're right. I guess we could all use some separation," he muttered. "Call me if there's any change or if you need me. I'll be out back somewhere."

Chapter 29

Josiah strode down the hall and out the back door. Once he was outside, away from Mattie's misery, his fury dissipated, replaced by hopelessness. He went to the kitchen and lit his pipe, then sat in one of the chairs on the porch. Pretty Girl came out from under the house and, after pausing to stretch, climbed slowly up the steps, sat beside him and pushed her head against his idle hand. He patted her, scratched behind her ears. She moaned in pleasure as her hind leg scratched a phantom flea and her tail thumped rhythmically against the floor. He tired of scratching her ear and quit. She pushed her head against his hand, insisting on more attention, but when she didn't get it, she flopped down on the porch with a sigh and rolled her eyes up at him and waited.

The tobacco in Josiah's pipe had burned to ash and still he sat, staring at nothing, not really lost in thought, just . . . there. He vaguely heard sounds—the chickens clucking and scratching, a pig occasionally squealing, the 'jrrrrrrr' of a jarfly, the sharp 'thwack' as an acorn dropped onto the smokehouse roof, the 'chk-chk' of a redbird in the rose-of-Sharon bush. The soft thud of a horse's hoof as it stomped in the barn finally brought him back to awareness of his surroundings and to conscious thought. The barn—Samson was working in the barn, but there was something else Josiah needed him to do.

Josiah returned to Mattie's room. Dorcas sat by the bed. Emmy had gone. Would she try to warn Luke? Probably. When Luke had departed there had been no hint he was about to be found out. He could come driving home late in the day into Josiah's ambush. Yes, she'd try to warn Luke. He'd better keep an eye on her.

Mattie, with her eyes closed, moaned and tossed and moaned again. She gave no sign of knowing Josiah had returned.

He went to his desk in the corner, opened it, and found two small sheets of paper, a quill, and a pot of ink. With his pocketknife, he trimmed a fresh nib on the quill, then tried the result against his finger. Drawing the paper toward him and dipping the pen in the ink, he wrote:

Creed,

Matilda Jane is sinking fast. She cannot hold on much longer. Please break this sad news to Mother Lorna, then come as quickly as you can. Send Samson back here, as I have further need of him.

Josiah

He folded and sealed the missive, then wrote a travel pass for Samson in case he ran into "regulators," cleaned the pen, and closed the desk. On his way out he kissed Mattie. She did not respond.

This time Josiah strode down the hall and out the door with true purpose. At the barn he found Samson finishing the leather halter.

"It's about done, Mistuh Josiah. You want me to put it on the cow now?"

"No. Right now I want you to take this letter to Mister Creed. Ride your mule, and go as quickly as you can. Give it directly to Mister Creed, not Miss Lorna. It's telling him Miss Mattie's dying."

"Yessuh."

"Stay by Creed. He's bound to be upset. He'll tell Miss Lorna in whatever way he thinks best. When you're sure he's all right, you come on back here."

Samson studied Josiah, then nodded. "Yessuh, I'll see it gets to Mistuh Creed."

"Take a saddle if you want."

"Yessuh." Samson took the letter and started toward the pasture but turned back. "Mistuh Josiah, I'm powerful sorry to hear Miss Mattie be so bad off. Powerful sorry."

Josiah looked away. He swallowed hard, then managed to say, "Thank you, Samson. I know you are. Me too. Powerful sorry."

Josiah returned to the house. He heard a child whimpering in the attic. He thought of Sally and had placed one foot on the stair when he heard soft murmuring. Emmy. And then he remembered Callie Belle's illness. Oh Lord, what else? Please don't let the child be seriously ill. How would they be able to cope with that on top of everything else?

He entered Mattie's room. No change. The clock began to strike. Noon. Dinner time. Food had no appeal for him, but the children might be hungry. "Dorcas, have y'all done anything about giving the children dinner?"

"Miss Emmy put on some beans this morning and she say she going to make some cornbread a while ago. It oughta be ready in a bit. I think she be upstairs, looking after Miss Callie."

"You go see about dinner, then. Call Sally and Jim. Feed Delia. Send Sally and Jim back outside after they eat. Maybe they can take Delia, too. Get them out of here. I'll sit with Mattie for a while."

"Yessuh."

"Oh, I've told Samson to ride over to McLain's with a letter. You might want to take him a bowl of beans and a hunk of cornbread before he leaves. Tell him I said for him to eat before he goes."

"Yessuh."

Josiah sat beside Mattie and mopped her brow. She didn't respond to him, and yet she moved fitfully and moaned. He felt her exposed toes and found them cold. The hot, close room choked him. He swiped the sweat from his own forehead. A foul smell lingered, drawing flies. They swarmed, buzzed, crawled over him, crawled over Mattie. He fanned and swatted but they kept coming back.

Once Mattie's eyes opened as though she were startled. She screamed. Josiah jumped up, not knowing what to do. He

211

grabbed the bottle of laudanum and held it to her lips as she thrashed about, but she didn't swallow and the medicine dribbled over her lips. He took a drop on his finger and stuck it well back into her mouth. She bit down, but he thought he felt her swallow. He had to wait till her jaws relaxed before he could extract his finger, which bore deep tooth marks seeping blood. The finger swelled immediately. It throbbed, compounding the stiffness and soreness from the beating he had given the porch post yesterday. He rubbed the tooth marks. Gradually the pain subsided.

The afternoon passed with agonizing slowness, the speed of time's transit inversely proportional to Mattie's agony. Josiah and Emmy and Dorcas all tended to her, sometimes one of them, sometimes two, spelling each other from time to time. No one could stand the constant strain of Mattie's passage for very long. When Emmy and Dorcas tended Mattie, Josiah went to the toolshed and started building a casket. True, a finished casket rode the rafters of the shed, but no way could he put Mattie in a box built by Luke.

More than once, when he sat with her alone, Josiah thought it would be merciful to press a pillow over her face, let the ensuing struggle be her last. But he couldn't do it. Finishing off a dying Yankee had haunted and tormented him. He knew he would go mad if he killed her, even as an act of mercy. And so he suffered when she did, and found himself praying to the God whose attention he doubted, praying for a merciful end to Mattie's protracted agony.

In the late afternoon Samson returned. Josiah heard the muffled clop-clop as the mule trotted up the dirt road. At first he stiffened, alert, but then he relaxed when he determined that only one mule approached. Dorcas sat with Mattie, so he could leave her without guilt, escape the torment for a while. He followed the mule to the barn.

"You give the letter to Mister Creed?" he asked as he caught up to Samson.

Samson dismounted. "Yessuh. It took me some while to find him—he was over to the Cawthorn's and I had to track him down there. He was some broke up, but he got hold of hisself. He hurried back home, had me come along with him. He wrote you this here letter." Samson handed a packet to Josiah.

As Samson unsaddled the mule and led it to water, Josiah stepped out into better light and read:

> Josiah,
>
>   I am sorely grieved to hear your news. We will be there as soon as I can tell Lorna and get her calmed down enough to travel. I hope Matilda does not pass before we get there. Tell her our love.
>
> Creed

"Did Creed say when he thought they might get started?"

"No suh. He hadn't said nothing to Miss Lorna when he writ this letter. I came right on back as soon's he give it to me. I reckon they'd be at least an hour, maybe two, behind me. I pushed the mule kind of hard on my way back, faster than he'll likely drive his buggy."

"Thanks for tending to these messages. Will you see to feeding the stock and milking the cow? I'll call Jim and Sally and have them help. There's so much turmoil in the house, none of us is thinking much about the routine things, but they've got to be done."

"Yessuh."

"And I'll have Dorcas fix you something for supper."

"No need for that. Mamie done give me some supper whilst I's waitin' for Mistuh Creed to write the letter. I done had plenty."

"Then I'd appreciate it if you'd see to the chores."

Josiah started back toward the house. In the middle of the back yard he stopped to call Sally and Jim. They came trotting out of the edge of the woods, each of them holding one of Delia's hands. "You children need to see to the chores. Samson'll help you. Feed and water all the stock. Milk the cow."

"But Aunt Emmy said we had to watch Delia," Sally said.

"Jim can help Samson see to the stock and you can take

Delia with you when you milk. She can stay in the stall while you milk, can't she?"

"Yessir. Only . . ."

"What?"

"Delia's bad to run off. I have to watch her real close. And sometimes she tries to eat all kinds of things she shouldn't. I don't know if I can watch her and milk at the same time."

"Well, tie a rope around her and knot it to the manger. Give her a doll or something to play with. That'll work, won't it?"

"No!" screeched Delia.

"Hush, Delia," Sally said, putting her finger to her lips.

"Nononono!"

"You can play with Callie Belle's doll."

"No. Your doll."

"Delia . . . Oh, all right. But you have to take real good care of my doll."

"I will. I pwomise."

Sally looked at Josiah and sighed.

"They'll both be all right if you put them where the cow can't step on them."

"Yessir."

"And when you take the milk to the house, ask Dorcas to help you fix supper for yourself and Jim and Delia."

"I know how to fix supper. And feed Delia, too. I don't need Dorcas to help."

"All right."

Sally started on to the house to get the milk bucket. Delia trotted to keep up. As they disappeared into the kitchen, Josiah could hear Delia chortling, "I gonna play with your dolly," and Sally warning, "You better take good care of her." By the time Josiah got to the house, Sally and Delia were leaving again, Sally toting the milk bucket and Delia a rag doll. Josiah smiled and winked at Sally, but she gave him a hurt frown.

Chapter 30

Josiah returned to Mattie's room in time to see both Emmy and Dorcas struggling to hold her as she jerked and twitched with more energy than he had thought she could possess. He helped and together they kept Mattie on the bed until the convulsions subsided. Then they let go, each trembling.

Emmy withdrew from the bedside and turned away from the others and sobbed. Dorcas remained by Mattie, ready to hold her if she convulsed again. Josiah flexed his hands but he hardly noticed their soreness and stiffness or the swelling of his bitten finger. He drew an uneven breath, then softly approached Emmy. He put his hands on her shoulders. She shrugged them off, kept her face turned away from him.

"Emmy, I'm sorry about all this. Sorrier than I have any words to express. I know it's hurting you about as bad as it's hurting me to see her like this. And I do know you've done your best to take care of her. I'm sorry if I hurt you when I hit you this afternoon."

Emmy's sobs diminished. She nodded twice and sniffed hard before she turned to face him. "I guess I should say everything's all right," she said. "But it's not. We can't save Mattie. It hurts to think Luke might've caused her suffering. I'm not at all sure he did. You're taking the word of a child."

"Sally didn't make up that tale. She didn't even understand the meaning of half of what she told me. No way did she make it up. And Mattie didn't deny it, either. She just pleaded for me to forgive Luke. You were witness to that."

Emmy raised her hands as if to ward him off and shook her head. "No. You're wrong." She gradually lowered her hands and drew a deep breath. "And you did hurt me. Your hatred hurt. I know you'll say it was Luke you hated, but it was me, too—I could see. You remember what you promised Mattie—about forgiving. You promised her." She looked up at Josiah with red-rimmed eyes as hard and sharp as shards of broken glass.

Josiah sighed, lowered his hands. "I remember what I told Mattie. For now, let's see if we can get through this night."

He regretted his apology. He had intended to comfort Emmy, but she wouldn't let him. He pitied her for the hardship she'd had at Luke's hands, but in his heart he believed she knew Luke hurt Mattie, no matter how she denied it. He didn't have the same love for her he had before.

What a mess. He shouldn't have told what he knew, should've let things ride until Mattie's ordeal was finished. They could've carried on as a united family through the worst and then later he could've taken care of Luke. But he had needed Mattie to confirm Sally's story, and she had with her plea that he forgive Luke.

"What will you do when Luke gets home?" Emmy asked.

With a weary sigh Josiah answered, "I don't know. Probably nothing right away. We have to get through Mattie's passing. I can't think beyond that."

The convulsions began again. And moans. And screams. Once again, it took all three to hold Mattie, to keep a rolled rag between her teeth to prevent her biting her tongue. They didn't always succeed. Blood trickled from her mouth. During the next hour it happened several times. Josiah and Emmy made a silent truce. Josiah pushed aside his doubt for the moment and prayed with Emmy and Dorcas for an end to Mattie's torment. Especially while they restrained Mattie, he prayed, "Oh, God, please take her now. Let her find some peace." He thought he prayed silently, but Dorcas said, "Amen," so maybe he had said it aloud.

The sun set and evening came on, the warm golds of sunset

216

cooling into lavenders, the whole world turning bluish, purple, darker and darker. Mattie survived another convulsion, then lay still, her eyes open but unseeing. She breathed raggedly, unevenly, the breaths coming less frequently, and shallower. And then there were no more. Josiah and Emmy stared at the utterly still form, not knowing whether to thank God for finally answering their prayers or to curse Him for letting the whole thing happen in the first place. The smell of feces joined the other foul odors that had been collecting in the room all day.

Dorcas pressed her fingers into Mattie's neck, then shook her head. She put her ear on Mattie's chest. She gently pressed her fingertips against Mattie's eyelids and pulled them down to cover the staring eyes. "She be gone. May God have mercy on her soul and on us all." She choked out an "amen" before she sobbed and began to wail.

Emmy keened, one long, shrill cry after another as though her lungs had infinite capacity and her grief no bounds.

Josiah stared at the disheveled broken shell of his beautiful Mattie. For some time now he'd known she would die. He'd even prayed for her death, there near the end. And now the finality hit him. Mattie was gone. Forever. His grief choked him. He could hardly breathe. His eyes burned and smarted as though he faced a roaring fire. His mouth twitched and quivered and he trembled all over. Forever. She was gone forever. But he did not cry. Not in front of the women.

He came out of his trance at the sound of rapid hoof beats, the rattle and clatter of a buggy coming up the road. He looked over at Emmy, whose keening had finally diminished to an occasional squeak interspersed with shuddering sobs. "I expect that's your mother and father," he said.

Blank-faced, she peered at him. "Who?"

"Your folks. I sent for them," he said.

"Oh." She looked about as though confused. "What . . . what should we do now? I don't know what we should do."

"Miss Emmy, you go on out and speak to your folks," Dorcas said. "Mistuh Josiah, you go on out there, too. You stay out of here for a little while, you hear? Miss Mattie need some tending to. I'll take care of it. Miss Emmy and Miss Lorna can come in here and help in a little bit if they want to, but you and Mistuh Creed stay out till I calls you. You hear me, Mistuh Josiah?" She had one arm curled around Emmy's shoulders, propelling her toward the door. She put the other on Josiah's shoulder, turned him, pointed him toward the door also. "Y'all go on now."

As Josiah stepped through the front door he saw Creed helping Lorna down from the buggy. Emmy ran out behind Josiah. Lorna took one look at her and collapsed in Creed's arms. Creed let his wife down to the ground, her skirt billowing as her legs melted beneath her. Emmy ran to them and fell beside her mother. They hugged each other and swayed back and forth as they cried. Creed stood beside them, trying to pat first one's shoulder, then the other. Josiah came up and put his arm around the older man.

"It's true, then? She's gone?" the old man asked.

Josiah squeezed Creed's shoulder. "Yes. A little while ago. Dorcas is with her, washing her, I guess. She said for me and you to stay out till she calls us."

The old man turned away, pulled a handkerchief from his pocket, wiped his eyes, blew his nose. He bent to Lorna, grasped her upper arms and lifted. "Come on, my lady. You can't sit here on the ground in the dew. Up you come."

Lorna got to her knees, then stood. Emmy rose and helped to lift her. They all stumbled into the house. Josiah and Creed eased the two women onto the settee in the hall, near the closed bedroom door.

Emmy turned to hold her mother, but for a moment she looked at Josiah and spoke. "There's whiskey and brandy in the kitchen, Josiah. On top of the pie safe. Mother needs some of the brandy, and I reckon you and Father could use a little of the whiskey. Can you see to that?"

"I can." He started down the hall and had almost reached the back door when he noticed four wan and frightened faces strung like beads up the stairs. "You children go on back to bed, now," he said. Callie Belle and Jim wordlessly turned and pushed Delia before them, but Sally stayed.

"I heard terrible noises, Daddy. Screaming. And crying. Did

218

Mama die?" she asked, only a slight quaver in her voice, far more composed than he expected her to be.

He turned back, nodded and reached toward her.

She dove into his arms, keening. He held her as she sobbed. She gradually regained her composure, sniffled and wiped at her nose with her hand. "She's gone to live with God?"

"Yes, baby." He thought she might break down again, but she remained calm.

"I have to get some things from the kitchen for Grandfather and Grandmother and Aunt Emmy. Do you want to come and help me?" She nodded and he put her down, then held her hand as they went out to the kitchen.

They found the liquor and glasses and returned to the hall. Sally sobbed and ran crying to Lorna's arms.

"Grandmo-o-other! Mama . . . Mama . . ."

"Hush now, child. I know. I know." Lorna held the child and cried with her.

Josiah poured the drinks. He set Lorna's aside. Emmy sipped her brandy then stirred restlessly. "I'll go help Dorcas now," she murmured. Lorna started to put Sally down, but Emmy stopped her. "We can manage, Mother. I don't think you want to see her yet. You stay here. We'll call you." She opened the bedroom door a sliver, passed through, and closed the door behind her before anyone could blink.

Josiah went into the other room, the former parlor, to fetch chairs for himself and Creed. Sally nestled on Lorna's lap, her cheek lying against her grandmother's bosom. She no longer cried, nor did Lorna. In the quiet Josiah heard the faint hiss of the two lamps burning, turned low, and the clicks and pings as moths collided with the glass chimneys and the occasional sizzle as one found its way into the flame.

The wordless silence became unbearable. They squirmed, wiped the tears from their cheeks, shifted in their seats. Finally, Creed said, "Son, there's things we need to do."

Josiah nodded. He remained quiet for a few moments, then said, "Yes. With the heat we'll have to hurry. I'll put Samson to digging at first light."

Lorna whimpered.

219

Josiah continued. "I'll ride over and get Preacher Thompson then. Mattie would want the preacher," Josiah added. Creed and Lorna nodded. "I'll stop by a few of the neighbors' places and let 'em know. The Pritchards and the Caruthers—Mattie set considerable store by Hetty Caruthers. Evie Jane Pritchard, too. Maybe the Wallers. I guess they can help get the word around."

"We need to build a casket, son," Creed said.

Lorna moaned.

Josiah nodded. "I started one already." He felt the blood rise in his face and his jaw tighten. "I knew we'd be needing one. I couldn't bear the thought of using the box Luke built."

Creed said, "When—"

"Where is Luke?" Lorna asked.

Josiah looked at Lorna, then at Creed. "The son of a bitch—your pardon, ma'am—has taken my team and my wagon and half my hogs and driven away with my blessing. Can you believe it? He's outraged and killed my wife, and I've sent him away with a sizeable part of what I own with my blessing. I'll just be damned."

Lorna gasped. "What?" Her mouth hung open as she stared at Josiah.

Creed breathed, "Oh my God." A protest, or a prayer. He stood. "Son Josiah, I think you and I better step outside and have a talk." He touched Josiah's arm and waited. Josiah unfolded from his chair in slow motion. They headed for the back door. Lorna stared open-mouthed as they left the house.

Chapter 31

Creed and Josiah walked out into the night, beyond the chicken coop where their passing disturbed an old biddy enough to cause her to shift on her nest and cluck in alarm.

"You want to tell me what you were talking about back there?" Creed asked.

"I do. But I need to get it straight in my head first."

"You do that."

They trudged on in silence. Creed shuddered as they entered the barn. Josiah led the way into the center of the hall, and then he put a hand on Creed's shoulder and turned him so they were face to face. Josiah drew a deep breath. As his eyes adjusted to the dark, he saw Creed's pained and doubting expression. He forcefully blew out a pent breath and said, "It happened right here."

"I know. It hurts me to think about it."

Josiah nodded. "There's a heap you don't know."

"Maybe so."

"They argued, him and Mattie. Right here. I don't know what about, maybe about the farm."

"Who?"

"Luke. Luke and Mattie argued and Luke went wild. He hit her. Beat her. Held her mouth to stop her screams and beat her. Hard."

"Not Luke."

"Yes, Luke. And he didn't stop with beating. He ripped up

221

her skirt and raped her. And beat her again, probably kicked her. Left her for dead."

"My God."

"When Sally raised the alarm, he came back to finish the job, only Sally and Emmy got there too quick." Josiah took a steadying breath and continued, "So, cool as spring water, he picked her up and carried her to the house and said maybe the cow trampled Mattie. Or maybe she fell from the loft."

"But the stranger—"

"Oh, he latched right onto that story as soon as Jim mentioned seeing a drifter. Gathered the neighbors and went tearing after the poor son of a bitch."

Creed, open-mouthed, shook his head but said nothing.

"I think Emmy had it figured out, or part of it anyway, but she never let on. At least not to me. If she let on to Luke, he must've persuaded her to keep quiet, probably with his fists. I came home and he kept coolheaded, as prickly and ornery as ever, but no more so. Just acted normal. He must've been kind of worried when Mattie roused up enough to talk. I caught him standing in her doorway, studying her, but he didn't do anything. Mattie was scared, but I was too blind to figure out she feared Luke. She never told, though. Never named him.

"Then I got worried about not having any money and owing Doc Wilson so much, and I wanted to sell some hogs. Luke played his part well—first objecting, then going along with the plan, then volunteering to take the hogs to market so's I could stay with Mattie. I shook the bastard's hand and sent him off with my good wishes. Don't that beat all?"

Josiah slammed his fist into a stall door, then grasped his injured hand and groaned.

"You all right, son?"

"Yeah. I'm all right."

"You don't sound all right. This tale—Josiah, it's hard to credit."

Josiah snorted. "I know. But it's true. And I sent him off with a handshake. I don't know if he has the balls to come back. He doesn't know I know, but he's got to fear that I'll eventually

222

figure it out. He's had more than enough time to take those hogs to Sand Springs and get back home. I think he's run."

They stood in silence for a few moments.

Creed rubbed his forehead, shook his head. "Josiah, I know you're upset and grieving. Maybe you need to blame somebody for our troubles. But Luke? I know Dorcas and Samson say Luke's a harsh and violent man, but this? No, I can't credit it. He's my son-in-law, too. I've known him a long time, trusted my daughter to him—well, two of 'em, really—"

"We all trusted him. He's betrayed our trust in the worst way possible."

"What makes you so damned sure Luke did it? How did you come by this wild tale? Did Mattie rouse enough to tell you before she passed? I know Samson and Dorcas said he hit Emmy, but it's a long leap from that to this."

"Sally told me. She saw them in here, heard everything."

As he uttered the last word sobs overtook him. In the dark, in the barn where it had happened, he broke down and wept. He appreciated the darkness. He didn't want Creed to see, wished he couldn't hear. He felt Creed's hands grasp his shoulders and pull him close. He cursed his weakness until he regained control.

As Josiah quieted, Creed gave him a firm squeeze, then released him. He pulled a handkerchief from his pocket and wiped his own eyes, then blew his nose. "This is a hard thing to bear," Creed said. "A hard thing." Josiah nodded. After a pause, McLain went on. "Sally's just a child. Children . . . get confused, don't understand what they see and hear sometimes. Or make things up. You think she could've made this up?"

Josiah shook his head. "No. She didn't make it up. To her it was her mama and Uncle Luke had a bad argument that scared her. She hid and heard the rest. She's too young to understand all of what she was describing, but it was a beating and a rape." He sighed wearily and continued. "And you know, when she raised the alarm and Luke got to the barn before her and Emmy? She says he had his hands on Mattie's throat. He turned loose when they ran up."

He caught his breath, then repeated, "No. Sally didn't make it up."

Creed drew a shaky breath. "All right. I believe you. But what do you want to do? This is a terrible shame upon this family. Terrible. Lorna and me, I reckon we could live with it being known. But it would dishonor Mattie's memory. And what about Sally? And Emmy? And Emmy's children? A thing like this could follow them all their lives."

"I know. But we have to do something."

"There isn't any law to turn to, not now—except those overbearing Yankees. I'll be damned if I'd turn a thing like this over to them and watch them snigger and gloat. We need to keep this within our family. It needs to be our secret."

"I agree. I can't see any way this was Mattie's fault, but there's those who would whisper behind our backs that she must've done something to cause it. It would dishonor her memory. But I don't want to let it go either. Do you?"

Creed remained silent for a while, then said, "No. I can't let it go." He paused, and Josiah heard the rustle as he ran his hand over his bearded jaw. "But I'm having a hard time sorting out what to do. If we go after Luke, make him pay, we'll widow Emmy and orphan her three. That's not right either, Josiah. There's no right way to end this. We have to make a devil's choice."

Josiah heard Creed's frustration and confusion and knew it matched his own. But Creed didn't know the whole story yet. He sighed, then plunged ahead. "There's something else. Mattie was selfless. She never would've told on Luke. Probably not so much because she wanted to protect him, but because she didn't want to injure Emmy and her children. After Sally told me, I was furious, so bent on revenge—I told Mattie I meant to kill Luke. She . . . she used almost her dying words to beg me not to. Begged me to forgive him. My God, I wanted to kill the bastard, but Mattie was so upset . . . I promised I would *try* to forgive." He hesitated before asking, "Am I bound by my promise? How hard do I have to try?"

"You promised her on her deathbed." Not quite a statement, not quite a question.

"I did. And Emmy and Dorcas witnessed it."

"You promised you wouldn't take vengeance on Luke?"

"No, that's not what I promised. I promised to try to forgive him. I don't know what Mattie thought I promised. Emmy heard it as a promise to spare Luke, but it wasn't, not in my mind."

"Have you tried to forgive him?"

"Yes." Pause. "No. Hell, Creed, I don't want to forgive him! After what he did?" He moaned and continued. "The promise I made to Mattie isn't the only problem, either. I promised Sally I wouldn't tell that she had told me what happened. I promised I would protect her. And I sort of told her I would punish Luke. Then, damn me to hell, I turned right around and told I knew Luke did it because Sally had told me. Right there in front of Emmy. I might as well have shouted it to Luke's face. Creed, I broke one of those promises to my baby, broke it almost as soon as I made it. And I'm sure I've put her in danger, especially if we don't—"

"Wait. You don't think Emmy would turn on the child? She must be mortified by all of this. After what he's done to her sister, she surely can't be taking Luke's part?"

Josiah snorted. "There's nothing sure in this world, Creed. Nothing."

"She's taking his part?" Creed's mouth dropped open.

"Yep. I don't understand it, but she is." Josiah sighed. "It's hard to credit, but maybe Mattie really forgave Luke and wanted me to forgive him, too. Part of her Christian faith, I guess, though it's hard to see how she could really take it so far. And she was really worried about Emmy and her children. But I don't understand Emmy at all. It's like she can't see what a low-down piece of shit Luke is. She won't admit she believes he did it. It's like she wants to protect him."

Creed groaned. "Then Sally may really be in danger. You owe a greater debt to the living than to the dead. God help us all."

Josiah drew a deep breath and blew it out again. "Amen. I've gone and said too much to too many. I can't unsay what I've said, and I can't keep all the promises I've made. It hurts to break a vow to Mattie, but I've got to protect Sally. Mattie'd want me to take care of Sally above all else."

He fought back tears. Eventually he continued. "I'm so tired

225

of fighting and killing. I thought I had put all that behind me. But ever since I got home and found Mattie'd been attacked I've flopped back and forth like a fish dragged up on the bank—hating the man who hurt her, wanting to track him down, but not knowing whether I could kill him if I found him.

"In the war I probably killed several men. Mostly it didn't bother me very much. But there was one .... Up close. Wounded. Unarmed. Maybe I didn't have to kill him, but I did. It's been bothering me ever since. So I didn't know if I could do it again—kill a man up close and watch him die."

"That would be a hard thing."

Josiah nodded. "Then Mattie wanted me to let it go, to forgive, and I promised her I would try. It seemed possible—not easy, but possible—before I knew it was Luke attacked her. But now ... Mattie's last hours—they were horrible. She suffered more than you can imagine. I'll make Luke pay with his life. I hate him. For what he did to Mattie, for what he might do to Sally, for what he's done to Emmy, to us all. No matter what it costs me, I'm going to kill him."

Creed reached out, put his hand on Josiah's arm. "Son, this kind of hate ... You're risking hellfire. I hate what he's done, too, but if he's run, maybe we should let him go. If he comes back, well ... we could run him off. We can protect Sally till he's gone. He's always seemed a good man. He must be ashamed. Surely, given the chance, he'll go away and we'll never see him again."

"There's nothing sure in this world. Remember?"

Creed sighed. "That's what you say."

"I know what this might cost me—my life, maybe even my soul. And I'll admit there's some complications. But I know what I'm going to do. I'm going to go after the son of a bitch. I'm going to kill him. I'm not going to let him walk away, free and easy, after what he's done. If I get caught I may hang for murder. So be it."

"It'll be dangerous."

"I'm not asking you to go with me, to be involved. I'd like to think I can depend on you to stay here, take Sally in and care for her until I've done what I need to do and get set somewhere so's

226

I can take her back. And if I can't return . . . You'll give her a good raising, won't you?"

"Of course we'll see to her. But . . ."

Josiah found Creed's hand and shook it, closing the bargain before Creed could raise objections.

Creed heaved a heavy sigh. "Son, you're putting me in a ticklish situation. From what you say, Emmy's going to be mighty unhappy. And taking care of my own means taking care of her, too."

"You'll find a way to handle her, and Emmy'll settle down, get used to it by-and-by. I reckon she won't ever forgive me. I guess I wouldn't expect her to." Josiah lapsed into silence. Then he added, "I'll write you out a deed to this place. I'll trust you to do with it what's right. If I come back and can live in this neighborhood again, you can hand it back to me. If I don't, you can use it for the support of Sally and Emmy and hers. You'll just have to do what you think right, what you're able. That all right with you?"

Josiah could hear Creed breathing, imagine him thinking.

Finally Creed replied, "I can hold your deed. I commend your willingness to put it in my hand. But Josiah, you must understand—your farm doesn't guarantee Sally's support, not the way things are now with the hands and the crops and the taxes. I don't know how it's all going to work out, this occupation, the do-gooders and the no-gooders."

"I know. But it's all I have to give. I hope it truly will help support Sally. And that it's not too much burden on you."

"Then that's the way I'll accept it. And I pray you'll be back to see to it yourself."

"I thank you, Creed. You take care of my baby."

"You're not leaving right now, are you?" Creed asked.

"Oh, hell no. You and I are agreed we need to keep this within our family. I owe Mattie a proper funeral. I have to do what all a widower has to do, else you have to make some sort of explanation to the neighbors. Tongues would get to wagging. No, I'll see Mattie gets a proper burial, then I'll slip off. We won't mention what I'm going to do, not even within the family. You'll explain to Mother Lorna how we need to keep the whole mess

227

quiet. I'll talk to Sally. I trust you'll be able to keep Emmy quiet after I go and she figures out what's happening. It's her shame. She shouldn't want it known."

"All right. We'll do the best we can to keep it normal and quiet." Creed sighed and scuffed his boot against the dirt before he added, "I expect we should be getting on back to the house. There's the watching to do."

"You go back. I'm going to work on the casket."

Chapter 32

As he entered the house near midnight, Josiah heard a child crying upstairs. Emmy emerged from the open bedroom and passed him without speaking as she went to the stairs. No one remained in the hall. He entered the bedroom.

Mattie lay on the bed, clean, combed, dressed in a dated but presentable blue dress. Dorcas and Emmy had done their best, but there had been no way to make her look peaceful. Her bruises showed and the lumpy swellings distorted her features. The splint had been removed from the right arm which looked only slightly off-kilter where her hands crossed on her chest. Lorna sat on the far side of the bed, holding Sally in her lap. The child looked tired but kept her eyes open. Creed sat near the door.

Josiah nodded at Dorcas who sat beside Lorna. "You did well. She would be pleased," he told her.

"Yessuh. We tried. At least she have some little bit of peace now."

He swallowed hard and bobbed his head in agreement. He pulled a chair around to sit beside Creed. "It's finished," he said.

Creed nodded. "You worked fast."

"I already had the boards cut," Josiah said. He sighed. "I believe I could use another shot of whiskey. How about you?"

Creed nodded. "I believe I could."

Josiah asked if Lorna would like more brandy. She declined. Josiah left. He returned shortly with the whiskey jug, placed it on the bedside table. He went back into the hall and returned with the glasses. He poured the whiskey, handed one of the glasses to Creed.

And there they all sat, wrapped in the silence again. Flies buzzed, enlivened by the lamplight. Dorcas discreetly brushed two of the bothersome pests away from Mattie's nose. The mugginess of the room made them all sweat, and the odor of hot bodies filled the air. An owl called far out in the night. They looked at each other. Josiah saw traces of his own fears mirrored. He heard Emmy moving around in the attic. When she rejoined them, she said Callie Belle seemed better.

Eventually Lorna began to nod off. Sally's eyes were closing. She'd jerk them open, and they would slowly close again, fluttering, fighting sleep. Creed's head had fallen onto his chest and he snored lightly. Dorcas sat straight and alert, as did Josiah. The clock began to strike. Josiah couldn't make out the hands in the heavy shadow, but he counted. Midnight. He stirred and cleared his throat.

"There's not any need for all of us to watch. Dorcas, you go on to bed. Get up and start breakfast at daybreak. Tell Samson to come up here to the house when you come to the kitchen. I'll be wanting him to start the grave."

"Yessuh. If you're sure y'all be all right here. I can stay, you know. I wouldn't mind at all."

Josiah nodded. "We'll be fine. We'll need you in the morning. You go on and rest now." She rose and tenderly rearranged a tendril of Mattie's hair before she left the room.

Josiah continued, "Mother Lorna, I can see you're about done in. Creed, too. Why don't y'all go get some rest in the other room?"

"Oh, I couldn't . . ." Lorna began to protest, but Emmy interrupted, "Yes, Mother. You can use my bed. I insist."

"Well, I am tired, but what about this baby?"

"I'll take her upstairs," Josiah volunteered. "That is, if Emmy will stay here and watch for a few minutes."

"Of course," agreed Emmy, but she eyed him warily.

He added, before any of them had yet moved, "And Emmy, I know you're exhausted. As soon as I get back downstairs, you go on and find a place to rest. There's nothing to be done now but

230

stand watch, and it won't take both of us to do that. I'll stay awake. You go on."

Emmy cut her eyes up at him, frowned, then stared straight ahead. "I'll stay up. Luke . . ."

"He's not likely to be coming back this late, Emmy. You go on and get some rest," Josiah said.

Emmy drew herself up, seemed about to continue her protest, but then she sighed and sagged. "All right, if you're sure you can watch alone. I'll take a quilt and make a pallet in the attic. I can keep an eye on Callie Belle,"

"This'll be best for us all." Josiah stood and took Sally from Lorna. Sally fluttered her eyes open and he whispered, "Go back to sleep. I'm going to take you upstairs to your bed." She relaxed against his shoulder as he carried her out of the room.

Lorna rose, creakily, arched her back and stretched. Then she came over to Creed and gently shook him. "Wake up and come to bed," she said.

He awoke with a start. "I wasn't asleep," he protested as he got up. They moved across the hall, leaning against each other.

*   *   *

When everyone had gone, Emmy opened the linen cupboard and retrieved a quilt, the same one she had offered to Josiah the night he had arrived home. She could hear him in the loft as he laid Sally in her bed. She could understand his fury, but she couldn't let him go after Luke, couldn't let him kill her husband. And she couldn't let Luke come driving back home to meet Josiah's wrath. What was she to do? And what if Luke never came home? How could she live?

If Luke didn't come back, Josiah would go out looking for him, as sure as the sun would rise in the east. He wouldn't honor his promise to Mattie. Men never kept their promises, not the ones they made to women. A distasteful frown settled on her features as his footsteps clattered down the stairs. When he entered the room she was already walking out with the quilt. "Don't go to sleep, Josiah," she said as they passed each other.

*   *   *

231

Josiah paced about the room. Mixed with his own footsteps he heard the rustles, splashes, grunts, mumbles of a household settling for the remainder of the night. Or maybe not settling—the noises continued long after he expected them to cease. He was sure everyone ached with exhaustion, but tension and grief haunted them. Sleep would come slowly for some and not be peaceful when it did. Quiet finally came, only occasionally interrupted by a complaining bed rope or mattress as someone tossed, trying to find comfort where little existed.

A distant rumble broke the stillness. He went to a window, pulled back the curtain. No breeze stirred. Far in the distance the sky lit briefly, diffusely. Lightning. Half a minute later he heard the rumble, faint, drawn out. He dropped the curtain and walked slowly to the bed.

He stood and stared—he didn't know how long—stared at Mattie's corpse. He tried to think back on the life they'd had together, but he couldn't organize any thoughts, couldn't even call up any definite memories. The corpse only vaguely resembled the Mattie he remembered from their good times. The clock struck twice—two o'clock—enough noise to get his attention. He noticed flies had gathered on Mattie's face. He brushed them away. Stirred to action, he walked over to his desk and once again prepared to write.

Dipping his quill in the ink, he frowned and bit his lower lip. He didn't know the exact form the document should take. It wasn't exactly a bill of sale, but was there such a thing as a "bill of gift?" He needed to convey his farm to Creed McLain so that, if and when he needed to, Creed could take the document to the courthouse and record his ownership. He drew a deep breath and began to write:

27 August 1865

I, Josiah Robertson of Red Lick, give for love and affection to my father-in-law, Creed McLain, also of Red Lick, my farm consisting of one hundred and sixty acres and the buildings and improvements upon it. It is his to do with as he wishes, without encumbrance, save he should

232

provide for my daughter, Sarah Catherine Robertson, as long as she has need and he is able.

He started to sign it, but stopped when he realized he should have witnesses. He didn't want to divulge the contents to any of his neighbors. No problem—only his signature had to be witnessed. He folded the document to conceal the message, leaving the space for his signature and those of the witnesses visible. He put it in one of the small drawers in the center of the desk. There should be several neighbors at the funeral. He would ask two or three of them to witness his signing.

He stood, massaged the back of his neck. He wandered around the room, brushed the flies off Mattie, peeked out the window. The lightning continued to flash far away. A slight breeze fluttered the curtains and brought a welcome breath of freshness to the room. A rooster crowed. He looked at the clock, couldn't make it out from where he stood. Couldn't remember when it had last struck, or how many times. He walked over to it, peered closely. Two forty-five. The rooster must be in a hurry to start this day.

One of the children upstairs cried out once. He thought about Sally. What if, when he faced Luke, he came out the loser? Or what if he killed Luke but got caught? If he was lucky, there'd be a trial. His actions ought to be seen as justified, but they might not be. He might be hanged. What would Sally think about her Daddy? Would she know he loved her, had done his best to protect her?

He returned to the desk and took out paper and pen and ink again. He began to write, hesitating and struggling to find the words.

My dear daughter Sally,

I love you very much. Always remember that. I said I would protect you, and I am trying my best to do so. What Luke did was evil, something no man should do to any woman. The Bible says 'an eye for an eye,' and I believe that is right. I intend to take his life like he took your mama's,

233

before he can hurt you. But that means I must be gone for a while. Grandmother and Grandfather will take you home with them and they will take care of you until I return. Be a good girl and mind them and help them all you can.

I do not know how this will end. It is possible I will have to search a long time for Luke. It is possible he will defeat me when I find him. When it is over, I may not be able to come back here, but if I live I will want you with me. I will find a safe place for us, but it may take some time. Be patient, Sally. I love you very much. If there is any way in the world to do it, I will be back for you.

With all my love,
Daddy

He folded the letter and wrote "Sarah Catherine Robertson" on the front. He sealed it and placed it in the drawer with the other document.

He heard shuffling footfalls and a board creaking. The faint light at the windows had not yet begun to turn pink. He went to the rear window and took a cautious look outside, half expecting to see Luke, but it was Samson who stood on the porch looking as if he couldn't decide whether to knock at the door. Josiah stuck his head out, breathed deeply and appreciatively of the fresh morning air, and called softly, "Samson."

"Yessuh. I be right here," came the reply, muzzy with sleep.

"Come on into the house. I need to talk to you."

"Yessuh." In a moment, Samson knocked softly on the bedroom doorframe.

"Come on in."

Samson stepped into the room. He stared at Mattie's corpse as he sidled his way through the room to Josiah. "Poor Miss Mattie," he whispered. "That poor, poor lady. She's gone to glory, but she sure had a rough passage. I'm so sorry, Mistuh Josiah. So sorry."

"Thank you, Samson. I know you are. Mattie cared deeply for you and Dorcas, and I think y'all thought highly of her."

"Yessuh. We did. She was a fine lady. She sure was."

Josiah nodded. "Samson, I need you to dig her grave. As soon's somebody else stirs and can spell me here, I'll show you where. I want to leave a space beside Pa for me, and then Mattie next to me."

"Yessuh, I think I know where you mean, but I guess it'd be better if you's to show me. Uh . . . what about a coffin?

"I finished it about midnight. I left it out in the shed."

Samson rolled his eyes. "I thought maybe I seen one out there yesterday."

"That's one Luke built."

"Oh, Lordy! Why Mistuh Luke want to go and bring on bad luck by having such as that around?"

"It's only a wooden box Luke built to store stuff he didn't want Yankee soldiers to find." Josiah stopped before he ran on and said Luke had killed Mattie. He didn't want that noised about. And then he realized Samson already knew. Dorcas knew. She would've told him. He continued, "I guess you know what we've found out. That Luke? . . . "

Samson nodded.

"Mister Creed and I, well, we don't want it to get around to the whole world. Can I depend on you and Dorcas to keep it quiet?"

"Yessuh, you can depend on me. And you can depend on Dorcas. The woman don't never gossip. I reckon she knows more about what goes on in these parts than just about anybody, but she don't never talk about it. She's like an ol' dry biscuit sopping up gravy—she soak up all the gossip gravy, she don't let none of it drip out. 'Bout drives Mamie crazy. Every now and then she tells me something, but I don't never pass it on, no suh."

"Good. You go tell her to keep those goings on to herself like she always does. And tell her to give you some breakfast soon's she can, so's you can get to the digging before the heat of the day."

"Yessuh." Samson said and quietly left the room.

Soon bumps and thumps over his head announced that

Emmy and the children had wakened. Creaking and rustling from the other room prefaced Lorna's appearance in the doorway. "You watched all night?" she asked. "There's been no sign of Luke?"

Josiah shook his head. "No, there's been no sign of him. He had plenty of time to get home yesterday. Maybe his nerve has failed him and he's started to run. It can't have been easy keeping up a normal, innocent front. I'm surprised he didn't run before I got home. He knew I was coming, that it would be only a matter of time till I got here. Maybe he thought something would happen to me, delay me. Maybe he thought Mattie would die quickly and there would be no way for me to find out about his guilt."

"I don't understand," Lorna said. "How can you and Sally accuse Luke of attacking Mattie? That can't be, Josiah. Luke may have some bit of a mean streak, but he wouldn't do anything so awful."

"Oh, it's true all right. It's not just an accusation—Sally was a witness. Emmy doesn't want it to be true—none of us do—but it is."

Lorna's hand flew to her lips. "Oh, dear. Whatever shall we do?"

"I don't know," he lied.

With a sigh, she said, "What a sad day for this family. For you. And you sat here alone with her all night?"

"Yes. I had some thinking to do. And some writing. And I've got to take care of several things this morning, so if you could watch now to spell me, I'd be much obliged."

"Of course. Is Emmy up yet? How's Callie Belle this morning?"

"I think I heard Emmy stirring, but I haven't seen her. I haven't heard any of the children crying, so I guess there's nothing too bad wrong up there."

Lorna gazed at Mattie, then walked to the window, pulled back the curtain, peeped out. "Looks like it's going to be a clear morning. That's some blessing. I thought I heard Samson?"

"Yes. I had him come in so I could talk to him. I want him to dig Mattie's grave. If you can stay here, I'll go show him where I want it."

Lorna's face crumpled and her lower lip quivered. She wordlessly waved him on his way.

Chapter 33

Josiah found Samson in the kitchen, sitting at the table, watching Dorcas prepare breakfast. He got up so quickly he almost knocked over the chair. Under the aroma of coffee boiling and sidemeat frying the baking cornbread produced only a hint of scent.

"How long, Dorcas?" Josiah asked.

"Oh, it be a spell yet. Oven's not been hot long."

"Well, then, you come on with me, Samson. We'll tend to a couple of things before breakfast."

They strode toward the shed, but as they neared it Samson hung back, eying the coffin-shaped boxes—the one set on two sawhorses and the one resting in the rafters.

"Mistuh Josiah . . . " he began but then trailed off.

"What?"

"That be bad luck, Mr. Luke keeping that there."

Josiah gave him a sharp look. "I guess I can't argue with that," he said. "We'll leave it to be his bad luck. He comes back here, we'll plant him in it."

"Yessuh." The corners of Samson's mouth turned up.

"Let's go. I'll show you where I want you to dig Mattie's grave," Josiah said.

The burying ground lay only a short way beyond the shed, a small plot with an unpainted picket fence and gate, partially overhung by a large chestnut tree. The small cedars near the heads of Josiah's ma and pa had grown considerably since he had

238

set them, and their clean pleasant scent seemed an affirmation comforting him against his doubts. Josiah felt at home here in this peaceful family place.

"Dig it here," Josiah said as he pointed out where the grave should be placed. He marked it with a few small stones.

"Yessuh. I knowed that's where you meant. Right after I get me a bite to eat I be out here digging. I'll make Miss Mattie a good place to rest."

They returned to the house to find breakfast ready. Dorcas filled a plate for Samson and he took it to the porch to eat. Josiah sat at the table and forced some of the food down. It would be a long day, a hard day. He recognized he needed sustenance even though he had no appetite. All of the family except Emmy had gathered, even Callie Belle. "How're you feeling this morning, Callie?" he inquired.

She glanced up, then back down again. "I'm all right, sir."

Josiah nodded and sopped the remaining egg yolk and grease on his plate with a piece of cornbread. He finished his coffee and said to Sally, "I'll walk you to the barn for the milking. I have to saddle Pepper and go to see some people."

Her eyes brightened. "Can I go with you, Daddy?"

"On Pepper? No. But we can go to the barn together."

Sally gulped down the rest of her buttermilk, then rose and scraped the few crumbs from her plate and Josiah's into the slop bucket. She hurriedly grabbed the milk pail as Josiah got up and moved toward the door. She caught up to him on the porch. He stood beside Samson who held a tin plate that looked perfectly clean, except for a slight greasy sheen when it caught the light a certain way. No leavings for the pigs there.

"Take Samson's plate back into the kitchen. I'll wait for you," Josiah told her.

When she returned, Samson was already on his way across the farmyard, heading toward the toolshed. Josiah had waited, as he had promised. They stepped off the porch together.

"Sally, I need to talk to you. About what happened to Mama. And about Luke."

"I don't want to talk about that anymore." She cringed away

239

from him as though she expected a blow. Her lower lip jutted. "You said you wouldn't tell on me."

"I didn't tell him," Josiah protested. "He hasn't been around here since you told me."

"I know. But Daddy, you told everybody else, and that's the same as. If he comes back, he'll know! Why'd you go and tell everybody?"

"Sally, I had to . . ."

But he knew better. He hadn't really needed to tell Mattie, upset her last few conscious minutes, let Emmy overhear.

He spoke again. "I had reasons to tell Grandfather. And I felt like it was important for me to tell Mama, so she could tell you it wasn't your fault. But maybe I should've waited till Emmy wasn't around . . . ." He trailed off in a guilty mumble.

"He'll know!"

"That's part of what I need to talk to you about. He left here yesterday morning to take those hogs to market not knowing you'd seen what he did. He should've been back by now. I suspect he's gotten nervous and finally decided to run. But I don't know that. He might be coming back. And if he comes back, he'll know you told." He looked away from her, then looked back with his face grimly set. "As soon as the funeral's over, I aim to make sure he can't come back, ever. Do you understand?"

Sally watched him, her eyes wide. She nodded.

He continued. "But it's better not to let Aunt Emmy know. And it'd be better if nobody else knows, either."

Sally nodded again.

"In fact, it's better if nobody outside our family knows about what Luke did, and what I'm planning to do. It needs to be our secret, something just you and I know. You kept your secret real good, until you told me. Now I want you to keep it again. From everybody. Forever. Can you do that?"

Sally whispered, "From everybody?"

"Everybody. Except maybe Grandfather."

"Why would I want to tell Grandfather? I don't want to talk to him. He smells like tobacco spit." Her indignant huff softened

240

as she continued, "But I want to tell Squeaky. I tell him lots of things."

"All right. Tell Squeaky. He can't tell anybody else. But be sure no one hears you tell Squeaky. If something happens so I'm not around to . . . If you have questions and I'm not around, I think you should talk to Grandfather. In private. Do you know what that means?"

"Just me and Grandfather?"

"Yep. Just you and Grandfather. Even if he does smell like tobacco spit."

They had reached the barn. No one had been out to feed yet. Josiah went into the loft and tossed hay into the cow's manger, then into the mangers for the horses and mules. Sally began to milk. Josiah combed and saddled Pepper. "Sally, I have to fetch Preacher Thompson. I'll be back in a while," he called as he mounted and put his heels to the roan's flanks.

He rode at an easy lope into Red Lick to tell Doc Wilson of Mattie's passing and to arrange for Caleb Thompson to conduct the funeral service early in the afternoon. Before returning home he rode by to tell Hetty and Andy Jack Caruthers and Evie Jane and Lem Pritchard of the funeral arrangements. They all promised to spread the word and to be at Josiah's house for the funeral.

As soon as he got home, Josiah watered Pepper, fed him corn, and fastened him in his stall instead of turning him into the pasture. He took the time to check his saddle and all of the equipment he had left in the tack room when he first got home. He filled his grub pouch with meal and a sack with corn for Pepper.

He returned to the house where he found Dorcas in the kitchen. "In a little bit me and Creed will bring the coffin in. I want you to get a quilt and line it, so it'll be soft for Mattie. Tell Emmy you need a nice one. We don't want the neighbors saying we didn't send her off right."

"Yessuh. I'll see to it," she said.

In the little cemetery Josiah found Samson had almost finished the grave. Sweat and red mud streaked the black man's bare skin and clothing as he steadily shoveled dirt from the bottom of the hole. He stopped his work, leaned on his shovel, and gazed up at Josiah, then dragged his hand across his face and flicked away sweat.

"I'll help," Josiah said as he started to the shed for another shovel.

Both men dug, taking turns driving their shovels into the earth with grating "kuh-shunks" and tossing the loosened clods out onto the growing mound. They finished the grave by midmorning. They pulled themselves out of the pit, stretched and limbered their backs and then placed one shovel discreetly behind the trunk of the chestnut. They carried the other shovel and the mattock back to the shed. They paused there beside the coffin. Samson nervously shifted from one foot to the other. "I'll go draw some water and wash this mud off," he said.

"Go on," Josiah said. Samson hurried to the well as though he were glad to put distance between himself and the coffin. Josiah looked at his own dirty arms and clothes. He remained staring at the box. He hoped Mattie wouldn't be too unhappy with it. It's the best I can do, he told himself, but deep down he knew if the heat weren't driving him so hard he could have built her a nicer casket. He followed Samson to the well and sloshed off, then went to the washbench on the porch and did a more thorough job before changing clothes for the funeral.

Chapter 34

Several horses and mules stamped and swished flies as they stood tied to the porch posts and the trees in the yard. Their saddles and harnesses creaked and clinked. The low hum of voices floated from the house. The community had come together to bid Mattie farewell.

Josiah went in and shook hands all around, nodding and murmuring responses as ineffectual as the condolences the neighbors offered, but that didn't matter—the intentions to solace and be solaced were genuine, even if the forms were worn. Preacher Thompson and his wife had arrived, along with everyone he had notified, and several more neighbors besides. The women wore their Sunday dresses. The men wore their suits, including their coats, although few of them wore collars. Everyone sweated. People sat in the bedroom, and the hall, and the former parlor. The odor of hot bodies filled the house.

Dorcas caught Josiah's eye and motioned for him to slip out for a moment. "The coffin be all right, I reckon," she said softly. "I put a quilt in it and I cut a little spray of rosemary and sage to put in her hands. That all right with you?"

"Yes. I thank you. That was a good idea. It's half past noon. I think we ought to proceed now, don't you? Has anybody mentioned somebody else coming who hasn't got here yet?"

"No suh, not that I knows about."

Josiah returned to the others and found Creed and Lorna, then Emmy, then Thompson, and suggested they get on with it.

Creed and Josiah slipped out to get the coffin while Thompson led a prayer and then marshaled the group outside so the family would have some privacy. Creed and Josiah returned with the coffin and placed it on the seats of two straight chairs. Dorcas arranged the quilt so it would lie beneath the body but could be wrapped back over Mattie. They lifted Mattie's stiffened body into the box. Emmy and Lorna straightened her dress and refolded her hands upon her breast. Dorcas placed the spray of herbs, tied with a black ribbon, their leaves subtly crushed to release their powerful aroma. She stepped back and the family crowded around the coffin, holding each other, the women weeping, the men stoic.

"I can't bear this," moaned Lorna.

"You have to, my dear," replied Creed.

Dorcas withdrew to the kitchen, where Samson had already sought refuge.

Josiah stepped out on the front porch and called Sally, who stood outside the circle of children playing in the front yard. She came to him, her head bowed and her feet scuffing the dirt.

"Do you want to see Mama? We have to go ahead with the burying soon. There's only this one last chance."

She shook her head. "No. I don't want to see Mama dead any more. You know I don't."

Emmy had quietly slipped out to stand beside Josiah. "Nonsense! You must tell your Mama good-by."

"No-o-o-o."

"Go back inside, Emmy Louise. Now."

Emmy winced at the harshness of his tone, and anger flashed from her eyes as she whirled and re-entered the house. He watched her go, then turned again to Sally.

"It's all right. I understand. You don't have to come and look. She doesn't look like herself, anyhow. And I don't see any need for you children to go to the graveside, either. Y'all keep on playing but don't be noisy. Dorcas will call you to dinner soon." He hugged the child and kissed her, then patted her behind as he gently pushed her away. She swiped at the tears staining her face and trudged back toward her playmates.

Josiah signaled for Thompson to bring the others back in for a final viewing. The neighbors filed past. Emmy and Lorna drew the quilt up around Mattie. Josiah and Creed fitted the lid on the box, and Josiah nailed it into place. Josiah, Creed, and four other men hefted the box and walked slowly toward the little cemetery. Emmy and Lorna followed, and the friends and neighbors. The preacher preached. They sang a hymn. The pallbearers slipped ropes under the coffin and lowered it into the grave, and the family crumbled symbolic clods onto it. They all turned away, except Samson, who had stood to the side with Dorcas during the ceremony. Now he went to the chestnut and retrieved his shovel.

Josiah hardly noticed any of the funeral activity. His mind had frozen at the point when he helped lift Mattie into the coffin. He went through the motions, but his surroundings, the burial service, the gathering of friends and neighbors floated past him like wisps of morning fog, making no impression and quickly drifting away in the heat of the day without leaving a trace.

At last he became aware that his feet were moving, that he was walking back toward the house, surrounded by the others who talked among themselves. He found himself between Creed and Andy Jack Caruthers. The rest of the group coalesced and milled about near the rear of the house, at first a mixed group, men and women. Then the women disappeared into the kitchen to put out a spread of the foods they had brought.

Josiah turned to Andy Jack and said, "There's something I need to sign. I need a witness. Would you?"

"Be glad to."

They made their way onto the back porch where Caleb Thompson stood with two other men. Josiah stopped and asked him also to be a witness. Thompson nodded and fell in with Josiah and Andy Jack. The two men who had been standing with Thompson stared after them, looking as though they were eaten by curiosity but polite enough to hold back.

The three entered the bedroom. Josiah retrieved the document from the desk, folded as he had left it so only the space for signatures showed. As both men watched, he signed and added the date. Each man took the pen in turn and signed his own name, followed by "witness."

"Thank you, Brother Thompson, Andy Jack. I do appreciate

this. I'll seal this now. Y'all better go see about the food the ladies are fixing. We'll be wanting you to ask a blessing, Brother Thompson."

Andy Jack left immediately, but Caleb Thompson tarried. "If there's anything else I can do, Josiah—"

"No, thank you. You've been a help and a comfort. There's nothing more I could ask of you," Josiah cut him off, aware of the other man's intense curiosity over the concealed contents of the document. Thompson left but craned his head back to try to see the paper, not once but twice as he walked out.

Josiah refolded the paper with its contents and the signatures to the inside. He sealed the packet and wrote "Creed McLain" on the outside. As soon as he could give this and the letter for Sally to Creed, he would be free to look for an opportune moment to slip away. He would have to wait until the neighbors had gone, though, or it would look strange and cause the tongues to wag.

He closed the desk and started to leave the room but hesitated. He stared at the bed for a while. The sheets had been smoothed and the counterpane drawn up, but in his mind he still saw Mattie's beaten body there. He heard people moving around in the house, and once someone started to come into this room but saw him, muttered a soft "oh," and turned away. He thought about his last words with Mattie. The promise she had extracted from him. Maybe she had been right, but he didn't think so. Right or wrong, he couldn't keep his promise.

"I'm sorry, Matilda Jane. For so much, I'm sorry," he whispered and turned away.

He circulated among funeral guests, thanked them for being there, shook hands, heard again and again the question, "How did it happen? I heard . . . but could that be?"

He answered, "We don't really know," wishing his words were as true as they had been a day ago.

Tongues did wag. Several asked after Luke. Josiah told them Luke had taken hogs to market and had not yet returned, didn't even know Mattie had taken a turn for the worse. Several of his acquaintances would piece together bits and pieces of the stories they had heard to fabricate possible explanations, then spread their speculations about until they took a life of their own and

246

became "facts." He hoped their "facts" wouldn't be as bad as the truth.

Gradually the neighbors left to tend to their own families and their own chores. The McLains, Emmy and her children, and Josiah and Sally remained, alone with their bereavement. Emmy and Lorna sat on the back porch, red-eyed, exhausted. Josiah and Creed walked around the farmyard with no real destination, idly discussing crops. Creed cut a plug of tobacco, offered it to Josiah. Josiah accepted, although he didn't much enjoy chewing. The mid afternoon sun pounded them, crushed the little energy they had remaining. In their distraction they had not thought to remove their coats when the last guest left, and now they sweltered and sweated in the heavy garments.

When they had walked beyond view from the back porch, Josiah fished the two documents from his pocket and handed them to Creed. "The one's to give you this farm, like I told you I would, for Sally's good, you know," he said. "The other's for Sally. I've talked to her about keeping her secret. And I've told her I would go after Luke if he didn't show up. But I didn't tell her when. It's going to be soon. Would you read this to her after I go?"

Creed took the proffered papers, flipped each of them over, read the names on each. He put them in his coat pocket.

"I will." He chewed and spat. "I wish you would think about this a little more. I have. There's no good way for this to end. Maybe he's gone for good. Maybe you should think about Emmy and her children. Let it go, after all. I know that doesn't give you any satisfaction. It doesn't give me any, either, but . . ."

"If he's gone for good, then what difference does it make? He won't be supporting his family, and him gone, any more than he will if I kill him. And the shame is in what's already done. I can't let it go. I can't. I'll be ashamed for the rest of my days if I don't avenge Mattie. And as long as he's alive, he's a threat to Sally. I have to make sure he can't hurt her."

Creed sighed. "I know."

They rambled on a while longer, circled the smithy, passed the toolshed, tramped around the garden, not talking much. As they came near the house again, Creed sighed again and said,

"Well, I reckon Lorna and me had better start on home so's we can make it by dark."

"I wish you wouldn't go yet. Stay the night. It'll be so lonely here. Emmy . . . Well, I probably won't be here. I don't think I'd be much company for her if I was. Y'all stay the night."

Emmy heard the last bit. "Oh, do. Please do. Don't go yet." Before she had finished she cut her reddened eyes warily from her father to Josiah.

Lorna joined in. "Creed, there's no reason for us to hurry home. Mamie and George will take care of our place."

Creed looked at his wife and daughter and accepted defeat.

They all sat on the porch and chatted idly, discussing nothing of consequence. After a while Josiah excused himself and withdrew to the bedroom. He removed his jacket, folded it. He checked his saddlebags and found his meager traveling supplies in good order. Head bowed, he stood leaning with one arm against the cupboard while he thought about how to slip away without giving Emmy any warning. He put the coat back on. He picked up the saddlebags, toted them hanging by his left side, put his hat on, and sauntered from the room.

On the porch as Emmy and Lorna discussed a new quilt pattern, Lorna's index finger traced figures in the air and Emmy watched with a puzzled frown. They paid little attention as he came out of the house. Creed turned to watch Josiah as he ambled onto the porch.

"I'm hungry. I think I'll grab a bite of whatever's left and then get to the chores," Josiah said.

Creed saw the saddlebags, knew their implication. He nodded and said, "I believe I'll have a bite, too."

As Josiah wolfed some beans from a pot, his eyes searched the kitchen for a sack or cloth he could use to wrap some of the food to take with him. He found a dishtowel, a little dirty, but usable. He wrapped several hunks of cornbread and two ears of roasted corn and a little bit of fried okra. No meat remained from the meal, and none of the other vegetables were packable. He stuffed the food package into one of the saddlebags. Creed munched a handful of fried okra, little crumbs of greasy cornmeal catching in his beard. Josiah took out his handkerchief and filled the center with coffee beans, then tied the corners into a pouch. That went into the saddlebag, too.

"I'll come help you with the chores, son," Creed offered, dusting off his hands.

Josiah shook his head. "I don't intend to do 'em now. After I've gone, see that Jim and Samson feed and water the stock and somebody milks the cow. For now, go on back to the porch and sit and pretend everything is fine. That way you won't have to admit you knew my plans."

Creed pursed his lips and studied Josiah. Finally he said, "All right." He shifted his weight from one foot to the other, then extended his hand. "I don't know if I should wish you good hunting, son, but I do wish you a safe return."

Josiah nodded as they shook. Then he clapped his father-in-law on the shoulder and walked away slowly as though he were off to the barn to do the chores. Pretty Girl slipped from beneath the porch and ran to catch up with him.

Creed came out right behind him and put the last piece of fried okra into his mouth as he walked heavily over to the ladies. "Good okra," he said as he licked the grease from his fingers and wiped his beard with the back of his hand. "Wonder who fixed it?" He kept their attention until Josiah had made his way almost to the barn. Neither of the women appeared to notice the saddlebags Josiah carried.

Josiah saddled Pepper and tied on his bedroll and the sack of corn for the horse. He removed his coat, folded and rolled it, and tied it on, too. He placed the saddlebags and swung up onto the horse. Pepper danced a couple of quick steps. Josiah pulled him back and guided him at an easy walk, staying on grass or soft dirt so they made little sound. They headed toward the side of the farmyard and kept the outbuildings between them and the back porch. Pretty Girl trotted along with them, sniffing at interesting odors on first one side of their path and then the other. Josiah intended to ride out the lane between the cotton and the corn, then cut over and pick up the road.

*   *   *

Emmy listened to Lorna's description of the quilt pattern

without really comprehending it. Out of the corner of her eye she caught a motion beyond the smithy. Focusing, she saw Josiah, mounted, his saddle laden for travel. Emitting a wordless, howling screech, she flew into the house, scooted a chair near the back door, climbed up on the seat, then jumped back down holding Luke's hunting rifle. It was long, longer than she was tall. And heavy. But she handled it well. She ran to the edge of the porch, leaped to the ground, and took off across the yard at a run, unmindful of the grasp and tangle of her skirt.

"Emmy, what're you doing? Whatever's wrong?" Lorna cried, getting to her feet as fast as her rheumatism would allow.

Emmy's scream and gun-toting run startled Creed into action. He scrambled after her. "Stop! Emmy, stop!"

She ran to the garden fence. Josiah rode between the fields, spurring the roan into a run. She drew back the hammer, braced the rifle on the top of the fence, and drew a bead.

Creed yelled, "No! Don't!"

She pulled the trigger. The recoil slammed her back and she took a couple of steps to regain her balance. White smoke billowed in the hot, still air. Its acrid scent stung her nose. She couldn't see the man on the horse, but she heard the hoof beats. Creed's arms wrapped around her and he wrested the rifle from her grip. The smoke cleared enough she could see Josiah, his unruly hair flapping as he spurred Pepper onward in an all-out run. She struggled against Creed's grip, sobbing, until her legs gave way. He lowered her to the ground and watched as she lay face down, her fists pounding the dust.

Chapter 35

My God! That was close! Josiah's heart raced as fast as the horse's pounding hooves. He had known Emmy would pitch a fit if she knew he was leaving. She had sworn she would stop him. He had expected screams and claws. Possibly the shotgun. That's why he had wanted to be well away before she knew he had gone. But a rifle? He had heard Creed yell at Emmy and he had urged Pepper to a lope, but he had been totally surprised when his hat had been snatched from his head, accompanied by the whine of the bullet and the sharp report. He had dug his heels into Pepper's flanks and the roan had responded. He didn't intend to slow down for a while.

But he did, though, when he quit shaking and could be more rational. Emmy wouldn't come after him. Well, maybe she would try, but surely Creed could keep her from it. And even if he couldn't, they owned nothing for her to ride that could come close to Pepper's pace. Knowing he might have a long, long ride ahead, he slowed the roan to an easy lope, a gait he could maintain for a long time but would cover ground fast. He turned and looked back once. Pretty Girl had given up on her attempt to stay with him and was nowhere to be seen.

He rode through Red Lick and a half mile beyond to a fork in the road with a house tucked into the wye. An old man sitting in a rocking chair on the porch raised his hand in greeting and watched Josiah turn toward Sand Springs.

Josiah met two men, one black, one white. Neither of them had seen Luke and the load of hogs.

The sun hung barely above the treetops when Josiah slowed Pepper to a walk and moved up the main street of Sand Springs. People moved about, going in and out of the general store, the drygoods store, the tavern. Some stared at him, then nodded, and he nodded back, but he didn't recognize any of them. He looked over the mules and wagons tied in front of the various establishments. None looked like his.

On the far outskirts of town the livery stable and a stockyard baked in their dusty stench. He approached those more cautiously. He didn't see his property. At the stockyard office he stopped and dismounted. He tied Pepper with enough slack to reach the water trough. A man lounged in a straight chair on the porch, tipping it back and leaning against the wall. He watched Josiah, turned his head to the side and spat a long stream of tobacco juice into the dust, sufficiently far from Josiah for etiquette. It beaded, dust grains rising up the sides of the droplets. But then the thirsty earth claimed the moisture and it flattened into a dark, damp stain.

"Can I help you?"

"I hope so. I'm looking for my brother-in-law. He headed over this way with some hogs to sell yesterday, and he isn't back yet. Wife's kind of worried. I told her I'd come look for him. Fellow about my size, light hair."

The tobacco chewer shook his head. "Nobody's brought any hogs here for a couple of weeks. You sure he was headed here?"

"Well, yeah. I mean, that's what he said." Josiah's forehead creased in a puzzled frown. "Does anybody else around here buy hogs?"

"Nope. Just me. Well, I suppose somebody might buy one. How many did he have?"

"Four."

"Ain't nobody been here with four hogs."

"Well, maybe he passed on through."

"I'd've noticed anybody droving hogs, that being my business."

"He wasn't droving. He had 'em in a stake-sided wagon pulled by a scruffy team of mules. He's got a gimpy leg."

"Ain't nobody come through here with a wagon full of hogs, either. I'd've noticed, f'sure. He ain't been here. Must've taken 'em somewhere else. Where was he coming from?"

"Over near Red Lick."

"Well, maybe he decided to take 'em to Henry's Ferry. It'd be considerably farther for him, but somebody told me the stockyard over there pays a little higher, it being on the river, easier shipping and all. I don't credit the higher prices, myself. But folks get greedy, you know. Want to believe they can get more. He might've gone there. I guess it'd explain his being late getting home."

"Yep, it would. I thank you. I'll go check the Henry's Ferry road."

As he mounted and turned Pepper back down the street the man called after him, "Good luck. Hope you find him all in one piece."

Josiah threw up his hand in answer, and urged Pepper into a trot, then a lope when they cleared the other side of the village.

Long deep shadows combed across the road and the sun neared the horizon as Josiah again came to the fork near Red Lick. The old man still sat on his front porch, watching the road. He raised his hand to the passing horseman. Josiah returned the wave and pulled Pepper down to a walk and turned in the drive beside the weathered picket fence. The old man watched him intently, perhaps a bit nervously.

As he drew near the porch, Josiah touched his hat and said, "Evening."

"Evening." He seemed friendly enough, but he watched Josiah very closely.

"I saw you out here when I rode by a while back. You look like you don't miss much that passes by," Josiah said.

The old man nodded. "I remember seeing you pass."

"My brother-in-law started out yesterday with some hogs to sell. Said he was going to Sand Springs. He hasn't come home. His wife's getting worried, so I set out to find him. I went to Sand Springs. He hadn't been there—at least so the stockman says. I's wondering if you saw him pass by yesterday. Man about my size driving a mule team pulling a stake-sided wagon with a load of hogs? Might've had a black dog with him."

The old man raised one eyebrow and snorted. "I did see a rig like that pass. Yesterday morning, fairly early. Driver was pushing his mules pretty hard and the hogs set in to squealing and carrying on when they got jostled in the turn. Caught my attention. You don't see a wagon load of hogs very often. Most everybody drives 'em on foot."

"Which way did he turn?"

"Toward Hope Hill and Henry's Ferry. Didn't stop and study on it, either. Like I said, he was pushing the mules hard and he whipped on around the curve there. I guess he changed his mind about where he wanted to go before he got here, huh?"

"I guess so. Wish he'd let somebody know." Josiah frowned. "You haven't seen him pass back by, have you?"

The old man shook his head. "Naw. I haven't seen him. I think I'd recognize the wagon and team if I saw them again, even without the hogs. I've been out here most of the time, too— except when I went in for supper a while ago. But I wasn't gone long. And I don't remember hearing any wagon pass. Heard a horse, but no wagon."

"Well, thanks for the information. I wish I'd stopped to ask you when I passed before. Would've saved me some time." Josiah turned Pepper to go back out the drive.

"I hope you find him all right. Henry's Ferry has a bad reputation—kind of rough, you know?"

"No, I didn't. I've been away for a while. Thanks for the warning."

He rode back to the road and turned toward Henry's Ferry. If he pushed on steadily he would cover the twenty miles before midnight, but not much before. He spurred Pepper to a faster pace to take advantage of the remaining daylight, but the horse couldn't maintain that gait for long. Later they'd have to move much slower even though the first quarter moon would rise in the cloudless sky to provide some light.

He covered perhaps a third of the distance, gradually slowing, before he could no longer see the dangers of the road.

Then he gave Pepper his head and let him pick his own way. Where they passed between fields the moonlight illuminated the road dimly. In woods the almost palpable darkness obscured all. An owl swooped silently in front of them to pick up a hapless young rabbit, spooking Pepper. Josiah heard the rabbit's terrified death cry over the irregular drumming of the horse's crabbing, dancing hooves. Reined in and settled, the roan snorted, then moved on down the road.

They passed farmsteads where dogs wakened and rushed, barking and snarling, to escort them beyond their territorial limits. It seemed as though the houses the dogs protected drew their breaths and held them. All lamps were extinguished, all sound and motion within them were suspended until the ruckus passed, their occupants having long ago learned to fear hoofbeats in the night.

The road wound through farms in rolling country and then through a loose gathering of houses and a small store and a church. Paradoxically, Hope Hill lay in a little hollow. The road rose up the narrow end of the hollow and over a hill. Then, in a small valley, Josiah noticed a little creek running beside them. Sometimes the road veered away from the creek for a ways, skirting a swampy thicket, but it always came back to the banks, sometimes even running in the creek bed. The stream flowed calmly, slowed in pools, then gurgled and burbled across stones and gravel in the shallows. As they went farther, the creek grew larger, claiming more land for its own. The valley deepened but didn't become appreciably wider. The forest closed in around them. The creek's voice grew louder, the road steeper.

Pepper picked his way over outcroppings of bedrock, his iron-shod hooves sometimes slipping on the hard surface, causing him to squat and scramble for balance. The creek cascaded below them on one side, at the bottom of a steep bluff. In the darkness, they hugged the other side of the road lest there be a hazard that would cause them to fall into the deep hollow. The bluff rose above them, so near Josiah had to lean away from it sometimes to avoid an outcropping stone or a bush that sank tenacious roots into the crevices between the boulders. He rode loosely, moving with the horse, keeping his mass balanced on the unevenly moving animal with the ease grown from natural ability and long, long practice.

The road became less steep. The creek quieted. The valley spread and once again fields flanked the track as it wandered away from the creek. Farmhouses appeared closer together, dark, the occupants long abed. At one farmstead a dog slunk off the porch and came silently, slipping low to the ground, hackles raised but not even growling, unseen until it was almost upon them. As it lunged at Pepper the horse reacted instantly, kicking powerfully and connecting his shod hoof to the dog's long head with a sickening pop. They traveled on, leaving the dog whimpering and twitching in the dust.

And then the houses beside the road clung together in clusters, their stables and gardens and chicken coops guarding their rears in a continuous phalanx. A town. Henry's Ferry.

Josiah pulled Pepper to a stop under a large oak that blocked the moonlight. A horseman riding through might attract more attention in the sleeping town than he wanted, but he planned to ride in quietly, on the lookout for evidence Luke had been there. If he didn't spot anything, he could go to the livery stable and bed Pepper for the rest of the night. Maybe he himself could rest in the hay. In the morning he could ask around, find out if Luke had been there, where he might be now.

He wished he hadn't lost his hat. He'd be too easily recognized without it. He didn't want Luke to have any warning. And he didn't want to be identified if anyone saw him with Luke. Then he realized it made no sense to worry about that—lots of people would know he had been asking after Luke. And a big, rangy roan like Pepper would be noted and remembered, too.

He eased Pepper into town, down the main street. Literally down. The whole town sloped off to the river. He peered along the cross streets and alleys but saw no sign of his wagon. He could see through some of the side yards into the stable areas behind the houses, but no stake-sided wagon sat there, either. He hadn't really expected to spot it here, unless maybe Luke had stopped at a boarding house. If he had money from selling the hogs he might've done that.

Josiah guided Pepper into the dustiest parts of the street to muffle the thud of his hooves. He entered the business district—a couple of general stores, a bakery, a drygoods store. A boarded-up newspaper office looked as though it had been closed for a long time. Something moved in the shadows beside the closed building. Pepper's ears laid back as his head swung toward the motion. Josiah saw the moonlight glint off the white of his eye. He gripped the reins firmly. The shadows grunted and rooted. Town hogs, foraging.

They came to a hotel and tavern. A lamp burned low in the hotel office. Light spilled from a room at the rear in the otherwise darkened tavern. A burst of laughter punctuated the quiet—some revelers making a night of it. As they passed on by, he noticed the stairs going up from the alley and the red lamp glowing dimly beside the dark smudge of a door near the rear of the building.

The main street dropped to the riverbank where it intersected the river road. A ferry lay moored at a small wharf just beyond the intersection, where the main street would've gone if the river hadn't been there. Josiah pulled up and looked both ways along the river road. He could make out stock pens and a large structure to his right. He turned that way.

He rode into the livery stable and dismounted. A lantern hung over the door and cast a faint light. He looked around. A black teenager materialized, his irregularly cropped hair sticking out at absurd angles, studded with bits of straw.

"Evenin' boss," the boy said, rubbing sleep from his eyes.

"Evening."

Josiah had opened his mouth to ask if the boy had seen Luke when he saw it, right there in the livery stable, beside the hire buggies: his stake-sided wagon. He stepped out of the lantern light.

"I'm looking for the man who drives that wagon," he said quietly, nodding toward the vehicle he now realized he could smell as well as see.

The boy looked at the wagon with disgust. "Don't nobody drive it now. It stinks. Man done drove it in here with hogs in it. Boss say I has to take it to the river and wash it out good, but I's busy today, didn't get it done. Wish now I had. It sure do stink."

257

"You're supposed to wash it before the man comes back for it?"

"No, before boss can sell it."

"Doesn't it belong to the man who drove it in here?"

"Did, boss. But he done sold it to Boss Dement. Them hogs and them mules and harness and the wagon all."

"What! That wagon and those mules belong to me. The hogs, too."

"I don't know nothing about that, boss. You just axed if it didn't belong to the man, yourself. Now you're saying it be yours. I don't know who it belong to. Man said he was selling up and moving on, going to Arkansas, or maybe Indian Territory. Axed Boss Dement did he want to buy the whole rig. Me, I'da kept the team and wagon. How he going to get to Arkansas? But boss offered him a hunnert and sixty dollars and the man said no and they settle on a hunnert sixty-five. I reckon the wagon be Boss Dement's now."

"Those mules alone are worth ten times that, and Dement knows it. So does Luke Elrod."

"You got to take it up with Boss Dement."

"All right. I will. How did the man take off for Arkansas?"

"He ain't took off yet, boss." The boy smirked, but quickly erased the impertinent look.

"He ain't? Where is he?" Josiah's heart pounded.

The boy looked as though he tried hard to hide amusement. "I don't know for sure, boss." He stifled a snigger. "But I heard even Miss Fancy Belle don't take no man smells like a hog. Sent him over to the barber shop for a bath." He giggled.

Josiah thought about the red lantern. "He's with Miss Fancy Belle now?"

"Naw. That was late this afternoon, when she be gettin' started, I reckon. He might be there, but it be a long time, you know? I heard he come out before too long. Went on in the tavern and got hisself some supper and then got in that poker game that's always goin' in the back. I don't know where he be now. Might still be there."

"Poker game? I never knew him to play poker."

The boy shrugged. "He probably be welcome then."

"The tavern. The one on the main street? Up the hill? With the hotel?"

"Yessuh."

"I need to talk to him. I'm going to water my horse and then maybe see if he's up there. If I don't find him, I'll be back to stable my horse."

"Yessuh, boss. If I don't hear you, jus' ring the bell yonder. They's a empty stall."

Chapter 36

Josiah led Pepper to the water trough and let him drink his fill, then he mounted and rode slowly back up the main street for half a block, musing about Luke's activities in Henry's Ferry. Luke the pious, humping a whore and gambling. Josiah snorted. None of them had known him very well, after all. Around him all those years, and hadn't smelled the rot within his righteous shell, hadn't seen past his Bible-thumping and praying. Josiah felt he should have recognized the evil, and yet he sometimes didn't know his own heart—how could he know the heart of another? Did he know his own heart now? He shuddered.

He turned into an alley between the shop buildings. Another dirty, cluttered alley ran behind them. He dismounted and led the horse, feeling his way as much as seeing. He spotted the red lamp in the side alley. Through the thin walls of the crib he heard grunting and squeaking—not the pigs.

Behind the hotel and tavern the alley smelled of the ripening garbage piled near a back door. Part of the pile moved and grunted. The pigs, again. On the other side of the door the smell worsened into the unmistakable odor of a pissing wall. The light of the quarter moon struck the other side of the alley, leaving the back of the tavern in deep shadow. He led Pepper a few feet farther, around the corner into the next side alley, then stopped. He scratched behind the horse's ears and patted his neck. Then he rubbed the velvety muzzle and whispered, "You stay here."

He heard a low growl that changed to a soft whine. Bo's dark form detached itself from the shadows and approached him.

He patted the dog and Bo's tail began to wag. Josiah whispered, "You stay here, too." The dog sat, his tail thumping the ground, and watched. Josiah pulled the knife from his boot and tested its keen edge. He stropped it a couple of strokes on his stirrup leather and tested again. Even better.

Don't do this, Josiah.

Hush, Mattie. He needs killing.

You promised me, Josiah.

I said I'd try, but I can't. I can't forgive him.

What you're about to do isn't for me. It's for you.

It is *for you, Mattie. I can't let him get away with what he did—to you, to all of the family.*

Do you hear yourself? You *can't let him get away with his evil.*

Do you hear yourself? *You know he's evil. What he did to you was pure evil. Do you know he's now deserted Emmy and his children? Do you know he's stolen our hogs and mules and wagon and is gambling with the proceeds? Do you really forgive all that?*

I'm supposed to . . .

You're supposed to forgive him, but in your heart, do you?

Maybe . . .

Mattie, you forgave me what I did to that poor wounded Yankee. Forgive me breaking this one promise.

There was nothing to forgive about that. You had to kill that boy. Do it or die yourself. Do it or not come home to me and Sally.

It's almost the same thing here. If I don't do this, I might as well be dead. I'll be ashamed for the rest of my life. I won't ever be at home in my own skin.

But you could take care of Sally.

Creed'll do that till I get back. When I get home, I'll take care of her.

If you survive. And don't get caught.

Will you look out for me?

Mattie?

Mattie?

Be very careful, Josiah.

261

Always.

He crept to the back of the tavern and listened for the sounds inside instead of those in his head. At first he could hear nothing. Then he picked out the shuffling of the cards and the slaps of the deal. He listened while four voices went through two rounds of betting. He smiled grimly when he recognized Luke's. The game ended and the players anted and started another one. Someone, not Luke, said, "I fold. Man, I've gotta piss. I'll skip the next round." A chair scraped and heavy footsteps came toward the back door.

Josiah melted back around the corner, out of sight of the man who stepped out, unbuttoned his pants, and relieved himself. The man returned to the game. Josiah crept again to where he could see the tavern door.

The men played on. After at least half an hour Josiah heard Luke say, "I fold." He heard the scrape of a chair followed by uneven steps toward the door. Josiah eased once more into the side alley.

Don't.

I have to.

No, you don't.

I do. Hush now, Mattie, dear.

Josiah waited until he saw Luke fumbling with his buttons. Then he moved quickly, catching his arm around Luke's neck, pulling tight and hard, and putting his knee into Luke's back. Luke grunted, no louder than the snuffling pigs. He struggled, his hands reaching back, trying to get a hold on Josiah, his body turning and twisting.

"You murdering bastard. You're going to pay for Mattie," Josiah spat into Luke's ear.

Bo dashed up, alternately whining and growling, and circled the struggling men.

Luke matched Josiah in size, and he bucked and kicked and pulled the conflict down the alley. They crashed into the abandoned newspaper building, breaking Josiah's hold.

Luke spun to face Josiah, hatred and desperation in his eyes. "She died?"

"Yes. Now it's your turn."

262

Luke lunged at Josiah. Josiah brought his knife up, edge to the side, point up. It pierced Luke's belly just below his sternum. Luke's eyes widened as his hands grasped for Josiah, but Josiah ignored their clawing. He drove the knife upward and jammed his free arm into Luke's throat, driving him back into the newspaper building wall with a dull thump. He gave the knife a savage twist and watched with satisfaction as Luke's eyes stared dully and blood ran from his mouth.

They sank to the ground together as Luke's legs folded and Josiah followed his knife down. He pulled the blade from the wound and wiped it on Luke's shirt. Blood oozed from the wound, forming a small dark spot barely visible in the murk of the alley. A trickle of blood dribbled from Luke's mouth. As his arms and legs twitched and jerked, his chest heaved twice more and air bubbled through the blood.

Then nothing.

Bo whined.

Josiah panted. His stomach heaved. His blood pounded. He went through Luke's pockets and found a purse. Reasoning the money came from the sale of his stock and wagon, he stuck it in his own pocket. He found a few loose coins and pocketed those, too. He left a handkerchief, but took a watch and a pocket knife—no sense leaving them for the gamblers. He would see they eventually got to Jim.

Then he heard noises—steps in the tavern, the door opening with a bang. He looked up at a heavy, bearded man in an unbuttoned waistcoat, his sleeves rolled nearly to his elbows.

"Hey, Luke. How long you gonna take? You in or out?" the man called into the alley. The dog whined. The man turned and saw Josiah bent over Luke's body. "What the hell's going on out here?" he yelled. "What the hell are you doing?"

Josiah leaped to his feet and ran into the alley as the man started toward him. He grabbed for his saddle, yelling at Pepper to run, as the heavy man pounded in pursuit. He clung to the saddle and ran alongside as the roan clattered out of the side alley, into the main street. Vaulting into the saddle, he bent low over Pepper's neck and dug his heels into the horse's flanks. Bo barked and ran after them for a few feet before returning to Luke.

Down the hill and to the right. Along the river. Racing in the dark and the fog forming on the river. Not watching for good footing now, just running. At first he heard commotion in the town behind him, but soon he left it behind. He slowed Pepper to a lope. If they really came after him he doubted the roan could outrun them. The horse hadn't had time to recover from their long trek yet, and he'd already covered a lot of ground in the last eighteen hours or so.

Josiah pushed on, frequently looking back over his shoulder, but he saw no pursuers. By dawn, lather covered Pepper. The horse could no longer lope or trot. He could barely walk. Josiah knew the horse's life depended on getting rest soon.

Josiah dared to pray for an escape route as he watched the river in the dim but growing light. He could hardly believe his eyes as they entered a curve and he saw the river ran broad but swift, indicating shallows. As he turned Pepper down to the edge of the stream he knew his tracks would not be noticed among the welter of those of horses, mules, and cattle that had watered at this spot over the past few days. He urged the horse a few feet out into the river and dismounted in the water. He scooped water to his mouth and filled his canteen while the roan drank.

As he straightened up and tied the canteen on his saddle, he studied the surroundings. A small, brush-covered island divided the stream. The far bank rose steeply above the river, but a narrow hollow cut into the bluff a short way downstream, behind the island. Maybe that was just good fortune, or maybe the Lord did look out for poor sinners sometimes, after all.

He gathered the reins and started to lead the weary horse farther into the swift water. The animal resisted. He pulled harder on the reins. Hesitantly, the roan began to pick his way through the ford.

They waded easily until they passed the tip of the island, where the water deepened and the current strengthened. Here large rocks littered the bottom, making treacherous footing. Josiah carefully felt out each step, and several times had to adjust their course to find a safer path. Near the far side they had to swim a few feet, but then they waded into shallower water.

Josiah stopped and let the horse drink again before he led him out onto the steep, brush-clogged bank.

Pepper shook his head vigorously, then stood shivering and panting while Josiah got his bearings. The mouth of the hollow opened a few feet downstream of their landing. He looked back across the river. The brush on the island screened the road and the watering spot. Perfect.

They made their way slowly up the heavily-wooded hollow, Josiah leading the roan. Several times both man and horse stumbled on the rough steep terrain. The most difficult passage came at the narrow cleft at the top of the ravine, but they made it through.

They stopped and caught their breaths. Huge trees surrounded them. The leaf canopies blocked the sunlight high above them. Uncluttered by underbrush, the forest seemed to go on forever, but Josiah knew it could end just beyond the reach of his sight. No path existed here. This was not a place for travelers.

He led the horse forward, farther into the woods. After they had gone about a quarter of a mile, he heard water dripping. He left Pepper and eased down into a small hollow. On one side the ground rose steeply, and water trickled from beneath a stone outcrop. The hollow had a fairly flat floor. He went back for the horse.

He unloaded the animal, removed the bridle and saddle, and snapped a line to the halter, then tied the line to a sapling, leaving plenty of slack. The sodden saddle blanket he spread to dry and used his own blanket to rub the horse down before he fed him some of the corn. Pepper moved around a little and pawed the ground. He sank to the earth with a roaring sigh and rolled in the crackling leaves, his legs kicking the air. Then he rolled back onto his side and stayed down, exhausted. Soon he slept.

Josiah unrolled his ground sheet and dropped onto it. He ate the fried okra and some of the cornbread. He licked his fingers, then wiped them on his pants, leaving light smears of grease. Despite the leaden weight of his limbs and the raw stinging of his eyes he remained too keyed-up to rest. His wanted his pipe, but he didn't want to strike a fire. He settled for putting a wad of tobacco in his mouth.

I did it, he thought. Luke would never be a threat to Sally again. He idly stirred the leaves beside him with a twig. He hadn't been sure he could do it, not till it was happening. The twig snapped. It was a hard thing to kill a man, no matter how much he deserved to die. A hard thing. Josiah broke the remainder of the twig in his hand, then picked up another and poked and stirred at the earth again.

He regretted having to break his promise to Mattie. She deserved better of him, but . . . The twig appeared to waver as tears filmed his eyes. She thought any vengeance should be the Lord's, but who's to say He didn't make Josiah Robertson His instrument? Josiah's eyes smarted and he rubbed them, drawing his fingers away damp. He felt if the Lord helps anybody, it's them who help themselves. He'd helped himself, but he'd certainly had some assistance. How else could he have found Luke, prevailed over him, and gotten away? Those men in Henry's Ferry must not've been very well organized. Pepper couldn't have outrun them, not for long. "So I thank you, God. I truly thank You," he whispered.

He sighed and tossed the twig away. Now he had to find a way to raise Sally. Maybe he could come back to Red Lick. Maybe not. He'd probably have to lie low for a while, but nobody outside their family would care much what had happened to Luke. They'd calm down and forget. Emmy wouldn't, but . . .

Josiah's eyes closed as he lay down and stretched out. He would sleep, maybe even all through the day and into the night. He squirmed, seeking a less uncomfortable position on the rough ground. Something hard and lumpy dug into his hip. With great effort he sat up and forced his eyes open. He scooted over and felt the cloth where he had lain. No bad lumps there. He patted his pockets and felt an unfamiliar bulge. His fingers fumbled as he pulled Luke's purse from his pocket.

He stared at the leather pouch for a minute or more, not really recognizing it. Then, with a start, he remembered. He shook his head and thought about getting up to put the purse in his saddlebags. But no. He sank back down as curiosity slowly pushed through his exhaustion.

Josiah's fingers trembled as he untied the string. Might as

266

well see what Luke had left him to live on till he could get home again. He felt in the purse and pulled out a few greenback dollars. Grimacing, he tore the purse apart, hoping Luke had concealed some of the proceeds from the sale to Dement. Nothing. He dug his hand into his pocket and retrieved the coins. A dime and a half dime. No gold. He jammed both the coins and the bills back into his pocket.

A memory scratched at his mind, but he couldn't quite retrieve it. Then it came to him, as if from the far past instead of only a few nights ago—Luke reading from Jeremiah. He barked a bitter laugh. Jeremiah was right. Beyond all else Luke was a fool, a fool to rape and kill, a fool to steal, a fool to take too little for his goods, a fool to gamble the little away. Josiah stood and threw the empty purse as hard as he could. It disappeared into a distant clump of bushes.

As he sank back to the ground sheet, he thought maybe he had been something of a fool, too. He had risked his life to avenge Mattie, but also to prove himself. Risked his life and Sally's future. He'd prevailed. Had there been divine intervention? He had to allow for that possibility. And he might need more help to get back home to Sally. He'd pray. Tomorrow he'd pray.

Why not now, Josiah?

I'm too tired, Mattie, dear. Your God will still be here tomorrow.

He lay back, pillowed his head on his saddle, and closed his eyes, confident that the bloody Yankee would not interrupt his rest, nor would Luke. Killing a man was a hard thing, but sometimes it was necessary. Sometimes it brought peace. He was sure Mattie knew that. She, too, would let him sleep tonight.

The End

267

Made in the USA
Lexington, KY
15 June 2016